Praise for

THE BLINDS

A Best Book of the Year at

Sun Sentinel • BOLO • Vulture Best • LitHub

"Wickedly entertaining. . . . This revisionist Western is a whip-smart addition to the literature of false reality." —*Chicago Tribune*

"Well-written. . . . An intriguing premise, strong narrative hooks and a brisk pace make this a riveting read." —*The Guardian* (UK)

"Sternbergh's characters are intriguing, his plot is suspenseful and his outlook is endearingly dark. . . . [He] is an original, grandly irreverent writer." —*Washington Post*

"A fun and inventive thriller that blends genres seamlessly." —Vulture

"Crackles with noir-ish delights. . . . Sternbergh writes a beautiful sentence, even when the subject is mayhem, and he has a talent for lean, propulsive plotting." —*Newsweek*

"Expertly melds the thriller with the western, adding a soupcon of medical science fiction while paying a bit of homage to Jim Thompson's novels." —*Sun Sentinel*

"[A] Coen brothers-like tale about a Texas backwater." —*Variety*

"Imaginative. . . . *The Blinds* expertly melds the thriller with the Western. . . . A truly original story." —Associated Press

"A quick-paced story of crime and deception." —*Dallas Morning News*

"The newest release from the riveting Adam Sternbergh." —PopSugar

"Sternbergh delivers cutting humor and devastating violence." —Paste

"Compelling. . . . A good old-fashioned beach read." —*Forward*

"[An] exciting new thriller. . . . This book doesn't pull any punches." —Bookish

"Genre fiction is made healthier through cross-breeding. In *The Blinds* Adam Sternbergh . . . has created a multi-layered hybrid of a novel strengthened by several different bloodlines." —*Toronto Star*

"*The Blinds* is an uncommonly ingenious thriller." —*Maclean's*

"Sternbergh shows again why he is one of the most inventive thriller writers working today." —*Booklist* (starred review)

"Adam Sternbergh is a genre bender of the highest caliber. Part thriller, part Western, part pulpy whodunit, *The Blinds* is a propulsive and meaningful meditation on redemption and loss. It's witty, electrifying, vivid, and thoroughly original." —Dennis Lehane, author of *Since We Fell*

"*The Blinds* is brilliantly original, fast-paced, ranging, and inventive. Adam Sternbergh's restless imagination once again conjures characters and scenarios with heartbreaking insight, peril, and startling stakes. Readers take heed; this is a hell of a ride."

—Smith Henderson, author of *Fourth of July Creek*

"Adam Sternbergh tops my list of drop-everything-and-read novelists. With hints of Charles Willeford and Philip K. Dick, *The Blinds* brings to vivid life a social experiment of the most compelling nature—a forgotten town where a collection of ragged souls hide from their respective pasts and their own violent natures in an unlikely bid for salvation. Rendered with achingly beautiful prose, the book plucks the strings of Sternbergh's favored themes—identity, loss, meta-reality—creating a symphony of noirish grit and improbable grace. As is the case with the best of genre fiction, this story has a depth that goes as far down as you're capable of riding it."

—Gregg Hurwitz, author of *The Nowhere Man*

"*The Blinds* is a wild fever-dream of a novel. Posing questions about the power—and peril—of running from the past, Sternbergh's vivid vision and the people he brings to life will haunt you long after you turn the shocking final pages."

—Julia Dahl, author of *Invisible City* and *Conviction*

THE BLINDS

ALSO BY ADAM STERNBERGH

Shovel Ready
Near Enemy

THE BLINDS

ADAM STERNBERGH

ecco

An Imprint of HarperCollins*Publishers*

This is a work of fiction. Names, characters, places, and incidents are products of the author's imagination or are used fictitiously and are not to be construed as real. Any resemblance to actual events, locales, organizations, or persons, living or dead, is entirely coincidental.

HarperCollins books may be purchased for educational, business, or sales promotional use. For information, please e-mail the Special Markets Department at SPsales@harpercollins.com.

A hardcover edition of this book was published in 2017 by Ecco, an imprint of HarperCollins Publishers.

FIRST ECCO PAPERBACK EDITION PUBLISHED 2018.

Designed by Michelle Crowe

Photography by ZAB Photographie/Shutterstock, Inc.

Map illustration by Michael Chen

Library of Congress Cataloging-in-Publication Data has been applied for.

ISBN 978-0-06-266135-7

18 19 20 21 22 LSC 10 9 8 7 6 5 4 3 2 1

For my parents

You could die just the same on a sunny day.

—James Joyce, *A Portrait of the Artist as a Young Man*

Who wants a smart sheriff?

—Jim Thompson, *Pop. 1280*

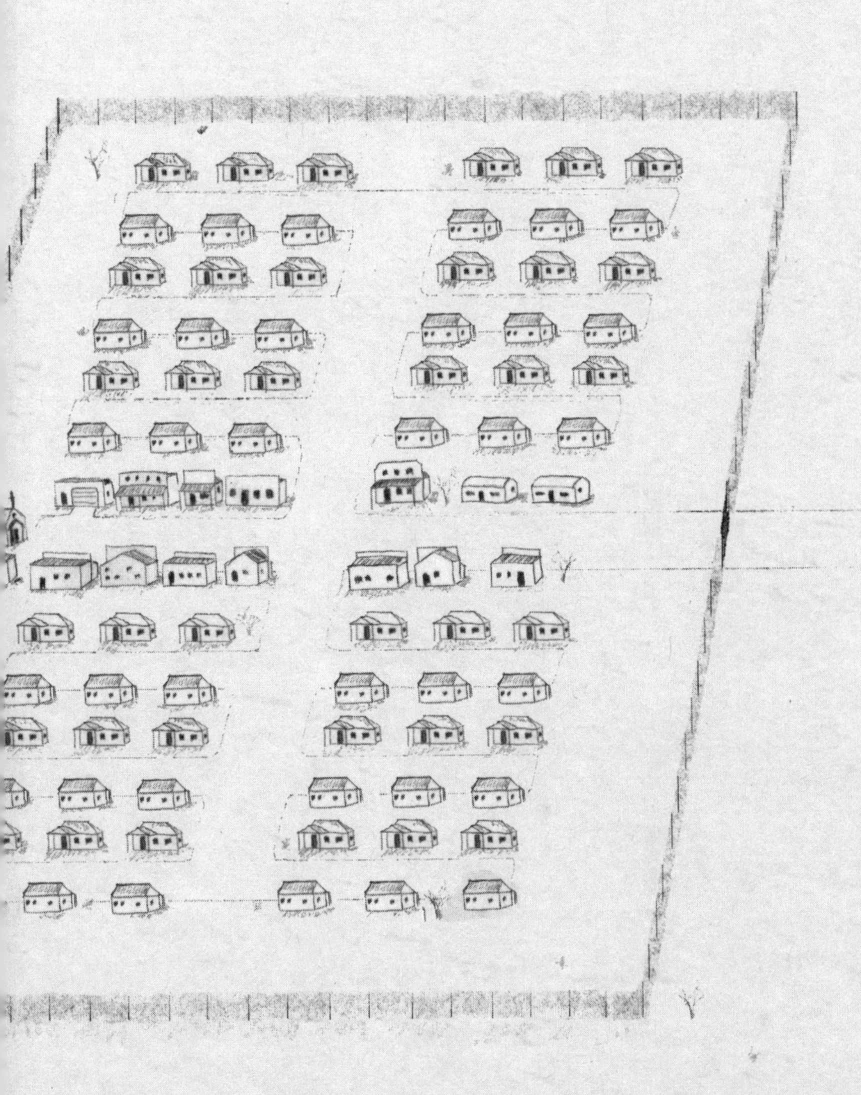

CAESURA, TX, A.K.A. “THE BLINDS”

POP. 48

SHE'S OLD ENOUGH, at thirty-six, to remember flashes of other places, other lives, but her son is only eight years old, which means he was born right here in the Blinds. She was four months pregnant on the day she arrived, her secret just starting to show. If the intake officer noticed, he didn't say anything about it as he sat her down at a folding table in the intake trailer and explained to her the rules of her new home. No visitors. No contact. No return. Then he taught her how to properly pronounce the town's official name—Caesura, rhymes with tempura, he said—before telling her not to worry too much about it since everyone just calls it the Blinds.

Caesura.

A bad name, she thought then and thinks now, with too many vowels and in all the wrong places. A bad name for a bad place but, then, what real choice did she have?

Reclining now at two A.M. on the wooden steps of her front porch, she pulls out a fresh pack of cigarettes. The night is so quiet that unwrapping the cellophane sounds like a faraway bonfire. As she strips the pack, she looks over the surrounding blocks of homes with their rows of identical cinder block bungalows, each with the same slightly elevated wooden porch, the same scrubby patch of modest yard. Some people here maintain the pretense of giving a shit, planting flowers, mowing grass, keeping their porches swept clean, while others let it all grow wild and just wait for whatever's coming next. She glances down the street and counts the lights still on at this hour: two, maybe three households. Most everyone else is sleeping. Which she should be, too. She definitely shouldn't be smoking.

Well, she doesn't smoke, she tells herself, as she pulls a cigarette free from the pack.

After the intake officer explained to her how things would work in the Blinds—the rules, the prohibitions, the conditions, the privations—he asked her to choose her new name. He didn't know her real name and, by that point, neither did she. He passed her two pieces of paper: a list of the names of famous movie stars and a list of ex–vice presidents. "One name from one list, one name from the other," he told her. She scanned the lists. She didn't remember much about who she used to be, but she had a feeling, deep down, that she wasn't an Ava. Or an Ingrid. Or a Judy, as much as she loved Judy Garland. That much she remembered.

"Did you do this, too?" she asked the officer, more as a stalling tactic than anything else.

"Yes, ma'am. That's the rules."

"So what did you choose?"

"Cooper."

"Like Gary Cooper?"

He nodded.

She laughed. "Of course you did." She pointed to a name far

down among the movie stars. "How about Frances Farmer? I'll take Frances. Fran for short."

The officer wrote the first name down on her intake form. "You'll need a last name, too," he said, and gestured to the sheet of vice presidents. She looked it over, then picked the first name she saw, right at the top.

"Adams. Fran Adams."

The intake officer wrote her full name on the form.

"You got a first name, Cooper?" she asked him.

"Calvin. Cal for short. Or so I imagine. We'll see what sticks." The officer signed the paper, held a hand stamp over it, then paused. "You sure you don't want to go with Marilyn? Audrey? Something more glamorous? They're all available."

"I like Frances. Frances was Judy Garland's real name. Frances Gumm. I like that."

The officer nodded, stamped her paper, then slipped it into a folder.

"Welcome to Oz, Frances," he said.

On her front steps eight years later, under a sky saturated with stars, Fran Adams wedges the unlit cigarette between her lips. She enjoys this drawn-out moment—the delicious anticipation that, in many ways, is better for her than the smoking itself. She leans forward, producing her lighter from a pocket, resting her bare forearms on her knees. She's still wearing the same jeans she wore during the day, and the same old plaid shirt worn loose over her sleeveless undershirt. She looks down at her slapped-together outfit, which taken together screams hot weather and housecleaning, which pretty much describes the day she's had. Pretty much describes the last eight years. If it weren't for Isaac, she'd have run already. Or so she likes to tell herself.

No visitors. No contact. No return.

With her sleeves rolled up against the stubborn night that's stayed just as warm as the day, she glances, unthinking, at the series of numbers tattooed like a delicate bracelet across the back of her left wrist.

1 2 5 0 0 2 4 1 2 1 4 9 1 1

No idea what it means. No idea how it got there. She can recall some ragged snippets of her previous life, childhood mostly, but she doesn't remember that. All she knows is that the tattoo predates her time in the Blinds, since she rode into this place with the numbers already etched on her wrist. No one else here has the numbers—she knows; she's checked. And she long ago gave up trying to decipher whatever coded message the tattoo's trying to send her. As far as she's concerned, it's just a souvenir of some past adventure she forgot she took, some past mistake she forgot she made. It belongs to someone else, some previous woman, not Fran Adams, who's only eight years old, after all.

Fran Adams, born eight years ago, just like her son.

She finally lights her cigarette and listens happily to the pleasing hiss of the first long drag. The paper flares in a vibrant circle, then withers. This is all she wants right now, right here. The crinkle of cellophane, the sour taste of the cotton filter, the sniff of butane, that first crackle of paper, then the fragrant heat-blossom in the fragile bellows of her lungs. In the stifling night, she loves this lonely ritual. She loves it so much, apparently, that she'll kill herself a little bit every day just for another chance to experience it.

If she smoked.

Which she doesn't.

Starting tomorrow.

She takes another long drag.

Then she stubs the cigarette out and brushes the ashes away, worrying Isaac might see the faint guilt rings of burn marks lingering on the painted steps in the morning. She flicks the spent butt in the bushes, far enough away that she can always blame it on a passing neighbor if Isaac finds it. He's still young enough that she can continue to pretend he doesn't know all the things he's clearly starting to understand.

If she could get him out of here, she would. It's time. It's long past time. If she had somewhere else to take him. If she had any idea what was waiting for both of them out there. Or who.

But she doesn't. So they stay.

She thinks about all the people who've arrived since she first came. She was in the first batch, the original eight, but there's been two or three new people who've come every few months ever since. She heard that four people arrived just today, the bus rumbling in after dark. Two women and two men. Of course, she can't help but speculate on what they did and how they wound up here. That's the kind of gossip people here tend to traffic in. Especially her next-door neighbor Doris Agnew, who always seems to know what's going on, gossip-wise. When she told Fran that she'd heard Sheriff Cooper was thinking of organizing a field trip outside the facility, just for Isaac, to a movie, in a real-live movie theater, Fran hadn't believed it, didn't dare to, but that rumor turned out to be true. The sheriff assured Fran it would be safe, but knowing what had happened to that poor boy years ago, and his mother, when they both left, Fran couldn't help but panic. Watching Cooper's truck leave with Isaac inside, his face pressed against the passenger-side glass, waving back at her, looking both lost and excited, was the worst and best she's felt since the day she arrived here.

Just come back, she said to no one, as the truck trundled off in a shimmer of dust, and the entry gates closed behind it.

He came back. He's growing up. And now he's seen the outside world. It was all she ever wanted for him, until it actually happened.

She stands up and wipes her hands on her jeans. Two drags. That's all she allows herself. The second drag is always a disappointment anyway, just an unsatisfying echo of the first. But she always takes that second drag, just to be sure.

She lingers a moment longer on the steps, savoring the silence, then starts to head inside, to shower off the smoky smell, and that's when she hears the shot.

A single gunshot. Far away but loud enough to startle her.

In the movies, people always mistake other things, like firecrackers or a car backfiring, for gunshots. But in real life, in her experience, no one ever mistakes a gunshot for anything other than what it is.

That's one thing she remembers from her previous life.

That a gunshot sounds like nothing else.

And even at this early hour, up and down the rows of houses, lights go on.

MONDAY

1.

HUBERT HUMPHREY GABLE, real name unknown, lies slumped on the bar at Blinders, his head resting in a curdling puddle of splashed beer and spilled brain matter, both of which used to be his. Gable's face is no longer useful for purposes of identification but the other three people assembled in the bar all know him well enough. Greta Fillmore, the bar's owner, stands newly awakened and angry, with the unkempt, hastily swept-up gray hair of a wizened frontier widow. She lives in the bungalow adjacent to the trailer that houses the bar and she dashed over at the sound of the shot. She's dressed, presumably hastily, in a colorful African-print dashiki. She looks pissed.

Calvin Cooper stands next to her, in his wrinkled brown sheriff's uniform, a concession to the propriety of his office that he considers important, even at this early hour. He wears his sheriff's star, too, and his gun belt, the full getup, though his revolver is not currently loaded, and hasn't been for the past eight years. Technically, he's not even officially a sheriff. He's a privately employed security guard with previous training as a corrections officer. The star he wears was a gag gift on his first day of work. But given that he's tasked professionally with keeping order in this town, the title of sheriff has proven to be a useful shorthand. Most often, what he deals with in Caesura are drunken fights or noise complaints, and the occasional teary breakdowns by residents who've spent too much time staring into the bottom of an emptied bottle. Now he stands at a remove from the body in question, studying the scene with the weary air of a man who's just returned from a particularly tedious errand to find that his car's been keyed.

Behind him, Sidney Dawes, his deputy, takes notes. She's always taking notes.

"'Execution-style' seems like the correct descriptor," Dawes says, scribbling her thoughts.

Cooper winces, or deepens his existing wince. "All that tells me is that, before you got here, you spent too much time watching TV, Dawes."

Cooper would be the first to admit that, as a sheriff, he's not much of a sheriff, but then this town's not much of a town, and this bar is not much of a bar. It's just a few stools set in a crooked row in front of a long sheet of stained plywood slung across two stacks of tapped-out beer kegs. There's a scatter of bottles on display on the shelves behind the bar, with enough variety on offer to allow patrons the illusion that what they're drinking matters to them. Blinders doesn't have to worry about customer loyalty, given it's the only bar in town, as well as the only source of liquor for about a hundred miles in any direction. During normal hours, it's reliably hopping. Right now, though, Hubert Gable is, or was, the only customer. It's nearly two thirty in the A.M. and well past closing time.

Cooper regards the body. To say Gable was a hefty man would be to extend a euphemistic posthumous kindness, given that Gable's impressive backside threatens to swallow the stool he's sitting on. Cooper recalls that when Gable arrived in this town, seven years ago or so, he'd been simply burly, a big guy, like a bouncer or a night watchman, someone you might even have called muscular. But time and booze and food and boredom conspired to engorge him. None of which matters to Gable anymore, of course, only to the other three people in the bar, all of whom are considering, to varying degrees, how he got in this current state and how exactly they're going to move him.

Cooper says to Greta, "Naturally, you didn't see anyone else in here after closing."

"Nope," she says. "I often let Hubert close the place down. I left him here around midnight and headed off to bed. Beauty sleep, you know." Greta's eyes have a youthful vigor, but her hands are veined and gnarled in a way that suggests her true age; like several of the longtime residents in the Blinds, she's on the far side of sixty and looks like she lived every day twice. On her fingers, she wears colorful rings with costume stones, each larger and more ornate than the last. As she talks, she twists and fidgets with the rings. "Hubert would usually lock up, then drop the keys in my mailbox," she says. "And he was always good about marking in the ledger exactly how much he drank."

"I don't doubt that," says Cooper. There's no cash exchanged in the Blinds, but people still have to account for everything they're consuming, be it food, liquor, clothes, or other sundries. And Greta, in turn, as town barkeep, must justify every bottle she orders as replenishment. Besides which, as Cooper has learned, in this town, everyone knows everyone, so tabs of all sorts tend to get settled, one way or the other.

"Do you want me to wake up Nurse Breckinridge?" says Dawes.

"Not much she can do about this now," Cooper says. "Just call it in to Amarillo. They'll send out an agent first thing. Hubert here won't be any less dead in the morning, and the cause of death should be fairly evident. Unless anyone wants to forward the theory that he was poisoned with arsenic before being shot in the head."

"How do I—" asks Dawes.

"You can call on the fax phone."

Dawes exhibits a flush of pride, which she tries to hide, unsuccessfully. She's never before been authorized to make a call on the fax phone.

"What about my bar?" Greta says. "When can I open up again? I have morning regulars."

"If you can stay closed until noon," says Cooper, "I'd consider it a favor."

Dawes stows her notebook in her left breast pocket, where it fits perfectly. She's the kind of person who's never happier than when someone's given her a task. She's just turned thirty, she's only six weeks on the job, and she keeps her uniform crisp and her hair shaved close, with daily touchups from the clippers she brought herself in a little box. When she started work here, she assumed she'd be the only black person in the Blinds, but it turns out she's not even the only black deputy. But the other deputy, Walter Robinson, is presumably sleeping soundly right now. He sets two alarms and once slept through a tornado drill, so it would take more than a far-off gunshot to rouse him.

As for Sheriff Cooper, so far he's yet to fully warm to the presence of his new deputy. She's a keen one, he'll give her that. She's wearing her uniform, even at this early hour, and she showed up minutes after the shot. No badge, though. There's only one badge to go around, even a toy one, and Cooper's wearing it.

"You'll have to meet the agent in the morning," he tells her. "I'll be busy with the new arrivals." He turns to Greta: "We got four brand-new residents, just arrived last night. They haven't gone through intake so they don't even have names yet. They came in late so I figured I'd let them get a night's rest first, get them settled. Just goes to show what I know."

"You think this is connected to them?" says Dawes.

"I don't think anything yet," Cooper says. "But since tomorrow's intake day, I'll be busy giving the welcome-wagon spiel bright and early. So I'll need you to talk to Amarillo and report this. Talk to Dave Brightwell. He's our liaison with the U.S. Marshals."

Dawes smiles to herself. Not unpleased to get this minor assignment. "And what should I tell Brightwell when I call him?"

"Tell him the truth, so far as we know it," Cooper says.

The truth being, he knows, that this is not going to be good for anyone, least of all for him. After eight years in the Blinds with little more than broken arms and bloody noses, this is the second violent death in the past two months. Granted, the first one was ruled a suicide, but it was suicide by firearm and, technically, firearms are prohibited in the Blinds. And now this. All of which is going to be an issue, he thinks, given there's only forty-eight residents living in the Blinds, and there's not supposed to be another human soul within a hundred miles of the town. And given that, theoretically at least, Cooper's the only person in town in possession of a gun.

2.

THE SIX OF THEM SIT in the windowless room. They look ghostly, like corpses, lit only by the harsh overhead fluorescents. There's two officers, Sheriff Cooper and Deputy Walter Robinson, along with the four new arrivals. A wall clock ticks off the minutes loudly. It's nearly nine in the morning.

The four new arrivals sit hunched and silent at school desks, scattered around the room in exactly the random, equidistant pattern that strangers who are suspicious of one another will always arrange themselves in. The room, contained inside a large brown trailer set up on concrete blocks, is bare and dingy with whitish acoustic tiles on the ceiling and a floor covered with linoleum that's shriveling at the corners. It looks like the kind of place you'd be sent to take a remedial driver's course after a particularly bad accident that was entirely your fault. Which, in a way, it is.

Cooper sits at the back of the room. He's still in the same wrinkled browns from several hours earlier. He hasn't yet been to bed, or strayed within arm's reach of a razor, and a person sitting close to him might smell evidence of a recent beverage not entirely appropriate to the early hour.

Walt Robinson sits on a metal folding chair at the front of the room. He wears the same brown uniform as Cooper. No badge, though. Just an arm patch that reads "Caesura" in a scripted arc over an embroidered crest of a river running through a scrubby plain. Robinson is giving the intake speech today. He's officially the officer in charge of intake, having taken over this duty from Cooper. Over the years, Robinson's gotten very good at the intake speech.

When the clock announces harshly with a loud jerk of the long hand that it's finally nine on the nose, Robinson stands.

He turns his back to the class. On a large whiteboard behind him, which still bears the faint smears of dozens of previous lectures, he writes:

WELCOME TO CAESURA

Then he turns back around to face the four arrivals.

"Rhymes with tempura," he says, then caps the marker.

Robinson is a fiftysomething African American man who's long since come to pleasant terms with his expansive middle-aged belly. Having a belly, he's realized, is the natural product of millions of years of evolution, a fat-storing reflex developed in the days when famine for humans was a constant concern. Robinson has come to accept himself as a creature programmed by nature to do what it takes to survive lean times. This is a good life philosophy in general, he suspects.

Robinson doesn't yet know that Hubert Humphrey Gable is dead, or that the slender population of Caesura, about to officially increase by four, just recently decreased by one. Robinson lives in a bungalow on the farthest, quietest edge of town, by choice, and his sleep patterns verge notoriously close to hibernation. He was long divorced in his previous life, currently unmarried, and his prospects for future coupling in the Blinds are honestly not great. Not because Robinson's not handsome. He's actually aged into a soft and pliant but trustworthy face that's surprisingly appealing and, if nothing else, he's kept his hair, which he wears very short, so his pronounced widow's peak looks like a bat taking wing on his forehead. Overall, he looks kind of debonair in a rumpled way, like someone who's gallant but tired. Still, his prospects for future marriage remain unpromising, in part because he's long since settled into his particular idiosyncratic patterns, and in part because getting romantically involved with a resident of the Blinds is an obviously bad idea, not to mention officially prohibited for staff. And, as stipulated in his original two-year contract that he's now re-upped twice, he's not allowed to leave the facility grounds, except under exceptional circumstances, which does not include blind dates. Which leaves Deputy Robinson with very few options. Deputy Dawes is his only potential onsite mate, but Robinson secretly suspects that Dawes is a closeted lesbian.

As for Cooper: Cooper's always had a more laissez-faire attitude toward both official prohibitions and obviously bad ideas, so his record when it comes to illicit relations with the residents of the Blinds is not spotless. Admittedly, even as he's aged into his mid-forties, huffing toward fifty like an aging slugger limping around third in a labored home-run trot, he benefits, in the Blinds, from an inherent lack of options among the citizenry. If you're looking for an ill-considered affair, it's not hard to find one, when there's only a few dozen of you, stuck together and cut off from the outside world. So, no, he has not been monastically chaste during his eight-year tenure as sheriff but, he figures, he's been good enough, and "good enough" is a standard he failed to achieve with such frequency in his life before the Blinds that it feels to him now like something akin to a moral triumph. Since his arrival here, he even once came perilously close to falling in love, but thankfully he managed to expertly fuck that up in the nick of time.

There are, in this room right now, he notes, four brand-new arrivals, two of whom are women and both of whom are attractive. The first one looks to be in her mid-forties, and she's arresting in a way that suggests she comes from money in whatever life she's just left behind. However, her carefully manicured nails and evident history of restorative skin peels suggest she might also find her new life among cinder block bungalows under the Texas sun to be an unwelcome adjustment. Given her obvious level of anxiety, as she mindlessly clacks said artfully manicured nails on her desktop, this new reality is likely dawning on her as well. The other woman is younger, possibly half-Asian, late twenties, with a tomboyish aspect, like someone who likes nothing more than taking a good early-morning hike. She has a pleasant, open, intelligent face, which suggests to Cooper that she'd stomach his particular brand of bullshit for about eight minutes. In any case, she's likely young enough to be his daughter, a realization that causes Cooper, lurking as he is at the back of the room, a physical pang of unease. Cooper wonders if maybe she's what they call "an innocent"—someone sent to the program because they witnessed some hideous crime, or imperiled their life by giving crucial testimony in some important trial, but who isn't, themselves, a former criminal. You're not supposed to speculate about things like that in the Blinds, but it's hard not to do, understandably. Of course, in Cooper's experience, everyone living here thinks they must be an innocent; they're certain of it. Which means that probably none of them are.

The other two new arrivals are men, and definitely neither of them looks like an innocent. One is thickly muscular and looks, honestly, Cooper thinks, like a goombah: you know, pinkie rings and pomade and chest hair and attitude. Hey, Cooper didn't invent this stereotype, he just encounters it very often. The other male is white and coiled and wiry and sits ramrod straight with a shaved head in a collarless white linen shirt. He has pale skin and the intense and bright-eyed and slightly shriveled look of someone who's been recently fasting. He has tattoos of little faces covering his neck, inked up from below the collar of his shirt to his jawline, like some worsening rash.

At the front of the classroom, Robinson launches into his speech. "I know you have questions. Let me answer the most common ones."

He turns and writes COMMON QUESTIONS on the whiteboard.

"We have three rules, and these three rules must always be respected." Robinson writes THREE RULES on the whiteboard. Under that, he writes:

1. NO VISITORS
2. NO CONTACT
3. NO RETURN

He turns back to the four newcomers. "No visitors—that should be self-explanatory. Whoever you knew, or think you knew, or half-remember maybe knowing in your previous life, you will never see those people again. Fortunately, most of those people probably want to murder you." No laugh from the crowd. *That's okay,* Robinson thinks, *that joke's always hit or miss.* He points to rule number two. "No contact. This means no letters, no emails, no phone calls, no telegrams, no carrier pigeons, no smoke-signals, no texts, no snaps, no pings, no whatever-the-latest-invention-is. No two-way communication with the outside world whatsoever. Period." He points to the last rule. "No return. This may be the most important for you to understand today. Caesura is not a prison. You are not being held here against your will. This is a program that you've entered freely, and you are free to leave at any time. But please understand: These gates only open one way. So, if you leave, you can never come back. Is that understood?"

The four new arrivals all mumble assent, in a way that suggests obedience more than understanding, which, for now, is good enough for Robinson. He continues.

"Also understand that if you exit the grounds unauthorized, for any reason, your safety cannot be guaranteed. Not only that, but you will have jeopardized yourself and, just as importantly, you will have endangered your fellow residents. So, if you leave, your participation in the program will be terminated immediately, and you will be out there, on your own, in the outside world, which, as I'm sure you can imagine, can be an unforgiving place, especially for the type of people who end up here. That said, you are in this program voluntarily. So, welcome."

At this prompt, the four people in the room eye each other, wondering how the other people came to be here.

Robinson goes on. "Beyond these three rules, we have a few other guidelines that I strongly suggest you take to heart. For starters, please respect your fellow residents. This is a community built on privacy and mutual trust. We don't ask pointed questions of each other or try to speculate about other people's pasts. We don't try to pinpoint regional accents or ask about sports-team affiliations or the origin or meaning"—and here he nods conspicuously to the skinny shaved-headed ramrod—"of people's tattoos. Whoever you were before, we are all now citizens of Caesura, located in Kettle County, in the great state of Texas, in the continental United States of America. Everything that happened to you before you got here has either been forgotten or is better off forgotten. Your new life starts today. Any questions?"

The young girl, the likely hiker, shoots up her hand. "Why Kettle County, Texas, of all places?"

"Kettle County is the third least populous county in the United States. The population of the entire county is, last I checked, about two hundred and sixty-eight, give or take a birth or death in the last twenty-four hours. That does not include the approximately forty-eight people, including yourselves, who live here in Caesura. Technically, we don't exist. At least as far as the census is concerned."

The hiker shoots up her hand again. "So why not situate us in the least populous county? Why third least?"

"Because the least populous county, which is also located in beautiful northwest Texas, seemed a little too obvious a choice, was the thinking, I believe."

Hiker's hand, again.

"What about the second least populous county?"

"The second least populous county in the United States is in Hawaii. Perception-wise, this was not deemed an acceptable location, since this is, after all, not a spa. And you are not here to work on your tans."

Robinson lets the four people in the room contemplate the fact that they could, right now, in an alternate universe, be living in Hawaii, rather than here, in this universe, in a glorified trailer park fenced in under the hot Texas sun. He savors their disappointed faces. Then he continues.

"Let me stress that, despite the perimeter fence and the various rules, your residency here is not a punishment. You are not in jail. You are not in hell. You are in Texas." He waits for a few dry chuckles; it's a long shot, but the line sometimes gets a response. Today, no dice. Tough crowd. "Beyond the prohibitions I've outlined, every *legal* recreational activity is accommodated and even encouraged. Books, films, and television are all provided. We have a library. We have a gym. We even have a bar. We have a chapel, if you're so inclined. We have a medical facility for onsite emergencies and treatments and a very good onsite nurse practitioner, Ava Breckinridge, who's also available for therapeutic visits. There's a well-stocked commissary that gets weekly shipments of goods, food, clothes, everything you might need. Though I'll warn you, it's not exactly Neiman Marcus."

This gets a dutiful snort from the fortysomething woman. It's something, at least.

"There is, however, no Internet access," he continues. "There are no personal phone calls in or out, and no personal mail. You will not be in contact with anyone from your past under any circumstances. Because, simply put, if we have access to the outside world, that means the outside world has access to us. Which is exactly what we are striving to avoid."

Now the goombah's hand flutters up briefly from the desk in what Robinson decides is an acceptable concession toward hand-raising. He nods to him. "Yes?"

"Are we hidden?" the goombah asks, in a goombahish voice. Cooper, from the back of the room, determines upon further consideration that the goombah's not Italian but from some more far-flung quadrant of Eastern Europe. His inflections, though, are pure American Gangster, probably picked up from a thousand Scorsese films. "You said we don't exist," the goombah continues. "Like, could people find this place on a map?"

"We're as hidden as you can be in an age when every shopping mall employs facial recognition scanners and every citizen can call up satellite photos on their phone," Robinson says. "But we're not on any official maps and you need binoculars to even see this place from the nearest public road. And we're a hundred miles from anything resembling civilization. As you may remember from your bus ride out here, we are smack dab in the middle of no-fucking-where, is the technical term, I believe." A few more chuckles, from everyone save for the skinny tattooed one. "In eight years, we have not had a single incursion or breach of security." That's not technically true, thinks Cooper, but he gets the purpose of Robinson's fib: Why scare the bejesus out of people on day number one, when they've barely had time to unpack?

"Now that we've got the rules out of the way," says Robinson, "let's talk about the more welcoming side of Caesura." He turns to the whiteboard and uncaps the marker again. "Caesura is not just a new home but part of a holistic program designed to ensure both your security and your future well-being in a larger sense."

He writes HOLISTIC on the whiteboard.

"As we like to say, we're not a place to hide, we're a place to flourish."

He writes FLOURISH on the whiteboard.

He turns back to the classroom, then points to the badge on his upper arm. "You see this? It's a river, in a desert. That's how we like to think of Caesura. Like an oasis."

The older woman pipes up now. No hand, which grates on Robinson.

"Has anyone ever left before?" she asks flatly.

"Yes. A few. Voluntarily."

"And what happened to them?"

"Once you're gone, you're gone," says Robinson. "You're no longer our concern. But from what I understand: nothing good."

The Tattooed Ramrod shoots an inked arm up, straight to the sky, like a parody of schoolboy obedience. As his arm rises, the sleeve of his loose shirt falls, revealing more tattoos of faces, from his wrist up his arm. "Excuse me, sir?"

"Yes?"

"What about pornography?"

Robinson stares at him flatly. Class clown. They show up occasionally. "What about it?"

"You said you have no Internet."

"We make magazines available. I'm sure you remember what those are." Robinson launches back into his spiel. "Does anyone here know what Caesura means? The word itself?" No one answers. "Caesura," he continues, "means a pause. A break. And that's what this is. You have entered this program voluntarily. This was not only to secure your cooperation and testimony, it was to ensure your protection and provide you with a *break* in your lives, a pause, a new start, which you have chosen freely to undertake. We encourage you to approach life here in that spirit. Now, if there are no more—"

Ramrod raises his hand again. "What about conjugal visits?"

Robinson sighs. "As I explained, there are no visitors."

"Even prisoners get conjugal visits," says Ramrod.

"You're not a prisoner, and that's not how this place works. If you were properly oriented before agreeing to enter this program, which I'm sure you were, then nothing I'm telling you should come as a surprise."

Ramrod raises his hand again.

"Yes?"

Ramrod says brightly, "So who are we supposed to fuck? Each other?"

"Well, you're fucking with me right now, aren't you?" Robinson says. The group titters. Then he quiets them again. "If you're unhappy with anything you've heard today, there are mechanisms by which you can withdraw and return to your former circumstance. Of course, there may be other repercussions for you to face. As I said: This gate only opens one way. So, before you leave, I'd encourage you to consider what kind of circumstances might have led you to agree to come to a facility like this in the first place." He lets the line linger, then says: "Now, if there are no further questions, I'll introduce Sheriff Calvin Cooper."

Cooper rises slowly from his seat at the back of the room and takes his time walking to the front of the class. The four arrivals are visibly restless, swapping agitated glances as their reality sinks in: *What exactly have we agreed to?* Yes, it's a new life, but a new life to be lived in a concrete bungalow with a lawn the size of a cemetery plot, in a town encircled by a fourteen-foot fence and surrounded by semi-arid plains for a hundred miles in all directions.

Cooper watches as they wrestle with this realization. He's seen this process before, many times. It always ends the same way: They stay. What choice do they have, really?

He waits for them to settle. Then he says, finally, in a slightly raised voice, "There was a murder here last night."

That quiets the room right quick.

Even Robinson looks surprised.

"Longtime resident," Cooper continues, "name of Hubert Gable, sweet guy, never harmed anyone, just liked to enjoy a drink. Shot dead in our local bar early this morning. Some of you may have heard the shot. The details are not yet public knowledge so I'd ask you not to repeat any of this until I have a chance to address the whole town."

He lets the information register, watches their faces as it settles in. He waits for eager hands to rise with questions. None do. He continues.

"Look, I don't tell you this to scare you. Just to let you know what exactly the stakes are here. This may not be a prison, and it may not be purgatory, but it's sure as hell not a paradise, either. This is the Blinds." Cooper leaves those words to linger in the air as well. Then he points to his arm patch. "It may say 'Caesura' on the badges, but the Blinds is what everyone here calls it. Because we don't see the outside world, and they don't see us, not anymore. So this town's continued existence—our survival—depends on shared principles, mutual interests, and trust, just like any community.

Except in this community, when those principles are compromised, people get hurt. People die. Understood?"

No one speaks. The room is silent. Cooper says, "The most important thing to remember is: The Blinds is both a last stop and a fresh start. Which, for most of us, is exactly what we need. That's why we're here. Now y'all have yourselves a pleasant day."

If Cooper were the type to wear a cowboy hat, this would be the perfect moment to don the hat and tip it to the newcomers. But Cooper's never been one for a cowboy hat. He's from the Northeast originally, New England, so he was not born a hat man and he's never learned to fake it. It's the great regret of his life. One of them, anyway.

So instead he just lets his practiced words linger, then turns on his heel and heads straight through the door, out into the sunlight, leaving the new arrivals to scan the two lists and decide on their new names.

3.

ROBINSON SLIDES TWO PIECES OF PAPER across the desk to the Probable Hiker. The other three newcomers sit silent and wait their turn. Robinson has his ledger open. He watches her as she considers the two lists.

"What do I do with these?" she asks.

"Mix-n-match," Robinson says.

"What do the red *X*s mean?"

"Those names are already taken."

She looks up at him. "Why can't I just choose my own name from scratch?"

"Because, left to your own imagination, we've discovered that people choose names linked to their past, even inadvertently. You borrow a name from an old best friend or some classmate from third grade. Or you name yourself after your first dog or the street where you were born. All of which connects you to your former life."

The hiker nods slightly, as if to say, *Seems reasonable*. Robinson can sense she's inquisitive to a fault. Not the type to sit in the back of the class and simply scribble down whatever you tell her. She's front row. She wants *answers*. She wants to know if this will be on the exam.

"So why movie stars?" she asks.

"Their names are generic but familiar, so they're memorable. Like you've heard them somewhere before."

She looks at the other list. "And why *vice* presidents? Why not presidents?"

"What could be more anonymous than a vice president?" Robinson says with a practiced smile. A joke that he's made many times before.

She laughs politely. She considers the lists again. She bites her lip in concentration and she is suddenly attractive enough that Robinson instinctively looks away from her and at the clock. Then he looks back at her. "Or I can assign you a name," he says. "It will be randomly chosen using an algorithm from the available options."

"I like Bette Davis and Aaron Burr," she says. "I'll be Bette Burr."

The goombah scans the lists. He seems acutely befuddled. "There's a guy on here named Hannibal," he says.

"Hannibal Hamlin, that's right," Robinson says. "Our fifteenth vice president."

"Can that be my name?"

"Hannibal?"

"Yeah."

Robinson leans in, like he's sharing a confidence. "It's available, but between you and me, I don't recommend Hannibal. There's a reason no one's taken it. In the very unlikely event that anyone ever comes looking for you, you want them asking around for a John or a William, not a Hannibal."

"I want to be Hannibal," the goombah announces.

"Fine. But you have to combine it with another name." Robinson points to the other list. "One of the movie stars."

"I want to be Hannibal Gore."

"Al Gore's not a movie star."

"Hannibal Bronson. Like Charles Bronson—"

"Charles Bronson's not on the list."

"He's a movie star."

"Sure. But he's not on the list."

"Okay, then Hannibal Schwarzenegger—"

"It's got to be a name on the list." Robinson nudges the list forward slightly.

The goombah nods, in a practiced imitation of comprehension, then reads the list again with great concentration. Robinson's irritated. He looks at the clock and thinks about lunch. He says finally to the goombah, as a prod, "How about Cagney?"

The goombah looks up, uncomprehending.

"James Cagney," Robinson says. "He was like the Charles Bronson of his day."

"Hannibal Cagney. I like it." The goombah grins. "Let them come," he says, now beaming. He fires two fingers in the air like pistols. "Let them come and try to take down Hannibal fucking Cagney!"

Robinson writes the name down in the ledger.

"Vivien King," says the fortysomething woman decisively.

The decision took all of five seconds.

"I do not want a Negroid name," says the Tattooed Ramrod flatly, staring straight at Robinson.

Robinson and Ramrod are the last two people in the room. Robinson remembers this stare-down game all too well from his previous life as a beat cop in Baltimore. He locks eyes with Ramrod to communicate that he has registered, but will not acknowledge, nor be rattled by, this punk-ass provocation.

"Jefferson, Johnson, Thompson. I do not want a Negroid name," Ramrod says again.

"They were your names before they were our names," says Robinson.

Ramrod breaks first. He glances at the list, then back at Robinson. "All the good ones are gone. I can't have Wayne?"

"No."

"How about Dean?"

"Already taken."

"Well, shit," says Ramrod.

"Forty-four people got here before you. The pickings are getting slim," says Robinson. "You don't have to take a male name, you know. You can choose from the women as well."

Ramrod scans that list, then points to Marlene Dietrich. "How about Dietrich?"

"That's available. But you need a first name, too. From the VP list."

Ramrod glances over the second list. "So strange, don't you think? To ascend to such a high position in your lifetime and then be totally forgotten? I mean, who even remembers Schuyler Colfax? Or John C. Breckinridge?"

"The history books do."

"In my experience, a history book is the last place you want to go looking for the truth." Ramrod consults the list again. While he reads, Robinson considers the tattoos that cover the man's arms and neck, stretching up to his jawbone like a priest's high collar. Tributes, all of them, from the looks of it. Faces, ringed in halos or roses. Women, men, even a few small children. All beaming beatifically.

"You know all those people?" Robinson asks, gesturing at the tattoos.

"Yes. Or I did, anyway."

"And they've all passed?"

"Yes, sir, they did."

"A lot of pain on those arms," says Robinson, and begins to reconsider his lack of compassion for the man in front of him.

Ramrod sticks his arms out straight and jacks up his loose linen sleeves and regards the tattoos like a man inspecting an expensively tailored suit. "Yes, sir, that is the gospel truth." Then he points to the bottom of the VP list. "What about Dick?"

"Dick? It's all yours."

"Dick Dietrich." Ramrod smiles. "Got a certain ring, don't you think?"

"It's definitely not a Negroid name," says Robinson, then writes it down.

"Dick Dietrich." Ramrod nods, pleased with his choice. "Now that's the kind of name that history remembers."

Fran Adams's house is just a five-minute walk from the intake trailer and the main drag of the town, but then, in the Blinds, everyone's house is just a five-minute walk from pretty much everything else. Cooper walks briskly, head down, up the main northwest street, casting a long, slanted morning shadow. The Blinds has one main dirt road that runs east-west, where the store and the services are found, and another unpaved artery that runs north-south, halving the half dozen or so residential streets into twinned cul-de-sacs, six houses per side. The streets have no names; the houses have no numbers, which, to Cooper, makes sense. It would be counter-intuitive, he thinks, to have street signs in a place that is primarily intended to help people hide.

He corrects himself.

Not hide. Flourish.

Just look at us all, he thinks. *Flourishing.*

The units are all single-story bungalows, wind-blasted, identical, constructed of cinder block, because the town is located in West Texas on the far west edge of Tornado Alley. So the Fell Institute, which established Caesura, decided to make indestructibility, rather than aesthetics, the town's top priority. And the residents dutifully run their tornado drills, ringing the bells at the chapel and gathering everyone inside, even though, in eight years, the town has never so much as touched the hem of a passing tornado. What weather they do get in summer is sun, sun, sun, and heat; in winter, it's sun and cold, with occasional wind. Cold is a concept that's difficult for Cooper to remember right now, given they're smack-dab in July's sizzling peak. As he passes the houses, he does his best to avoid the glances from the curtained windows, and only nods at the few lobbed greetings from people out sitting on their porches. He's not up for his usual, ambling sheriff routine this morning, and he'd rather not field any panicked questions about exactly what the hell happened in the wee hours last night. He'll address the whole town soon enough. He can quell their fears then, as best he can. But before all that, he wants to check in on Fran Adams. He knows the route to her house by heart.

He marvels again at the little things—the flower boxes, the stubborn gardens, the stained-glass decorations on rubber suckers stuck inside windowpanes to catch the sun—all the ways people try to personalize their tiny, identical parcels of the town. Each house has a scrap of front yard, but no driveway, since no one in the Blinds has a car. Cooper's the only one in town with regular access to a vehicle—another perk of his position, if you can call a dented pickup with a slippery transmission and 250,000 miles in the rear-view a perk—and the town keeps another car on hand, a Chevy Aveo, for emergencies, though that vehicle is usually up on blocks at the repair shop, under Orson Calhoun's care. It doesn't matter much; no one ever uses either vehicle, not even Cooper. Unlike the residents, he's technically allowed the occasional twenty-four-hour furlough to civilization in extraordinary circumstances, though he can't remember the last time he requested one from the Institute. Once you're planted here, he's found, you get pretty much settled, and civilization starts to feel very far away.

As he turns the corner toward Fran Adams's house, he spots her sitting out on the front steps. Cooper waves as he approaches.

"Morning, Ms. Adams," he says.

"Morning, Sheriff." She stands. She's wearing the same torn jeans and plaid shirt and t-shirt she'd worn the previous night and her hair's pulled back in a ponytail that says, *I'll deal with you later.* "So," she says, "you planning to tell me just what the hell happened last night?"

Before Cooper can answer, which he's not eager to do, Isaac runs out the screen door, letting it slap closed behind him.

"Look at these cards," Isaac says. He holds up a fresh pack of trading cards, a souvenir from the movie they'd gone to see together offsite a few months back. That wasn't an official furlough—Cooper just snuck that one in himself. He sat beside Isaac in the air-conditioned theater for two hours, munching popcorn, keeping watch, though he can't recall a single thing about the movie now. Some animated action film for kids with guardian robots in it and monsters who eventually learn to accept themselves.

"I got these, they just came to the store," Isaac says, fanning the cards out, fresh from the pack, the cardboard still dusted pink with the residue of the bubblegum they arrived with. The cards depict battling robots; apparently, it's some kind of game. Isaac holds them out proudly. He has his mother's dark hair, though on his head it's scalloped into tight curls. He's a sweet-looking kid, Cooper thinks—he looks a lot like his mother. Kids always look to Cooper like the as-yet-unruined version of their parents, like some remnant of the you that existed before you made all your bad decisions.

"You going to share that bubblegum with me?" asks Cooper.

"I already confiscated it," says Fran. "Or did we finally get a dentist in this town?"

"Can we go to another movie?" asks Isaac. He speaks in a clipped, insistent, urgent bark, like he's never had to wait his turn, and he's accustomed to everyone's instant attention. Maybe that's what happens when you grow up the only kid in a town full of adults, Cooper thinks. There used to be another kid for a while—Cooper wonders if Isaac remembers that boy. No one expected kids here; no one planned for it. Once Isaac arrived, the town just made it work. But that was back when he was only a baby, a toddler. Now that he's going on eight, it's just not a tenable situation—Cooper's known this for a while. And he knows that Fran understands that, too. It's just convincing her to go anywhere else that's hard. Not that he blames her. Nothing good ever happens to people who leave the Blinds. Including that other boy.

Jacob was his name. Jacob Mondale. And his mother, Jean. It's important to remember their names, Cooper thinks.

"We'll see," he says to Isaac. "I sure had fun last time. But we'll have to ask your mother." He winks at Fran, who doesn't soften.

"Isaac," she says, "why don't you go inside and put those cards somewhere safe." Isaac runs back into the house. She says to Cooper, "I asked Spiro to order those cards a month ago. They finally came through the commissary. I thought they'd make for a nice souvenir. He really did have a good time. Though I still don't know if it was a good idea."

"He's got to see the world eventually. He can't stay here. Not forever."

"I thought that was the whole point of this place. To hide from the rest of the world."

"For most of us. Not for him. He's not—"

"We've had this discussion, Cal. Now are you going to tell me about that gunshot?"

Cooper considers his words. "We had an incident, it's true. Not a good one. At the bar."

"An incident? Like, the kind of incident that involves a gun going off into someone's body?"

"I'm calling a town meeting about it this afternoon. I'll explain everything then."

"Can you give me a sneak peek? I have a kid here, Cal. Was it a suicide, like the other one?"

"Not likely, no." Cooper nods toward the house. "Did it wake him?"

"No, thank God. He sleeps like a teenager."

"Count that as a blessing."

"For him or for me?"

"Depends how many late-night bad habits you're hoping to hide."

Fran eyes Cooper, then smiles slightly—finally, a concession, a crack. "There was a time when you were very familiar with my late-night habits, Sheriff Cooper."

For the second time today, Cooper thinks this would be an excellent moment for a hat. Instead, he just rubs his forehead and squints out at the block. "I can't let you know anything until I let the whole town know."

"No special privileges, huh?"

"Not with this."

She unfolds her arms and squeezes his shoulder. This is as much of a physical intimacy as they've ever allowed themselves in public, even back when their private meetings were much more intimate. "Just let me know he's safe, Cal."

"He's safe. You're both safe. I can promise you that." He regrets this promise as soon as he's spoken it. He's had a lifelong habit of offering promises he's in no position to deliver. But it's too late to back down on it now, so he says, "I'll ring the bell for the town meeting sometime around one. Then I'll tell you everything I know. I promise that, too."

As he walks down her steps and back into the street, he regrets that last promise even more.

4.

SO WHAT DO WE KNOW about Hubert Humphrey Gable?" asks Dawes, flipping through her notebook.

"Nothing. Not a fucking thing. That's precisely the founding principle of this town," Cooper says. "But more to the point, Dawes—what are you doing sitting at my desk?"

"I warned her," says Robinson, who's standing over a pair of uniform pants slung across an ironing board, affecting an earnest but clumsy imitation of ironing.

"I just thought I'd see what the view looked like from here, while we waited for you," says Dawes, looking up from Cooper's swivel chair, at Cooper, who's standing in the doorway of the trailer, having just arrived back from his entirely unsatisfactory visit to Fran Adams.

The three of them have gathered in what passes for the town's police station: a single room housed in a trailer at one end of the main thoroughfare. The office is crammed with filing cabinets and discarded furniture of various fake wood grains, in various stages of disrepair. A sadly failing and mostly ornamental A/C unit sits wedged in the lone window. Only Cooper gets a desk. Cooper gets the desk because Cooper's the boss, he was here first, and when he started, it was only him. When they hired Robinson five years back, Cooper ordered a second desk. They're still waiting for it to arrive. Cooper never bothered to order a desk for Dawes.

Situated behind Cooper's desk is Cooper's swivel chair, another perk of his position, and behind that, in a place of honor on top of a low-slung filing cabinet, sits the idle fax machine. Only Cooper gets to touch the fax machine. Since there's no Internet and no cell service in Caesura, the fax machine and its dedicated phone line are the town's only link to the outside world. Next to the fax machine sits an impressively sturdy paper shredder. If you get a fax, you read the fax, and then you feed the fax into the shredder's hungry teeth. Once upon a time, not long after he arrived, Robinson nicknamed the fax machine Cain and the shredder Abel. Now Cain and Abel sit attentively behind Cooper's desk, waiting, under his watch, like two heeled dogs.

Dawes rises from Cooper's desk and returns to her own spot, a hardback chair by the wall. "I meant, what do we know about Gable since he got here?" she continues. "Any feuds? Debts? Disputes?" As she says this, she flips back through her notebook intently, as though the answers are already written there by some previous, wiser version of herself.

"Gable mostly kept to himself, best as I know," says Cooper, unbuckling his gun belt and coiling it heavily on his desktop. Thus unburdened, he settles back into his swivel chair, where he twists idly, the king returned to his throne.

"I've always meant to ask—why is it that Deputy Robinson and I aren't issued gun belts, sir?" says Dawes.

"Because you don't carry guns," says Cooper. "One sheriff, one gun—that's the theory, anyway. We used to keep an emergency firearm in a locked safe but look how that turned out. Speaking of—" He unlocks his top desk drawer and slides it open and pulls out a box of .38 ammo. He shakes six bullets into the palm of his hand. Then he flips open the cylinder of his pistol and feeds the bullets, one by one, into the revolver. "Eight years, and I never had to load this thing." He flips the cylinder shut, then slips the pistol back into the holster in his gun belt, and locks the box of ammo away again. "This belt isn't even Institute issue. It's my personal property, a souvenir from my last job, before I signed my life away to work for the Blinds."

"And what was that?" says Dawes.

"Wish I could tell you, Dawes, but you know the rules." Cooper raises a finger to his pursed lips like an old librarian shushing a rowdy room. "But this here? This was my lucky gun belt. Good thing I brought it with me, too. It's hell trying to convince the Institute to supply us with anything." He gestures to the ramshackle office. "As you might intuit."

"So what's your plan on informing people?" asks Robinson, continuing to torture those pants with the hissing iron. Cooper suspects that it's taking everything in Dawes's power, as the clear subordinate, not to leap up and offer Robinson remedial instruction in crease-making, given that her own uniform is always pressed to a military crispness.

"I'll ring the bell and call a town meeting this afternoon," says Cooper. "That gives us a little time to put our heads together and figure out what we're going to tell them."

"We might want to hold off until the agent from Amarillo has weighed in," says Dawes.

Cooper stops swiveling. "Wait—someone's coming out here?"

"Agent Rigo, from Amarillo. He's on his way right now. He's scheduled to arrive in a half an hour or so."

There is nothing about Dawes's statement that is welcome news to Cooper. "Who's Rigo? What happened to Agent Brightwell?"

Dawes shrugs. "I called it in first thing this morning from the fax phone just like you asked me to. This Agent Rigo answered. Said he's our liaison now. Said he wanted to come out personally to have a look at the crime scene." She delivers all this with the slightly defensive, slightly befuddled tone of someone relaying news she had no idea would be controversial. "He also said he had some questions about Colfax."

"Errol Colfax?"

"Yes, sir."

"What about him? Colfax was months ago. Colfax was a *suicide,*" says Cooper.

"Agent Rigo was very insistent," Dawes says, then looks to Robinson for reinforcement, but he keeps his head down, studiously trained on the ironing. She looks back to Cooper. "I just assumed—"

"Please, do not do that," says Cooper. "This is just great. Dr. Holliday is going to be *delighted.*"

"We'd have to tell her what happened eventually," says Robinson.

"Of course, we'll tell her," Cooper says. "I'd just—I'd like to have a little more to tell her when we do. Like a fucking suspect, for starters."

"Sheriff, I don't mean any disrespect—" says Dawes.

Cooper turns to Robinson. "Why do I suspect I'm about to be disrespected?"

"—but it would seem," Dawes continues, "to be in everyone's interest to follow procedure on this, yes? It is a homicide, after all."

Cooper stands and leans forward on the desk. "While I'm certainly delighted to be reminded by you about the necessity of procedure, I am also interested in sparing the fragile residents of this town from a parade of nosy outsiders. Residents who, I'll remind you, are made jittery by law enforcement agents who come bearing intrusive questions."

Dawes has the quizzical look of someone being chastised for something she's still confident was entirely right. "I'm sorry, sir. I didn't—"

"No, you didn't. That much is for certain." Cooper picks up his gun belt and straps it back around his waist. The belt and its holster—and the pistol inside it—are almost entirely for show, but then Cooper's learned that showmanship—the appearance of authority; the illusion of order—is a crucial part of his job. "Dealing with our citizenry's sensitivity to these issues"—he pulls the belt tight and buckles it—"is something I have learned a lot about over my eight years of doing what you've been doing"—and here Cooper comically checks his watch—"for all of six fucking weeks. So, before you don your goddamned deerstalker hat and start the Sherlock Holmes act, will you please consider the nature of our situation. Which is delicate."

Cooper also considers the nature of their situation. Now, instead of gathering the residents to give a calming, don't-worry-folks-we've-got-this-all-under-control speech, he's going to have to lead an officious stranger right down the middle of the main street while the entire jittery town looks on and speculates. He turns to Robinson. "Any thoughts you care to share on this subject, Walt?"

Robinson props the iron on its haunches, where it looses a long exhausted sigh of steam. "I never knew that's what they called it."

"Called what?"

"That Sherlock Holmes hat. A deerstalker. I never knew it had a name."

"Any other thoughts?"

"It's not good," he says.

"No, it's not good," says Cooper. "It's not fucking good at all."

5.

THE AGENT FROM AMARILLO arrives at noon exactly. His bright black car appears down the dirt road in a shimmer of undulating heat. The tires spray a continuous plume of yellow dust as the long sedan approaches the town's fence, then stops, and Cooper and Robinson roll back the entrance gate and the sedan enters slowly. The driver pulls the car over and parks. The three of them, Cooper, Robinson, and Dawes, stand attentively aside.

The driver's door opens. A very tall man with very blond hair unfolds himself from the front seat, then reassembles himself to stand straight again, like some new brand of expensive and complicated umbrella. He wears a black suit, white shirt, and black tie, the whole outfit entirely inappropriate to the heat. On his face, he wears wraparound sunglasses that look as though they've been stolen from a surfer. His white-blond hair is gelled straight up in the air in an almost aquatic crown of spiny spikes. He's very pale, Cooper thinks, like he crawled up from the bottom of the sea to emerge blinking in the Texan sun.

He steps forward and extends a white hand.

"I'm Agent Paul Rigo," he says.

Cooper shakes his hand. "Sheriff Calvin Cooper."

"I know," says Rigo. "Now where's the bar?"

As the quartet walks through the center of town, faces appear at windows. Curtains are parted. This is exactly what Cooper had hoped to avoid. He's relieved when the four of them finally reach the trailer that houses the bar, Blinders, where Greta Fillmore is already waiting outside to receive them. Robinson offers a mumbled pleasantry, then excuses himself to dubious-sounding duties. Cooper's hoping Dawes might similarly recuse herself, but no such luck—she sticks around to observe. The four of them step into the darkened bar together. When Greta flicks on the lights, a defeated ceiling fan begins its exhausted rotation. Rigo steps forward and inspects the plywood bar, which still bears a large kidney-shaped stain. Then he inspects the stool where Gable sat. Then he walks around the bar and inspects the shelves behind the bar. He finds a hole basically at a plumb line from where Gable's head would have been while he was seated. Rigo pats his pockets, pulls out a Leatherman tool, then wrenches free a bent slug from the wall. He puts it in his palm and peers at it like a prospector appraising a nugget. Then he sets the slug on the bar, and requests a beer.

"Thoughts?" says Cooper, now nursing his own beer and seated next to Rigo on a barstool. Dawes hovers, beerless, behind them, scribbling notes.

"It's a nine-millimeter round," says Rigo. "You know anyone in town with a nine millimeter?"

"I don't know anyone in town with a gun," Cooper says, smiling, "save for me. Which is our dilemma in a nutshell." He unholsters his gun and presents it to Rigo. "It's a thirty-eight, in case you're wondering. Never even carried it loaded, until today."

Rigo inspects it disinterestedly, then hands it back. "You had another shooting a while ago, yes?"

"That's right. A suicide."

"*Suspected* suicide," Dawes interjects from behind them. Cooper shoots her a glance that, if there were any justice in this world, would send her scurrying to the other side of town.

"You folks seem to be suffering from an epidemic of unexplained shootings," says Rigo.

"In the case of the suicide, we did keep an extra handgun in a locked case in the police station," says Cooper. "Couple months back, someone broke in, smashed the case open, stole the pistol."

"You weren't concerned?"

"We were plenty fucking concerned at the time. Then we found out what had happened to it two days later. Fellow by the name of Colfax, Errol Colfax, one of our original eight, he'd stolen it to end his own life. I found him myself, with the gun in his hand, in his living room La-Z-Boy, having ushered himself from this world."

"That seems like an awful lot of trouble to go to just to off yourself," says Rigo. "Breaking into a gun safe like that."

"Well, some people don't like ropes," says Cooper. "And we're a long way from the nearest bottle of pills."

"What happened to that gun?"

"We bagged it and sent it to the Fell Institute in Amarillo to let them handle it," says Cooper. "That's the institute that runs this place."

"I know," says Rigo. "I work for the Fell Institute. They sent me out to assess this situation."

"You're not Justice Department?"

"Ex-Justice."

"So you work for Dr. Holliday now?"

"Indirectly," Rigo says.

"What happened to Brightwell?"

"Reassigned."

"Shame," says Cooper. "He was a good man."

"I wouldn't know," says Rigo. "The point is, the Institute is"—here he considers his words, in a very ostentatious manner—"concerned. About this killing. As you would imagine."

"As are we, I can assure you," Cooper says.

"Who sent that gun in to the Institute? You?"

"It was my ex-deputy, Ellis Gonzalez. That was his real name. His name out here was Marlon Garner."

Rigo laughs. "That's right, you've all got these funny names here. What's your real name, Cooper?"

"I can't tell you that. Not while I'm still employed."

"What about her?" Rigo nods to Dawes.

"Deputy Sidney Dawes, sir."

Rigo says to Cooper, "So what happened to Marlon Garner?"

"He quit, not long after Colfax killed himself."

"And where is he now?"

"I have no idea. We haven't kept in touch. Why?"

Rigo picks up the slug from the bar and studies it, pincering it between two long fingers. "Because my guess is that the pistol you gave him never made it back to the Institute. And that if this slug here matches the one from that gun, we might have two murder mysteries on our hands. You pulled the slug from Colfax, right?"

"Sure did—I sent it back to Amarillo with the gun." Cooper did no such thing.

"And the body?"

"Colfax? Cremated. Our local nurse has an arrangement with a town nearby. Same fate awaits Gable, is my understanding. You want me to hold them off?"

"No need. You go ahead and deal with your dead." Rigo finishes his beer, pulls a few bills from his pocket, and slaps them on the bar.

Cooper slides the cash back toward him. "You know your money's no good here, Agent Rigo."

"The Institute's got it covered."

"No, I mean it's literally no good here. We don't exchange cash."

Rigo glances at Cooper. "That's right. No names, no cash—quite an operation you've got going here." He pockets the bills and retrieves the slug from the bar and pockets that, too. "You got any kids living in this town?"

"Just one."

"They let you raise a kid out here?"

"It wasn't exactly planned."

"Does he have a funny name, too?"

"He's a good kid."

"No doubt. This town seems like a regular Mayberry."

Cooper stands, in hopes of ushering Rigo out of the bar. "I know you're new, Agent Rigo, but traditionally the Institute more or less leaves us alone to handle our own affairs."

"That might be changing. After all, you've never had a murder before." Rigo stands. "Nice to meet you both. I'm sure I'll be seeing you again soon."

"Would you mind doing me one favor when you leave?" asks Cooper.

"What's that?"

"Outsiders tend to make our residents a wee bit nervous. So drive a little faster out of town."

With Rigo gone, Dawes occupies the barstool next to Cooper. He uncaps a beer and hands it to her without asking, knowing it's the only way she'll accept it, given she's still on duty and it's still the middle of the day. And she does accept the beer, showing only the slight hesitation of someone faced with the conundrum of having to either disobey a written regulation or disobey a direct request from a superior. But Cooper's always considered this a useful rule of thumb: Always obey the request in front of you over the one written in a book somewhere. If he can teach Dawes that, he thinks, then maybe one day they can move on to the more valuable lesson of when to disobey both.

He holds up his own bottle, his second, and offers the longneck for a toast. "Here's to following proper procedure."

She hesitates. "I'm not a cop, you know. I was an EMT before this."

"And I was a corrections officer. So maybe neither of us should be expected to play Sherlock Holmes on this one."

They toast. Cooper swigs. He tips his beer back slowly, careful not to race too far ahead. It's not like he's an alcoholic. It's just that he can't usually think of a good reason, when the opportunity presents itself, not to fuzz the edges of the world just a little bit. "You like that work? An EMT?"

"I trained for it because I thought I'd be saving people's lives. Turns out you spend most of your days helping really fat people get out of bed." She pretends to take a sip of beer. She hates beer.

"I'm sorry I was hard on you earlier."

"You weren't hard. You were right."

"It's possible to be both." Cooper looks her over. "Why the hell did you choose the name Sidney Dawes, anyway?"

"Do I look like a Barbara Quayle to you?" She picks at the label of her beer, unscrolling it from the sweating bottle. "To be honest, I thought you could choose any name you liked when you got here, and I wanted to be called Darwin."

"Why Darwin?"

"Because Darwin means change." She fakes another sip. "I don't know shit about Charles Dawes, but 'Dawes' seemed close enough."

"And why Sidney?"

"For Sidney Poitier. He's the only black person on either of those lists."

Cooper finishes off his bottle, slightly ahead of schedule. He starts to think about number three. He gets up and walks around the bar, rummaging in the fridge, then surfaces with another cold one and pops the beer open.

"What about you, sir?" she asks. "Why Calvin Cooper?"

"Cooper for Gary Cooper, the greatest movie sheriff of all time. I guess I figured if someone had to take that name, it might as well be me."

"And Calvin?"

"I just liked the comic strip, the one with the kid and the tiger. Besides, I always had a boring first name so I wanted something a little fancier. It was John, if you're curious. Unlike the residents living here, I know who I used to be."

"Really? And what was your last name?"

"Now you know I can't tell you that." Cooper swigs. "Okay, your turn, Sid—what's your real first name?"

"My first name is just a bunch of syllables my mother thought up five minutes before I was born, then slapped on my birth certificate, then stuck me with. I never liked it."

"Let me guess. LaToya?"

"Don't. That's not even funny," she says sharply.

Cooper considers this onset of defensiveness. For the first time, he starts to think he might grow to tolerate her. From what he's seen so far—well, for starters, the notebook's got to go. But she's smart, and persistent, and not afraid to be a stickler. "Your secret dies with you," he says.

To Cooper's disappointment, Dawes pushes her beer away and pulls out her notebook. "Tell me about Ellis Gonzalez."

"We've got to get back to work."

She nods to the notebook. "This is work, sir. Why'd he leave?"

"To be honest, he wasn't cut out for this place."

"I'd like to try and contact him."

"Why?"

"Ask him about that gun. What if he never sent it in? That would answer a lot of questions. I bet I could track him down."

"Off-grounds? Absolutely not. We're only cleared to leave the facility under extraordinary circumstances."

"And this doesn't strike you as an extraordinary circumstance, sir?"

Cooper stands behind the bar, glaring at her. Here he is, trying to reach out, sharing a slightly illicit midday drink, *making connections,* and now this: a blatant flirtation with insubordination. "You seem to be under the impression that you can say anything to me just so long as you follow it with 'sir.'"

"That's not true. Sir."

"My theory is, someone got drunk, staggered home to retrieve a rusty old firearm he'd kept stashed under the floorboards or who the fuck knows where, came back here and settled their argument for good. People do smuggle things in here, Deputy, despite our best efforts. In any case, whoever did this will likely come crying to us and confess before week's end. It's not like they have anywhere to go."

Dawes sits up a little straighter, like a student in a seminar, poised to deliver the argument she's been formulating for weeks. "To the contrary, I would argue that, given this is a facility dedicated to sheltering sensitive government witnesses, even the *possibility* that someone's found a way to target these witnesses represents the most serious kind of breach—"

Cooper cuts her off. "Let me share a secret with you, Sidney Dawes. These people"—and here he gestures toward the door, the bungalows, the town—"they agreed to be part of an experiment.

That's what this really is. You ever hear that expression: 'If you want to truly keep a secret, you have to keep it from yourself'? That's the notion this whole place is founded on. You flip. You talk. You get your past sins wiped away. In most cases, so thoroughly that even you don't even remember who you used to be. For these people, that's a blessing, believe me."

"But they're not all criminals, right?" Dawes asks. "Some of them are innocents. Just victims, hiding out from some bad person they agreed to testify against."

"Sure. But here's the magic of this place. We don't know which is which. And neither do they." Cooper leans in toward her and speaks low—he doesn't want Greta, wherever she got off to, or anyone else, to hear this next part. "Look, if you are worried that this incident will somehow imperil your potential for professional advancement—"

"That's not my worry—"

"Let me assure you that, to anyone in the outside world, this town basically doesn't exist. As far as they're concerned, these people have served their purpose. This place is just a landfill to store them all until they die."

"But Agent Rigo—"

"Agent Rigo works for the Institute. His only concern is to make sure nothing happens here that would let anyone shut this place down." Cooper walks back around the bar. "Now, if you'll excuse me, I've got a lot of nervous residents with a lot of pressing questions, and I've got to think of something to tell them."

"I'm going to stick around here," she says. "Maybe have another beer."

"You barely touched the first one."

"I want to look over my notes."

"I'll see you at the town meeting then. When you hear the chapel bells, head over to the main street." Cooper pushes the door open, letting in a rush of sunlight.

Dawes calls to him from the bar. "One more question, Sheriff."

"What's that?"

"Agent Rigo said"—she checks her notebook—"he said, 'Does he have a funny name, too?' About the child in town."

"So?"

"So how did Agent Rigo know the child in the town was a boy?"

Cooper shrugs. "He works for the Institute. I'm sure he knew about Isaac already."

"So why's he asking us then?"

"Another mystery to ponder."

"I guess so. One more thing, sir."

Cooper grimaces. "What is it?"

"Happy birthday."

He looks at her, his hand still propping open the door. "How in the hell do you know that it's my birthday?"

Dawes raises her barely touched bottle. "I guess it must be all that time spent wearing my deerstalker hat."

Alone now at the bar, Dawes sets her beer at a distance. She's a lightweight, even after a few sips. And it's not like she doesn't have plenty of cautionary tales in her background when it comes to the consumption of alcohol.

She looks at her watch. Nearly one. Many hours left yet in the workday. And a crime scene, all to herself. She stands up and decides to question Greta, then scouts around until she spots her in back, standing in the cramped, dirty kitchen behind the bar, washing glasses. She wonders if Greta heard any of what they were talking about.

The kitchen's barely bigger than a phone booth. Greta looks up at Dawes leaning in the doorway.

"So can I replace that blood-soaked plywood now?" Greta says, with the edge of irritation of someone whose life has been upended through no doing of her own.

"I believe so, ma'am," says Dawes. "I'll arrange to take it to the station as evidence. We can certainly replace—"

"I'm good," says Greta. "I'll replace it. And fuck 'ma'am.' That's not a title I aspire to."

"May I ask you something? How long have you lived here in Caesura?"

Greta laughs, her hands in sudsy rubber gloves, poised over the basin. "Me? I'm an original sinner, dear. One of the original eight."

"And you didn't notice anyone else at the bar last night? With Gable?"

"No, but I like to turn in early."

"Cooper said Hubert always drank alone."

"Not always. Just last night. He closed the place down, like usual. But he used to drink a lot with Gerald Dean—you know him? Short fellow. Not the prettiest. Lives on the north side of town, over by the old Colfax home."

"I don't know him," says Dawes, inching into the room. "And I—and please forgive me, I'm new here—but: How exactly does this bar work?"

"I sling, you drink," says Greta. "It's a bar."

"I mean to say—the provisions. The liquor. Where does it all come from?"

"It comes in with the weekly shipment, on Wednesdays, same as anything, from Amarillo. Clothes and boots and toothpaste and booze, everything a growing town needs."

"I'd like to come by on Wednesday morning. Meet the driver, if that's all right. Come to a better understanding of how things work around here. You mind?"

"He's not cute, if that's what you're wondering."

Dawes laughs. "No, that's not what I'm wondering."

Now fully wedged into the cramped kitchen with Greta, Dawes grabs a towel and starts to dry.

6.

THE CHAPEL BELLS RING.

The town assembles.

They come quickly, in a rush, like they've been waiting all day.

The crowd is bigger than Cooper expected, maybe thirty, maybe forty, which is nearly the entire population of the town. Only the usual introverts and invalids don't show up, people like William Wayne—the shut-ins and loners who you might not lay eyes on for an entire calendar year. Everyone else, though, is gathered in a jumpy mob in what passes for the town square just outside the commissary. As the crowd gathers, it's reflected in the ripples of the store's huge plate-glass window, people's faces wide and anxious, waiting for Cooper to start his address.

He steps up on an overturned apple crate to be better seen by all, then immediately regrets it—now he feels like a target, like some clown at the fair you throw balls at to dump into a barrel of water.

He waves his hands to get their attention.

"I'm sorry to report we've had an unfortunate incident," he says.

The crowd pulsates in the heat, murmuring, fluid and combustible.

"Call it what it is, a fucking murder!" someone yells. A male voice. *Well, that didn't take long to escalate,* Cooper thinks. He tries to place the voice; it sounded like Lyndon Lancaster, though Cooper can't quite make out faces as he squints against the sun-glare.

"That's right. A murder. A fucking murder," says Cooper. "Hubert Gable was shot dead last night."

The crowd ripples again, roiling, the nervous chatter of a rumor confirmed.

"Okay, settle down," says Cooper, pointlessly. He's trying hard not to slip into vice principal mode. He's got eight years of hard-won collateral on the table here, eight years of cultivating trust, house by house, handshake by handshake. In the Blinds, he's learned, people run hot and skittish, their anxiety fueled by mistrust. That's what happens when you wipe out a big chunk of a person's memories: Fear breeds in the empty space that's left behind.

"Call in the real police!" someone else yells, a woman's voice this time, followed by an angry counterpoint from another man: "Yeah, that's a fucking great idea—more police!" The crowd falls into angry factions, bickering. Cooper calms them again, or tries.

"We're going to handle this in-house," he says. "The way we always do."

"There is no 'always' when it comes to a killing," someone says loudly enough to settle the crowd. The man steps forward. It's Buster Ford. He wears denim overalls with a paperback stuck in the front pocket, his white hair ranging wildly, letting the world know he has more important things on his mind than combing his hair. He's one of the original eight as well, got to be near seventy by now, and as such, he commands respect in the town. "There's never ever been a killing here, Calvin. Not once. Not inside the gates."

"Yes, I know, Buster," Cooper says. "I've been here since day one, same as you." Then, to the crowd: "Longer than most of you. We've never had a murder and I don't plan on having another."

A woman's voice now. This one he knows very well. It's Fran Adams. "So who was that man here this morning?" she calls out. Cooper spots her in the crowd, her hand cupped over her eyes to shield them from the sun.

"That was a, uh, liaison. From the Institute. Visiting from Amarillo," says Cooper.

This news pleases no one.

Cooper continues: "It was strictly some logistical assistance, which will aid us in figuring all this out."

Fran speaks up again: "Will they be sending more men? More *liaisons*?"

"We are not anticipating any further outside involvement at this time," Cooper says. Goddamned press-conference-speak. Snap out of it.

Another hand goes up, like a submarine's periscope rising in choppy waves. Thank God for the civility of a raised hand, Cooper thinks. He peers out and sees it's Spiro Mitchum—well, of course it is. Spiro, who runs the commissary, is nothing if not orderly. He wears an actual apron to work every day, like an old-time shopkeeper, bless his heart.

"Is this an outside breach," he asks, "or are you looking at someone here. A resident." The crowd communally echoes the question, restating it chaotically.

"That's ongoing," Cooper says. "But we have no reason to suspect a breach—"

"What about the newcomers?" someone yells.

"As I said, we have no reason to suspect a breach. But either way, it's a serious matter. Because someone is in possession of a firearm in this town." He shifts on the crate, which feels unstable under his boots. "Now, I know some of you might have, shall we say, *secrets* you keep in your bungalows. Contraband items kept as extra precautions or whatnot. And you know that, normally, as long as there's no trouble, I don't like to pry. But in this case, if you know anything at all, please come forward to me or to Deputies Robinson or Dawes." Cooper nods to the pair of them, standing dutifully nearby. "This is not—" Cooper pauses. Then restarts. "Look, as you know, the Blinds is not like any other place. We have our own rules, our own customs, and, I like to think, our own sense of what's right. I don't want to bring up the threat of expulsion, but we need to get this sorted out. If you know something and you come to me, we can work this out, I promise you that. But if Amarillo or the Institute or, God forbid, the federal law enforcement gets involved, then I can't protect you. Any of you. This is a fragile ecosystem we live in here. Someone out there knows who's behind this. So I'm counting on you to come forward. Thank you."

More questions are being lobbed now freely from the crowd but Cooper's done, it's over, he's said his piece and he's already stepped off the crate. He starts to walk away and motions to his deputies to follow.

"That could have gone better," mutters Cooper, as the three of them retreat.

"You were expecting different?" says Robinson.

Cooper's spent and pissed and frankly tired of questions. He looks at Dawes's placid, maddening face. "You've got something to contribute, Deputy?"

"Just observing," she says, as they walk.

"And what, pray tell, did you observe?"

"People are scared. For good reason. And if we don't figure this out, or at least give the impression that we've got a hunch, I'd worry that mob is going to go door-to-door until they find someone to blame it on."

Cooper wants to cut her off right there, remind her again that she's barely six weeks on the job, except he knows she's exactly right.

"It's our duty to make sure that doesn't happen," he says. "You got any better ideas on ways to do that, you let me know. Now, if you'll both excuse me, I've got a birthday to celebrate."

As Bette Burr watches the crowd disperse, she tells herself it's a simple question of numbers. She has two days, maybe three tops. She's been here one day already. There's forty-eight residents in the town, give or take. And there's three things she knows about the man she's looking for: He's old. His name is William Wayne. And he's been here the full eight years. She thinks she'll recognize his face, too, given they showed her pictures of him, and he's the only one in this town who was once famous enough to have been on TV. She remembers those newscasts vaguely, the outrage, though she didn't pay attention at the time. She didn't know then what she knows now about him. About him and her father.

She can guess at roughly how old he'll be because she knows how old her father is, which means the man she's looking for must be seventy, at least.

Was.

How old her father was. Past tense.

Not a change she can get used to. Or wants to.

When she heard the bells and saw everyone assembling, she hoped she'd spot William Wayne here. No luck, but she's not discouraged. There's only so many doors to knock on in this town. Just knock and ask, knock and ask, until a door opens and it's him.

William Wayne.

People here act funny when his name comes up, she's definitely noticed that. They whisper. Withdraw. Few claim to have ever even seen him. Yet everyone has a story. A rumor. A myth.

She's tried to act casual, just asking questions, the new kid in town, orienting herself. Hanging around outside the commissary on the main drag ever since that intake session ended. Chatting up people as they exit the store, asking them to explain how all this works. The Mexican shopkeeper, the one in the apron, Spiro Something, he was friendly. He told her the shop is pretty much picked clean by this time in the week, but not to worry, a new shipment arrives every Wednesday. He said they even get apples and bananas on Wednesdays, fresh produce, though it's usually all gone by the afternoon. Save up your allotment of chits, he told her, don't waste them at Blinders on booze, and you can trade them for different treats when they come in every week. Clothes, books, games—sometimes they even get mangoes. He hinted that, if they did, he'd stash a few away for her. Ah, the advantages of being young and cute, she thinks—she's never had a problem getting people to do her favors, especially older men. It's kind of her hidden superpower. She's friendly, approachable, she's got an "open face," that's what everyone tells her, which she hates, because she thinks "open face" is just a euphemism for stupid, which she definitely is not.

Yet her open face has certainly helped her today—pretending like she's one of them, these people with no pasts. She watches them leaving the town square slowly and talking in their worried whispers about the meeting and the news and what's happened here and what might happen yet. She wonders what it's like to uproot yourself from everything you know, everyone you loved, everything you'd ever earned, and damn yourself by choice to a life in a place where you've forgotten it all. To be given the chance to forget every bad deed you've ever done. In a way, she's almost envious.

Not that everyone here had a choice, of course, she understands that, too. Sometimes the decision finds you. Sometimes the decision kicks in your door or wakes you in your cell or presents itself in stark terms in a bare room with an attorney present while you're handcuffed to a table. The decision: a lifetime of fear in prison somewhere, dreading death in every moving shadow, or a new life unburdened of all your past sins, with a new name, a new home, new neighbors, hidden away in this place. A decision that's laid out to you in hard-to-follow legalese, as the Institute's representative slides a silver folder across the table, with a single, unfamiliar word embossed on the cover: Caesura.

Will I remember what I did?

You won't.

But will I know that I've forgotten it?

You will.

So I'll know I did something bad, but I won't know what it was.

You'll know you made the decision to come to this place.

That's the sales pitch, delivered calmly, even soothingly. Like they're hoping to sell you a piece of land, except this piece of land is in Texas, in the desert, behind a fourteen-foot fence, and you can never come back and, by the way, you won't even remember this conversation. Then they explain, in an effort to close the deal, that no matter where you go, you will always have a secret, and that the best way to keep a secret is to keep it from yourself. That the one thing in life you can never outrun is the guilt over what you've done. That follows you everywhere. Except here. Because they can make it all go away. They tap the folder.

She spots the sheriff walking away alone, breaking from his two deputies, and she scrambles to catch him. "Sheriff Cooper?"

He turns. "Can I help you, Miss—" He squints. "I'm sorry, I remember you from intake, but I left before you took your new name."

"Burr. Bette Burr," she says, then laughs. "Well, that sounds weird. Bette Burr." She rolls the *R*s and pops the *B*s. "Bette. Burr. I guess that's my new name now. I'm looking to meet someone."

"You just did—Calvin Cooper," he says. "You can call me Sheriff or Cal or Hey You, they all work fine by me." She's got freckles sprayed like buckshot across the bridge of her nose, he notices. Pretty. Seems friendly. From out west originally, he'd bet—her skin looks too sun-toasted to have come shrink-wrapped from the pale-faced East. Late twenties, maybe. You don't get many people that young in this place. She definitely must be an innocent, he thinks—a victim, not a perpetrator, and a victim of something so traumatic she chose to wipe it from her memory and start fresh. "So how can I help you, Ms. Burr?"

"I'm especially curious to meet William Wayne."

Cooper chuckles. "Oh God, you're not a groupie, are you?"

"I just remember all the coverage he got before he came here."

"That was ages ago. How do you even know his new name? That's not supposed to be public knowledge."

"Sheriff, there are entire websites dedicated to him. People drive out to the desert with telephoto lenses to try and snap pictures of him."

"They used to. That kind of died down. And we do our best to chase those folks away, with a little help from the local U.S. Marshals office." Cooper wonders if, in the wired world beyond their fences, there's any such thing as a true secret anymore. "I'll warn you that William is not much for new friends. He never comes out of his house, just gets his groceries dropped off on the doorstep. Hell, I haven't seen him in months—and I go out of my way to check on him every so often, make sure he's still with us."

"I was just intrigued. I mean, imagine the stories he could tell."

"But that's the thing, Bette. He doesn't have those stories anymore. That's why he's here. That's why you're all here."

"Of course. I just thought maybe he remembers some of it."

"Not if the Institute did its job."

Bette smiles, like she can't believe she's been so silly. "Sure, it's stupid. I shouldn't have bothered you. I'm sure you've got other things on your mind."

"I'll tell you what, stop by the police station tomorrow and we can discuss it," says Cooper. "I'll tell you all about old William Wayne."

Bette looks him over. He's handsome, or used to be once, with a few intriguing scars, including one that descends in a faint white arc across his forehead and through one eyebrow like a falling meteor. He's probably used to the easy attention of women. That can be a handy quality in someone you're trying to get something from, she's learned. The genial, vain, eager-to-save-the-day sheriff—she may have just cut her work in half.

"That would be great," she says. "Nice to meet you in person, Sheriff."

"Cal."

"Cal." She smiles again, pausing like she's about to say something more, then she just nods, gives him a little wave, and walks away. *Don't lay it on too thick,* she thinks. *You're simply here to find a door and you just need him to point the way. Once you find the door, you knock.* And she has a feeling that when she does, the famous recluse William Wayne will open for her. Once he learns who she really is. Who her father is. Or was.

The knocking will be the easy part.

After that, all she needs to do, this newly christened Bette Burr, with her approachable manner and open face and irresistibly pleasant demeanor, is deliver to William Wayne the most unwelcome news of his crooked, wayward, broken, blood-soaked life.

Fran sits and flips through an obsolete magazine, which somehow washed ashore in this Laundromat from several years in the past. There's no one else in the place, of course, just her, as usual. Following the welcome interruption of the town meeting, she returned to finish the one task that seems to occupy her every waking hour: the never-ending cleansing of the clothes. Our Lady of Perpetual Laundry. She wonders if anyone else in the town has this many soiled socks and jeans to clean, but then, no one else in the town has a kid. Just her. The only parent. On top of everything else she's dealing with, lonely doesn't begin to describe how that feels. Isaac's off playing right now, alone, in the sad little playground they installed for him not long after he was born, just a patch of dirt, some scrubby grass, a slide, and a swing set with just one lonely swing. Getting his clothes dirty. And so the cycle goes.

As she glances idly at the magazine's glossy pages, she wonders if these hairstyles are still stylish. Are these fad diets still the fad? Are these time-saving recipes still saving time? There's a breezy story about a celebrity marriage, a tell-all about a singer's comeback from addiction, and a Q&A with a handsome tech guru sharing his lifestyle tips. *Buddy,* she thinks, *you're a billionaire, so finding time for calming daily meditation is probably not an issue for you.* She tries to remember a time in her life, before Isaac, before this town, when she cared about hairstyles and fad diets. She can't remember a goddamn thing. Just trying to remember gives her a headache. How old is this magazine, anyway? She checks the cover—eight years old, holy shit, it's the same age as her son. That celebrity couple is definitely divorced by now. That singer is back in rehab. She tosses it aside and glances up, listening to the washers' throaty grumble, watching her and her son's clothes tumble, slosh, and paw at the glass, trying to escape their sudsy fate.

The TV hinged to the concrete wall above the long bank of washers is turned to the all-news channel, prattling disposable headlines piped in from the outside world: new arguments, new advances, new fronts in distant wars, new studies, new polls, new perils. She searches for the remote to mute it. No one here can contact anyone on the outside, but they sure as hell get all the endless news. She was surprised, when she first arrived, how quickly she stopped caring about the ceaseless chatter of current events. Now she actively avoids it, which is easy enough. There's no Internet, just the TV in the Laundromat and the few stray newspapers that show up at the library. A couple of people keep radios, but she doesn't bother. She's come to value the silence. There is certainly plenty of that.

As she hunts for the remote, she catches what's happening onscreen: *Coma Tycoon Considers Senate Run* reads the news crawl, as a handsome man in a well-tailored suit stands at a podium in front of some flags. "Some call it a miracle, some call it impossible, but I just want my old life for me and a better life for all Americans," he says. *Holy shit!* She picks up the magazine to confirm: Yes, it's that same stupid tech guru with the daily meditation tips. So he's a politician now? He has time to make a fortune and meditate and run for the Senate, and she can't even get to the bottom of the laundry hamper.

She watches him; he's handsome, she'll give him that. He thanks the crowd, cameras click in reply, his smile blossoms. Reporters shout questions. Her headache barks again. She finds the remote on top of a washer and changes the channel, flipping until she lands on that station where they show exhumed game shows from the seventies all day long. Now this is more like it: no hubbub of the daily news, just polyester lapels and canned laughter, lightning rounds and mystery prizes.

Why the Institute didn't think to put washers and dryers in each bungalow when they built this place, she can't imagine. She wished they'd told her that before she came here—it might have been a deal breaker. Someday maybe she'll live in a place with a washer and dryer in the basement. A backyard, a real yard, for Isaac. And playmates. A school. That's what Cooper's always talking about, like it's an actual possibility. Like what happened to poor Jean Mondale and little Jacob never happened. Jean, wild Jean, who got herself knocked up within a month of arriving here and then, a few years back, when Jacob was barely two, decided the Blinds was no place to raise a kid. She was right, of course, she was absolutely right, so they packed up and left, the two of them, and everyone here wished them well. They were dead, mother and son, within a week. The residents can't contact the outside world, but they sure as hell get the endless news. Everyone gathered around the TV watching the news reports. Now there's a new rule: If you get pregnant in the Blinds, you don't have a choice but to end it. There won't ever be another kid born here. There will never be another kid to swing on that lonely swing. Isaac was the first and, now, he's the last, for as long as they choose to stay here. Sometimes Isaac still asks about Jacob, what happened to him, where he went. She never knows what to tell him.

The washers slosh to an end, stilling, the clothes slumping into a sodden heap. She pulls them out, tosses them into the dryer. Everything about this feels so familiar to her. Not just like she's done it before, but like she's never not doing it.

She hits Run on the dryer and turns her attention back to the game show. Someone's winning something. Someone's getting hugged. Someone's jumping up and down with joy. She's always thought it strange that there's a whole channel dedicated to reruns of old game shows. Why does she care to see who among these contestants will triumph or stumble? Who will choose the cash in hand and who chooses what's behind Door Number Three? These are all repeats anyway, so these people's fates have already played out. Whether they won or lost was decided for them long ago.

7.

COOPER STANDS IN THE DOORWAY of Errol Colfax's darkened bungalow.

There's no light; it's long past dark; the carpeted living room is striped by stray shards of errant outdoor glow. The town's other residents have all retired to their homes, to their VCRs, their crossword puzzles, their bottles of various potencies, the few distractions kept on hand to tide them through the long silent hours of the night. There's no tape over Colfax's doorway anymore, no padlock on the door, it's been left open for anyone to enter. But best as Cooper can tell, it looks exactly as it did the night Colfax died. No one's been here in the two months since, save for a band of volunteers, including Greta Fillmore, Spiro Mitchum, and Buster Ford, all among the original eight, who offered to come with buckets and bleach and clean the place up as best they could, out of respect for Colfax. Cooper himself didn't join them. This house was not a scene he cared to revisit.

After a long moment spent lingering in the doorway, he steps inside and shuts the door. He stands alone for another moment in the murky dark. The air is still stagnant, just as stale as he remembers it from that night, but now it's tinged with an ambient tang of cleaning products. He flicks on his flashlight, swings its beam around the room, focusing his search. He figures it's better not to turn the overhead lights on and spook anyone who might notice him poking around. Part of him doesn't want to be here at all—more than part of him, to be truthful. Cooper shines his beam over the chair where Colfax died. He spotlights the dark brown oval stain on the floral upholstery. No amount of scrubbing could remove that, apparently.

He gets on his hands and knees and rubs his palm lightly over the shag carpet, a foot or so from the chair. When Greta and her crew were cleaning up, they would have focused on the blood, not on finding a shell, which would have ejected in the opposite direction. Maybe one of them thought to check for it and never mentioned it to Cooper, or maybe they vacuumed the carpet and sucked up the shell with a rattle without even knowing it, and the shell is gone forever, but he doubts it. Just as he's contemplating these possibilities his palm rolls over a hard cylinder in the shag, and there it is. He picks it up and holds it in the flashlight's glare: a spent 9 mm shell. He pinches it between his fingertips and inspects it, then pockets it.

Then he stands up and walks to the wall adjacent to the chair and shines his light over the painted cinder block. Now this wall, they did a real good job of scrubbing. Cooper remembers well just how much blood there was that night. Now there's not a trace. Maybe a faint tint, if you look long enough. And the bullet shouldn't be too hard to find, he thinks. One nice thing about cinder block is that no round is going to penetrate it, and given how close Colfax's chair is to the wall, the gun was basically fired point-blank into the cinder block, with only Colfax's skull to impede its journey.

Cooper traces his flashlight beam over the wall until he finds the point of impact, a small but unmistakable pockmark. He rubs his thumb over it. No bullet lodged in there—not deep enough. So he gets on his knees again and searches. He wonders again if maybe they found the slug in the cleanup. No one mentioned finding a bullet, but then, he's not sure they would have thought it worth mentioning. After all, there wasn't any doubt among them about what had happened in this bungalow: Colfax put a bullet in his brain. In a way, it made sense. Colfax was always a recluse. A gun had gone missing in the town. And who among them hadn't thought at least once of ending it, in that way or some other, during their long tenure here?

As Cooper searches blindly, groping along the floor, he remembers Colfax's body, the way it slumped awkwardly sideways in that floral La-Z-Boy chair. Colfax was not the first dead body Cooper had ever encountered, but it was the first he'd seen that had been so violently ended. During his time as a prison guard, he'd seen a few stiffs gurneyed out: diabetic shock, a heart attack, each body gray and unmistakably stilled. Colfax was different. Cooper was profoundly struck at the time by the disorder of it all—the anarchic pattern painted by bodily innards so powerfully ejected. The thought of just how inadequate the body's natural defenses—skull, bone, brain—were in the face of the advanced physics—lead, gunpowder, momentum—of invented death. It all seemed so absurd to him: that a life comprising so many accumulated years could be interrupted with such indifferent swiftness. The fundamental fragility of it. The truth of it lingers with Cooper still. How quickly and casually it all ends. Unlike the other longtime residents of the Blinds, the ones he's been tasked to protect, he does not enjoy the privilege of forgetting what he's seen. He remembers everything.

His fingers find it first. It's wedged in a crack in the baseboard where the floor meets the wall. Cooper wiggles his finger in until he gets hold of the slug, then retrieves the misshapen round and studies it under his flashlight. God, he's getting old, he thinks, his eyes are going, especially in low light. He holds the bullet closer until his eyes can finally focus and it snaps into detail, this misshapen killer. He's amazed that the bullet's still here, frankly, after all this time, just waiting for him to find it, but then, where else would it go? Its job is long over. Just like the people in this town. It served its one purpose and now it's been discarded and forgotten.

Except this bullet has one more job, Cooper thinks: To be a witness. To be bagged and sent to Agent Rigo, in Amarillo, to tell him everything it knows. To be compared with the bullet that killed Gable and, possibly, to confirm that they were both fired from the very same gun. Which, if true, would mean that both Colfax and Gable were likely murdered, and likely by the same hand. It's possible the bullet is too damaged, too mashed, to reveal anything useful, but then again, as the people in this town can attest, even the profoundly damaged sometimes have useful stories to tell. Even if those stories are later wiped away. Some stories are probably better lost forever, never remembered, never told.

This bullet here, for example, thinks Cooper, has quite the story to tell, if it's ever allowed to tell it. For starters, it was definitely fired from the same gun that killed Hubert Gable.

Same finger pulled the trigger both times, too.

But then, Cooper already knows the story of this bullet, from the moment it left the gun.

Given he's the one who fired it.

He considers the bullet a moment longer, then drops it in his pocket, alongside the spent 9 mm shell.

Cooper raises a glass.

Happy birthday. To forty-five.

He drinks.

Forty-five, he thinks, is basically a quick spit's distance from fifty. And fifty, he knows, is the moment in life when you stop looking forward and wondering what kind of person you might become, and start looking backward and wondering how you became the person you are.

He sits at his kitchen table under the light of a single pendant lamp. It's nearly midnight. A half-drunk bottle of bourbon is on the table before him, and the half-drunk Cooper contemplates it.

He refills his glass. Holds it aloft.

Here's to the person you might have been, and to the person you have become. May they never meet in a dark alley.

He downs it.

Then Cooper sets the glass aside and begins to count his scars.

It's an annual ritual, every year on his birthday, like revisiting a topographical map of his past misadventures and mistakes. He starts with the crescent-shaped scar on his elbow, earned at age eight, during a brief experimentation with skateboards. Eventually, he decided that it was hard enough to keep your feet under yourself in this world without adding the complication of wheels.

Scar number two: A faint straight line on his left hand, over his thumb, from a slipped chisel in tenth-grade woodshop. Seven stitches. He got better with the chisel, eventually.

Number three: The blanched-white lightning-bolt zigzag on his left shoulder, acquired while bow-hunting in the woods of Vermont. Age sixteen. An errant shot, loosed by a friend who either had terrible aim or who was finally acting on long-simmering suspicions that Cooper was fucking his girlfriend. Those suspicions were never proved, Cooper thinks, which isn't the same as saying they were unfounded. Had the arrow sailed six inches to the left, it would have soared right past him, an effective warning shot; six inches to the right and it would have put him in the ground. He knew the friend well enough to know his aim wasn't that good either way. The friend never out and out copped to it—he always insisted it was an accident. But he couldn't muster any tears at the ER. And Cooper didn't talk much to either of them after that, the onetime friend or his girlfriend. Eventually, they got married, and Cooper moved away. The shoulder still aches from time to time, but only if he thinks too hard about it. Sometimes he can forget it's even there.

Number four: Hairline scar threaded across his right knuckles. Age seventeen. Courtesy of a concrete dugout wall punched in frustration after allowing a game-tying home run. Missed six weeks of pitching. Probably cost him a scholarship.

Number five: The arcing surgical scar on his right shoulder, age twenty, where a doctor went in and tried to save his bum rotator cuff and his slim hopes of a baseball career. The doctor saved one but not the other. Cooper was in community college at the time, a local star of sorts, and still nursing the eroding dream that his pitching arm might carry him to some better life. Truth is, he was good but not that good, even before the surgery. He could blame the injury for halting his career, and has, out loud to many people in his life, but secretly, he knows. To this day, he can't raise his right arm to shoulder height without a little bit of wincing, and the famous Cooper curveball died on that operating table, along with a few other things.

Number six: The showstopper. Age thirty-two. A faint but unmistakable fissure arcing downward across the left side of his forehead, cutting his eyebrow in half. The consequence of his head being slammed in a door, intentionally and repeatedly. It happened at Highsbury Federal Correctional Institute, where Cooper worked as a guard. A surly inmate caught him looking the other way, wrong-footed, and jumped him. Goddamned low-security facility, too, full of frauds and cheats and embezzlers, not grizzled murderers, so where's the good story in that? The inmate was not exactly some cutthroat lifer, just a finance dude with rage issues and an aggravated assault prior doing a stretch for insider trading, who filled his time in the weight room and got his girlfriend to smuggle him steroids. Definitely not a scar to be proud of, thinks Cooper, feeling it now with his whiskey-numbed fingertips. But it's the one most people ask about. It probably even got him laid a couple times. That's never changed the fact that he often wishes, in the later hours of the evening, that the inmate had finished the job.

Number seven: He threads his fingers back through his hair and feels the long ugly scar along his scalp. This is his most recent acquisition, obtained right before he started working at the Blinds, the barroom mystery. A souvenir of the dark years, the Austin years, when he'd regularly go out to new bars looking for drinks and fights and usually find both. This was all before he landed his plum job as sheriff in Caesura. This was back when he was working as private security for an old baseball teammate from community college who'd made good, and who basically gave him the job out of charity. That job mostly entailed watching nothing happen on multiple security cameras for ten hours a day, or patrolling the grounds and throwing rocks at rats. As for his off-hours, he spent those becoming well acquainted with the local constabulary, particularly the inside of their drunk tank, even if he was not always clear on the specifics of why he'd ended up there. He fingers the jagged ridge. This scar is a remnant of a particularly nasty barfight, one that got away from him, or so it was explained to him later. Honestly, he doesn't even remember that fight. All he'd asked afterward was which bar it happened in, so he'd know which one not to go back to, because they likely had a Do Not Serve photo of him hung over the cash register.

Lucky for him, not long after, he stumbled into this job at Caesura. Friend of a friend of his old boss, who was happy to pass along the tip. Lucky for him, and lucky for all the fine residents who've since been placed under his protection.

Well, lucky for all but two of them, he thinks.

He's eight years in, with two to go—that was the deal from the start. Put in ten years as de facto sheriff of the Blinds, babysitting memory-wiped felons, then retire on half-salary and full benefits, with no further obligations. It's a hell of a pension plan, frankly, if he can just stick it out for two more years. Which, until recently, he was more than happy to do.

Then another even more compelling offer came along.

He raises the near-empty bottle. He proposes a toast to all his scars. The whole collection, another birthday tradition. They are, all seven of them, a year older, as is he.

Here's to you, my lifelong companions. Happy birthday.

This time he skips the glass.

Not drunk. Not really.

Just fuzzing the edges of the world.

Cooper puts down the bottle, wipes his mouth, and then refills his glass. He pulls the misshapen slug, the one he retrieved from Colfax's bungalow, from his pocket and holds it up and looks at it under the kitchen light. This wayward bullet, with so many secrets to spill, should it ever be allowed to share them. He turns the slug in his fingertips, slowly, examining it. Then he drops the slug in the shot glass. It sinks with a *plop* into the amber bourbon and hits the glass's bottom with an audible *plink*.

Tiny bubbles flock to the bullet and stick to it.

Cooper picks up the glass, toasts the world one last time, then downs it all in a single gulp, the whiskey, the bullet, everything.

A crackle of static shakes him awake.

He's still in his kitchen. Apparently he'd nodded off. It's well past midnight now. Cooper rises and fumbles around for his gun belt. On the belt, his walkie-talkie. He retrieves it. Clicks the button. "Yes?"

Only Robinson and Dawes have walkie-talkies. It's how the local police force keeps in touch. They don't usually need them to keep in touch at five in the morning, though.

"Sheriff, it's Deputy Dawes."

"Do you know what time it is?"

"I do."

"Well, what is it?" says Cooper, irritated in this moment for about twelve different and equally pertinent reasons, not least by the whiskey headache pounding full-fisted at the door of his addled brain.

"I think I've found something," Dawes says, through the static.

"Found what?"

"For the murders," she says. "I think I've found the missing link."

TUESDAY

8.

ORSON CALHOUN DOESN'T KNOW WHY, but he's always been good with tools. He can't remember where he learned to use them, or to what purpose, but they just feel right in his hands. The heft of the pliers. The surety of the wrench. The momentous arc of a ballpeen hammer, perfectly weighted and well suited to its job. It all just feels so natural, like he was born to wear overalls. He remembers something vaguely, as a kid, with his dad, in a dusty basement with small windows, and the sound of tools clattering, but that's where his memory gets ragged. Orson's case, the doctors told him before he entered the town, was a deep dive; the relevant memories required something like a root canal for his brain. Plus, he was one of the early ones, the original eight, back before they'd perfected the precision of the technique. Some of the newer people, they remember almost everything—childhoods, first crushes, wives, kids—except for the part of their lives they chose to forget. With Orson, they scoured most of his memories, just to be sure. So there's a lot of empty space in Orson's mind. It's left him a little slow, he understands. Common objects can sometimes puzzle him, and every emotional reaction feels unexpected and brand new. But not tools—tools feel *familiar*. They feel good. They sound good. They even *taste* good, he thinks: that metallic tang you get on your tongue when you spend all day in the workshop. Which is where Orson spends almost all his time, out at the repair yard at the far edge of the main drag, in the shadow of the westward fence.

The scrubby patch of grass out front of his shop usually looks, to the unaccustomed eye, like a junkyard, with various machines in states of disassembly, their inner workings strewn across the dirt. There's a rider mower that Sheriff Cooper located for Orson as a reclamation project, which he's been tinkering with for weeks. There's a rusting and broken-down washing machine salvaged from the town's Laundromat. There's the dormant Chevy Aveo hatchback, the town's emergency vehicle, half-covered under a blue plastic tarp with its hood propped open, waiting for Orson to spark it back to life. It all looks terribly disordered, to anyone but Orson. Yet even from a distance, in the morning's first shadows as Orson approaches, he can tell that something's wrong today. What would look like the usual sprawl of the yard to anyone else looks to Orson like chaos. Parts kicked and scrambled. Tools broken and destroyed. Machines upended. And that's just outside.

Inside, the workshop's much worse.

Orson feels a terrible clenching as he flips on the light switch to reveal the damage.

His workshop's wrecked. Tables overturned. Tools and parts scattered everywhere. Whoever did this even found his cache of spray paint and emptied every can, leaving vandal's scribblings. Graffiti. Something scrawled that's not even English. And underfoot, he notices, in among the overturned boxes of nails and screws and bolts and scattered drill bits, is a bunch of playing cards. They definitely don't belong to Orson; he doesn't have the attention span to play cards. His scrambled brain can barely remember which suit is which, let alone actual rules.

He stoops to pick up a card. Turns it over. It's not a playing card.

It's a trading card. Fresh from the pack. Bubblegum powder still on it. He picks up a few of the others. They're cards for some movie for kids, with robots in them, scattered all over the floor of his shop.

Orson drops the card. No sense to any of it, he thinks, despairing, as he surveys the damage again. Assessing what he's lost, he feels an ugly stirring. The kind that usually only tugs at him in the night's last moments before he falls asleep. Something dark. A rustling in the bottomless chasm of his mind where all his memories used to be.

He fends it off. And does the only sensible thing he can think to do.

He sets out to track down Sheriff Cooper.

Sheriff Cooper will know what to do. Sheriff Cooper will help him. Orson believes in Sheriff Cooper, who's always been very good to him.

As he's leaving, Orson notices that a gas can has gone missing from the workshop. What the hell? Given that no one in this town has a car, except for Sheriff Cooper, what in the world would anyone in town want with a can of gas?

Dawes is waiting for Cooper at the police trailer when he arrives just before six, which is an unpleasant surprise for Cooper, since he purposefully showed up fifteen minutes earlier than their meeting time to get a few minutes to collect himself. No dice. She's already seated in a hardback chair, hands resting on her knees, like someone in a banana republic stationed patiently outside the office of an elusive bureaucrat. She smiles at him pleasantly when he enters, and he smiles back, less pleasantly. Cooper looks around the trailer, groggy, a little hungover, a lot suspicious, and still recalling foggily how that half-drunk bottle on his kitchen table last night got whole-drunk in a hurry.

"You call a meeting for the ass-crack of dawn, Dawes, you're at least obliged to provide coffee," he says.

"Commissary's not open till seven."

"So what the fuck are we doing awake at this hour?" Cooper halts by his desk to fiddle with a cheap plastic coffee machine, then realizes there are no filters. Or, for that matter, coffee. He takes off his gun belt, coils it on his desk, and slumps into his swivel chair, which wobbles uneasily beneath him.

"A fax message arrived for you," Dawes says, nodding toward the machine.

Cooper turns in his chair. Sure enough, a long white tongue of shiny fax paper lolls out of the machine. "What time did this arrive?"

"It was here when I got here."

"Did you read it?" he asks, trying his best to sound casual.

"Of course not. Fax machine is sheriff's eyes only."

He nods thoughtfully, as though to acknowledge that she's spoken some wise old gospel truth that they'd all be well served to remember. Then he rips the scrolled paper clear of the fax machine, turning in the chair to make sure she won't see it, even though she's risen from her seat, carrying a thin file folder, and come to hover by his desk. He hunches over the fax. It says, simply, *2 P.M.*, in handwritten scrawled block letters. He reads it again, then folds it, stands, and feeds it into Abel, the shredder, which gobbles it with a mechanical roar.

"Anything important?" Dawes asks with, to Cooper's ear, a little too much interest.

"Just a routine ping from Amarillo, checking in on the investigation. I'll call them this afternoon." Cooper slumps back into his chair, the springs whining beneath him. "Now tell me about this grand theory of yours. The one that couldn't wait until a reasonable hour."

"It's not really a theory. Not yet, anyway," she says. "It's just a name. Gerald Dean."

"Okay. Gerald Dean. What about him?"

"He drank with Gable, regularly. Real barstool buddies. According to Greta."

"For this you woke me up at five in the morning?"

"It also turns out he and Gable arrived in Caesura together, in the same batch, in the first year, about six months after the facility opened."

Cooper has no idea where this is going, but he's sure of one thing: It's not leading in any way back to him. He does his best to subsume his relief in a wave of exaggerated irritation. "Sure. Lots of people arrive together, Dawes. They usually come in groups of three or four. That's how this works."

"Then there's this—" Dawes drops the thin file folder on Cooper's desk.

Cooper opens it, while saying, "Feel free to spoil the surprise."

"I looked back through the old records. Housing requests, medical records, that sort of thing. Right after he arrived, Dean put in a request to be moved across town. To the north quarter. So he'd be next-door neighbors with Errol Colfax."

Cooper scans the papers in the folder and thinks, *Is this it? Is this really all that Dawes has?* "I remember that," he says. "Dean wanted someplace quieter. The north quarter is where all the shut-ins are: Colfax, William Wayne—you know, the mummies. We had a free bungalow at the time, so I approved the move. So what?" He hands the folder back to Dawes. "I'm still not sure what this has to do with Hubert Gable."

"Don't you think it's odd," says Dawes, "that Dean requested to move so close to Colfax? Who ends up dead? And now he turns out to be our second victim's closest drinking buddy?"

"Maybe. But he moved seven years ago. What do you think he was doing all these years—biding his time?"

Before she can answer, the door to the trailer swings open—it's Robinson, arriving for his shift. He looks mildly surprised to see Dawes and Cooper already at the office, insofar as his face can register extreme emotions like surprise. "I'm presuming my invitation got lost in the mail," he says.

"Dawes has a *theory,*" says Cooper.

"Worth waking with the roosters for?" says Robinson.

"Jury's still out on that," Cooper says.

"Well, when you two are done with this little powwow, we've got a noise complaint to deal with," Robinson says. "One of the new arrivals, Vivien King. Lives over by Ginger Van Buren. Says she was up all night."

"Let me guess," says Cooper. "Our beloved coydogs."

"In fine form and full voice last night, apparently." Robinson shrugs. Then he eyes an open box of pastries on the table. "Remind me when the last delivery from Amarillo was?"

"Last Wednesday," says Cooper. "New truck's due tomorrow."

"So those are a week old?"

"What is it they say about beggars and choosers, Walt?" says Cooper.

Robinson frowns. He's amassed an impressive collection of frowns over the years, to go with his extensive arsenal of shrugs. These frowns and shrugs, deployed in various combinations, serve him perfectly well for roughly 99 percent of whatever each day might present. He ponders the pastries a moment longer, frowns again, shrugs again, then passes. "So what's this grand theory?"

"That Hubert Gable and Gerald Dean like to drink together. And Gerald Dean and Errol Colfax used to be neighbors," says Cooper.

"Sounds open and shut to me," Robinson says.

Dawes pipes up. "I think it's at least enough of a connection to justify putting in a formal information request to unseal the files on Colfax, Gable, and Dean."

Cooper laughs outright. He knows it's rude, ruder maybe than even young Dawes deserves in this moment, but he can't help himself. "Do you know how many successful information requests we've put in over eight years? Walt, help me out with the math here."

"I believe the answer you're looking for is zero," says Robinson.

"Somewhere in that ballpark," says Cooper. "It's definitely a number between zero and zero."

"How many information requests have you made in that time?" Dawes says, in a way that let's Cooper know she's already tracked down the answer, which he finds a little infuriating.

"Also zero—and there's good reason for that. Do you know why we don't know anything about the backgrounds of the people who reside here? Because if we did, it would make our jobs impossible."

"I'm happy to put in the request myself to Dr. Holliday," she says, "and make it clear to her I'm acting against your objections."

"And I'm happy to say no to that, too," says Cooper.

Dawes finally breaks. "Why?" she asks sharply.

Cooper almost smiles, knowing the break in her composure means he's won. "Because Dr. Holliday will just say no. And you'll gain nothing but a notation on your official record suggesting you misunderstand the fundamental mission of your place of employment. I'm trying to protect you, Dawes. An information request like that is a huge ask that, frankly, you don't have the equity here to make. I have built up a number of important and crucial relationships over my eight years here, relationships I am not eager to endanger. Meanwhile, you, in your short six weeks, haven't even managed to charm me."

"So I can't contact Ellis Gonzalez and I can't make this request. Is there anything I can do, sir?"

"Yes, there is—LaToya."

"LaToya?" says Robinson. Something like a chuckle tumbles from his throat.

"That's not my name, and it's not funny," Dawes says.

"I want you to go door-to-door this morning and engage in some *community outreach,*" Cooper says. "Reassure the residents, let them know we've got this under control."

"It's not even seven A.M., sir," she says.

"You're certainly welcome to wait until the day gets even hotter."

"And what exactly am I supposed to tell them, reassurance-wise?"

"Tell them what we know. Our victim is Hubert Gable. Killed by a nine-millimeter pistol, smuggled in to our premises at time unknown, by persons unknown, and currently stashed at whereabouts unknown." Cooper stands. "And while you're out there canvassing, see if anyone heard any noises last night over by Orson Calhoun's repair yard. Someone trashed it overnight."

"Drunks?" says Robinson. "Greta's open for business again."

"Maybe—though it may be more complicated than that." Cooper thinks of the bubblegum card he's got stashed in his breast pocket. "They scribbled some graffiti on the walls, too. Some gibberish"—he searches both pants pockets for a slip of note paper, then finds it and reads it—"*Damnatio Memorae.* That mean anything to either of you?"

Robinson shrugs, and Dawes shakes her head.

"My kingdom for a Google, right?" Cooper crumples the paper and tosses it in the trash. "While you're formulating grand conspiracies, Dawes, I've got an actual town to govern." He grabs one of the week-old pastries and bites into it—it tastes about as good as he expected. Then he searches reflexively for the phantom hat he doesn't own. "I've got to go see a lady about some coydogs that won't shut up."

"Anything you want me to do, chief?" says Robinson.

"Maybe learn Latin," says Cooper. "Then, if you've got another spare moment, figure this whole fucking thing out."

Walking along the sunbaked gravel, out toward the farthest corner of town, Dawes is happy to let Cooper think she's out here dripping, sweating in agony, being punished, but the truth is she's never minded heat. Not this kind, anyway. Not Texas heat, not *dry* heat. Even now, in the first hours of the morning. Where she grew up, in the South, hot meant sticky; hot meant *sodden;* hot meant barely tickling eighty on the thermometer but with humidity so suffocating that your heart felt like a wet dishrag hung in the cavity of your ribs. *Compared to that, this Texas heat can sun-kiss my ass,* she thinks. *In fact, this whole town can kiss my Georgia-born ass, starting with the sheriff,* she thinks.

And she's happy, too, as she makes a beeline to the north quarter of town, and the former place of residence of one deceased Errol Colfax, to let Cooper assume her real name is some collision of random syllables, like LaToya, like she's hiding it to outrun some shameful secrets from her past. Truth is, her Atlanta background is all upper-middle-class cul-de-sacs and kente cloth formal wear and faculty parties glimpsed from between the railings of the staircase as a kid. Her real name isn't LaAnything. It's Lindy, short for Lindiwe, the Zulu word meaning "I wait." Her parents chose it for her because it took them so long to have a child, and once they did, she often wondered why they even bothered, given how absent they both were for most of her childhood. They were ambitious academics who tried for a late-life kid, then got one. Good for them. The most vivid memory she has of her childhood is the two of them retreating behind their respective office doors.

She always hated Lindiwe, and hated Lindy even more. It was only once she got older that she learned Lindiwe has another meaning. It means "I wait," but it can also mean "I watch," or "I guard."

That meaning suits her better, she thinks.

And she's happy, too, to let Cooper think he's had the last word. She still has a few secrets of her own. For example, she now knows Cooper's real name.

John—that part he told her already, back at the bar. Got skittish about the last name, given exchanging any information about names or your past is against regulation, but he probably figured, rightly, that John's a common enough name to share—not like Lindiwe. Then this morning she played a hunch and stole a glance at the inside of his gun belt on his desk while he was reading his precious fax. His lucky gun belt, the one he toted along with him from his previous job. A keepsake like that, she figured, you don't want to lose it. Don't want some coworker accidentally walking off with it at the end of a shift.

Might even write your name in it.

Which he did, in block letters, on the inside of the belt.

Barker.

Nice to meet you, John Barker, she thinks.

Not that there's much she can do with this info, or even that she thinks it adds up to anything. But right now, it feels good to know something about him that he doesn't know she knows. Just a name, but that's a little bit of power, and she'll take it. Just like how she didn't mention to Cooper when he asked that she knows damn well what *Damnatio Memorae* means—she slept through enough prep school Latin classes to know that. *Damnatio Memorae:* the

Condemnation of Memory. Now, why someone would scrawl that in spray paint on the wall of Orson Calhoun's workshop—that's just another mystery for her to solve. She pulls out her notebook, writes the phrase neatly inside with her pencil stub, right under the name "John Barker," then stashes the notebook in her breast pocket again, all without breaking stride.

For now, though, she's got her stupid door-to-door reassurance tour to worry about. Cooper told her to do it, but he didn't tell her where to start, or with whom, which she figures is tantamount to official clearance to head over to the north quarter and knock on some doors. The north quarter, where they house the so-called mummies: the former home of Errol Colfax and current home of Gerald Dean and, most curiously, the fabled William Wayne. Dawes has never seen him in the flesh and she's been told many times never to disturb him. In her six short weeks, she's become well acquainted with the legend of William Wayne, which looms over the Blinds like a long shadow at dusk. Taller than a totem pole and craggier than driftwood, so they say, those few people who've glimpsed him. Wayne's willful retreat from the community breeds all manner of unkind speculation, like he's some mythological creature sliding along in the shadowed depths beneath the surface of a placid lake. He's said to have a large scar on his face, or maybe a whole bunch of scars. Some say his face is blood-splashed, permanently marked. Some say he's a killer whose past is a swath of carnage, while others swear he was a mere accountant, some factotum adjacent to violence, but one who witnessed something so chilling and gruesome that even the head scrubbers at the Fell Institute couldn't uproot those memories. Now he lives alone with them, haunted.

As she rounds the corner toward his house, she hears footsteps—someone running. She turns and sees a young woman jogging toward her.

"Deputy Dawes!" the woman calls out. She's carrying a manila envelope. "Sorry to startle you. My name's Bette Burr. I'm hoping you can help me. I'm looking for someone's house. William Wayne?"

"I'm headed there right now. You're welcome to tag along." Dawes nods to the envelope in Burr's hand. "What's in the package?"

"Just something I want to deliver to him," Burr says.

They walk a bit, not speaking, then mount his steps together. "After you," Dawes says.

Burr raises a fist to the door, then pauses. She turns to Dawes. "Just knock?"

"Sure. Though if he answers the door for you, that would be a first."

Burr knocks.

They both wait.

No answer.

Burr knocks again.

Nothing.

Dawes steps to the side and peers as best she can into the bungalow's large picture window. The curtains are drawn tight and the glare from the early sun turns the glass reflective, into a bright painting of what the window faces: an empty, dusty street, the other quiet houses, the shimmering heat, and Dawes and Burr, standing side by side on the porch.

"No luck, I guess," says Dawes finally. "Though you're welcome to keep trying. I've got a few dozen more people to call on this morning." Dawes retreats down the steps, then turns back. "By the way, the sheriff wants me to tell you: Everything's fine. It's all under control."

"What is?" says Burr, confused.

"Everything," says Dawes. Then she smiles, turns away, and walks off toward the next house.

Burr stays on the porch and stares at the window, toward her reflection again. Still clutching her manila envelope. *At least I found you, William Wayne,* she thinks, and she contemplates the door again. *Now all you need to do is open up. Maybe this will help*—and she pulls a piece of paper from her pocket and unfolds it. She's already affixed a piece of tape to it; already written the note. It reads:

I am John Sung's daughter.

She places the note against the plate-glass window, tapes it there, and smoothes it flat against the glass, so that the words she's written face the darkness inside.

9.

GINGER VAN BUREN is, at sixty-eight, one of the oldest living residents of Caesura. The oldest known resident is William Wayne, who's well past seventy, and their respective presences in the town couldn't be more different. Wayne is whispered about, never seen, and barely ever heard from. Ginger Van Buren, on the other hand, is seen, and heard from, often. She's well known to everyone in town. And, for the most part, what she's known for is her dogs.

Not dogs, exactly. Coydogs, actually. Bastard offspring of dogs and coyotes. Just four of them, though you'd never know that from the amount of noise they make.

Cooper still remembers the day, six years back, when Ginger arrived for her intake. She came with no name and no past and no worldly possessions, save for a lime-colored polyester pantsuit, Jackie O sunglasses, and her dog. The dog was a short-haired, long-limbed, and vocal hybrid of a Doberman and whatever lesser breed her Doberman ancestor managed to pin down and force himself upon. At the time, there were absolutely no pets allowed in Caesura—there still aren't—but Cooper's overlords at the Institute explained that they'd made an arrangement with the Justice Department. The agents in charge of the investigation for which Ginger had served as a crucial and indispensable witness had made it clear that taking her dog was a nonnegotiable part of her amnesty deal. It made sense, sort of. Because if she left her beloved hound behind in the outside world, whoever sought to punish Ginger for whatever it was she said could simply find and enact their revenge on her precious pooch, which, to her, would be a much worse punishment than anything they might do to her. So the town made room for the lady and her dog. They've regretted it ever since.

They'd located her and her dog in a bungalow at the farthest end of the final street in town, in a cul-de-sac, a stone's throw from the outer perimeter fence, the thinking being that the dog, in her mature years, might live another two or three years, tops. Unbeknownst to Cooper, however, Ginger started squirreling away food scraps from the commissary and leaving them out by the fence. Pork chops. Raw hamburger. Left by the fence as bait. Hoping to attract some of the area's wilder denizens. And she used some pliers borrowed from Orson Calhoun—himself easily hoodwinked under any pretense—to snip a small doggie-door in the bottom of the fence. All in hopes, to her credit, of midwifing exactly the kind of amorous union that eventually took place. Coyote meets dog. Coyote mounts dog. Dog births litter. And the tangled lineage of her beloved pooch became even more compromised.

Her bitch got pregnant, birthed four mewling coydog hybrids, then passed on from the stress of the delivery. The coydog pups were small, cute, loud, wild, and nasty—naturally, Cooper submitted a request to the Institute to eject the whole brood. Ginger protested to her overseers, successfully, claiming emotional support. Of course, no one at the Institute who approved the coydogs' continued presence had to actually live with them, or listen to them crooning every night.

Eventually, a compromise was reached. The pups got neutered, the illicit doggie-door got sewn back up with plastic ties, and the town built a small, fenced-in kennel adjacent to Ginger's bungalow, right by the perimeter fence, where the four coydogs could howl and paw the dirt and gaze longingly at the wild expanse just beyond. Sometimes Cooper sees the arch of that sewn-up doggie-door in the fence and it looks to him like a hellmouth, the portal by which the town was invaded by these infernal, yapping beasts. Once the coydogs grow to adulthood—or Ginger passes from this world—they will be released back into the wild, or, in Cooper's secret fantasy, shot. The beasts are half-wild already, he figures, with no hope of domestication. Ginger thought she could tame them; she was wrong. Now they live as accidental bastards, the untamable offspring of the ersatz civilization that exists within the fenced-off confines of the Blinds and the acres of empty nothingness on the other side. Robinson once joked that the Blinds should adopt the coydog as its mascot and form an official football team: the Caesura Coydogs. Cooper never saw the humor in all that. To him, the coydogs were snarly, mean-spirited mistakes, an ill-advised experiment gone wrong. True, most people get used to their howling—eventually. You can get used to almost anything, he's found. But not if you're brand-spanking-new to the town, spending your very first week in the Blinds.

Cooper knocks, and waits patiently, until Vivien King answers the door. Her hair's tousled and she looks tired and pissed off and desperate, standing in the doorway, wearing a chiffon robe.

"Morning, ma'am. I'm Sheriff Cooper. I understand you had a complaint."

"Those *dogs,*" she says, nearly in tears.

"Technically, they're coydogs. Part coyote, part—"

"Whatever they are, they were barking. All. Night." She looks wrecked.

"I do apologize."

"I'm not—look, I *love* animals."

"Trust me, these animals are not lovable," says Cooper. "The best thing is to just move you clear across town. We'll have to fill out a few forms, but I can get you moved to a different bungalow, in the north end, where it's quieter."

King smiles, then says in a ragged voice, "It went on all night. I didn't sleep at all. Just lay there—thinking."

"I understand."

"I have no idea what I'm doing here, Sheriff."

"It's a common reaction on the first few nights."

She stares out past him, past the fence. "I thought it would be liberating, you know? Not to remember? But I just feel"—she pauses, searching—"untethered." She looks back at him. "I remember some of it. I remember my childhood. Everything up to a certain point."

"The experience is different for everyone. The goal of the Institute—"

"But then it just stops," she says. "Like a whole portion of my life is just . . . missing."

"That's the way it's supposed to work," Cooper says. "You should consider yourself lucky. Some of the earliest people lost *everything*. Over the years, the procedure got more precise. They only target the parts of your life you don't want to remember. That's how you get a fresh start."

King looks dismayed, like all of this is dawning on her only now, as she's saying it. "I just can't stop thinking about that emptiness." She looks up at him, bewildered. "Does that feeling get any better?"

"It does," Cooper lies.

She smiles, comforted a little bit, at least for now, and once she's tucked away back inside her bungalow, Cooper exits her porch and lingers for a minute in the dusty street. He checks his watch—still early, still several more hours until two P.M. He considers the coming agenda for the day. Thankfully, Dawes's vaunted theory turned out to be a bunch of nothing, just a few happenstance overlaps. Still, it's not like he hasn't wondered himself if maybe Colfax and Gable were connected in the real world. Well, it's not for him to ask questions, not those kinds of questions, anyway. In the meantime, he has to go talk to Fran about this incident at Orson's, because they found Isaac's trading cards sprinkled all around Orson's trashed workshop. Cooper pulls a card from his pocket to examine it. No mistake: It's a trading card for the movie he and Isaac went to see a few months back. Which puts Cooper on a collision course with a very unpleasant conversation with Fran. He feels a painful twinge in his gut and wonders if it's guilt or that stale pastry, then remembers hazily how he swallowed a bullet in a glass of whiskey last night. Probably some combination of all three.

Cooper's set to leave when he notices a man on the porch adjacent, watching him but saying nothing. It's another one of the new arrivals from yesterday's intake. The man's head is shaved, like a new recruit or a monk, and he's wearing loose pants and a white sleeveless undershirt. His taut, wiry arms are covered with tattoos.

Once Cooper catches his eye, the man nods. "Good morning, Sheriff. What you got there?"

"Just a good luck charm." Cooper pockets the card again. "I'm afraid you have me at a disadvantage, since I didn't stick around yesterday when y'all chose your new names."

"Now what did I end up calling myself?" The man adopts an exaggerated pose of rumination, stroking his stubbled chin with spindly fingers. "Oh, yes, Dick. Dick Dietrich."

"Those coydogs keep you up last night, too, Mr. Dietrich?"

Cooper stands in the street, cupping his hand over his eyes, squinting.

"No, I slept like a baby. Or a corpse." Dietrich laughs. "I suppose the corpse of a baby would be the soundest sleeper of all."

"I don't believe I saw you at the town meeting yesterday."

"I was busy getting settled in."

"And how's that going?"

Dietrich looks up and down the street, then smiles. "Already feels like home. This meeting I missed—was that about the killing you had here the other night?"

"That's correct."

"You see a lot of killing in this town?"

"Never before, and never again, if I have anything to say about it."

"But that's always the question, isn't it?" says Dietrich. "Will you have anything to say about it? Or will something else happen instead?"

"I guess so." Cooper's in no mood for this, not today. "Y'all have a nice morning," he says, then turns to go.

Dietrich calls after him. "You don't come by that 'y'all' honestly, do you, Sheriff Cooper? My ear can pick out a carpetbagger at a hundred yards."

Cooper turns back to him. "Really? Are you a Texas boy, Dick?"

"I'm from all over," says Dietrich. "Now I guess I'm from right here. Fancy calling this place home."

"We do our best to be neighborly," says Cooper, with a cold smile.

"Then I'll do my best to do my best," Dietrich says.

"You do that," Cooper says, then walks away. At the end of the street, he taps the trading card in his pocket again, like a talisman, then turns the corner and points himself on a path to Fran Adams's house, which happens to be the very last place in town he wants to go right now.

The Chevy Aveo has two rear windows smashed by the vandals, but Orson's vacuumed out the shards from the backseat and cleaned out the empty panes and covered the empty windows in black plastic. The tires are solid, the engine's tuned, so otherwise, he explains to Dawes, the car runs good. "Once you get north of sixty miles per hour," he says, "she'll start to shudder on you." Dawes assures him she takes her driving slow, which isn't exactly the truth.

"You planning on taking a trip into town, Deputy?" he asks.

"Just curious if it's an option," she says. She'll have to figure out a story for Cooper to get his permission to leave for the day, but she's not too worried about that. She's allowed to request a twenty-four-hour furlough in case of emergency, and she's confident she can cook up something convincing. She just needs to get to Abilene for a couple of hours, tops. During her rounds, knocking on doors, she managed to slip in a few questions to the residents about Marlon Garner, aka Ellis Gonzalez, aka the man she was hired to replace. Aka the man who up and quit and took off the week after Colfax shot himself. *Allegedly* shot himself. Everyone remembered Garner, of course, though no one knew where he went. But Lyndon Lancaster remembered him talking often of Abilene, like maybe he had family there, or at least a reason to visit. It's not much, but it's not nothing, she thinks. A real name and a real place. It's a start. Now all she has to do is get there. That's where the Aveo comes in.

"It's beautiful countryside beyond these fences, or so I recall," Orson says. "It's been a long, long while since they drove me in the bus to here." He nods to the half-organized refuse in the yard. "You see what they did to my shop?"

"I'm very sorry, Orson."

"They scrawled some foolishness, too, on the wall to scare me. You have any idea what that means?" He points to the graffiti: *Damnatio Memorae.*

"I don't," she says, another not-exactly-true statement.

"Well, if you do need the car, she's ready to go and the tank is full. Thankfully I filled her up before my spare gas can disappeared."

"What happened to the spare gas can?" she asks.

"Whoever broke in here up and stole it. Must have done. I've searched everywhere else. Though you know my mind's not always the clearest."

"What would someone want with a gas can?" asks Dawes, though she knows Orson won't have an answer. And if she's honest with herself, she knows there's only one reason someone would steal a gas can in a town without cars, and that's to burn something down.

10.

COOPER KNOCKS AGAIN and Isaac answers the door. He seems excited to see Cooper, which just makes Cooper feel worse about the business that's brought him here. He considers confronting Isaac directly with the telltale trading card, but he can't bring himself to do it. *Geez, he's just a kid,* thinks Cooper, *a little weird, but innocent and unruined.* Or so Cooper had always assumed.

"Your mother home?" he asks.

Isaac hollers and Fran appears, her arms wrapped around a basket of half-folded laundry. She invites Cooper into the living room and, after exiling Isaac back to his room, inspects the trading card that Cooper just handed over. While she does, Cooper marvels at the living room again—he's been here plenty of times, but he's always struck anew by all the books. Since the day she arrived she's surrounded herself, patiently building a collection. She quickly filled the small, standard-issue bookshelf they all get—Cooper's got maybe two, three throwaway paperbacks on his shelves right now—then she squirreled away the other volumes, discards mostly, collected from the library or from the new books that arrive sporadically with Spiro's weekly commissary supplies. It doesn't matter: Fran wants them all. Every surface in her living room now holds a small collection, in haphazard piles or standing up straight, spines rigid. That's all she does when she has the time. She reads.

"Sure, it's his," she says finally, "but Isaac would never do anything like that." She holds out the card to Cooper with finality, as though the issue is settled and the topic is closed.

"I know it seems unlikely, Fran, but someone trashed that shop. It wasn't me, and I'm pretty sure it wasn't you, and I don't imagine it was old Buster Ford. And you know Isaac has been acting out lately—"

"Come on, Cal, that was months ago."

Cal—it's been a long while since she regularly called him that, he thinks. She turns away from him and goes back to folding her laundry—another signal to tell him she's done with this topic.

"He set a fire, Fran. These things escalate—"

"It was a pile of grass and sticks in my front yard. He found some matches in the kitchen. Boys do that. I bet you did it, too, when you were a kid. I bet you did a lot worse."

Cooper did—plenty worse. He doesn't mention that. "Plus, he broke that window—"

"You don't know that was him—"

"We both know it was him, Fran. Doris Agnew saw him do it."

Fran sweeps stray hairs back from her ponytail, tied hastily. She picks up a kids' t-shirt. In her fingers the shirt looks frail and impossibly small. When she answers, it's in a low voice, to be sure Isaac won't hear from his room. "Look, I'm not saying he doesn't misbehave. Or that living here isn't taking a toll on him. We both know that it is. But I was up until midnight last night. He was sound asleep the whole time."

Cooper holds out the card again. "Then explain this."

"That's my whole point, Cal. I don't know how someone got those cards, but I do know for a fact that Isaac would never leave any of his cards behind. He *loves* those cards. They're like treasures to him. He even stores them in a special box. He would never scatter them all over the place. It makes no sense."

"I'm not saying I'm sure it was Isaac," says Cooper. "In fact, there's reason to believe it wasn't. There was graffiti there, too, in the shop, some Latin saying. But if it wasn't him, then it's someone who wants us to think it was. And that makes me nervous, too."

"Then I don't know why you're wasting your time here," Fran says. "Accusing me? Accusing my son?"

"You know I'm only concerned about him. About both of you."

"And what is that supposed to mean?"

"There's just something happening right now," Cooper says. "The thing with Colfax. Now Gable."

"Funny you didn't mention any of this at the town meeting yesterday." She folds a pair of jeans, her motions controlled and precise, her creases crisp. "Is that why you broke things off between us? To give me an easy way out?"

"I've told you I'll help you any way I can."

"Look, I'm happy to leave, if you, or anyone, can give me some idea of what exactly is waiting for us out there if we do."

As she folds mechanically, Cooper glances at her left hand and the series of numbers tattooed like a cuff around her wrist. He asked her about it once, in a very different moment of intimacy, one which seems very long ago to him right now. Calling each other by first names, quietly, huddled together in the dark.

"There may not be anyone out there hunting you," he says. "Maybe you just—"

"What? Maybe I'm an innocent?" She almost laughs at the thought. "Isn't that what everyone here wants to believe? I may not know why I'm here, Cal, but I do know, at some point, it was my only option. And that scares the hell out of me."

"Look, just ask him about the card," says Cooper. "I'm not going to punish him. But I do need to know what's going on in my town."

"You worry about your town. I'll worry about my son," she says.

Cooper wants to say more, but what exactly, he's not sure. But he does have an idea. Not a new one exactly, but one he's been waiting for the right moment to act on. *Well, this sure as hell feels like the right moment,* he thinks. He nods to her, then excuses himself from the house without another word.

Cooper eats his lunch alone at home. The shades are drawn. It's nearly two P.M.

At quarter to two, he rises, clears his dishes, and washes the plate in the sink. He sets the cutlery in the drying rack. He wipes his hands on a towel, then heads out to the police station.

Back in the harsh sunlight, ambling through the middle of town, Cooper watches as people gather in front of the commissary, collecting provisions; it's Tuesday, so end-of-cycle allotment discounts kick in to clear out space for the new shipment Wednesday morning. Cooper spots white-haired Buster Ford in his overalls loading up a little red wagon with groceries. Ford gives him a friendly nod.

"Any leads?" he calls out.

"We're working on it, Buster," says Cooper. "Closing in on a few promising possibilities."

A few other stragglers, their arms freighted with bags, free their hands to wave a greeting to the sheriff. He smiles back each time, doing his best to look calm, optimistic, and in control. It's a look he's practiced enough to pull off.

He heads to the police trailer, which is empty, thankfully, so he doesn't have to make any excuses to chase off his deputies. Cooper closes the door behind him. He takes his seat by the fax machine and checks his watch.

At two P.M., the machine barks to life. Paper starts stuttering out. He rips the page clear of the machine.

The paper contains one word in large letters across the top: *Tomorrow.* Then, in smaller script, beneath that: *9 mm in the mail.*

Under that: a photo.

A mug shot actually. He recognizes the person right away.

It's a photo of Gerald Dean.

Gerald Dean—the same guy Dawes decided to focus all her attention on. That's got to be a coincidence, right? There's no way Dawes—no, she's on the wrong scent. Still, the connection—Colfax, Gable, now Dean—makes Cooper uneasy. If Dean and Gable were drinking buddies, maybe they did know each other in their previous lives. Maybe they were drawn to each other, without knowing exactly why.

What did you do in your past life, Gerald? Cooper thinks, studying the photo. *What evil deed brought you to this place?*

Either way, it doesn't matter to Cooper, or to what he knows comes next. Besides, he'll find out all about Dean's past soon enough.

He's about to feed the paper into the shredder, but he stops and folds it up instead. He slips it into the breast pocket of his shirt, just under where his sheriff's star is pinned.

Then he sits again in the silent gloom of the shuttered office. He's got one more decision to make. Not about Gable, not about Dean—about Fran Adams and her son. He's considered this option before—his final option, really—but hesitated to pursue it, knowing it was the last and only card he had to play. But he's out of ideas now and, frankly, after tomorrow night, after Gerald Dean, all this will come to an end. He's decided that already. Recent events have only made him more sure. He's honestly not certain what happened at the repair yard—drunkards, vandals, roustabouts—it wouldn't be the first time a few boisterous residents got out of hand. Right now, it's just a distraction to him. But what he sees more clearly than ever is that there's no good reason for Fran and Isaac to stay.

He takes another moment to talk himself out of it, fails, and so he scribbles his note on a sheet of paper. He feeds the paper into the fax machine. He dials a number that only he knows. His belly gives another painful twang. He recalls the bullet he swallowed last night.

He sends the fax.

His note bears a simple message:

We need to meet.

An unusual request. But these are unusual times.

He sits back in his chair and waits. He thinks about a little boy on the other side of town, and all the years that boy has spent here, and all the years he has ahead of him.

Then Cooper thinks about another little boy, from long ago.

Maybe a minute later, maybe two, maybe twenty, Cooper can't tell, he loses count, the machine whines back to life, and his answer comes stuttering out. Handwritten on official Fell Institute letterhead.

It's been a long time, Calvin, but I'm always happy to see you—come by the ranch tomorrow afternoon.

There's no signature, but the long, looping letters are unmistakably written in Dr. Holliday's impeccable hand.

Bette Burr waits on his porch again.

Knocks again.

Still no answer.

No worries. It's only the second day. She's still got one more day—that's what they told her. Three days to find him and deliver the news.

Don't think I can't wait you out, Mr. William Wayne. Or that I'm going away.

She knocks again.

Then she steps back and peers into Wayne's window, but sees nothing. The curtains are still drawn tight. Only her searching face reflects back to her in the rectangular pane of glass.

She does notice one thing, though. Something encouraging.

The faint residue of the Scotch tape she used to leave her note, lingering in a tacky rectangle on the glass.

Someone took that note down. Must have read it, too.

I am John Sung's daughter.

And I'm still out here, she thinks.

She knocks again.

No answer. Again.

That's okay. Neither of them is going anywhere.

In her other hand, she clutches her manila envelope. Inside is a photo of her father.

Once William Wayne opens up, she'll show it to him.

To see if he remembers.

11.

FRAN SLIDES OPEN THE DRESSER DRAWERS in Isaac's bedroom and lays in the folded laundry. The dresser looks like a baby's dresser, she thinks, still covered in appliqué and painted baby blue. The whole room is now years out of date, she realizes, with a Noah's Ark mural and a zoo-animal mobile hanging from the ceiling. She feels a sudden flush of embarrassment, ashamed that she's kept the room frozen in time like this. As if that would keep him from growing up and save her from making her decision. When he was born, she thought she had a year to decide. At a year, she gave herself two more. When he reached age five, she wondered if this life would ruin him, but also admitted to herself that what lay beyond the fences was far too scary for her to contemplate. She dreamed of Jean Mondale and Jacob nightly; in her dream, they were both in a school bus, trapped, submerged underwater, drowning and pounding the glass. Then the bus filled with blood. Then she woke up. Sometimes she dreamed a man was watching the whole thing on his computer, his back turned to her, so she could never see his face. That same dream, night after night, for years. How could she plan to move away with Isaac after that?

In the meantime, as she waffled, frightened, Isaac turned six, seven, eight—he's got race-car posters taped up over the rainbow in the Noah's Ark mural now. Is that how the story of Noah ends? With a rainbow? She struggles, but she can't recall. She remembers the part about the storm, and the flood, and everyone piling into the boat to seek salvation, but not how it all ends. A rainbow? And dry land somewhere. A mountaintop. Maybe a dove.

She lays the clothes in the drawers carefully, creating neat little piles. At the bottom of the laundry basket, she finds one lonely sock. Shit. She searches the basket, then the carpet around her feet. Socks, especially kids' socks, are so fucking hard to get in this town, mostly because shipments of kids' clothes are so infrequent, since there's only one kid. She has to beg and plead with Spiro just to get what few provisions they can. He does his best, but Isaac outgrows everything so fast. These clothes. This room. This town.

She gets down on her hands and knees to check under the dresser. No luck. And there's something else missing, she realizes: Isaac's box, the one where he keeps all his treasures. The one where he put his trading cards. The one she was telling Cooper all about. The wooden cigar box, covered in shiny NASCAR stickers that arrived one blessed Wednesday morning years back, on the supply truck, ordered specially by Spiro for Isaac as a surprise. She remembers Isaac bringing the stickers home; she remembers him sitting patiently, applying each one to his cigar box as lovingly as an attending nurse might apply bandages to a suffering patient.

He keeps that box tucked under his dresser, she's sure of it. She's cleaned around it a hundred times, each time sliding it out carefully, then placing it back just so, for fear of upsetting him.

His treasure chest.

Now it's gone. No box, no cards, no bubblegum, no treasures, no nothing.

She can even see the faint impression in the shag carpet where the corners of the box once lay.

Well, that's about the worst news you could get right now, she thinks.

Then she stands back up, dusts off her jeans, and resolves, quite easily and with surprisingly little internal dissension, to share this information with precisely no one else.

Dawes finds Cooper alone in the police trailer, in his swivel chair, boots up on his desk.

"Are you busy? I can come back," she says.

"No. Come on in," he says, and sits up. "And, yes, you can take the car."

"I'm sorry—?"

"The emergency car. Orson Calhoun told me you were asking about it. I assume you want to track down Ellis Gonzalez and ask him a whole bunch of those questions you've been collecting in your notebook."

"I—" She's stumped. She had a whole lie prepped and ready, a good one, but apparently she won't be needing it now. "Yes, I had considered it."

"I saw Lyndon Lancaster earlier," says Cooper. "He told me you were asking about Ellis. He mentioned something about Abilene to you?"

"That's right."

"Sometimes you seem to forget—people in this town love to talk. And I'm the closest thing they have to a shrink. So things tend to get back to me." Cooper glances over the paperwork on his desk, as though he's ready to move on to the next order of business. "I think it's definitely worth a follow-up. You should go."

"Really? Because before—"

"What is it they say about gift horses and mouths, Deputy Dawes?" Cooper looks up at her and gives a little smile. "You were right. This is a serious matter. If it means heading off the reservation for a day, so be it. I'd offer you my truck, but I've got my own errand to run tomorrow. I just made an appointment to see Dr. Holliday."

Dr. Holliday is not a name that comes up in conversation very often, and when it does, it's typically spoken with reverence. Dawes can't help but ask: "What's it about?"

"I considered what you said about Gerald Dean and Hubert Gable. This incident with Gable is a serious breach. So I'm going to personally visit Dr. Holliday and put in an information request. Get Gable's file unsealed, and hopefully Dean's and Colfax's, too. Let's finally get some real answers, right?"

"I've never met Dr. Holliday," Dawes says. "Is she—what they say she is?"

"That all depends on what they say she is."

"You know—*impressive*."

"That, she definitely is. If you think about it, none of this"—Cooper gestures toward the door to the town beyond—"would exist had it not sprung from the depths of her fertile mind."

"I thought it was Dr. Fell who founded this place."

"Fell pioneered the technology, but I think he had other applications in mind," says Cooper. "In any case, he died before Caesura ever opened. So this particular forsaken experiment?" He leans back in the swivel chair and holds his hands wide. "This is all Holliday's baby. She makes the rules. And, if I prove charming enough tomorrow, we'll see if she's willing to make an exception." He looks back down at his paperwork, by way of a dismissal. "You have yourself a good trip, Deputy." Let her drive off and track down Gonzalez, he thinks, as he pretends to peruse a form. Let her marry Gonzalez for all he cares. So long as she's out of his hair for one day. Just one day—a day that promises to be quite eventful here in town.

"Thank you, sir. I'll let you know whatever I find out." When he doesn't answer, Dawes lets herself out of the trailer.

12.

FRAN CHECKS EVERY DRYER for the missing sock but finds nothing. She rummages through the lost and found box—also nothing. Isaac, meanwhile, has enacted a temporary speedway, with a single toy race car, on the peeling linoleum floor of the Laundromat. He races the car in a noisy circuit, around and around, making rubbery race-car gear-shift sounds with his mouth. She watches him for a moment: lost in a world of his own invention. How easily he escapes. To a hidden place with its own rules and regulations, its own dramas and crises. That's no surprise, she thinks. It's all he has. An elaborate imaginary realm that only he can access. She hasn't asked him about the missing cigar box and doesn't plan to, not yet, at least. He's so alone in this world, she thinks. He needs the solace of his own secrets.

From above the row of washers, the TV drones—someone switched it back to the all-news channel, apparently.

—has become a national story. Vincent, the tech tycoon who was injured in a brutal domestic assault and lay in a coma for over a year,

attracting national headlines—she looks up to see a man in a polo shirt, handsome, smiling, at a podium—*and only now, after many long years of recovery, is looking to restart his political ambitions*—this apparent politician has a warm smile, he's appealing, she has to admit—*after making his fortune in the science of predicting elections, he'll now try his luck at his own Senate run. Addressing the media earlier today, Vincent*—the man, familiar to her now, she knows this face, she realizes, he's the same man from the news report she saw the other day, it hits her with a painful twinge, the whine of the TV now making her head throb slightly; the man's talking now, seated, in an interview, coolly answering questions, in soothing tones. He's a natural, she thinks, though his voice, she can tell, is still affected somehow by whatever accident he endured, his words ever so slightly slurred—*what's in the past is past, and I can only wish her the best. What I'm interested in is moving forward, together with the good people of the state of California, if they see fit to entrust me with this. For years, I studied the best ways to predict how people would vote. Now I'm just trying to win those votes the old-fashioned way*—he chuckles, warmly, on cue, but believable nonetheless—*but it certainly is unusual to find myself on the other side of the ballot, so to speak*—the interviewer nods, volleys a few more questions and the sharp chatter of the TV surges, stoking Fran's burgeoning headache; the edges of her vision blur; this one's worse than ever; her stomach lurches; she feels like she might tumble; she shoots an arm out to steady herself on a nearby machine. Now Isaac's tugging at her shirt, now he's asking if she's okay, his voice distant and tinny—

Then it passes. She finds the nearby remote and mutes the TV. Now the hopeful politician is simply smiling and nodding warmly in muted silence.

So strange that once upon a time that kind of ambient electronic gibberish was the soundtrack of her everyday life, she thinks. That she actually found the staccato of the TV comforting as background noise. Once you spend enough time alone out here in the middle of nowhere, with silence as your counsel, on your steps at two A.M. counting endless stars, you'll forget how you ever managed to filter all that toxic white noise out, let alone find it welcome.

Given all the peace she's found out here.

Save for the occasional gunshot.

At the thought, she flinches reflexively, standing in the Laundromat among the mechanistic whir, as though she's heard a gunshot just now, they sneak up on her, these phantom shots. She glances back at the TV, bewildered for a moment, wondering if maybe something happened on the screen. But the wannabe politician on-screen is still smiling and talking, nodding, the sound's still muted, the only noise the perpetual sloshing of the washers, and it's nothing, the moment's over.

Isaac, below her, looks up, still worried.

Poor Isaac. She's literally all he has.

She shakes it off, does her best to smile, and reaches out to give his shoulder a reassuring squeeze, and she glances at the etched tattoo that encircles her wrist, the forgotten numbers that she almost never thinks to notice anymore.

Cooper unfolds the fax on his kitchen table. Smoothes it out under the overhead lamp. Reads the single word again. No reason to, it's not going to change, but he does it anyway.

Tomorrow.

He folds the fax and puts it back in his pocket. Checks the clock. Nearly ten P.M.

Cooper has set his last unopened bottle of Old Grand-Dad

bourbon on the table. A new shipment of provisions comes in tomorrow morning, and Greta will definitely set aside something just for him, she always does, but this is his in-case-of-emergency-break-glass secret reserve. You can't open it lightly. He picks up the bottle, considers the unbroken seal.

Dean is the last one—Cooper's decided that already. Colfax, Gable, Dean, then he's done. Not that he went into this with much of a plan, just an offer in hand, a bag of dangled cash, but he definitely has a plan now. And three should be enough. More than enough. It should be plenty.

He hates to break into his last bottle, his emergency reserve, just on principle.

Besides, he's got one more important thing to do tonight.

He needs a drink. But he needs a clear head more.

He taps the cap. A nervous drumbeat.

Checks the clock again. Just past ten.

Isaac will be asleep by now.

Cooper remembers when he used to visit Fran late at night for entirely different reasons. How she always told him it was safe to come after ten.

How he'd sneak over, under cover of darkness, hoping none of her nosy neighbors would spot him. Hell, Doris Agnew, who lives right next door to Fran, is the worst wag in the town.

How Fran would answer the door without a word and he'd slip inside and spend an hour or so with her, pretending they were somewhere that's not here. Being as quiet as they could. Pretending they were people who aren't the people that they are. A few hours in the darkness, together, complicit in indulging that luxury. Just like a normal couple somewhere. You could almost believe it, in the dark. Imagining some other story for themselves, some escape.

He hated breaking it off. Hated it. Hated watching her take the news. Hated seeing this strong woman try stubbornly to keep her face from falling at his weak excuses and pathetic dissembling and obvious lies. Hated watching it dawn on her that even this lowly, inadequate, compromised scrap of human contact they'd forged together was going to be denied her. Cooper doesn't fool himself into thinking he's some prize catch. Far from it. He understands that her sorrow in that moment was spurred entirely by the realization that she couldn't even have something so broken and cheap, so compensatory, not even that, so she could forget about ever finding anything worthwhile.

And most of all he hated watching her realize right before his eyes that those stolen hours they'd spent together were nothing but mutual lies, told to each other in silence in the dark, with the understanding that they'd both pretend to believe that they were true. That in the light of day her life is nothing more than what it is, and always will be. That whoever she used to be, whatever she can't remember, it doesn't matter, she's here now, within these fences, with her son, with nothing but fake names and endless days and no escape.

That's what she thinks, unless he can convince her otherwise.

He unwedges the bottle from his thighs and sets it aside on the table, unopened. He'll have to break that emergency glass another time.

Tonight, he needs his head clear.

He hated to do it, he hated to end it. It was the one good thing he can remember in his life, that one weekly hour of escaping, but that's exactly why he had to break it off. He had to think of the bigger picture. Which, for her, can't include him. For her, or for her son.

Keep telling yourself that, Cooper.

He checks the clock. It's time to go.

You've got one more chance to save the day, he thinks.

She answers the door, drying her hands with a dish towel, after his second knock.

"You want to come inside?" she says.

"Maybe it's better if we speak out here. Or walk a little. Will Isaac be okay?"

"Sure, for a moment. He's asleep."

They walk up the street together, in the dark, toward the perimeter fence. At the end of the block, she pulls out her pack of cigarettes. "You mind? I like to multitask."

"You still hiding that habit from Isaac?"

"I'm still pretending he doesn't know," she says. "Or that I don't know he knows—I've lost track." She sticks the cigarette in her mouth and pulls out a lighter and sparks it. Cooper's about to speak but she hushes him with a raised finger. Takes a long drag. Then exhales.

"That's the only part I really enjoy," she says. "So it's important to maintain a proper reverence." She puts the cigarette to her lips again and takes a long second drag. She exhales, then says, "Second drag's never as good," then drops the cigarette to the dirt and grinds it out with a little halfhearted twist, like a weary dancer at the end of a marathon, just trying to stay upright and keep dancing.

They walk a little farther, until they're standing right under the fence. Looking out beyond the chain link: Nothing. Total darkness. The watching world, presumably.

"I'm sorry about today," says Cooper.

"No, I owe you an apology. I looked for his treasure box. The one where he keeps the cards? It's gone."

"Look, that doesn't mean—"

"Don't bullshit me," she says. "Sometimes I wonder if I even know him at all anymore."

"Kids are hard."

"Easy for you to say, given you don't have one."

"There's a parenting book you could read," Cooper says. "It's called *Raising Icarus*. Just sound advice about kids, you know, keeping them close but not too close. It's written by a single mother who did a hell of a job with her son. I'm sure we have it at the library. I asked them to order a few copies a while back."

She turns in the dark to look at him. "What the hell are you doing reading parenting books anyway, Calvin Cooper? Aren't you just full of surprises."

"I heard about it on the radio once," he says. "Before I came out here. Recommended it to a few people over the years. They seemed to find it useful."

Off in the distance, they can both hear a rising whine as Ginger's coydogs start in on their nightly serenade.

"Believe it or not, there are things about this place I would definitely miss," Fran says.

"That's what I want to talk to you about. I came to tell you that you need to go. As soon as possible."

"We've talked about this—"

"It's different now. Trust me. Take Isaac. Tomorrow."

"What the hell, Calvin?"

"Trust me."

"Sure—like Jean Mondale and Jacob?"

"I had nothing to do with that, you know that. She made her own decision. She knew the risks."

"So do I. The world's not safe out there. Not for us." She pulls the pack of cigarettes from her pocket again and fumbles with it. Thinks better of it. Pockets it again. "I have nothing, Cal. No money. No prospects. No fucking clue even who I am. So where would we go? I thought coming here would be a fresh start, you know? But it's not. It's just a fucking hole you fall into and you can never climb back out again."

"I can help you," he says.

"How?"

"Money, for starters."

She laughs a brittle laugh. "I used to think one of the only appealing things about this place is you don't have to think about money. You really want to help me?"

"Of course." Cooper strains to see her in the dark. He hears her strong voice wavering. There's an unsteady twang in her voice now, a vibration, like the sound of struck steel.

"Then how about instead you start by telling me who the fuck I really am?"

"I don't know that. But I can try to find out," he says.

She turns toward him. They're standing close now. She reaches out a hand in the dark for his face. Lets her palm rest on his cheek. It's been a long time since they touched like this. Cooper wants to resist, but he doesn't. It's too dark by the fence for anyone to see them out here anyway. They can barely see each other.

"It's funny, right?" she says. "We used to expend so much energy pretending we were someone—anyone—else. When all I really want to know is who I am." She pulls her hand away. "Look, I'm sorry. It's not your fault I'm here."

"You're not alone. We all have secrets," Cooper says.

"Sure. But at least you know what your secrets are."

"If I can tell you about your past, the circumstances that brought you here, would you consider leaving?"

"Can you do that?"

"I'm seeing Dr. Holliday tomorrow."

"Really?" Fran's surprised. It's unusual for anyone to mention Dr. Holliday, let alone visit her. "Why?"

"She's got access to all the files. It could be you're an innocent, Fran. You could walk out of here tomorrow. And even if you're not, at least you'll know which direction to run."

"I can't."

"Just consider what I'm saying. About leaving. A little money. A head start. You could do well, I know it."

"I am—" She starts to say something else but the next words are swallowed by a sudden rising clamor. Barking, and then a heavy *whoosh* like a gas burner lighting, and then a scream.

A long, loud woman's scream that keeps on screaming.

Cooper turns toward the sound of the ruckus. Fran says instinctively, plaintively, "Isaac," then runs off, back toward her house. Cooper feels a sharp tug to follow her, but she's already gone, and the scream is still screaming, so he raises his hand to get a sense against the fence of where in the darkness he is, then he starts to run toward the howling, his fingertips tracing the fence, toward the sound of the scream, a woman's scream, and toward the barking, a clatter of discordant yelps that now swells in an unsettling way into a wail.

He runs faster.

Cooper follows the fence, stumbling; he hears the coydogs baying, their cries now disturbed and constant and piercing, an unholy choral howl. He rounds the corner to the block where Ginger Van Buren lives and runs across the scrubby grass and falters again in the dark, then rights himself, and as he stands straight he sees a brightness dancing in the middle of the street.

A flame like a bonfire, circling.

He sees Ginger out on her porch with her nightgown pulled around her, her mouth open and her shrieking face lit by the flames. Cooper reaches for his pistol. On the street, he sees now that several fires are moving as though synchronized, hemorrhaging dank black smoke into the sky, and the sounds of the coydogs keening unfurls like a hellish siren that rises and recedes in piercing waves. He watches as the bonfires move and dance until he understands what he's seeing. Her coydogs are on fire. Two of them gallop down the gravel road like torches in the hands of a running mob. Two of them have fallen and are burning dead in the dark where they fell. The smell of hair and fat sizzling unfurls in an inky smoke. The stink of it chokes the air. Cooper gags and bends double, then straightens again and peers past the two felled beasts, toward the pair that are running in the street ablaze. Threatening the houses. He smells gasoline intermingled with the smell of burning fur. Cooper unholsters his pistol and his right shoulder barks as he raises the gun and he aims at a coydog and fires. The bullet kicks the gravel yards away. He fires again. Misses again even worse, a plume of dirt spouting harmlessly from the road. That's two bullets wasted. He's only got four left in the gun.

Then beyond the flames and black smoke and the ripples of heat in the road, Cooper sees a figure walking slowly toward him. A lithe form silhouetted in the shadow of the fire. The figure approaches, backlit, and reaches a hand out to Cooper. It's Dick Dietrich, and he's asking for the gun. He says warmly, as though in confidence, "Let me take a crack, Sheriff. Trust me. I'm a very good shot."

Cooper stands a moment agape and confused by Dietrich's sudden appearance, his outstretched hand, his calm request, which rattles in Cooper's brain before it registers. He looks at Dietrich and then at the burning dogs loosed and howling in the street behind him. Then Cooper hands over his revolver.

Dietrich nods and seems to almost smile and takes the gun and turns. He raises the revolver smoothly and there's a sharp report and a muzzle flash. The first burning coydog buckles. Now only one beast remains, circling in slow tortured rotations as though befuddled by its curious change in circumstance. A black smear inside a bright flame, like a matchhead at ignition. Other residents have gathered now and stand silent on their porches, clutching robes or simply watching.

Dietrich raises the pistol again. As calm and confident as a shepherd.

He sights the pistol and shoots again, his placid face lit by the fire.

The resonant clap shatters the stillness.

The last burning coydog falls in a crackling heap.

WEDNESDAY

13.

DAWES HOLDS UP A HAND to halt the supply truck as it pulls up in a growl of gravel just outside the front gate. She rolls open the entrance and waves it through. The driver gives her a smile through the window but already he can tell, just from her brown deputy's uniform and her refusal to smile back, that something's wrong, something's up, and he's going to wish he never got out of bed this morning.

It's a small delivery truck, with Texas plates and a cargo box that's covered in graffiti. Dawes walks around the back and slaps loudly on the rear door as the driver disembarks to open up. Greta, who normally receives this truck alone every week, at least for the drop-off of bar supplies, stands just behind Dawes. She's fidgeting nervously with her rings.

"You have a manifest?" Dawes asks the driver.

"Sure—you mean, like, what? Invoices?" he says. "I got a list of what's aboard." He grabs a clipboard from the cab and walks over and hands it to her. There's a sheath of pink and yellow carbon papers clipped haphazardly to it. Dawes looks them over as he rolls open the back door of the truck. Inside, it's half-full with crates of food and stacks of cardboard boxes.

Dawes looks the driver over—he's a yokel-for-hire who's been conscripted by the Institute from some nearby backwater town to do the weekly supply runs from Amarillo. Dawes flips through the carbon papers, then looks up and catches Greta giving the driver a look that says, *Stay cool.* The driver, for his part, looks nervous as hell. Dawes hoists herself into the back of the truck and quickly counts the boxes inside, checking the contents against what's listed on the clipboard. There's a crate of softening mangoes, a crate of browning bananas, a crate of bruised apples—the usual haul for the produce section of Spiro's general store. There's two cardboard boxes containing plastic-wrapped t-shirts, socks, and undergarments in various sizes, listed on the invoices as "sundries." There's an open box with a few used paperbacks, romances mostly, along with a small pile of local newspapers bundled together with twine, some of them a few weeks out of date and already yellowing. There's a plastic crate full of assorted liquors, the bottles separated by cardboard dividers.

"Not too much produce this time around," the driver calls into the back of the truck. "Refrigerator truck's only available once a month. So no dairy on this haul. In case you were hoping for some cream in your coffee." He turns to Greta. "But don't worry, I got your bottles. Two of everything, just like you asked. Should hold you till the end of the month, at least." He stands rocking with his hands jammed in the pockets of his jeans, while Dawes says nothing, just keeps counting. The driver gives Greta a look like, *What's with the third degree?* but Greta just watches Dawes.

"I should probably get those mangoes to the shop before they spoil," the driver says loudly. "Though feel free to grab a couple for yourself. I hear they're a hot commodity, likely won't last too long."

Dawes ignores him, though she notes an increasingly anxious edge to his voice.

She checks the invoices again. Eighteen boxes. Then she counts the boxes again.

Nineteen boxes.

There's a box marked MALLOMARS on the top of one pile that's been opened already and then taped up sloppily. If the commissary has ever carried Mallomar cookies, she's sure she would have noticed. Out here, indulgences are rare and valued, and they don't tend to go undetected.

She pulls out a penknife, then pauses, blade open, and calls back to the driver, "You mind?" Right away, she knows from his face that she's found something he didn't want her to find.

The driver doesn't answer, just glances nervously at Greta, who looks resigned to whatever's coming next.

Dawes slices the tape on the box and opens the box flaps.

Inside, there are letters. Envelopes. Postcards.

Mail.

"I don't—" says the driver, but Greta hushes him with a bejeweled hand placed gently on his arm.

Dawes steps out of the back of the truck into the road, holding the box of mail. She puts the box down on the rear gate of the truck and starts fishing around in it, pulling out a handful of envelopes and shuffling through them. All are hand-addressed to real names, names she doesn't recognize: Eduardo Figueroa. Anthony Mancuso. Theresa Benedict. And all of them are addressed to the same P.O. Box in Abilene, where they were presumably picked up and brought here. No return addresses on any of them.

She peers inside the box again. Shakes it. Maybe a dozen letters in all, plus a small paper-wrapped package.

Dawes looks up at Greta. "You know about this?"

Greta steps toward her, her face set defiantly. "So we run a little mail. People need some kind of contact. It's not humane otherwise."

"So you know who all these people are? These names?"

Greta shrugs.

Dawes looks down at the envelope in her hand. Figueroa. Her mind swims—it doesn't make any sense. Because even if these envelopes are addressed to the real names of people who live in the Blinds, how does Greta know who those people are? What's more, how do *they* know who they are? And how do people on the outside know that they're here to send them mail?

She's about to ask Greta these questions, and when she holds up one of the envelopes as proof, that's when she spots it. On the back of the envelope. A photograph. A small, smiling snapshot, like a passport photo. Taped to the back.

She recognizes Eduardo Figueroa. He's Spiro Mitchum.

Dawes drops the envelope back in the box and starts turning over the others. They all have photos stuck on the back, of people she recognizes from the town. Doris Agnew. Ginger Van Buren. Marilyn Roosevelt, the librarian.

"How do people out there know these people are living here?" says Dawes.

"I don't ask a lot of questions," says Greta. "I just deliver it. If it's got a photo, and I know the person, I drop it off. Trust me, we get a lot of mail addressed to people I've never seen before, people who never lived here, as best I know, and I've been here since day one. I think some people find out about the P.O. Box and just send letters in hopes that a person they're looking for might be living here. And sometimes they're right."

"Who sends this mail?"

"Relatives. Friends. Old neighbors," says Greta. "You might not remember the world, but the world remembers you. Sometimes the world even takes some pains to track you down. Let you know you're not forgotten."

Dawes shuffles through the mail again. There's a postcard with a photo of Lyndon Lancaster on it; real name: Sam Lemme. There's an envelope addressed to someone named Kostya Slivko; when she flips it over, on the back, there's a photo of Errol Colfax, who's been dead for two months. She looks up at Greta. "This is serious," Dawes says softly, almost like she's reaffirming it to herself. She can't believe this. She looks back into the box. Every one of these envelopes links a resident to their former identity, which is a fundamental breach of Caesura security. And every one of them means that someone in the world knows who's living here, and knows how to contact them. She thinks a moment, then turns to the driver and says quietly, by way of dismissing him: "You better get those mangoes to the store."

He glances at Dawes, then at Greta, then back to Dawes, then, without another word, steps quickly back into the cab and starts the truck, happy to escape his punishment.

As the truck trundles away, Dawes turns to Greta. "Does Sheriff Cooper know about this?"

"Why don't you ask him yourself?" Greta gestures toward the box. "Please. People are expecting those." She sounds plaintive now, pleading, like a child who let you look for a moment at something valuable and is now worried you're never going to give it back.

Dawes nods toward the box she's still holding in her arms. "Do you know what this means?"

"Sure," says Greta. "It means someone out there still remembers you. That you had a life before this place that hasn't been forgotten. Once you've been here five, six, eight years, you might understand how that feels."

Dawes clutches the box closer to her chest and says simply, "I'm sorry." Then she peers inside the box again. At the bottom, she spots the small paper-wrapped package. About the size of a box of matches.

She picks it out. Puts the box down. Shakes the package. Like a kid on Christmas.

It rattles.

Addressed to someone named Lester Vogel.

"You know who this is? This Lester Vogel?" Dawes asks.

Greta says nothing. Dawes turns the box over. There's a photo. It's Gerald Dean. Dawes can't believe what she's seeing yet is also not surprised in the least. She unwraps the package.

It's a brand-new box of 9 mm bullets.

She hefts it in her hand, then holds the box up to Greta. "Is this the kind of thing you usually deliver?"

"Look, I'm not customs. I'm just the postmaster," Greta says. "If it comes in on the truck and has a photo on it, I deliver it."

Dawes puts the package back in the box. She closes the flaps, hoists the box in her arms, and heads off with her contraband toward the police trailer, confident that the day ahead will prove to be the best one she's enjoyed yet here in the Blinds.

14.

COOPER HASN'T SLEPT. He hasn't had time to change his clothes. He spent the night awake on his sofa, nursing the dull burn in his shoulder and staring at the ceiling, visited by bright visions of burning beasts turning in endless circles. A few visions of Errol Colfax, too, and the back of Hubert Gable's head. Now, as morning beckons, he finds himself on Dick Dietrich's porch. After last night's commotion, he was too busy calming everyone down to deal with Dietrich—people pooling in the street, panicked and yammering, some with flashlights, some with lanterns, all with insistent questions about what the hell just happened. Some hauled buckets of water to try to stanch the burning corpses, but the water just splashed over the stubborn fires with an impotent hiss. Finally, Robinson arrived in his bathrobe, armed with a fire extinguisher, and snuffed out the fires, the extinguisher roaring. Foamy water ran in rivulets in the dusty gravel road; Cooper sees puddles of it still lingering this morning. The burned-animal smell is still on his tongue, in his throat, in his lungs, on his clothes. He recalls, too, how last night people circled Dietrich, thanking him, clapping him on the back, applauding the newcomer, stepping up to shake the hero's hand.

Cooper's barely finished his first knock when Dietrich swings open the door and welcomes him in.

"I heard the dogs—"

"They're coydogs," says Cooper.

"—the coydogs wailing," says Dietrich, now standing in his kitchen, pouring two mugs of black coffee. "So I came out, and I saw what was happening, and I knew they were in pain. It seemed like the humane thing to do." He hands a mug to Cooper, who's seated in a chair, and Dietrich sits opposite him on the sofa. His feet are bare and he wears jeans and a white linen pullover shirt with an open mandarin collar, and he crosses his legs at the knee and smiles. Save for the tattoos, he looks like an annoyingly optimistic therapist. If he brought an extra stitch of clothing with him to Caesura or a single other personal effect, Cooper notes, there's no evidence of any of it in his bungalow. There's nothing in the room save the standard-issue furniture: the cheap sofa, the modest coffee table, a lonely standing lamp. The closet door is ajar and the closet sits empty. If Dietrich spent the last two days getting settled, it's hard to see what exactly he was settling.

"Thanks again for your help," says Cooper.

"Just trying to be a good neighbor, like you said." Dietrich holds up his mug. "I'd offer you something stronger, but when I made my way to the commissary for provisions yesterday, there wasn't much left for the taking."

"That's okay, it's a little early in the day for me."

"I thought one of the benefits of this place is that you get to dispense with those kinds of proprieties." Dietrich sips his coffee.

"That Mexican grocer told me the new shipment of goods comes today."

"Spiro. His name is Spiro Mitchum."

"You ever look at that ink he's got on him? Speaks to a cartel background."

"We don't speculate on that kind of thing here," says Cooper. "Besides, you're a fine one to talk about excessive ink."

Dietrich jacks his loose sleeves up and inspects his arms. The tattooed portraits of beatific faces crowd into one another. "I like to keep track of the people I've encountered."

"That's a lot of people."

"I used to work in community outreach. Or so I'm guessing!" Dietrich laughs and slaps his knee. "Either way, I'm pretty handy with a firearm, if you're ever looking for a wingman. You never know when you might need to put down another animal in pain."

"Ex-military?" asks Cooper.

"What do I know? My memory's been wiped clean, right?"

"Not everything. Most people remember some things. Just not the bad things."

"I'm afraid for me that's most of it," says Dietrich. "The bad things."

"Well, I already have two deputies, but thank you for the offer," says Cooper. "Speaking of which—one of them, Deputy Dawes, found an empty gas can last night over by the coydog kennel. It had been stolen that morning from Orson Calhoun's repair shop."

Dietrich takes another sip, as though he's pondering this information, like Cooper's come to him to ask advice. "And what do you make of that?"

Cooper sets his mug aside, in hopes of signaling to Dietrich that the niceties portion of the conversation is now concluded. "As much as I'm grateful to you for helping me stop those poor animals,

I'm just as interested in finding out how they got on fire in the first place."

"It seems to me you've got all manner of miscreants holed up here. Any one of them seems capable of that kind of cruelty. Maybe even Spiro." Dietrich fans his hands dramatically like he's telling a ghost story at a campfire and Spiro is the mythical beast.

"We've gone eight years in the Blinds without any sort of trouble."

"And yet that seems to be coming to an end." Dietrich leans forward and sets his own mug on the coffee table. "The Blinds? Why does everyone keep calling this place that? I thought it was called Caesar salad or something."

"Caesura. The Blinds is just a nickname we original residents came up with. You know—blind leading the blind, that kind of thing. And when there's trouble here, in the Blinds, we know how to take care of our own."

Dietrich seems curious to hear what comes next. "How so?"

"As I like to say, these gates only open one way. So, if anyone has trouble integrating into the community, we send them right back out into the arms of the waiting world. Which, for most people here, is not a fate that ends too well for them. Especially people with bad things in their pasts."

Dietrich considers this solemnly, then leans forward again and picks up his mug. He points to the lingering moisture ring. "Coasters," he says.

"I'm sorry?"

"I looked everywhere, Sheriff, but I couldn't seem to find any. You'd think they'd anticipate that kind of thing."

"I'll see what I can do," says Cooper.

"And I will thank you for your visit and see you to the door." Dietrich puts his hands on his knees and stands with a smile. "I do appreciate you coming by. And as to those mutts," says Dietrich, "if

I were you, I'd be less concerned with how this all began than with how it's going to end."

"And how's it going to end?"

"Bang, whimper—how does that old expression go?" says Dietrich. "Either way, I sure can't wait to find out." He reaches out to shake Cooper's hand.

Cooper takes it, then leans in ever so slightly, holding Dietrich's hand tight. "You may be a crack shot, Dick, but don't forget, I've still got the gun." He releases Dietrich's hand and gives him a nod. "You have a good day now." He turns to the door.

And at that moment, good goddamn, Cooper really wishes he wore a hat.

From the window, Dietrich watches him go. Disappearing again down the dusty road to whatever it is he does all day. Tin-star sheriff. *I could break that badge in my teeth,* Dietrich thinks, then chuckles.

Maybe this whole thing will be a little bit of fun after all.

It felt good to shoot those coydogs, he can't lie. Moving targets, obscured by flame. Good practice. Stay sharp.

And those wild bastard beasts were never meant for this world.

Felt good to shoot them.

Felt even better to set them on fire in the first place.

He wants to say he never set an animal on fire before but that's not true. There was that time in the desert, with the dogs, the wild ones, the ones that haunted the platoon's camp, searching after scraps.

Stupid towelhead dogs too dumb to run.

See, but that's the kind of shit that gets you kicked out of the military.

That, and other kinds of shit.

Bad things.

Out in the desert. So many dunes. So much time spent sitting around and waiting.

So many bad memories. A lifetime's worth.

Damnatio memorae, he thinks.

The waiting around is making him itchy here, too, despite his diversions, but at least he's only got to wait another day or two at most.

Until then: Be patient.

Keep busy.

Get creative.

As he holds the curtain open, he looks at his arm and all the silent faces tattooed up and down his skin. He wants to ask them for their thoughts, but he knows they'll just stare back up at him, mute and reverent. Thankful, even.

Same for the ones on his chest. Even the three new ones on the small of his back, still bandaged and healing.

Dietrich remembers Cooper's face again, so serious, pulling him close. Whispering his empty words.

Then compares that face to one of the new tattoos freshly etched on his back.

Turns out it's a pretty good likeness, he thinks, as he lets the curtain drop.

15.

BETTE BURR SITS in her nearly empty bungalow. She slept well and woke up early, folded her pajamas neatly, and got dressed and sat at the table with her manila envelope set squarely in front of her. She has two empty suitcases piled up in one corner of the kitchen, both of which she brought with her to maintain the illusion that she'd be staying here for life when, in fact, she expects to be here three days, tops. It's been two days already.

So far, nothing. But that's okay. She's got another day.

She'll go, and knock, and wait. Again.

Expecting no answer. Again.

No sign of life even. Except that he took the note. That's something. And, if he still won't answer his door today, she'll show him the photo.

She empties her manila envelope onto the kitchen table. A large glossy photo slides out, along with a small Polaroid.

The large photo is a portrait of her father, smiling, handsome, taken in his younger days. She sees herself in him, a little, even though she never knew him. In the eyes, maybe.

She checks the second photo, the Polaroid, to confirm if the resemblance is real.

It's a snapshot of the two of them, standing side by side, in a modest house in Hawaii. Her father stands with his arm uneasily around her shoulders, a head taller than she is. He's smiling, or trying to. An oxygen tube snakes up from a tank on the floor beside him, draped over his ears and plugged into his nose, keeping him alive. He looks emaciated, diminished—a sunken husk that hardly resembles the robust man in the first photo.

The first photo. The one she brought for William Wayne.

The second photo is hers. The only one she has of them together.

It was taken the day he gave her his message to deliver. Now all she has to do is find Wayne and deliver it. Assuming Wayne even remembers who her father was.

That's what the first photo is for. To see if Wayne remembers.

Today, she intends to find out.

Fran walks into the library as soon as it opens in the morning, dragging Isaac behind her. She's not letting Isaac out of her sight today, or ever again, not after what happened last night. The whole town is talking about it. She didn't see any of it go down. She ran back to her house, with all the shouting and screaming and gunfire behind her, and she ran up the steps of the porch and into the house and into his room and found him curled up on the bed. She'd left him alone—just for a moment, but she left him alone.

That's not going to happen again.

And this morning, first thing, she decided to head to the library. After spending the night soothing Isaac back to sleep, then lying restless and helpless in her own bed for hours, she felt like she had to do *something* today. She's not convinced that the book Cooper recommended to her will hold any answers, but she's certainly willing to look. Guidance. Advice. Wisdom. Something.

Isaac trails her grudgingly into the library, clutching his toy race car, and plants himself on the floor among the shelves of books. As libraries go, it's a makeshift affair: just a storefront on the main thoroughfare, just down the street from the Laundromat. Yet it's surprisingly well stocked, the rows of shelves jammed with a wide range of books. The Institute seems to be committed to giving the residents this one amenity, at least. Fran knows. She spends a lot of time here. She feels like she's read every book in here, twice.

As Fran walks in, Marilyn's threading the new shipment of local papers onto the long wooden poles that serve as reading spines and which allow her to hang the papers, like inky laundry, on a wooden rack. Marilyn keeps the place admirably tidy and well ordered. She's in her mid-fifties, with a matronly air, and a meticulously maintained bouffant hairstyle that can't have been fashionable at any point during her lifetime. She's pleasant and helpful and perfectly harmless, which leads Fran to wonder frequently what exactly Marilyn did, or saw, to wind up here in the Blinds. If Fran had to peg anyone here as an innocent, she'd probably pick Marilyn Roosevelt. But, no doubt, Marilyn has her secrets, like everyone, even from herself.

Marilyn shakes her head with neighborly concern. "Quite a commotion last night."

Fran ignores the prompt and gets right to business. "I'm looking for a book—it's called *Raising Icarus*. It's a book about parenting."

Marilyn laughs. "Did Sheriff Cooper recommend it? I'm sure we have a copy—parenting books aren't in such hot demand around here." Marilyn turns to the old-fashioned card catalog on her desk, pulling out the narrow drawers and riffling through hand-lettered index cards. She pulls a card out. "Here we go—it's filed under Social

Sciences. The call number is on the card." She hands the hand-lettered index card over to Fran; it's got the call number up top, followed by the title, author, and a long sequence of numbers on the bottom.

"What's this number?" asks Fran.

"That's the ISBN. Helps you know you're getting exactly the book you're looking for."

Fran smiles and pockets the card, then turns to go scour the shelf. It's only once she's found the book that she stops and retrieves the card from her pocket. Something about the sequence of numbers scribbled on it nags at her.

The ISBN is a string of ten seemingly random digits.

She feels a sudden hollowing in her chest as she turns her back to Marilyn and holds the card up next to her wrist.

12500241214911

Fourteen digits on her wrist. Too long.

She's almost relieved.

She puts the card back in her pocket and admonishes herself for being so dumb as to think she'd stumbled on a clue.

She pulls the book that Cooper recommended from the shelf. It's a hardcover, with the title, *Raising Icarus,* written in looping script above a photo of a young boy and his smiling mom. There's something weirdly familiar about the boy's eyes—

Then she stops.

Puts her thumb over the digits at the end of her long tattoo. Covering all but ten of them.

She walks back over to Marilyn's desk, where Marilyn is puttering over her newspapers.

"Would you check another book for me?" says Fran, as calmly as she can. "I don't know the title. I just have a number for it. Can you do that?"

"The ISBN?" Marilyn says. "Well, for that, I'll need my books-in-print catalog." She unshelves an enormous hardcover, the size of an encyclopedia, and opens it. "The Institute sends me these every once in a while. The irony is, it's so out of date that it's probably out of print itself." She chuckles as she flips it open. "I keep telling them we need a computer to look these books up but, you know, prohibitions. All right—what's the number?"

Fran pulls the index card from her pocket and pretends she's reading from it, as though she's scribbled the number down. It doesn't matter either way, since Marilyn's back is turned and she's concentrating on her catalog. Fran holds up the card but recites the first ten numbers from her wrist.

1250024121.

It's not hard. She knows them by heart.

Fran watches as Marilyn flips through pages.

Waits an excruciating moment.

Then another.

Telling herself this is stupid. This will all be for nothing.

"Yes, here it is," Marilyn says. "And you're in luck." She spins on her swivel chair back toward the card catalog. While Fran waits, she notices that the library has suddenly gone very quiet, and Isaac's motor-car noises sound very loud, but very far away. She feels her chest constrict.

Marilyn plucks another card from a narrow drawer and holds it aloft triumphantly. She turns in her chair and holds out the card to Fran.

Fran almost doesn't want to take it, but she takes it. Once she has it, she doesn't want to read it. But she reads it.

As Consciousness Is Harnessed to Flesh: Journals & Notebooks 1964–1980, by Susan Sontag.

"That's the one," Fran says feebly, trying to sound convincing, forcing a smile.

"We have a copy," says Marilyn. "Should be filed under Biography."

Fran nods and turns to go search for the book. In truth, neither the title nor the author's name means anything to her. The title sounds kind of ridiculous, to be honest. But there's no way this is a coincidence—not all ten digits. She finds the section and runs a fingertip across the spines.

Snowden, Solzhenitsyn, Sontag.

Here it is.

She pulls it from the shelf.

It's a volume of diaries. She flips through it. There's a second book, a sequel, with a matching spine, still on the shelf. She pulls that book down, too.

"Certainly looks thought-provoking," says Marilyn, cheerily, from behind her.

"Something to pass the time," says Fran, then shoves both books, along with *Raising Icarus,* under her arm, grabs Isaac's hand again, and tugs him toward the door.

Cooper watches himself in the mirror as he buttons a fresh new brown uniform shirt. He has five identical brown shirts, all with identical pearl snap buttons, and he tries his best to make sure at least one of them is clean for work every single day. It's the little things that keep you sane.

He smoothes a hand over the front of the shirt. Good enough. Got to look presentable, especially if you're going to meet with Dr. Holliday.

It's a big ask. He's got a little leverage, and a little charm, and he's hoping, together, that will be enough.

He checks the clock. It's nearly nine in the morning already.

He looks over at the unfolded fax laying faceup on his dresser.

He should have fed it in the shredder the moment after he first received it. No need to hang on to it—the message isn't going to change.

But he did hang on to it, maybe because shredding it might give him a moment's pause, like maybe he's going to wriggle out of it.

Looking at the dead-eyed mug shot of Gerald Dean.

What did you do, Gerald?

The fax doesn't say what Gerald did. It just says the same thing it said yesterday.

Tomorrow.

Except now tomorrow is today.

Cooper's got the fax folded up again and tucked in his breast pocket, just under his star, as he walks down the main strip past the general store. He spots Spiro, who's out front, in his apron, unpacking the morning's shipment of supplies. Looks like they got mangoes; Cooper makes a note to grab a few before they get snapped up. He gives Spiro a friendly wave.

Then he sees Fran and Isaac rushing out of the library, just down the block, in a hurry. Fran looks harried, tugging Isaac by the hand. She's got three books in her other arm. He waves her down.

"Morning, Fran."

"Hey, Cal," she says, distracted.

Cooper tousles Isaac's hair, then looks her over. "Everything okay last night?"

"Yes, in the end. Isaac was home. Scared out of his wits, but okay. Walt Robinson came over later to check in on us. I assume you sent him by. Thank you for that."

"What happened, Sheriff?" says Isaac. "I heard a gun shooting."

"Now how do you know what a gun sounds like?" says Cooper.

"From movies."

"Just an accident," says Cooper. "It's taken care of."

"Morning, Sheriff," comes a woman's voice from behind them. Cooper turns and sees it's Dawes. She's walking toward them, up bright and early, carrying a cardboard box under her arm.

"You headed to the station?" Cooper says. "I'll walk with you."

"No, I'm just getting ready to head off to Abilene."

"You really got Mallomars in that box?" says Cooper.

Dawes laughs. To Cooper's ear, she sounds nervous. "These are just some supplies I asked Spiro to order for me."

"I bet it's full of Mallomars, and you just don't want to share." Cooper winks at Isaac. "That wouldn't be very nice, now would it?"

"They're personal items."

"Come on, Dawes, are you going to make me confiscate it?"

"They're"—Dawes leans in—"*feminine* items."

"In a Mallomar box?"

Dawes shrugs. The sun to her right now feels hotter than it's felt in a long time.

"What's a feminine—" says Isaac.

"I understand, Deputy," says Cooper. He glances at Fran. "You found the book?"

"Yes, at the library."

"What's with the other two?"

"Just something that looked interesting—"

"All those books you have at home," Cooper says, "I'm surprised you still go searching."

"Good morning, Sheriff." Cooper turns at the voice and sees Bette Burr approaching, with an envelope in her hand.

"We've got a regular town meeting happening," he says.

"Just on my way to the commissary to check out the new supplies," says Burr. "That's today, right? The new shipment?"

"Sounds like you're finally figuring out how this place works," says Cooper. "Any luck with Mr. Wayne?"

"Not yet," says Burr.

"If you don't mind," says Dawes. "I've got to get—"

"Of course," Cooper says. "You'll be back tonight?"

"Yes, definitely."

"I want you here by the time I get back from my trip."

"Understood."

Cooper turns to Fran. "I may have some news for you later."

"You know where to find me," says Fran, who smiles, then tugs at Isaac's hand.

Cooper gives each of the women a quick nod and, the impromptu meeting implicitly adjourned, the four of them head off on their separate missions: Fran with her son, Bette with her photos, Cooper with his folded fax, and Dawes with her stash of purloined mail and her secret box of bullets.

16.

THE TORN BLACK GARBAGE BAGS taped by Orson over the smashed back windows of the car rattle frantically as Dawes speeds south on the highway. But the noise doesn't bother her; it sounds like freedom to her.

This is her first trip away from the Blinds in the six weeks since she started working there. Frankly, she's surprised that Cooper agreed to let her take the furlough. She understood the deal when she took the job; you live onsite for the length of your contract, and leave only in case of emergency and only at Cooper's discretion. He seemed to change his mind about her trip awfully quickly but then, as he likes to say, gift horse, mouth, and so on. She wonders as she drives how it's going to feel to be back among strangers. Abilene isn't exactly a raging metropolis, but, compared with the Blinds, it might as well be Times Square.

The Aveo jitters whenever the needle brushes sixty, but she presses the gas all the same. This drive reminds her of the last time she was in a hatchback, fleeing from somewhere—driving away as fast as she could from Atlanta with her every worldly possession crammed in the back of her car, squeezed in under glass. What she couldn't fit in the hatchback she left behind on the sidewalk because, fuck it, she wasn't staying a moment longer. Not with him. Not with the stink of booze on his breath and the sting of his fist on her jaw. Not when the other bruises hadn't even had a chance to heal yet. Not when her life became lies on top of lies, bruises on top of bruises, excuses on top of excuses, for him, for her, for how she looked, for how he acted, for how they lived. She'd always grown up hating liars, then she married one, then she became one. It's hard not to lie when you've got new bruises all over your face all the time. And there are only so many believable excuses for being banged up. She got good at concocting them, but they do run out eventually. So she ran out. Eventually. In hindsight, she just considers herself lucky to have found a job where they let you change your name.

She guns the Aveo to sixty-five.

Caesura's residents aren't the only ones in hiding.

Lindy.

I wait.

Lindy.

I watch.

Lindy.

I guard.

The job opening was a miracle, really, a way forward, and thankfully her résumé was strong enough to land an interview. And there wasn't much competition—it turns out not many people want to up and relocate to a place where you forswear all contact with the outside world. But she did—she was glad to. She signed on for two years, with an option for more. For her, this town was a place to catch her breath and plot a way forward. And let's see that fucking asshole find her in the middle of the Texas plains, working under a brand-new name, in a compound cut off by design from the outside world. She didn't expect to play Junior Sherlock once she got there, and certainly not so soon, but now that she's got the deerstalker cap on, as Cooper likes to call it, she finds she likes the way it fits.

I wait. I watch. I guard.

On this trip, her only cargo sits on the seat beside her, rattling lightly—the open Mallomar box full of mail and someone else's bullets. Sent to Lester Vogel, aka Gerald Dean, who just happened to be the prime suspect in her personal murder investigation. She'd already decided, once she took this box from Greta, not to tell Cooper about it, not yet. She wants to contact Ellis Gonzalez first and find out what he knows. Then maybe corner Lester Vogel back in town and confront him with these bullets. She wants to gather enough evidence that, when she *does* tell Cooper, he can't dismiss it, refute it, or, even worse, co-opt the whole theory and take credit for it and claim it as his own.

Because this truth belongs to her. She uncovered it. Now she owns it.

Gable drinks with Dean; Dean lives next to Colfax; Colfax winds up dead in his home and Gable dead at the bar. And Dean's getting bullets sent to him in the mail. And Ellis Gonzalez was working in the Blinds when Colfax died, then he left in a real big hurry. He's got to know something, she figures—and now she's discovered that someone's running mail to the residents, through a postbox in Abilene, which happens to be where Ellis Gonzalez likely now lives. She doesn't have an address for him, but she's got a pretty good hunch.

She's also considering whether she should stop somewhere in Abilene and purchase a firearm. There's certainly plenty of places that won't bother her about a wait period, though she doesn't have much in the way of cash. Not to mention that she's never held a gun before, though this seems to her like it might be a good time to start.

Just in case she runs into trouble.

Don't get ahead of yourself, Lindy, she decides. *There's no situation that a gun doesn't complicate. Besides, you've got the truth in a box beside you. And that should be enough, right?*

Just wait. Just watch. Just guard.

The truth rattles as she tickles seventy.

Cooper's visited Dr. Holliday's ranch before on a handful of occasions but, even so, the sight of her homestead never fails to amaze him. Driving for hours on endless ribbons of West Texas highway—the same sun-bleached land and wind-scrubbed grass looming flat around every bend—then suddenly, boom, there it is. Dr. Holliday's oasis, rising from the rough plains like a hallucination, like some new Garden of Eden, an explosion of flora and flowers. Her home is a low-slung, very modern, very boxy poured-concrete affair, lined along the outside with dark-tinted glass, which makes no effort or concession to blend in with the surrounding Texas landscape. And then there's the grounds: a sprawling garden that spreads out from the main house in a tangle of exotic foliage, palm trees and ferns and forsythia and Japanese maples and palmetto plants. As if a jungle fell straight from space and landed with a thump on this patch of arid plain. A large stone patio stretches out from the house, shaded by grapevines that dangle from an overhead trellis. This is where Dr. Holliday entertains her guests. This is as close to the main house as Cooper's ever going to get.

His pickup pulls into the roundabout driveway and Cooper quiets the engine. He's practiced his pitch a dozen times on the long drive out here. This is it, he thinks: Do this, then do the other thing, and then it's over. He taps the folded fax in his pocket, like he's about to embark on a dangerous journey, and the fax is a relic he expects to keep him safe.

Dr. Holliday is already out on the stone path in front of her door, waving, greeting him in a loose white blouse, light linen slacks that drape over leather biker boots, with some kind of expensive necklace, stones of high polish, hanging heavy on a loop across her chest. Her white hair is pulled back in an intricate braid. Cooper doesn't have a clue how old she is, but he guesses she's older than him, maybe in her sixties, though she could be even older than that; either way, she's definitely more well-preserved than he is. Cooper's lifelong inability to achieve her brand of effortless Zen-like self-presentation is one reason, he thinks, he's always gravitated professionally toward uniforms. Including, today, this rumpled, sweaty, and now slightly truck-stale brown shirt he's wearing. So much for first impressions, he thinks, then steps out of the truck and says hello.

She motions him toward the patio, where a sweaty pitcher of pale juice sits waiting on a long stone table. She offers him a seat on a roughhewn wooden bench across from her. The table itself is made of some cool stone and looks like the kind of slab you might perform an autopsy on.

"How have you been, Calvin?" she asks, then nods to the pitcher. "Can I offer you a glass of apple cider? It's cold-pressed. I have it shipped in especially."

"At this point, I'm happy for anything wet," says Cooper. He fills her glass from the pitcher, then pours a glass for himself. Their rapport has always been friendly, the few times they've met before; she's his boss, technically, but more than that, she's the den mother of Caesura. She runs it—she runs the whole Fell Institute now—and she helped create it, along with her ex-partner, the legendary Dr. Johann Fell. Cooper met her at his first job interview, just after Dr. Fell died.

"I see you're still wearing your star," Holliday says with a laugh. "I got you that as a gag gift, you know. To celebrate your first day on the job. I didn't think you'd wear it."

"Feels too funny to take it off now," Cooper says. "Thanks for answering my fax."

Holliday smiles. "People laugh when they see that old machine sitting in my office. But it's the best way to keep your communications discreet, especially in this day and age. No satellite is going to eavesdrop on a fax machine." She taps her fingers on her glass. "Speaking of discretion, I'd love an update on your recent incidents. I trust you have things under control in my town?"

"That's what I came to talk to you about."

"You met Agent Rigo, yes? He's our new liaison. He's a good man, Cal. I met him through our work with the Justice Department. He used to refer potential residents to us."

"Sure, he came by."

"Don't hesitate to lean on him. He could be useful," she says. "So what brings you out here today?"

Might as well just come out with it, Cooper thinks. "I need to see a few of the files. The blind files."

She laughs. "Now, Cal, you know I can't do that."

The blind files—that's where the town really gets its nickname, Cooper knows, though he's never shared that information with anyone. Every person living in the town is considered a blind file. Their cases are closed, their lives warehoused away, and their fates now in the able hands of Dr. Judy Holliday and the Fell Institute. She was the secondary researcher on the project that gave birth to Caesura a decade ago, along with her mentor, Dr. Fell. Cooper never met him—Fell was dead by the time Caesura opened and Cooper got his job. Killed in a random car accident, a hit-and-run, a real tragedy, given his stature in the world of science. By building on treatments pioneered to deal with traumatic memories, Fell had found a way to isolate specific memories in a subject's brain, using MRI imaging, and then erase those specific memories completely. A memory is no more than a cluster of chemicals, a tiny clump of proteins, is how Dr. Holliday once explained it to Cooper. In the beginning, Fell's technique was less like a scalpel and more like a scythe, cutting out huge swaths of people's memories. Over time, it became more surgical.

After Fell's death, Dr. Holliday proposed the idea of memory erasure to the Justice Department and the U.S. Marshals as an alternative to WITSEC, the traditional witness protection program. In WITSEC, you get a new identity and a new home, but you're still fundamentally *you*—with all your criminal history, proclivities, predilections, and expertise—and you're planted in an existing community full of unsuspecting innocent people. Over the years, this proved problematic for WITSEC—when, for example, ex-criminals got back into illegal trades, or used their new freedom and anonymity to go on murderous sprees. Caesura, Holliday argued, offers the ultimate alternative: Not even you know who you are or what you've done. *If you want to keep a secret, you must also hide it from yourself*—this was Caesura's founding credo. A new you, a new life, a new start. WITSEC was attracted to the Caesura program as a way to deal with its most repugnant witnesses: the killers, the serial rapists, the child predators, the ones who had knowledge and leverage, who could trade their testimony for amnesty, but for whom it was most difficult, politically, to justify making a deal and then loosing that person back into the world. The notion of a voluntary memory wipe, followed by consensual internment in a secure and isolated government-monitored community, under the Institute's watchful care, seemed both more palatable to the public and more humane to the witnesses—that's what everyone told themselves anyway, on the day they cut the ribbon on Caesura.

And in among these criminals, Holliday proposed, they'd seed a sprinkling of true innocents: witnesses whose lives were forever in peril for whatever they'd seen or known, or victims of crimes so terrible that the best recourse was to wipe their memories clean and let them start fresh. In this way, Dr. Holliday envisioned a humanitarian aspect to Caesura: as a refuge for the most severely traumatized witnesses. Don't force them to struggle through years of tedious therapy to learn to live with their trauma, she argued; instead, just erase it and let them start again. A new life under the Institute's benevolent watch, in exchange for their testimony. Given the alternative—a life on the run, haunted by pain, and dwelling in perpetual fear—this option seemed not only appealing but merciful.

Holliday further insisted that the residents of Caesura could never be allowed to know for certain which one they were: an innocent witness or a flipped criminal. This is crucial, she argued; otherwise, the town would collapse into a caste system of the innocent and the guilty. So all of them, criminals and innocents alike, were classified as "blind files"—basically, wiped from the system. Only the Justice Department knows who they were and only the Institute knows who they've become. That's how the Blinds got its name. When people outside of the town say "the Blinds," they're not talking about the town, they're talking about the people who reside there: blind to their own pasts, their own sins, their own selves. And the world is blind to them.

The first eight cases, the original eight, were experimental and brutal. Some people, like Orson Calhoun, wound up with thirty-year memory gaps, just a ragged hole where their life used to be. Then there's the man now known as William Wayne, whose case history leaked to the press, and who became so notorious that it nearly toppled the program before it even got started. Most of the original eight, like Fran Adams, remember almost nothing of their previous lives. A little bit of childhood, maybe, but that's it. Cooper always thought Fran got the worst deal of anyone: She arrived with a kid in her belly, and no idea of who the person was who'd fathered him. Yet she raised him all these years. She deserves a better life, and so does her son.

The criminals and the innocents—even Cooper doesn't know who's who. That's by design—it's what he agreed to, way back at the start, and he's never questioned it, until today.

But now he has to know. Which brings him here.

Because if Fran's an innocent, she can just go free. He could open the gate for her tonight and send her and her son on their way. And if she isn't, at least Cooper will know what exactly she needs to prepare for. Because he's already decided that she has no choice but to leave, and he's already decided that he's the only one who can make that happen.

"So whose histories are you interested in, exactly?" asks Dr. Holliday.

"Four people," says Cooper. "Errol Colfax, Hubert Gable, Gerald Dean, and Fran Adams."

"Why those four?"

"Colfax is the one who committed suicide a couple months back. Gable just turned up dead this week. Dean is our main suspect. And my deputy, Dawes, thinks there might be some connection between the three of them, from the outside, before they arrived. Gable and Dean came in as part of the same cohort, about six months after the program started."

"But that can't matter," says Holliday. "People don't know who they used to be. So it's hard to keep a grudge from your life before, let alone act on it."

"Maybe someone reminded them. Maybe from the outside. Either way, I'd like to know for sure."

"What about Fran Adams? How does she fit into this?"

"I just need to know if she's an innocent or not. Just tell me that."

"Why, Cal?"

"Because she needs to leave. She has the only remaining child born in the Blinds. He's eight already. She can't hide him from the world anymore—or the world from him. But if she's going to leave, she needs to know what's in store for her out there."

Dr. Holliday considers this, then motions toward his untouched glass.

"You haven't touched your juice," she says. "It really is excellent cider."

"With all due respect, I didn't come for the refreshments and the pleasant conversation. I came to help these people and come back with some answers."

She nods. "The funny thing about Johann Fell," she says, "is that he never wanted any of this. He perfected the technology, but he resisted this application of it. So as much as I owe to him—an immeasurable debt, really—his death was, in some ways, the event that made all this possible. But Caesura was my idea—my baby, really. Do you know why he opposed it?"

Cooper shakes his head and sips his juice.

"He thought it was inhumane," says Holliday. "Imagine that: inhumane to let people live again with no memories of their past. He worried that this hole in the mind, this abyss, would simply be filled with doubts and fears and questions about what exactly used to be there before. I disagreed, obviously. Do you know what that abyss looked like to me, Cal?"

"What's that?"

"Freedom," she says. "So the idea of seeding the Blinds with innocents—with letting people believe maybe they were simply witnesses to the unimaginable, shielded from their own traumas—that was my idea. My concession to Johann. After he died, I discarded it completely. There are no innocents in Caesura. But I allowed the fiction to persist."

"But why?" Cooper's throat is drier now, tighter, despite the drink. He feels the hot tendrils of the day's climbing sun snake through the shade of the vines overhead and find his neck and set him to sweating.

"To give them hope," she says. "It was the one flaw in Caesura, from the conception. If you leave the world and lose not only all contact but all knowledge of your previous life, what will keep you going every day? What gets you out of bed? The answer is simple: the same thing that keeps any of us going—hope. The hope that you're different. That you're special, somehow. That maybe, after all, you're innocent."

"But Fran is not an innocent. None of them are. They're all criminals."

"I'm afraid so," says Holliday. "That's the nature of the experiment."

"That's an awfully harsh experiment to carry out on actual people."

"Remember, Cal, these people didn't come to us with a whole lot of other options. For them, this program is an opportunity. Really, it's a kind of gift. But what kind of gift, exactly? Answering that question—that's what keeps me going every day." Holliday takes another sip, her eyes on Cooper, watching him like a vivisectionist, her dissection now complete, she's laid him out on that cold slab of a table and learned all she needs to know.

"Either way, she needs to leave," says Cooper, his mouth parched, the words whittled to a dry whisper.

"She's free to leave at any time," says Holliday. "She just has to weigh the consequences." She tents her long fingers in front of her face. She has an intelligent face. A kind face. A face that expertly camouflages the kind of mind that is well accustomed to twisting people into useful knots. "Go back to your town, Sheriff. Keep the peace. Don't concern yourself with matters beyond your position."

"I want her file," says Cooper, cornered, stubborn, with no cards left to play but not yet willing to rise from the table.

"Trust me," she says. "I'm tempted to show you. I'm a scientist. I like variables. But are you sure you want to know who she really is?"

"I want her file. Don't forget, Doctor, that I've been there, in your town, in the middle of your experiment, every day for eight years. So I know a few things, too. Things people might want to know."

Holliday folds her hands on the cold table. "Should I take that as a threat?"

"Take it as a variable. For your experiment."

"I said I like variables, Cal, not tantrums."

"Someday you can explain the difference to me." He stands. "I want her file. I want you to fax it to me by the end of the day. If you're worried about whether it will compromise my ability to do my job, then you can consider this my resignation. You either send me those files and I'll quit and keep quiet, or you don't send me those files, and I'll quit and start writing my memoirs."

She regards him like he's a well-trained animal that's disobeyed an order, and now she's wondering if the fault lies in the animal, the training, or both. "Don't forget—we're on the same side, Cal," she says finally. "I'll consider your request and let you know what I decide. But I won't endanger the fabric of this entire undertaking for one resident. I can't do that."

"It's two residents. And one's a child. Who never asked to be here, and who's innocent. Truly innocent."

"As I said, I'll consider it."

And it might just be Cooper's imagination, or some trick of the shadows from the strangulated sunlight streaming through the vines overhead, but as she rises from her bench, she seems not angry but almost impressed with him, even proud, in the manner of a researcher watching a favorite rat, after years of struggling, years of failing, finally nose its way out of a maze.

Then again, Cooper thinks, as he starts his truck and pulls out of the driveway, if he's come to understand anything in the last eight years of his life, it's that the only reward for the triumphant rat is a bigger, trickier maze.

17.

DAWES PULLS INTO A PARKING LOT by a row of town houses in Abilene, then checks the address again.

She already stopped at the shipping store that houses the P.O. Box, a rented box that was a month in arrears, so she easily convinced the teenaged manager to hand over Gonzalez's information. Her hunch—that the postbox was rented out by one Ellis Gonzalez—turned out to be correct, which means Gonzalez was running the mail into Caesura. Now Dawes sits in the dented Aveo in the parking lot, looking at a slumping row of gray town houses. A few laundry lines crisscross the cramped lawns, which are separated by peeling wooden partitions.

She gets out of the car and rings the bell of Gonzalez's apartment. She's not sure what she'll ask him if he answers. Why he's sending bullets to residents of the Blinds, for starters. But there's no one home. *Okay, now what, Lindy?* She's got only a few hours before she has to make the long drive back to the Blinds. She spots a kid on a low-slung BMX bike, turning circles in the parking lot. The kid's maybe ten, eleven, dirty-faced and sullen, wearing a San Antonio Spurs ballcap with a brim so flat you could set a teacup on it.

She waves him over. "Hey, do you know the gentleman who lives here? Do you know when he might be home?"

The kid smirks. "I dunno—never?"

"What is that supposed to mean?"

"Lady, that dude's dead. He got shot in some gas station robbery like a week ago."

"He robbed a gas station?"

"No, he was a customer, wrong place, wrong time." The kid makes *crack-crack-crack* gun sounds while pistoling the air with his fingers. "What the fuck do you care?"

She thinks of the brown uniform she's wearing, with its unusual badge, and figures she'll give it a shot. "I'm a police officer."

"No, you're not," the kid in the cap says.

"Thanks for your help," she says, and turns back to the locked door. *Well, this is a fucking disaster,* she thinks. It was nearly a three-hour drive just to get to this stupid town. *Dumb,* she thinks, *to come all this way without a backup plan, or even a clue of what you'd find—so much for your vaunted deerstalker. You drive all this way in the heat and the emptiness, back to the fringes of the big, bad world, just to come up empty—*

Wait. The big, bad world. And all that it has to offer.

She turns and asks the kid, "Where's the nearest library?" and hopes to hell this Podunk town even has one, and that this little brat ever visited it.

It does, and he has, and it's not too far, it turns out, and, thankfully, it's still open when she arrives. It's not much of a library, but that's okay—all Dawes needs is one computer terminal. That, and the exact thing everyone in the outside world takes for granted every single day, but which she can't ever access in the Blinds.

The big, beautiful, information-rich Internet.

She sits down at an open carrel. It's a small local library branch, underpopulated, save for a few homeless guys napping and a couple of kids playing violent games on computers. The sound of electronic gunfire rattles in the background as she settles in and clicks open the Internet. She thinks how routine this all used to be—the process of connecting to every other computer in the world and thereby gaining instant access to virtually every piece of information you could ever want. What was it that Cooper said? My kingdom for a Google?

Well, look who's got a Google now, she thinks, and types in "Ellis Gonzalez."

A torrent of Facebook pages pop up, websites, blog posts, all the crisscrossing digital vapor trails of the identically named. She limits the search to "Abilene" and Recent News. There are a few local stories about the gas station robbery, in which he's listed as an unfortunate bystander. Beyond that, nothing. No mention of his previous employment, or his reentry into the community. Only the end of his life has been documented, and even that in passing, a footnote to a footnote, buried in the depths of the fathomless Internet.

So Ellis Gonzalez is dead. She knew that already.

She's about to close the browser when another thought occurs to her. She types in "Caesura." Gets a bunch of results related to poetry. So she adds "Caesura" and "criminals."

There's not much to find, but there's something. Conspiracy websites, mostly. Chatter of secret government camps and black helicopters, mind experiments and covert crackdowns. A few fan sites devoted to serial killers, speculating on their current whereabouts. There's a Wikipedia page for the program, but when she opens it, the entry is short, and mostly full of dead-end speculation. And she finds a few sites dedicated to someone named Esau Unruh—some super killer, by the looks of it, with long paeans written to his supposed exploits. But among the pages there are so many divergent and contradictory accounts that it's impossible to tell what, if any of it, is true.

She clicks back to the search engine. Slightly drunk with the heady power of unlimited information. She tries to think what else she can search for.

Types in "Damnatio Memorae."

It turns out to be an ancient Roman practice, which literally means "the Condemnation of Memory." When a Roman disgraced himself—a traitor, a tyrant, a failed conspirator—he would be cleansed from the official histories. His name chiseled out of monuments. His statues toppled and destroyed. His likeness scrubbed from coins. Erased from the historical record. As though he never existed. A permanent exile from history itself.

Whoever wrote that in the repair shop certainly knows their history, she thinks. Not a bad official motto for their town.

Damnatio Memorae.

What else? The search box waits, patiently.

Remembering the box of bullets sitting in her car, she types in "Lester Vogel."

A new series of articles comes up. About a trial. And a conviction. She leans in to read the results.

Holy shit.

As she scans a few articles, her pulse begins to thump. After a few more, her stomach lurches.

Lester Vogel's history is . . . unpleasant.

In this moment, she realizes exactly why they never let you know about the history of the people in the Blinds. She certainly knows she'll never look at Gerald Dean in the same way again. She also realizes that if she ever gets caught doing this—searching for background information on the residents—she'll get fired. Or worse.

Maybe end up like Ellis Gonzalez.

But she keeps reading. About Vogel's history, before the Blinds.

When she's had enough, she closes the browser. Stands unsteadily. Takes a moment to collect herself.

She's about to leave when another thought occurs to her. This is her most ill-advised notion yet. And, naturally, the most irresistible.

Fuck it. She's come this far.

She sits back down.

She hesitates, nearly talks herself out of it, then opens the search engine again. She's about to type in "Calvin Cooper," when she remembers that's not his real name, any more than her real name is Sidney Dawes.

But she knows his real name.

She types in "John Barker."

Hits Search.

Again, she gets a torrent of histories, the spilled ephemera of a thousand different John Barkers across the world.

So she types in "John Barker" and "Caesura."

Nothing.

So she types in "John Barker" and "Fell Institute."

A page of results unfurls.

Even before she starts to scroll through them, she knows she's stepping through a door, one that can't be unstepped through, and one that's about to close behind her for good.

18.

BETTE BURR SITS on the porch of William Wayne's house, her back resting on the railing, knuckles sore from pointless knocking. The manila envelope is balanced on her knees. It's getting dark. The day's nearly done. If knocking alone was going to work, it would have worked by now, she thinks. And she wants out of this place, badly, this town where no one knows who they are, what they've done, where they've been. This town where she has to pretend to be like them and live like an imposter. Unlike the rest of them, she knows who she is. She's Eleanor Sung. Her father's daughter. And she made her father a promise.

She slides the large portrait of her father from the envelope and considers his face for a moment longer. She had spent so much of her life wondering who this man might be. Then, once she finally found him, he made her erase the memory of meeting him.

She doesn't remember meeting him at all.

So if she wants to rediscover him, she must deliver his message. The message that he's dead.

She says goodbye to the image of her father and slips the photo halfway under the door.

Fran sits on the sofa with the three books beside her. Isaac is finally asleep. She picks up the parenting book, *Raising Icarus,* and gives the cover a glance. Still weird, she thinks, that Calvin Cooper, of all people, is recommending parenting books. The mother and son who are pictured on the cover, smiling and confident, definitely do look happy. There's even something of Cooper's cockeyed smile on the boy's beaming face—maybe that's why Cooper likes this book; he sees something of his former self in this little kid. Or maybe Cooper pushed this book on her to show her an alternate life for her and Isaac. *You could be like these two, Fran, smiling and confident.*

We'll never be like them or anyone, she thinks. *Not anyone normal.*

She puts that book aside.

The cover of the second book with the lengthy title, *As Consciousness Is Harnessed to Flesh,* features a photo of a severe-looking woman, a lone streak of gray in her black hair, smiling slightly, as though her mind's elsewhere, on bigger, more substantial things. Fran wonders what connection she may have once had with this woman, this book, if any. The photo does look familiar, though she can't say why, or from where.

She turns the book over. Finds the ISBN on the back, above the barcode. Holds her own arm up to check, though she already knows.

1-250-02412-1

She feels a little thrilled and a little sick to find they match.

Save for the last four numbers. The extra numbers on her arm.

4911

Can't be a year. Not a page number, either—this book isn't that long. Maybe a chapter?

She flips through the book.

It's a collection of journals, fragments, stray thoughts.

Fran turns to page 49.

She counts down to line 11.

She's almost relieved to find it's just some random reference to a movie, something called *Marked Woman*. It's strangely appropriate, actually, and she could certainly try to find meaning in this if she really wanted to. But, out of context, the fragment means nothing to her and she can't believe this is the message someone left for her to discover. Or that she left for herself.

She flips through the book again.

4911, she thinks.

She riffles through pages all the way to the back.

Finds page 491.

She realizes now that this page does look familiar—or, at least, a different, past version of this page, from a different, past copy of this book. A copy that's underlined. Dogeared. Highlighted. Circled. The book bent, folded, creased, read and re-read, she can remember it now, she can picture it, as though it's the page right in front of her.

She counts down one line from the top.

Just one.

Finds a lone sentence and reads it.

God may forgive, but He rarely exonerates.

She reads the line again. For the first time. For the millionth time. She feels its warm familiarity. The letters practically vibrate.

This is the message from her past self, she knows it, cast like a letter in a bottle, to be opened on some other shore by her future, stranded self.

God may forgive, but He rarely exonerates.

Forgive who? And exonerate who? And for what?

She looks up, and only then does she notice the title of the second book, the sequel, which she also took out from the library.

Another volume of diaries written by the same woman, with a simpler title.

Reborn

The sky is just starting to consider darkness as Cooper steers his pickup home. He can see the bright dusk on the distant horizon, negotiating the handover from the day. As his truck hums over the two-lane highway, he hasn't seen another car in at least an hour, and he doesn't expect to see another one tonight.

This is one benefit to the Blinds, Cooper's learned—it offers you a cleansing kind of loneliness. It's the blessing of exile and it's something he never expected. Life out here on the great flat plains with barely a human whisper to be heard from the outside world. Just you, and the sky in all directions, and the barest scrap of land to hold it all up, to keep you from tumbling into the emptiness of space.

The highway lines zip by hypnotically as he drives. The tires of his truck serenade the road. No street lamps, no houses, no nothing. Just road.

Cooper thinks about Fran, and Isaac, and the great, big world spreading out in all directions, and the dangers, known and unknown, that it harbors.

About how having a kid makes you think constantly about all

the ways the world might hurt him. And how tempting it is to hide from all that. At least until the hurtful world finds you.

And it always finds you.

Cooper taps his star.

His finger feels the folded fax that's tucked in his breast pocket.

And he thinks about the one last thing he has to do tonight.

19.

GERALD DEAN KNOCKS at the door of the police trailer, which is already ajar.

"You wanted to see me, Sheriff?"

It's late and the town is sleeping. Cooper welcomes him in. The night is cooler, finally, so the lack of air-conditioning in the trailer isn't nearly so vexing. Robinson's already home in bed and Dawes isn't back from her daytrip yet. The two of them, Cooper and Dean, are alone in the trailer.

Cooper pulls Robinson's chair around to face his desk and offers Dean the seat, then sits down in his swivel chair.

Dean's always been a skittish sort, keeping mostly to himself. He and Cooper have never had any run-ins before. Dean's squirrelly manner suggests not so much someone who's guilty and worried about getting caught, but someone who's worried about being wrongly blamed for something he didn't do. As though that was a theme in his life prior to his arrival here, and it somehow seeped into his manner. A learned habit he never could shake.

And one not entirely appropriate to the situation, Cooper thinks.

Cooper's revolver is sitting on his desktop. He picks it up, flips the barrel open, checks it.

Four bullets.

"Eight years, Gerald, and I never had to carry a loaded weapon," he says. "Times are changing, and not for the better."

He flips the barrel shut and puts the gun back on his desk. Dean shifts in his chair uneasily.

Cooper continues. "So I take it you know what's been happening in the town."

Dean nods. He's hefty and his posture resembles that of a toad on a rock. He has thinning hair and a wide speckled forehead and a face that's inscribed by transgressions that even he can't recall or recount. Cooper can see all that now. It's all so obvious, once you know to look for it.

"How long have you been here, Gerald?"

"Nearly eight years. A long stretch."

"That's right. You came in the first year, maybe six months after we opened, by my recollection."

Dean nods. Still waiting to learn why he's here.

Behind Cooper, the fax machine sparks to life and begins to whir.

"Deputy Dawes—you know Deputy Dawes, right?"—and here Dean nods again, trembling his chin wattle—"Deputy Dawes," Cooper says, "has a theory. About you."

"What theory?" Dean's voice a croak.

Watching him, Cooper thinks: There are hard people living in this town. People who look for excuses to detonate. Their minds may not remember who they are, but their muscles do. People like Dick Dietrich who are wired to do damage. But Dean is not one of those people. Dean is not a coiled trap, waiting to snap. Dean is more like a malfunctioning valve, a faulty weld, a crack in a storage tank leaking toxins into the world. Dean is a mistake, an aberration. He leaches a different kind of harm.

A long sheet of fax paper spits haltingly from the machine behind Cooper, coiling extravagantly as it ejects, but Cooper ignores it.

"Seven years ago, you submitted a request to be moved to another part of the town," Cooper says. "Closer to Errol Colfax."

"Sure. I wanted somewhere quieter."

"And how did that work out?"

"It's pretty nice," says Dean, suspicious, still wondering when Cooper will circle around to the point. "I mean, aside from that nastiness with Colfax."

"True. And you drank frequently with Hubert Gable. May he rest in peace."

"I don't know if I'd say frequently. We liked each other's company. I was sorry, what happened to him."

"Still, you can see how all these connections might raise an eyebrow. Given your curious proximity to these two dead men."

"I didn't even know Colfax—"

"I'm not accusing you of anything, Gerald. I just want to let you know what kind of talk there is out there."

Cooper pulls a ring of keys from his pocket, and thumbs through them until he finds a small desk key.

"You know how Gable died, yes?" he asks Dean.

"He got shot, right?"

"That's right. By a nine-millimeter pistol."

Cooper slides the key in the lock on his bottom right drawer and unlocks it. Pulls the drawer open. Retrieves a handgun. Holds it up to show Dean.

"This one right here, in fact." Cooper puts the gun down on the desk, next to his revolver. "Same gun that killed Errol Colfax, too. Never did make its way back to Amarillo as evidence. Wound up stranded here in my desk drawer."

Behind Cooper, the fax machine stops. There's a sudden jarring quiet in the absence of the whirring. A long ribbon of paper, its sheen catching the fluorescents overhead, hangs languidly from the machine.

Cooper stands and turns, at last, to the fax machine. He rips the paper from the machine. It looks almost comically like a Christmas list in his hands—like he's Santa, checking who's naughty or nice. He turns back to Dean and passes him the sheet of paper.

"I thought you might be interested in this," Cooper says.

Dean takes the paper but keeps his eyes locked on Cooper, searching for some clue of what's in store. Finding nothing, Dean smoothes the paper on the desktop and starts to read.

Cooper stands over him. Watching as Dean's face drains to an even paler, near-impossible whiteness.

On the paper. Dean's photo. A mug shot.

The rest of the paper a rap sheet.

For someone named Lester Vogel.

Some vile twin.

Sixty-eight counts of conspiracy to create child pornography. Sixty-eight counts of possession of indecent material. Twenty-two counts forcible confinement of a minor. Eighteen counts kidnapping. Twenty-one counts statutory rape. Twenty-seven counts conspiracy to pervert a minor. Eighteen counts—well, the list goes on. A litany of unimaginable perversion. The chronicle of a broken valve, a mistake, an aberration, leaking toxins, poisoning the world.

The figures and phrases on the page sound loudly in Dean's head as he reads them, like thudding explosions from very far away. Dean hears a rushing, a roaring, all around him, in the trailer. His mind is now a vacuum that threatens to collapse in on itself, to swallow itself whole. He doesn't understand.

Yet the picture is of him.

The deeds described are his.

He looks up at Cooper, with nothing to say.

"That's you," says Cooper. He points to the rap sheet. "You're Lester Vogel. You did those things. All of them."

Dean sits, shaking, confused, his hands quaking, the fax paper rattling in his grip.

"I'm not supposed to see this," Dean says finally, quietly. "I'm not supposed to know this."

Cooper picks up the 9 mm from the desk.

"They're children, Lester."

At the sight of the pistol, Dean flinches. Then Cooper grips the pistol by the barrel and holds it out to Dean.

"Take it, Lester," Cooper says, calling him by his real name.

Vogel puts down the paper and takes the gun, as he's told to do. He regards the pistol quizzically. Then he seems to figure something out. Something dire. When he speaks, his voice quavers. "What do you want me to do with this? Am I supposed to shoot myself now? Is that what happened to Colfax? To Gable?"

"No," says Cooper. "You're supposed to shoot me."

Vogel looks around, wondering what fresh trap this is, and what new horror will visit him next. He holds the pistol limply in his hand.

"Don't worry," says Cooper. "It's not loaded. Though I believe some bullets arrived for you in the mail today. They were scheduled to, anyway. That's what the fax machine told me."

Vogel squirms and considers running, his chest rippled through with dread. But his body's not built for flight, he knows that, and in the panic of a dead man he's gripped with a last lunatic notion of survival and he points the gun at Cooper and pulls the trigger and hears it click.

"I told you it's not loaded," says Cooper. "I am many things—many bad, bad things—but I am not a liar."

Vogel keeps the pistol raised, his arm still stiff and shaking. As though he believes that as long as he keeps it aloft he can hold his fate at bay. His eyes swim. He looks to Cooper. He looks at the sheet of paper in front of him. Then back to Cooper.

Then he says, simply, "Why?"

"I might ask you the same thing," says Cooper. "Given the choices you've made."

"That's not me," Vogel whispers.

"That's your history, Lester," says Cooper. "Your record. Your deeds. Your life. You thought they wouldn't find you here. But they did."

Vogel barely gets the words out. "I wish I didn't know this." Then he drops the hand with the gun to his lap.

"I'm sorry," says Cooper, not without sympathy. "I can honestly say, I wish I didn't know it, either."

Then Cooper picks up his revolver and shoots Lester Vogel once through the chest.

As Vogel slumps in the chair, Cooper gathers the long fax paper and feeds it into the shredder. As the hungry blades gobble and swallow the detestable record of Lester Vogel, now deceased, Cooper prepares himself to greet the panicked citizens of the Blinds, who are even now bound to come running, frantic, full of questions, their peaceful evening shattered for the third time in a week by the rude intrusion of a gunshot.

THURSDAY

20.

YOU CAN'T KILL A MAN without consequence.

Calvin Cooper understands that now.

Even if that man's continued existence on this earth runs contrary to any notions you may hold about fundamental or celestial justice. Even if that man has laid a trail of grievous harm and pain and death, inflicting misery on innocent others in some previous, despicable, and since-forgotten life. Even if that man's manifold sins are enumerated plainly to you in a straightforward and pitiless accounting, and even if the terms of his subsequent protection and clemency under your watch were granted by powers you no longer have faith in and to which you no longer feel any loyalty.

Even then.

Even if that man is Gerald Dean, aka Lester Vogel.

Even then.

Or Errol Colfax. Or Hubert Gable.

Even then.

Take Colfax, for example. Because he was the first.

Real name: Kostya "Costco" Slivko. A debt collector for the Russian mob in New York. On the face of it, a standard thug, perhaps more enthusiastic than most. He'd earned the nickname "Costco" because he liked to kill in bulk. But this was not the quality that made him most valuable to his employers. Killers are a common enough sort, even enthusiasts. There are many sociopaths for whom a lack of access to the normal range of human empathies proves a formidable vocational asset. Slivko was one of those people. He possessed the kind of ill-formed mind, likely twisted in the womb, that came into this world with no interest in anything other than blood and no aptitude for anything but spilling it.

But that's not what made him valuable, or feared, or infamous, among the kinds of people who employed him. What made him all those things was his particular psychological innovation to the enforcement trade.

Something Slivko liked to call *krovnyi sled.*

Translation: blood trail.

It worked like this: If you owed a debt to his bosses, he would not kill or even hurt you, or threaten you, or even contact you directly. Instead, he would find your furthest relative by blood. The further, the better. A distant aunt. Some second cousin's niece. A person in some other state or distant country who did not even know you personally and with whom you had little or no contact. Certainly not someone you would feel a fierce loyalty to, or even a passing attachment.

Then he would kill that person. This distant relative. This blood relation.

Then he would work his way back toward you.

A gardener, pruning the family tree.

With the first person, he wouldn't notify you. He'd just let word of their ill fortune wind its way back to you through the family grapevine. *By the way, did you hear about poor cousin so-and-so. Very gruesome. Such a tragedy.* Or perhaps you'd catch a stray news report. A face you vaguely recognize, come to a terrible end.

It might dawn on you at that point but the connection's so unlikely. You might think nothing of it.

And then he would continue.

A cousin. A nephew. A grandparent.

Inching closer.

Until you start to put it all together. That your debt had set this in motion.

A brother. A sister. Then your child. Then your wife.

Until the debt was paid.

And all the while, you would come to know: You loosed this plague on your house. People were dying violent deaths and their only crime was sharing your blood.

This was a far more effective and ultimately devastating technique, Slivko had found, than some of the more traditional persuasions, such as, say, cutting off someone's appendages: a toe, a finger, an ear. People don't want to lose those, but they can carry on. Slivko's technique, by contrast, was designed (he explained later to the federal agents who finally apprehended him, one of whom, an eighteen-year veteran of law enforcement, excused himself from the room to be sick) to inflict a particular kind of psychological torture. You would, at first, upon hearing your second cousin's daughter had been tragically and inexplicably murdered, recoil with horror and yet—and *yet*—a wound like that, you could survive. Especially if you were the sort to incur debts you had no hope of ever repaying. Flowers and weeping and funerals aside, a second cousin's daughter's death is by nature a distant shock, a muted cry, an easily recoverable harm. It might not be enough to motivate you to action. Until you understood. That it was just the start.

That realization would definitely motivate you, Slivko had found.

Then, of course, you had to scramble to assemble the repayment, which would obviously be difficult, and by that time, Costco Slivko was working his way back through your more dearly held relations. Like some viral congenital epidemic, affecting only people whom you love. You would come to dread the very passage of time. Your debt of course would quickly become unpayable. Never mind the money. You'd find the money. But your entire family's ruin was now on your hands.

A very effective form of terror.

Krovnyi sled.

Blood trail.

Slivko worried his technique might lose its capacity to terrorize once it became widely whispered of, his modus operandi quickly recognized. But he found, to his pleasant surprise, that there was no dilution of terror; in fact, when debtors recognized his work early on, from the very first victim, it made the whole ensuing process even more palpably devastating. Still, he came to miss the early days, when his technique was in its nascence, not yet infamous, and he could savor the slow accretion of tragedy as the debtor continued, clueless. Only eventually, over months, understanding the connection. Like Job in the Bible. Slowly figuring it out: Wait, this isn't all just really shitty luck. Slowly figuring it out: My God has abandoned me.

By the time the FBI apprehended Kostya "Costco" Slivko, the most conservative guess put his personal body count at somewhere in the range of sixty killings. He was always coy to particulars. But to the FBI, catching Costco Slivko was like finding the cure to a lethal disease.

And the moment he was arrested, word came down from the pinnacles of the shadowed criminal hierarchies that employed him: a hefty bounty for a quick result. He'd served his masters admirably but now, like a rabid dog, he must be put down before he barks and wakes the neighbors. The first attempt on Slivko's life came on the very first night the feds had him in custody, during a transport, an amateurish approach, clumsy and easily foiled by Slivko, but he knew that this would now be his life. An endless procession of petty attackers with their makeshift shivs and awkward ambushes. It all seemed so very tiring to him.

So it took little convincing, on the part of the federal agents, to sell Slivko on the notion of providing enough evidence to put three of his bosses—top men, long hunted, masterminds for whom twisted soldiers like Slivko were little more than disposable tools—in prison forever. Big catches, all three of them. And, sure enough, those three men are now interred in three different supermax facilities, serving thirty-six consecutive life sentences between them, with no possibility of parole. Moreover, the agent who solicited Slivko's testimony is now associate deputy director of the agency.

As for Slivko, his part of the deal was that he got all memory of his transgressions wiped and he got shipped out to live in a place called Caesura. In peaceful oblivion, as the newly christened Errol Colfax. A quiet type who kept to himself and showed little taste for socializing. Those sixty or so lost souls who died at his hands now as forgotten to him as he was to the rest of the world.

So, no, Cooper did not feel remorse for killing Errol Colfax.

Of course, the $50,000 didn't hurt.

But the killing was not without consequence. Spiritual and otherwise. Cooper understands that now.

Cooper learned of Slivko's backstory by anonymous fax. The first of which arrived over two months ago.

Cooper was alone in the police trailer, working late, fussing with paperwork, when the fax machine started chugging. That infernal whir. A single sheet, unfurling.

On that sheet: A proposal. Addressed to Cooper.

A proposal. A task. And a price.

To this day, Cooper still doesn't know who sent it.

The incoming number was blocked, untraceable.

He assumed at first it was a joke, of course. Some clown in Amarillo, probably Brightwell, who got hold of the fax number, having a laugh. Cooper fed the fax into the shredder and thought nothing of it.

Until, a few nights later, the second fax arrived.

This time, it came attached to Slivko's arrest record. His mug shot. The charges against him, which were never officially filed. A summary of his "alleged" crimes.

This required a much longer piece of fax paper, curling endlessly from the machine.

At the end, another proposal. And an account number. For an offshore bank.

Twenty-five thousand dollars had already been deposited, the fax explained. Cooper could call and confirm.

The other $25,000 on completion.

It took three more days before Cooper finally called the bank, from a phone booth at a gas station a few miles outside of Abilene. Hot as Hades and Cooper crammed into that phone booth, sweating, like Houdini in an upright glass coffin. The booth as small and airless as a confessional. Flies smacking like buckshot at the glass.

On hold. Waiting for confirmation.

Receiving it.

Twenty-five thousand dollars. Fully accessible.

He pondered that figure over whiskey later that night in his bungalow with the ceiling fan turning slowly overhead. This was two months ago. Cooper had just recently celebrated his eighth year as Caesura's unofficial sheriff.

There are plenty of people in the world, Cooper figured that night, twirling the amber whiskey in his shot glass absently, who would pay good money to find someone like Colfax and make an example of him. Though he didn't know exactly who was making him this offer, the "who" was not what concerned him. The "who" were bad people, with resources, that much was obvious. The kind of people in whose employ, or debt, you would not want to be. The "why" was not difficult to discern, either: Cooper knew there were many people beyond this town's fences, from criminals betrayed by testimony to law enforcement officers offended by Caesura's particular form of clemency, who might wish certain of the town's inhabitants dead. Slivko once made a habit of hurting people by killing their distant relatives; maybe a distant relative of one of his victims had decided to enact an ironic revenge. In any case, the motive of the proposal, while never made explicit in the faxes, was not difficult to guess or imagine. The "why" is revenge. Retribution. Some distant relative of justice. The "why" was written out in plain English on the long, curling fax that enumerated all of Colfax's former sins.

Twirling the whiskey.

Twenty-five thousand dollars, already waiting.

Sixty restless ghosts, waiting as well.

Cooper was a good man, or so he liked to believe. There was not much in his previous life to fortify that opinion and, forced to defend it, he'd have scant evidence to present, but he clung to the notion nonetheless. Not a great man—that much he understood; he'd long since given up hope for that and had made his heavy peace with it—but a good man, or good enough. He'd done selfish things, certainly, hurtful things, awful things, made terrible choices, abandoned people who'd offered him love, lied straight to the faces of people who'd offered him trust. There were things buried in his history that he'd do anything to go back and change, but who doesn't have a few of those? The kind of cold decisions and thoughtless betrayals that had sent his life careening in regrettable directions, before he finally crashed and found himself marooned here, in this town, at this table, with this choice.

But he'd never done anything like this, he thought. Not kill a man.

Not even a man like Colfax.

You can't stay good after that. If good was a thing you'd ever been.

Whatever his decision, Cooper wondered how he could possibly continue to live with Colfax in the town, now that he knew the full accounting of who Colfax was and what he'd done and what he was capable of. Cooper wondered how exactly he could let Colfax remain, living side by side with the other residents, as just another happy neighbor. Colfax, it's true, was a homebody now. Almost meek. Rarely smiled. Kept to his darkened bungalow. *Maybe he's haunted,* Cooper thought, *and he just doesn't know by what.* That twisted brain, now unburdened of all its worst memories. All its guilt. All its remorse. If ever there was any.

Yet still haunted by those sixty restless ghosts.

Cousins. Nieces. By definition, innocents.

Cooper swirled the whiskey.

As for the outside world, as far as they were concerned, Kostya Slivko no longer existed. He'd given his testimony. He'd flipped his bosses. Those cases are closed, those files sealed, those sentences passed, those promotions granted. And as for the man himself, he just disappeared. His exploits are now legends. Whispered of. He lives nowhere now.

Except that he lives here, thought Cooper. *A couple of blocks away.*

And all those crimes—

All those names—

All those ghosts—

They're forgotten.

Most criminally, by Slivko himself.

Cooper downed the whiskey.

He remembers it well, the turning point, at his kitchen table in the light of the single fixture under the stir of the fan blades: The moment that the realization hit him.

It's not often in this life that someone offers you $50,000 to do something you already believe to be right.

And if the price in return was his goodness, that seemed a fair sacrifice. There are other good people in the world, or so he'd heard. He even knew a few, right here in this town, and now he knew how he might help them.

At which point the decision seemed simple. Because it's not like the money was for him.

After that, he just needed a plan.

That first one was easy, thinks Cooper in hindsight, so easy that he was stupid and sloppy. But he also knew that ultimately there'd be no one to investigate the death except for him. A faked suicide seemed the obvious route. Colfax barely looked up when he entered. Cooper faked the break-in of the gun safe, and the story afterward told itself: Old Errol Colfax, the haunted man, finally got his hands on a pistol and ended it. This surprised exactly no one. Truth be told, there weren't many people living in the Blinds who hadn't at least contemplated a similar escape. It's hard enough to live with what you've done. It's immeasurably harder to live with knowing you've done something, but not knowing what exactly it is you did.

But that's the nature of the experiment.

Either way, Colfax ended it, took the coward's way out, that seemed obvious. And afterward, Cooper simply needed to let the fundamental first rule of the Blinds—the essential truth of its existence—prove itself again to be true. Which is: No one gives a shit. Not outside these fences. Was anyone in Amarillo going to sit up straighter at the news that a piece of human garbage, warehoused in some godforsaken facility, had found a way to put a bullet in his head? Cooper recalled dimly the time when the serial killer and cannibal Jeffrey Dahmer had been murdered in prison by a fellow prisoner, brutally, with an iron bar. The public was not outraged. The public practically cheered. They practically threw the guy who did it a parade.

So, no, Cooper did not expect the weight of the law to come calling. He went through the motions of an investigation, of course: the break-in, the pistol, and so on. A week later, Ellis Gonzalez up and quit and fled, and for a moment Cooper thought that maybe he could pin it on Ellis, but by then the other $25,000 was deposited and everyone had bought the suicide. Case closed.

Colfax was easy in hindsight.

Though it was not without consequence for Cooper.

For starters: another fax.

It didn't come for a couple of months—long enough for Cooper to start believing the Colfax deal was a one-off, engineered by some old nemesis. Long enough for Cooper to start calculating just how much freedom $50,000 could buy.

Some, but not much. Maybe not enough.

Then he got another fax.

This time: Hubert Gable.

And Gable—well, Gable's history, chronicled in all its lurid detail on that curling sheet of fax paper, made Colfax look like a choirboy who'd stolen a few coins from the rectory's money box. Gable's real name was Perry Garrett. A former professional bodyguard with an amateur taste for call girls and a penchant for sexual pain. Not his, of course.

Call girls, or whoever else was handy. And disposable.

His sordid hobbies were apparently later discovered by his employers and discreetly covered up. Until such time, Cooper assumed, that Garrett became expendable or, more likely, found a way to leverage the more mundane but politically enticing transgressions of his employers in exchange for a free pass, a new name, a fresh start, a memory wipe, and a one-way passport to Caesura.

For Cooper, this decision required decidedly less whiskey-swirling.

Fifty thousand dollars became one hundred thousand.

That much closer to his personal fund-raising goal.

A second suicide wasn't feasible, of course. Cooper knew that would raise too many questions, maybe invite a raft of psychiatrists to descend on Caesura, concerned about the apparently fragile mental health of the community.

So no suicide.

However, the fax offered not just a paycheck, but it suggested a narrative. Colfax's gun is used to kill Gable. Maybe during a drunken argument. After all, Gable was a friendless grouch who spent most of his time drunk and getting drunker. Anyone might find a reason to plug him out of anger.

Gerald Dean, aka Lester Vogel, for example.

The faulty valve.

The best way to frame him, the fax suggested, was a box of bullets sent to him in the mail, which could be arranged and which Cooper would then conveniently intercept. What Cooper hadn't counted on is Dawes, the new girl, being so persistent—but even that had an unexpected upside. Dawes beat him to the bullets, but that's all right, Cooper knows they exist. The stories will still line up. And Dawes, with her notebook and all her fanciful dot-connecting, wound up providing the beginnings of a theory. Something about Colfax and Gable and Dean all being linked, having some outside connection, and Dean stealing the gun, staging Colfax's suicide, then killing Gable and ending, neatly, with Dean pulling that same stolen gun on Cooper and then being killed in self-defense. The last loose end. A satisfying ending.

The fax offered him $100,000 for Dean. Whoever they were really wanted Dean dead, apparently.

Which would bring the grand total to $200,000. And that was more than enough for Cooper's purposes. The purchase of freedom. To start a new life.

Not for him. For someone who actually deserves it.

Two people, actually.

So whether Holliday gives him the information he's looking for on Fran Adams or not, Cooper knows it's almost finished. He's already got Fran halfway convinced to leave the Blinds, take Isaac with her, and find a better life. And while $200,000 can't buy back your memories or your past life, it can go a long way toward getting you safely set up in a new one. New identities. New papers. A new home, somewhere rural. A place to live that's safe and far and remote from all this madness. Maybe with a view. Maybe with a yard. Near good schools, and other people. Good people. That doesn't seem too much to ask, all in all. A life far away from this town and its fences and its befuddled denizens and their unspeakable, buried crimes. If Cooper wasn't convinced that Isaac needed to leave before—and he was, he definitely was convinced—then the arrival of an animal-burning psychopath like Dietrich has proved more than persuasive enough. Something is unraveling in this town; Cooper feels it. The very experiment itself is coming undone. And Fran and Isaac can't be here when it does.

And once they take his money and leave, then Cooper's done. No more faxes. No more proposals. No more killings. And if the Institute shuts down Caesura, so be it. He would be glad to know he had a hand in closing it down. He's watched over it for eight years, watched what it does to people, living with a giant hole in the middle of your mind and the knowledge that once you did unspeakable things and you don't even know what they are. It kills you a little bit, day by day, without killing you. That's why Colfax's suicide was so easy to sell. The other residents weren't suspicious. They were envious.

If the Institute shuts this place down, Cooper can live knowing he's made one right choice in his life. Set one thing right, as best he could.

After all, wouldn't you kill three murderers to save one child's life?

But it is not without consequence for Cooper, he knows that.

For example: Lester Vogel's eyes.

Looking up at Cooper from the other side of the desk. Holding that fax paper. Hands vibrating. Fax paper rattling. His eyes drained once and for all of any hope.

I wish I didn't know, he'd whispered, which turned out to be his final words. Clutching the revelations of his past. This accounting of who he really is.

I wish I didn't know.

Cooper understands that sentiment completely.

He feels that way himself nearly every day.

21.

ALONE IN THE POLICE STATION, in the stillness of dawn, Cooper sips his morning coffee. He, along with Robinson, already hefted Gerald Dean's body and lugged it over to Nurse Breckinridge's infirmary—she's making the arrangements right now to have the corpse picked up later today and taken to the nearest town to be cremated. By this time tomorrow, Dean will be ashes. And, if all goes well, Fran will be gone. In the meantime, Cooper's got paperwork to do. Wrap everything up, file an incident report to the Institute, give them a plausible explanation: How, confronted with Cooper's theories and the irrefutable evidence of the box of bullets in the mail, Dean confessed that he'd killed Colfax and Gable both, then pulled his 9 mm pistol on Cooper, and that's when Cooper was forced to shoot him dead.

Cooper puts the mug down and unfolds the fax from his breast pocket, the one he's been toting around for a day, the one with Gerald Dean's real name and mug shot, and he stands and feeds the fax into the shredder.

Almost over, he thinks.

Two hundred thousand dollars is plenty. More than enough.

He's so lost in this comforting thought that he nearly doesn't notice when the fax phone starts to ring.

He stares at the phone. It rings again.

No one ever calls this number, he thinks.

Then he answers it.

Just as he's lifting the receiver to his ear, Robinson and Dawes come through the door together to start their shift. Cooper raises a finger to hush them and says into the phone: "Cooper here."

"—"

"Of course, I remember you. I was just—"

"—"

"As a matter of fact, last night we had a break in the case—"

"—"

"Well, I'd sure hate for you to waste your time coming all the way out—"

"—"

"Okeydokey. Well, we're here. We're always here. So I guess we'll see you then."

Cooper hangs up the phone.

Robinson asks, "So who was that?"

"Agent Rigo, the liaison from the Institute who came by on Monday. He says he's coming out with an investigative team today."

"A team? How many people?" says Robinson.

"Six."

"Seriously?" says Robinson. "Well, shit, looks like we finally got *someone's* attention."

"Apparently, there's a lot of 'top-level' concern about the recent 'incidents' in the town," Cooper says. "His words, not mine."

"And it only took three dead bodies and some barbecued coyotes," says Robinson. "You tell him we got a fresh body on our hands this morning? Not to mention a full confession?"

"I tried, but he didn't seem too interested in chatting."

Dawes, for her part, just watches the proceedings unfold.

"As long as they're making the long trip out here," says Robinson, "can they talk to those top-level types about bringing some better-quality toilet paper out to us? Something softer than that surplus sandpaper they've been sending?"

Cooper gives a distracted smile, but keeps staring at the fax phone. Like it might jump to life again. Offer up another surprise.

Almost done. Almost over.

Well, be patient, Cooper thinks. *You've got a story. Stick to it.*

Then he says abruptly to Robinson and Dawes: "He said they'd be here in an hour, so we better get busy putting out the welcome mat."

22.

THIS TIME, Rigo arrives bright and early, in a black SUV that looks, in the distance, like a hearse. It barrels ahead on the private approach in a convoy with a second SUV, sleek and identical. As they rumble up, Cooper rolls open the gate and then motions them forward, and the trucks enter and curl to a halt. The agents disembark, three from one car, three from the other, all of them dressed in black suits, like pallbearers, waiting for the hearse to unload.

Rigo steps out from the backseat of the first truck and stretches in the sun, smiling and shaking off the long drive. Beside him, a woman strides out from the shadow of the first SUV: petite, all business, maybe five feet in heels, and dressed in a black pantsuit. Her white blouse crisp and open at the neck, her black hair pulled back harshly in a ponytail. The other four agents are uniformly beefy and inexpressive in a way that identifies them as supplementary muscle. They array in a loose spread pattern and survey the scene like soldiers in an occupying army.

Cooper raises a hand in greeting to the party.

"Sheriff Cooper," says Rigo. "Anything notable happen in my absence?" He steps forward and claps Cooper on the shoulder like they're old buddies, then gestures back toward the woman behind him. "This is my partner, Agent Iris Santayana." She nods. Doesn't move. Says nothing.

"Pleased to meet you," says Cooper, stepping forward. "I'm Calvin Cooper. I'm the sheriff of this town. Sort of." He starts to offer a handshake but aborts at the last minute, thus saving himself the humiliation of holding his hand out in the air while she ignores it. Instead he shoves the hand into his pants pocket, like something he's ashamed of.

Rigo doesn't bother to introduce the other agents individually—he just waves in their direction and calls them "the team." Rigo and Santayana are the ringleaders, clearly, and, standing together, one of them seems like a vigilant master and the other like an exotic, expensive pet, though it's impossible for Cooper to tell which one is which. He introduces them to Robinson and Dawes, who've been lingering on the periphery like shy children. "My deputies are at your disposal, as am I, of course," says Cooper.

"We'd just like to get settled in," says Rigo. "And then get started."

"And what exactly are you here to do?" says Cooper.

"We're here to find some fucking answers," says Rigo.

Cooper lets this rebuke linger in the air, then turns to address everyone. "All right then—let's get you set up in some of our finest lodging. Then I can give you the grand tour." He even claps his hands together feebly, feeling like a yokel innkeeper under the scrutinizing eye of city slickers who've just arrived and can't believe that this backwater shithole is where they're going to have to spend the night.

Cooper arranges for the agents to stay in a single empty bungalow. They've brought their own bedding, military cots, and Rigo insists they bunk together.

"We'll need an operations center, too," Rigo says.

"You can use our intake trailer," says Cooper. "It's just off the main drag."

As the three of them, Cooper, Rigo, and Santayana, thread their way straight down the main street, they leave the other agents behind to unload their party's luggage, which seems to consist of an endless supply of identical large black and very heavy suitcases. Leading the party, Cooper gestures toward the strip of buildings ahead of them. "So, this is the town, pretty much," he says. "We've got a commissary, stocks our sundries and whatnot. We've got a library for books and such. There's a small medical center for emergencies, and there's a gym, though it's not much to look at. Basically a bunch of free weights, if you need to blow off steam." As they pass the commissary, townsfolk are already loitering and gawking at the side of the street, regarding this advancing trio in agitated silence. Cooper waves and offers a reassuring "Morning, folks!"—then says to Rigo in a lower voice, "We don't get many visitors, as you know."

Rigo nods up the street. "Your medical center—how many people is it equipped to handle?"

"We've got just the one nurse, Ava Breckinridge," says Cooper. "The infirmary is really just a Band-Aid-and-aspirin shop. We've been asking for a medical doctor for just about eight years but, given the terms of employment—no contact with the world and such—the search has pretty much dried up. But Ava takes good care of us, and if anything really serious comes up, we contact the Institute and they arrange to pick up the person and transport them to a private hospital, under close watch. Whole thing is very hush-hush. Thankfully, we've rarely had to worry about anything more serious than the occasional busted nose or a bad bout of pneumonia. Until this past week, of course."

Rigo and Santayana look over the main street, saying nothing further, like two unimpressed buyers who've realized they're house-hunting in the wrong part of town.

"There are a couple of other facilities scattered here and there," Cooper continues. "A repair yard, run by one of our locals, Orson Calhoun. A small playground just past that with a slide and a swing—"

"That's right—you have kids here," says Rigo.

"We have one," says Cooper. He points up the cross street. "The rest of the bungalows up yonder on the cul-de-sacs are all private residences. We have seventy-two bungalows in total, thirty-six on either side of town, so our total capacity is roughly seventy residents, give or take, though we're at just over half that now."

"Wow, they had big plans for this place once, didn't they?" says Rigo.

"I just mind the store," says Cooper. "I don't get much word from the outside world about plans."

"And you have Esau Unruh living here, don't you?"

"I don't know who that is," says Cooper.

"What do they call him here?" Rigo snaps his fingers and grimaces. "Wayne something—?"

"William Wayne?"

"That's right." Rigo smiles. "I've been reading up. He was quite something in his day."

"Technically, I'm not allowed to know who is living here, or anything about their history. Though I do understand Mr. Wayne has quite a reputation."

"He did, once. Who knows what's left of him." Rigo points

up the street to a small, single-story brick bunker, painted all-white and set off from the main road. "And what's that building up there?"

"That's our interfaith chapel," says Cooper. "Truth be told, it doesn't get a lot of use these days."

"You see that?" Rigo says to Santayana. "That's the chapel. You know, in case you want to say a prayer." She nods distractedly, still taking in the town. Troubled citizens amble by silently on the sidewalk, stealing glances, then hurry off. The trio walks another block to the intake portable where Cooper mounts the steps and swings open the door. "And this here should serve you pretty well in terms of an HQ."

Rigo pokes his head through the doorway. "What's this building usually used for?"

"It's where we do our orientation meetings for new arrivals."

"And who has access to it?"

"Anyone, really," says Cooper. "We're not real big on locks in this town."

"We'll need to install some locks. For starters," says Rigo.

"You planning on staying that long?"

"As long as it takes," Rigo says, then steps inside and inspects the trailer: the small school desks all pushed up against the walls, the stained acoustic tile on the drop ceiling, the fluttering fluorescent tubes, the peeling linoleum on the floor. He turns to Santayana, who's now peering through the doorway. She nods.

Rigo turns to Cooper. "This will do. Give us an hour to get set up, then send over Deputy Robinson. I'd like to start with him."

"Start with him—how, exactly?" asks Cooper.

"Questioning," Rigo says. "Oh, and, Sheriff—I understand you have two working vehicles on the premises. I'll need the keys."

"What for?"

"We can't have anyone leaving."

"We're a hundred miles from the closest town, Rigo. If someone runs, where are they going to run to?"

"I'll need the keys. Drop them by this afternoon. And send over Deputy Robinson." Rigo gives Cooper a smile. "Don't worry. You'll get your turn."

Santayana slips past Rigo and Cooper and walks into the room, inspecting it like someone considering a new home. She walks to the whiteboard and runs three well-manicured fingertips over the leftover scrawl from Robinson's intake speech. She leaves three swipe marks, like claw marks, through the word FLOURISH.

She looks at the marker on her fingertips, rubs them, then turns to Cooper and Rigo. "We'll take it!" she says, then laughs.

Dawes watches the four agents as they unpack the luggage from their trucks and tote it into the bungalow. She's curious about the unending stream of hardware. She's curious, too, about how all this is going to go down. She's been prepped, naturally, by Cooper, earlier this morning, before the agents arrived, on the events of the previous night: On how, spurred by Cooper's faith in Dawes's intuitive and quite ingenious suspicions, he'd called Dean into the police trailer for a late-night chat. How he'd explained to Dean that Dawes had pieced together a compelling trail of evidence that connected him to Gable and, before that, Colfax. And how Cooper then mentioned to Dean that Dawes had intercepted the box of 9 mm bullets addressed to his real name, Lester Vogel, in that very morning's shipment of contraband mail. And how Dean, confronted with this evidence, had cracked and confessed to killing Gable and then, in a panic, pulled his 9 mm gun on Cooper, the same gun that had killed Gable and Colfax, Cooper was sure. And how, so confronted, Cooper had been forced to draw and fire first with his revolver, killing Dean.

A remarkable feat of quick-draw survivalism, Dawes thinks, given what she knows about Cooper's surgically reconstructed right shoulder.

But that's the official story, as relayed to her and Robinson by Cooper. As long as they all communicate this story clearly to these agents, Cooper explained, he was confident these agents would wrap up their business shortly and be gone quickly out of everyone's lives. Everything would return to normal, or as close to normal as this town gets.

It might even be the truth, Dawes thinks. Maybe that is how it went down.

She's certainly not about to mourn Lester Vogel, not after learning what she did at that library computer terminal about his copious and hideous crimes. She did not mention to Cooper, of course, that she'd been to a library in Abilene, or that she'd run a search on "Lester Vogel," so she knew all about his past transgressions. She also didn't mention that, as a result, she now finds herself peering at every person in the town, wondering what abominable sins they, too, might be hiding, forgotten, in their buried histories.

People like Spiro Mitchum. Orson Calhoun. Marilyn Roosevelt. Fran Adams.

People like Calvin Cooper.

When she ran her search on "John Barker" and "Fell Institute," she got a hint of his sins.

She also didn't mention that to Cooper.

But that's not what's truly troubling Dawes this morning, as she watches the agents unpack.

What's truly troubling Dawes is this: She never told Cooper about the box of bullets in the morning's contraband mail. So how did he know about it when he confronted Dean last night?

As she watches, and wonders, she feels idly for the notebook she keeps tucked in her breast pocket, just to make sure it's still there.

23.

BETTE BURR STARES into an empty suitcase and wonders if she should bother to pack it.

She arrived with two suitcases, mostly for show, one of them full of bedsheets to give it heft, and the other with barely enough of her clothes in it to last for a week. She figured she'd be in Caesura for three days, tops—that's what they told her—but now it's already day number four. When the Institute contacted her about her father, she was very curious to meet him. She had spent her whole life trying to figure out just who exactly her father was. He was never spoken of by her mother, and when she finally got old enough to press, her mother would only say that Eleanor was the product of a very short and long-forgotten relationship. Possibly as short as one night. Possibly as short as an hour. Her mother would never elaborate.

When she got to be a teenager, Eleanor found out a few things about her father on her own. For example, she knew that her father was a criminal. That he went to prison. Her mother let that slip once late at night after too many drinks. And after many more years of badgering, cajoling, and persistent coaxing, Eleanor even managed to convince her mother to tell her the man's name.

John Sung.

But when Eleanor searched the public records for any trace of John Sung, there was no mention of any such man, living or dead, in the prison system. And that was pretty much it.

Until she got a call one day.

Eleanor was living in Palo Alto at the time, doing graduate work at Stanford, a promising student with the plan of becoming a clinical psychologist. (Something about her open face made people open up to her, it seemed.) She knew the work of Johann Fell and Judy Holliday vaguely—she'd studied their research in one of her seminars on radical alternate treatments for trauma survivors. Johann Fell, who'd worked closely all his career with damaged refugees and torture victims, pioneered a method by which you could chemically nullify traumatic memories in someone's brain. It was crude, but it was a notorious breakthrough, and promised an entirely new tool in helping people move on from horrifying pasts. Since his death, however, his protégée, Dr. Holliday, had taken the research in a different direction.

Eleanor hadn't realized just how different until she sat one day across a table from Dr. Holliday in a large, empty boardroom on the Stanford campus. Dr. Holliday cut an impressive figure. She was well-spoken, elegant, and incandescently intelligent. She outlined to Eleanor the broad parameters of a project called Caesura—a small and privately funded element of the Fell Institute's overall mission, but a crucial one, Holliday explained. Eleanor spent most of the early part of this interview wondering what exactly she was doing there. Then Dr. Holliday asked Eleanor what she knew about her father.

I know his name, and that's about it, Eleanor told her.

There's a man, Dr. Holliday explained, *currently in the Caesura program whose backstory might shed some light on your history. His name is William Wayne. He's been the beneficiary of a unique arrangement in Caesura, and that arrangement involves another man, who's currently living under house arrest in Hawaii, and has been for eight years.*

A criminal by the name of John Sung.

After that conversation, Eleanor traveled to Hawaii—to Kauai, specifically—where she was met at the airport by a police officer in a panama hat and a floral Hawaiian shirt, who took her on a two-hour drive in an open-topped Jeep through the lush and picturesque mountains, to a remote shack off an unpaved laneway, almost totally obscured by overgrown foliage, where she met her father and sat with him in a quiet living room, alongside the policeman who'd been her father's minder and sole friend for the past eight years.

She even has a Polaroid to prove it. Given to her later by Dr. Holliday. Which is helpful, because Eleanor remembers none of this.

Her father was thin and feeble, and he wore shorts and no shirt and his chest was sallow and seemed to cave in on itself, and on one ankle he wore an electronic monitor, and he had an oxygen tube entwined around his face and in his nose, and next to him, like a loyal pet, sat an oxygen tank on a stand on wheels.

She doesn't remember any of that, either.

The room was dark and smelled stale. There was a half-completed card game laid out on a small rattan table. Her father offered her a seat on a tattered wicker chair. He was dying, he explained. He coughed a lot.

She doesn't remember that, either.

His story, insofar as it concerned Eleanor, was not that surprising, in the end. An hour turned out to be a generous estimate as to the length of her parents' relationship. It was a drunken collision between strangers that yielded a child. As for the rest of his life, or at least the parts he was willing to hint at, it all seemed compelling in a sordid way, though he purposefully avoided going into details. He claimed he didn't remember much, including anything at all about her mother. About his own childhood, his own origins, the reasons for his current circumstance, he revealed nothing. *It's better forgotten,* he told her.

She doesn't remember any of this because, after she returned from the trip, Dr. Holliday arranged to have her memory of the trip erased. Fell's technique, so crude at its inception, had been honed by Holliday to the point that specific memories could be targeted and nullified, especially very recent ones. They are the easiest to eliminate, Holliday explained to her later. Johann, she said, was concerned mainly with victims of unspeakable atrocities and had developed a way to erase whole decades from people's memories. But Holliday had perfected the method such that it could erase a week, a day, even an hour.

And it was Dr. Holliday who explained to Eleanor, in that same enormous boardroom on Stanford's sun-slanted campus where they'd first met, that her trip to Hawaii had even happened at all. Eleanor had no memory of it. She sat there, befuddled, her mind feeling muddied and scrubbed. And it was Dr. Holliday who gave her the Polaroid of her and her father, as proof. Who explained to Eleanor that her father had requested to meet his daughter, just once, before he died, so he could give her a message to deliver—a message for a man named William Wayne. Dr. Holliday also explained that it was her father who had insisted, to both Dr. Holliday and Eleanor, on the lone condition of this meeting: That afterward, Eleanor would have all memory of the meeting erased. And that Eleanor had agreed to this beforehand. There was a signature sheet to prove it. Holliday slid it across the table. Eleanor looked it over. Sure enough.

She looked up at Dr. Holliday. "But why did he want to do that?" she asked, feeling, in that shadowed boardroom, confused, disoriented, and betrayed, and suddenly aware of a dark and malignant blot in her mind, this absence, like an ink drop spreading in water.

"Because your father did not want your only memory of him to be of an old, feeble man trapped in a shack," Dr. Holliday said. "You have to understand—in his time, before his incarceration, John Sung was a very *robust* man. If you're going to remember him, he wants you to remember him that way. As the man he once was. As the man William Wayne knew."

"But how can I possibly do that?"

"By finding William Wayne. And delivering your father's message to him."

"And what's the message?" Eleanor asked.

"That your father is dead."

"Is he?" Eleanor asked.

"He is now," Dr. Holliday said. "He was very sick. He knew what was coming. He died just a few days after your visit."

After that, Dr. Holliday arranged for Eleanor to visit Caesura, under the guise of a new arrival. She would have to pretend that she, like the other residents, had no memory of who she'd previously been. The employees in the town, the sheriff and his deputies, wouldn't be informed that Eleanor—or Bette Burr—was any different from anyone else. Once inside the town, her job was to find Wayne, deliver her father's message, and, in return, find out what, if anything, Wayne remembered about her father, John Sung. Then, after three days, the Institute would extract her. That was the arrangement.

Eleanor had two more questions in that boardroom for Dr. Holliday, sitting at that long table, after Holliday had laid this all out to her.

The first question: "Why me? Why not just deliver this news to Wayne yourselves?"

"Because Wayne won't believe it coming from anyone else. But he'll believe you."

The second question: "Why would I do this?"

"Because it's your only chance to know who your father really was."

Her only chance to know—yet here she is, thinks Bette Burr, four days in with no progress. And no desire, really, to stick it out for any longer, here in the middle of nowhere, struggling to deliver a message to a man she's never met from a father she never knew.

So, when Bette saw the two black SUVs roll into town this morning, while everyone else in the town chattered and wondered who these people were and what they were doing here, she figured, *Okay, this must be my ticket out of here. I gave it my shot. I knocked. I knocked again. Now I just want to go home.*

As she looks now at the empty suitcase again, the one she toted in just for show, she thinks, *Fuck it, forget the second suitcase, forget the whole masquerade,* and she zippers the first one shut, with her few pieces of clothing in it, and her manila envelope, and her Polaroid, and she hefts that suitcase and heads over to where the agents seem to have gathered, across town, at the intake trailer.

There's a big one in a black suit standing guard at the door. She marches up to him, suitcase in hand.

"Okay, I'm ready to go," she says.

"I'm sorry?" says the agent.

"My name's Bette Burr. I mean, Eleanor Sung. You're here to take me home, right?"

The agent resumes his disinterested stance. "No one in, no one out."

"I'm sorry—what's your name?"

"Agent Burly."

"Agent Burly, I understand you've got some other business in the town, but I'd like to go. Now. Maybe one of you can drive me out of here?"

"I think you misunderstood me," he says.

Bette sighs. "Contact Dr. Holliday. She knows all about this."

"No one in, no one out. That's all I know."

"Okay, yes, but when are we leaving?"

"I suggest you return to your home."

She stares at the agent. She stares at the closed trailer door. Neither is budging. Maybe someone inside—someone official—"Can I at least talk to whoever's in charge?"

"No one in, no one out."

She hefts her lone case and walks away, figuring she'll have to identify whoever's in charge later. She'll be okay, she thinks, she's got an open face. In the meantime, if nothing else, she wants that photo of her father back—*let me at least have that as a souvenir of all this,* she thinks. She decides to walk past Wayne's house, one last time, just to see if the photo she left is still half-sticking out from under the door, so she can snatch it back. Which she's sure it will be. She's starting to wonder if William Wayne even exists. Or if maybe he died years ago, and there's no one to notice, or care. Maybe he's just a bogeyman, a legend languishing behind a locked door. As she trudges down his block and approaches his house, suitcase held in one hand, she must look like a traveling salesman, she thinks, with her bag of cheap inducements—and then she sees the photo. It's not under the door anymore. It's taped up inside the window, facing out to the street.

Her father's face.

Left like a message. From William Wayne. To her.

She walks up to the door and knocks.

24.

MARILYN ROOSEVELT LOOKS UP from her desk when she hears the bell ring over the door to the library. "May I help—" she starts, but something in Fran's face halts her usual chipper greeting.

"This week's papers," Fran says, tugging Isaac behind here. "Do you still have them?"

"Sure, they're all out on the rack."

"What about the last few months? Do you keep those, too?"

"I'm supposed to recycle them, so I bundle them up every week. But no one ever comes to pick them up. If you want, you can find them all in the back room. Is there something specific you're looking for?"

"I just want to have a look through." Fran steers Isaac off toward the YA section to flip through paperbacks.

"But I've read all those—" Isaac starts to whine, but Fran gives him a look that cuts him short. He sulks over to the shelves and starts idly flipping. Fran gathers the stacks of inky papers on their long, stiff wooden spines from the rack and lays them with a clack out on a large table. They're mostly local papers from the castaway towns within a few hundred miles, filled with coupons and news items about fires. The national news sections are thin collections of wire-service copy. Fran's not even sure what she's looking for. But something about those pages, in the journal with the quote, the way they came alive under her eyes, convinced her to keep looking; that maybe these papers would have more words that would trigger something in her.

She sits, begins at page one, and starts flipping. She scans through each rippled newsprint page for a spark. Ink blackens her fingertips as she traces the headlines, hoping for—she doesn't know, exactly. She avoids the local news, the sports, the entertainment—she scans only the national news. It's like looking for a memorable quote in a book you once read. She'll know it when she sees it, or she hopes she will.

God may forgive, but He rarely exonerates.

Who sent her that message, and why?

Who left those numbers on her wrist before she even got here?

More gray boxes. Small type, and all gibberish. Studies, protests, polls: the usual cacophony of inconsequence. She glances at the dates of the papers—they're all out of order, and seem to be from random days. She calls to Marilyn: "These papers are old, and weeks apart."

"I just put out what comes on the truck," says Marilyn.

Fran turns back to her papers and keeps flipping. What's common to all these papers? She looks for recurring articles, echoed headlines. Her fingers are so ink-stained now that she's leaving her own fingerprints in the margins.

She sniffs an inky finger, idly. It smells like gunpowder.

No. Like ink. Right?

Like gunpowder.

She remembers smelling gunpowder. The acrid stink of it in the air. On her fingers. The acrid stink and a jarring, numbing shudder sent back up her right arm.

A recoil.

Her shoulder aches at the recollection of it.

She's remembering.

She flips.

More pages. More columns. More headlines.

Wait.

MIRACLE MOGUL MAKES SENATE RUN OFFICIAL

A smiling photo. The same man she saw making speeches on the TV in the Laundromat.

She grabs another paper's national section and flips through it—there he is again. She rummages through the other editions she has piled on the table. Each one contains an article about him, charting his progress as he prepares to run for the Senate seat in California. Detailing his past as a billionaire tech titan, his political ambitions, and his long recovery from a gunshot wound to the head.

She turns back to the first article. About the miracle mogul.

God may forgive, but He rarely exonerates.

She reads.

If Fran looked up, she would see through the library's front window the figure of Cooper, heading back to the police trailer, alone, right down the middle of the main street. As he walks, head down, the restless assemblage of a dozen or so townspeople that has been hovering at the edges of the thoroughfare, conspiring and speculating, converges around him. Buster Ford is the first to speak: "Calvin—"

"It's under control, Buster," says Cooper tersely, not breaking stride. "These agents are from the Institute. They're just here to wrap things up."

"How long are they staying?" shouts Lyndon Lancaster from the edge of the crowd. Cooper turns; he can tell Lancaster's out of sorts, because he's unshaven and looks like he hasn't slept in days, and his usually impeccable, Brylcreemed hair flops in long strands over his face.

"I can't imagine it will be longer than a day or two," Cooper says, though he's starting to imagine it might be much longer than that.

"So do they—do they know?" says Spiro Mitchum.

"Know what, Spiro?"

Mitchum clutches at his apron anxiously. He says quietly: "Who we are?" Cooper can't tell from his voice if he's fearful that they might know or hopeful that they do.

"Of course not," says Cooper. "No one has access to those files, not me, not them, not anyone. You know that." He turns to walk away.

"I have a question—" comes a reedy voice from the crowd, and Cooper knows it right away: fucking Dietrich. He turns and spots Dietrich lingering near the back of the group.

"What is it, Dick?"

"When whatever comes that's coming, how do you plan to deal with it?"

Cooper stares him down. "Dietrich, what are you asking me?"

Dietrich repeats himself, as though presenting a delightful riddle he expects everyone will find enchanting. "When whatever comes that's coming, how do you plan to deal with it, Sheriff?"

"The same way I deal with everything in this town," says Cooper. "Quickly, resolutely, and definitively." Cooper's about to walk away, to let it drop—he should, he knows—but instead he says: "What's your game, Dietrich?"

"I'm just biding my time, Sheriff. Just waiting."

"For what?"

"For whatever's coming to come. It's almost here."

Cooper's about to press this further, but he feels the anxious eyes of the crowd on him, nervous, combustible, so instead he turns and starts to walk again. He barks over his shoulder: "If anyone's feeling uncomfortable, I suggest you stay in your bungalow until this blows over. As always, you can find me at the police trailer. Have a good day, everyone."

He strides off, eager to shake the crowd, and annoyed at the pleading insistence of the townsfolk and the blatant insolence of Dietrich, not to mention this whole unannounced intrusion from the Institute. Dr. Holliday didn't even warn him about this when they were sitting face-to-face a day ago? And *six* fucking agents? For what? No wonder Rigo's got everyone in town shitting their drawers. This doesn't look like an investigation; it looks like an invasion.

Cooper's already at a low boil as he approaches the police trailer—and what he encounters there stops him dead.

One of the agents, a runty redhead, his brush cut the garish crimson of a dime-store lipstick, is standing by the entrance of the police trailer, crisscrossing the closed door with yellow tape that reads SECURITY LINE DO NOT CROSS.

"Excuse me?" says Cooper.

"This is an active crime scene," says the agent.

"I know. I'm the shooter, remember?" says Cooper.

The agent doesn't smile or even turn to look at Cooper, just keeps taping the doorway. With each tug of the roll, the tape screeches.

"I have to get in there—" says Cooper. "I have personal effects—"

"You'll need clearance from Agent Rigo."

"To access my own office?"

"You'll need clearance from Agent Rigo."

"You work for the Fell Institute, right? Do you even have legal jurisdiction here?"

The agent stops taping. "We both work for the Fell Institute, Sheriff. And this is a private facility on private land. If I were you, legal jurisdiction is the last thing I'd be worried about right now."

"And what is the first thing I should worry about?"

The agent says nothing, just starts taping again.

"Look," says Cooper, "I'd love to get a sense of the parameters of your investigation. Since we'll be working together—"

"You'll need clearance from Agent Rigo."

"I'm thinking of taking a shit later. Will I need clearance from Agent Rigo for that?"

The agent keeps taping.

"Don't worry, I'll ask him myself." Cooper turns and heads right back toward the intake trailer he just came from. Nothing about any of this feels right. He does take some consolation as he walks in the fact that the most important piece of evidence from the agent's active crime scene behind him is still safely in Cooper's possession. He rests the heel of his hand on the grip of that evidence, his pistol, still nestled in his holster.

Robinson shifts his admittedly ample ass in the uncomfortable plastic chair. He waits for this long-legged prick in the black suit to look up from the screen of the electronic tablet he's so intently focused on. It's not lost on Robinson that this is the exact position, in this exact building, in possibly even this exact chair, that new arrivals to Caesura sit and squirm while he, Walter Robinson, sits pretty much exactly where that long-legged, black-suited prick is sitting now, staring them down. Robinson's never had to feel this way before—the way the new arrivals must feel on the other side of his desk. Asked to pick a new name. Asked to start from scratch. Feeling like you're in a little rubber dinghy, and behind you rests your whole unremembered life, and Robinson sits before you holding a comically huge pair of scissors, and he's about to cut the rope and let you drift.

He doesn't love the feeling, to be honest.

But it's not like he's the one who goes in and scoops out all their memories—he's just the one who welcomes them here after that's done. So don't blame him. He just answered an ad for a job. Sure, it's true, he used to wonder about newcomers. He used to sit at the intake table and silently size people up, trying to guess, *to speculate,* even though you're technically not supposed to. He'd think: *Okay, what did you do, buddy? Where did you go wrong, lady? What brought your ass to the Blinds?* But that phase only lasted maybe six months, tops. After that, he stopped wondering. What's the point—you could never know, and they could never tell. So he decided just to take people as they come. And as had happened at many previous junctures in his life, Robinson ultimately came to understand that not asking questions is just a lot . . . *easier.* It's even a kind of relief. Everything got simpler. Chase down noise complaints. Break up drunken fistfights. And at night, watch old movies on the TV they gave you, on the old VCR they let you have. Then go to sleep with earplugs and an eye mask, shut the world out, then wake up and do it all again.

Simple.

And Robinson's been doing that for five years now, even though he never expected to stay that long. But when the first two-year contract was over he re-upped without a second thought, then re-upped again two years later. It's quiet here. Peaceful. Not that he hasn't had moments of boredom. He has a certain proficiency with small appliances, just hobbyist stuff, and, once, he took the back off his standard-issue walkie-talkie and tried fiddling with it to see if he could pick up a different signal—someone from the outside, some new person to talk to, some stray transmission from civilization drifting on the ether. But he abandoned that project pretty quick after he got worried that, if the Institute found out what he was doing, he'd be censured, fired, or worse. Maybe he'd even get wiped. Maybe they'd kick down his bungalow's door in the night, shining flashlights, and take him away in leg irons and erase his memory, too. He'd considered the possibility. That they might erase someone's memory without their consent. How would you even know if they had? Maybe it had already happened. It's the kind of thing he used to read about a lot on the Internet, back in his other life. Black helicopters and chemtrails and secret government camps and all sorts of shit they never talk about. You don't know the half of what's going on in the world, is how he figures it. So why wouldn't they wipe your memory, then wipe your memory of it being wiped? Who knows what the Institute is capable of?

So he stopped fiddling with the walkie-talkie.

Instead, he watches his VHS movies. Tapes worn so thin in certain parts that the screen just fills with fuzz.

Maybe he'd even ask the Institute to do it one day, before he retires. Wipe his mind clear. Why not? You have nothing to lose but your past. For example, he'd sat out one humid night in his backyard in Baltimore and destroyed all the photos of his ex-wife with a Zippo lighter in a small trashcan, after he'd quit the force and been put on disability but before he'd packed up his apartment and moved all the way out here. Burning those photos—wasn't that just a low-tech, homemade version of doing what the Institute does? He remembers the acrid smell of them. The emulsion catching fire. Her smile bubbling, curling. Then gone.

She'd already left him, and took that smile with her, which, to be fair, had been underused of late. He burned her photos, and packed up his apartment, and answered an ad for a job, and here he is. He feels like most of his life is only half-remembered at this point anyway. He barely remembers her smile. He wishes he'd kept one of those photos. Saved it from the fire. All those years they'd spent together seemed like someone else's years to him now, someone else's life, someone else's smile.

There's nothing special about this place, he thinks. *We all forget. Then we forget what we forgot. And that's how we survive.*

Rigo taps the tablet screen and finally looks up.

"Tell me about Calvin Cooper," he says.

"What would you like to know?" Robinson says.

"For starters, would you say he is a violent person?"

"Define 'violent,'" Robinson says.

Fran sits at the library table, hunched over the articles, making her way through them, one by one. Isaac's curled up in a corner of the kids' section, lost in a YA novel.

Fran reads the first article again.

The story of the tech tycoon in California who was shot in the head by his wife.

A domestic dispute, is how the article describes it. An argument that escalated. Crime of passion.

She knows that's not what it was.

It's very unusual to be shot point-blank in the head and survive.

Unusual. But not impossible.

A miracle, really. No other word for it. Nearly a year in a coma.

He was written off, for sure. Then he came out of it. Then four years in rehabilitative therapy. Relearning to stand. Relearning to speak. Then three more years of—what? she thinks. Just waiting. Searching, maybe. Planning, perhaps.

Shot, he survives. In a coma, he awakens. Bedridden, he rises. In a wheelchair, he walks again.

Runs.

Runs for office.

Mark Vincent, tech titan, noted philanthropist, victim of a terrible tragedy and, armed with an inspiring backstory, soon to be the next senator from the great state of California.

An American miracle.

He was a well-known figure at the time of the incident, a billionaire in his early forties who'd made his fortune in predictive algorithms applied to political campaigns. Better than polling, was the promise, and better than polling was the result. His software could collect and collate consumer information, then tell you, with unnerving accuracy, how someone will vote.

"I thought, I've spent my life perfecting a way to predict how people will vote," he says, quoted in one of the stories. "Maybe I'll try to win some of those votes for myself." He was well on his way to laying the track for a Senate run eight years ago, when he was derailed by a senseless attack. A gunshot wound to the head. It nearly killed him.

Nearly.

Fran's been too long out of touch with the news, after eight years of tuning out the chatter of the TV in the Laundromat, of ignoring the yellowing newspapers on wooden spines in the library. But from what she can gather scanning these pages, things in the outside world aren't going too good right now. Economy is down. Violence is up. People are scared.

Yet amid all that, there comes reason for hope.

The American Miracle.

That's what they're calling him now or, at least, that's the slogan festooned across his podium when he speaks.

"I think America can rise again as well," he says. The medical miracle is promising a national miracle. It's a narrative that can only end in the White House. It should have no problem lifting him to the Senate. And after that, who knows?

He's even forgiven his wife, he says. Wherever she might be.

He doesn't like to talk about it, but he will if the press insists.

He has no memory of the event itself—*the incident*—and really that's for the best. Memories can hinder you. He's all about moving forward. He believes there's a larger plan for his life, and when you believe there's a plan for your life, then everything *in* that plan becomes an instrument *of* that plan. Even a disloyal wife.

Even a coma.

Even a bullet.

He wishes her only the best, he says. No, he hasn't heard from her in years. Not since that night. When you spend nearly a year in a coma, he jokes, you tend to fall out of touch with people. [*Laughter.*] Imagine my email inbox, he jokes. [*Laughter.*]

The press nods and jots down his remarks.

His wife was a PhD student in English lit at UC Berkeley when they met, a good fifteen years younger than he was. Part of a group of top students he'd brought in to help make his algorithm more *poetic*. The kind of tech project you undertake when you have shareholders to dazzle and unlimited money to spend. Nothing came of the meetings, but the two of them fell in love. A real storybook romance, he says. [*Laughter.*] She was a bookworm, with a vast collection of volumes that arrived at his home in dozens of boxes after he finally convinced her to move in. He built her an incredible library. An entire room inlaid with built-in bookcases floor to ceiling, all her own, her vast collection of books shelved, ordered, tagged, archived, and neatly tucked away.

They're not married anymore, not legally, of course. She's in prison, somewhere in solitary, receiving appropriate treatment for her mental illness, so he understands. Probably for life. He wishes her the best. He'd rather not say anything more about these personal matters. Let's move on. Next question.

In truth, it's the kind of story that fades after a few months, after the bang, after the headlines, after the trial. She's just the answer to a trivia question now. Of course, she told a different story at the time, but no one listened. And then she disappeared into the bowels of the penal system. And her memories of the whole event—of the man, of the night, of the shot, of the different story she once told—all that disappeared, too.

She remembers a book she'd been reading at the time, after the bang, after the headlines, after the trial. A book she brought with her to prison. A collection of journals by a woman with a faraway look and a strident mind. What was she looking for in it: strength, wisdom, succor, something? But she read it every day. She remembers scribbling and highlighting and underlining each page, the book marked up like a treasure map that refuses to yield its treasure. As though every line contained some secret coded message just for her. She sat in her cell and read and scribbled all over it. She slept with that book under her pillow every night.

It's not even a process of remembering, she thinks. Memories are something you recall. You recollect them—you literally *re-collect* them. Dredge them up from some secret hollow where they've been lying in wait to be rediscovered.

They took her to a room.

Explained how it would go.

You won't remember any of this, they said, and she immediately thought of the book back in her cell.

The clatter of prison. The tang of antiseptic. The sharp steely pain of the homemade needle in the skin of her arm.

She looks down at her tattoo now. Rubs it.

12500241214911

Then keeps reading. The article continues:

Vincent, having amazed his doctors and defied all expectations, would now run unopposed for his party's nomination. His replacement stepped aside willingly. "Honestly, I was just keeping the seat warm," he joked stiffly at the press conference. [*Laughter.*] After all, who stands in the way of this kind of story?

The article continues:

"If I learned one thing during my recovery, it's the importance of taking life one step at a time," Vincent said.

The article continues:

Vincent is newly engaged to be remarried. "My past is my past," he said. "And that's that. Some things are better left forgotten."

He has no children.

The article ends.

The night before they were to come and give her the procedure, she found someone in the prison, a heavyset woman with kind eyes, she remembers now, who knew how to do it. It took hours, and it was painful, she remembers.

The woman said to her, *You really want this whole thing?* and she said to the woman, *Yes,* and the woman said, *Right arm or left arm?* and she looked down at her two bare arms and the flesh of her wrist and said, *Left.*

The clatter of prison. The tang of antiseptic. She can smell it, in the library, right now.

She remembers a circle of women formed around them in the cell to block what they were doing from the sight lines of the guards, and she remembers she turned the paperback book over in her hand and searched for numbers on the back and said, *Here,* and pointed out the numbers to the woman and the woman said, *You sure?* and she said, *Yes, I'm sure.*

She remembers the pain of the needle. She feels it, right now, on her wrist, like an itch, like a burn, like the tattoo is re-etching itself.

She remembers that she held out her pale left arm and, as the woman started to etch in the numbers painfully over her wrist, she said to the woman, *Sinister,* and the woman said, *Sister what?* and she said to the woman, *No, sinister, that's from the Latin word for "left,"* and the woman nodded and got back to work with the needle. She remembers the ballpoint pen with a sewing needle taped to it, dipped rhythmically in an overturned cap filled with homemade ink. She remembers wondering halfway through the procedure if the ink would hurt the baby, but it was too late. The baby that no one knew about but her. The baby so young and her not even showing. She said nothing about it, and at some point she remembers the woman while she worked said, *You're new here aren't you?* like she was trying to distract her from the pain, and she answered, *Yes,* and the woman said, *It's painful but it will all be over soon,* and she said, *It's okay, I won't remember any of this, that's what they told me,* and the woman shrugged, and as she worked with the needle the woman said, *Well, this you'll have forever, like a keepsake of this place, like a souvenir,* and she said to the woman, *Do you know what "souvenir" means?* and the woman shook her head and kept working and she said to the woman, *"souvenir" is the French word for memory, it literally means "to remember,"* and the woman nodded and said, *Don't worry, you'll remember this,* and got back to her work and to the pain until she finished.

1 2 5 0 0 2 4 1 2 1 4 9 1 1

On her left wrist.
Her sinister souvenir.

God may forgive, but He rarely exonerates.

Something to remember him by.

25.

I WANT HIM GONE," says Cooper.

"Who gone?" says Rigo.

"Dick Dietrich. I want him out of here."

"I have no idea who that is," says Rigo, barely glancing up from his tablet's screen. Behind him, the intake trailer is jittery with activity: two of the muscular, black-suited agents, Corey and Bigelow, sort through boxes full of files, all lifted from Cooper's office. When Cooper entered the trailer, shouldering past Burly, the goon outside, the door opened and Walt Robinson exited, giving Cooper a funny look as he passed, Cooper's sure of it. He might even interpret the look as a warning. Cooper watches now as one of the agents hoists the 9 mm pistol he confiscated from Gerald Dean and left in his desk drawer—it's wrapped in an evidence bag. The agent tags it and tosses it in a box.

"You can't just barge in here, Sheriff," says Rigo. "I know you're used to having the run of this town, but we're trying to conduct an investigation." He keeps swiping at his tablet with a long white finger, like a tree branch scratching at a window. Cooper wonders how Rigo's even getting a signal out here.

Another agent hoists a long black case onto a desk, then with two sharp clicks opens it, and when he lifts the lid, Cooper spots an AR-15 rifle nestled in egg-carton foam inside the case.

"You expecting a war?" says Cooper.

Rigo just smiles, distracted.

"You do realize no one in this town has a gun, right?" says Cooper.

"And yet people keep getting shot."

"Dietrich is the menace, I'm telling you. Do you know what he did to our pack of coydogs? He set them on *fire*."

"Wait—what's a coydog?" says Rigo.

"Dietrich's unhinged."

"All due respect, Sheriff, my mandate here is to get answers, not settle old grudges."

"He's a danger. To all of us."

Rigo glances around at the agents in the room, unpacking their weapons, then says to Cooper: "I think we can handle him. In the meantime, if you'll excuse me, I've got interviews to conduct." He nods toward the doorway of the trailer, where Dawes is now standing and waiting. Cooper spies her, too: Sidney Dawes, watching the action in silence, avoiding his eyes, or so it seems to Cooper. Rigo waves her in, and she sits down at a school desk without so much as a word to Cooper.

"We'll be right with you, Deputy," says Rigo. Then, to Cooper: "I'm going to have to ask you to leave. You understand."

"Dietrich's the one you need to focus on," says Cooper, sounding increasingly desperate, even to himself.

"Sure. I'll get right on that. In the meantime, don't wander off too far."

Cooper shoots another glance at Dawes, hoping for—something.

Some indication. But she stares straight ahead and ignores him. So he heads for the door and, before Cooper exits, he says to Rigo, "Where exactly am I going to go?"

Once Cooper's left the trailer, Dawes settles into her chair, her knees bumping up against the underside of the little school desk. She waits and watches as the agents unpack boxes and tack photos of Errol Colfax, Hubert Gable, and Gerald Dean to the whiteboard. She thinks back to the day just six weeks ago when she first arrived here—her own unofficial intake day—and all that had preceded that moment: how she fled Atlanta and that starter home and that abusive dead-end husband and how she thought, as she drove in her dented hatchback over those long stretches of look-alike highway, pointed southwest toward a friend in Austin and an uncertain future, that the best parts of her life were likely behind her and that they hadn't even really been that good. She sat there in her car, on the highway, that idea filling her with dread. To be barely thirty and already feel like your life is irreparably off the rails. The evidence was piled up against her: from her decision to skip college, mostly to annoy her academic parents; to her failed and dispirited attempt to become an EMT; to her quick marriage and even quicker divorce; to her hasty exodus to Austin—all those choices had led her to apply for this job, in this place, and they could not reasonably be regarded as steering her toward some greater destiny. Yet here she is. And, every day, she irons her uniform. Every day, she updates her notebook. Every day, she asks questions, and waits patiently for improbable opportunity, even though she has no clue what opportunity might look like, especially one that might find her all the way out here.

Well, maybe, she thinks, settling into the chair, tapping the notebook in her breast pocket, *maybe this is what opportunity looks like.* A trailer full of outsiders in suits with questions that she just might have the answers to. After a life spent too long on the wrong side of other people's lies, it feels good to be on the side of the truth. And she's pretty sure she knows the truth. She knows plenty, that's for sure.

I wait. I watch. I guard.

John Barker, for example. She knows something about him. It's certainly not part of the story he told her to tell these people. But that's okay—she's not telling anyone else's stories today.

The tall agent with the spiked white hair and the sunglasses, Rigo, is conferring with the female agent, Santayana. "I have to go and deal with this guy Dietrich," he says to her. "Can you handle this?"

Santayana glances at Dawes and nods.

When Rigo exits, Santayana strides crisply over to Dawes, her heels tapping the linoleum floor. *Imagine wearing heels out here,* Dawes thinks, *in all this dust and heat.* She can't tell if it makes you confident or obstinate. Agent Santayana pulls up a plastic chair. "My apologies. We're just getting everything up and running."

"No problem," says Dawes.

Santayana sits. She offers Dawes a warm smile, like the smile you might get from the person at a crowded party who finally makes you feel welcome, like it wasn't a huge mistake for you to come. Up close, the agent's age is impossible to ascertain—she could be twenty-five or forty-five or anywhere in between. She's quite well groomed, even in this Texas heat, and she smells pleasantly of summer orchards, Dawes notices, the scent drifting lazily toward her in the stale air of the windowless intake trailer.

"Sidney—that's an unusual name," she says.

"I prefer Sid."

"Okay, Sid. I prefer Iris. Nice to meet you." She gestures back toward the commotion in the room, then turns to Dawes and mouths the word "men," then laughs. "Am I right? They're useless without us. I'm sure you know what I'm talking about." Then she picks up her deep black tablet and starts stroking the screen. A few moments pass. Dawes, anxious, decides to speak: "About the shootings—"

"Yes, we'll get to that." Santayana keeps her eyes trained on the tablet.

Dawes waits. Then says, "Do you know about John Barker?"

"Hold that thought, Sid." Santayana taps the tablet again, then holds it up and turns it toward Dawes. "Tell me, do you know this woman?"

Dawes looks at the tablet. It's a photo of Fran Adams, but not the version of Fran Adams that Dawes is familiar with. This version of Fran Adams is dolled up, laughing, her hair swept high for some fancy function. She's smiling with an intensity and fervor that Dawes has never seen from her in here—or, really, from anyone in here. She wears glittering earrings that dangle. She looks like she knows the person taking the photo. She looks, honestly, like she's in love.

Dawes stares at the photo, confused, her throat constricting slightly for reasons she can't quite pin down, then says finally, "Yes. I know her."

"Very good. You're being very helpful. Second question, Sid." Santayana's smile is gone, she's suddenly brusque now, all business. "Do you know where we can find her right now?"

26.

THE AIR IS IMMOBILE. Dust motes hover, indecisive, in the pale shafts of what little light penetrates the curtains. The bungalow smells of old man, moth balls, and wet wool, which is to be expected, Bette thinks.

William Wayne offers her a seat.

He's unshaven. A white spray of whiskers spreads across his neck, chin, and cheeks, speaking to habitual neglect. The scruff seems coarser over the kidney-shaped port-wine stain that covers one side of his face. The splotch spreads, large and puffy and crimson, over his cheek and under his eye and crawls up the bridge of his nose. His eyes above the stain are small and hooded, like the eyes of a cave dweller, long ago adjusted to inadequate light.

"What made you open the door for me?" Bette says.

"It's a door. That's what it's made for," he says. "I'd offer you something to eat or drink, but I don't have anything to offer."

"That's okay," Bette says.

He has a wild crown of impressive ghost-white hair, swept up and back in a careless pompadour. He wears a black cowboy shirt with tarnished pearl snaps, and stained black corduroy trousers, and weathered leather boots. The knuckles of his gnarled hands are ballooned with age, like knots in an ancient tree trunk. Bette watches him. She'd imagined someone different. Someone gallant and strapping. Someone fearsome. Someone dangerous. Not this man. This cannot be him.

The famous killer known as William Wayne.

"How can I help you?" he says. His voice has a rasp to it, a wheeze, like a punctured accordion, gasping.

"You knew John Sung," she says. Despite herself, her voice ticks up at the end, as though she's asking him a question, or asking for confirmation of her statement.

Wayne winces, regarding her. Doesn't answer. She continues.

"I'm his daughter, Eleanor. I'm Eleanor Sung."

"Did I ever know you?" asks Wayne.

"I don't know. But I don't think so," she says. "I only just met my father. And I don't remember him at all."

"Can you tell me how he is?"

"He's dead."

Wayne hears this, then sits silent for a very long moment.

"Do you remember my father?" she asks finally.

"In a sense," says Wayne. "They don't let me forget. That's how they keep me here. Or at least that's what they believe."

He points toward the kitchen with a finger so crooked that it's no longer suited to the task of pointing. "I have a kettle. I can put some water on. I can offer you hot water."

"I'd like that," she says.

He stands. He's so tall, she sees now. As he unfurls himself, like a flag, for the first time she sees perhaps what her father saw.

This fearsome, gallant man.

The famous killer, William Wayne.

The love of her father's life.

William Wayne was born Esau Unruh and loosed in this world like a plague. As a boy, he knew nothing but whippings and darkness, these being the preferred punishments of his father—the strap or the closet, or both. One punishment would follow the other without reason or restraint. Exiled in a farmhouse on the coldest plains of Manitoba, Canada, he soon learned there was little point in crying out at his father's hand. His mother, for her part, always screamed as his father beat her; as a young boy, bruised, Esau fell asleep nightly to the lullaby of his mother's further wailings. She was a woman haunted, by visions and dread, and his father was convinced that fists, relentlessly applied, were the only remedy for her sickness. She rarely raised a hand to intervene or spare Esau from his own whippings. The fact that Esau was marked as a newborn by a wine stain like Cain only furthered his mother's conviction that her son was tainted at birth by something corrupt and otherworldly. And she may have been right.

He left home at an early age. He lived for two years on the streets in the closest city, with nearly nothing to his name but a fierce will to protect what little he had. The stain on his face had long since taught him not to anticipate human kindness as a rule. Cain, not Esau, struck him as his biblical precedent. And he quickly learned two lessons: to defend his personal possessions with a vigor that far exceeded their actual worth; and to counter his attacker's violence with a savagery that far exceeded the original aggression. If they shove, you kick; if they punch, you puncture. Brutality that's swiftly and almost inexplicably escalated can be a very effective deterrent, he found.

A reputation can serve as a kind of armor.

Then, at age fifteen, he returned home, finally succumbing to a persistent, nagging compulsion to intercede on his mother's behalf. As it happened, on the night he returned unannounced to his homestead, he walked in on one of his father's beatings, not that such beatings were rare events. His mother, bruised and cowering; his father looming over her with the posture of a prizefighter in training. Esau stopped it, first with his newly expert fists and then with the family shotgun. After he shot his father, his mother, unhinged, distraught beyond reason, and cursing him as the earthly manifestation of some unbound demon, came after him wielding a long kitchen knife. She had already cut herself many times with the blade in a rabid fervor, and blood trailed over her person like festive ribbons. Esau killed both his parents that night. He believed the trigger-pull, the sharp report, the echoing boom, represented a kind of spiritual release for her. He hoped it did.

Then back to the city. What friends he'd made were of a type well versed in criminal enterprises, and they weren't really his friends, and he understood this. They used him. They recognized in him an exploitable ferocity. He understood this, too. It didn't bother him. The fact is, once you've killed your own parents, there's no one in the world you can't kill. This is a truth passed down from Bible times.

As a young man, he became the type of nomad who trails fatalities. He never killed out of malice or anger, only from a plain recognition that death is as natural a feature on the landscape as the trees, the water, the earth itself. The human instinct to avoid death at all costs seemed to him the basest form of folly, a grand misunderstanding of our fleeting place in the cosmos. And, like many who come to a quiet peace about the inevitability of their own demise, he came ironically to avoid that fate almost as if by divine protection.

He ventured south. Bound for the United States, a country where his skills and attitude attracted no end of eager suitors. As a professional, he developed a reputation for finality, once dispatched. He was efficient but he did not relish cruelty. The problem with many professional killers is that they themselves become problems: greedy, ambitious, sloppy, disloyal. He was none of these.

He lived this way for many years. He never married. He had, on occasion, sexual relations with women but the act seemed unnatural to him. It was one he pursued mostly out of curiosity, until he abandoned the pursuit. With no desire to procreate, it struck him as pointless, even laughable, to go through the clumsy motions.

He was aware of an emptiness inside himself but could not name it. Rather, his life drifted toward the monastic. This was not a choice he made but rather a return to what felt to him like a natural state.

Over time the kind of men who'd once employed him came to fear him and, eventually, to avoid him. Most men who are drawn to a violent life are driven by an appetite for fear, a desire to generate sufficient fear in others that it might temporarily nullify the smallness and fear in themselves. Either way, fear is the currency of their world. For that kind of man, to encounter a person like Unruh, who had no appetite for instilling fear in others and no apparent occasion for fear in himself, can be almost existentially unnerving. Such a person is impossible to comprehend. So these fearful, violent men came to avoid him. Which bothered him not in the least.

He retreated into further solitude. This seemed, to him, the natural path. He was nearing seventy. He settled in California. The coastal aspects of the state never suited him, but he found a pleasant refuge in the Inland Empire. Communications between himself and his sporadic employers were infrequent and uncluttered by niceties. All the vicious men he had known in his earlier days were, for the most part, now either dead or incarcerated, the natural conclusions for such lives. Still, someone of Unruh's history and reputation will never fully be unemployed, as long as damaged and angry men have access to grudges and money.

So, at a certain point, he was connected with a younger man of similar vocation and temperament. A killer by the name of John Sung, who was half-Hawaiian, half-Japanese. Sung's ethnicity was unusual among the network of people who employed him, which was comprised almost entirely of white men of European heritage. In this sense, Sung seemed marked in a similar way to the marking of Esau Unruh's wine stain: a man set apart, for reasons of happenstance. This endeared him to Unruh.

Sung's background, Unruh later learned, was tainted in similar ways to Unruh's own. Sung had been brutalized from an early age by most everyone who came across him, from relatives to teachers to state guardians, the kind of child who draws the attention of predators, and who is therefore taught from the earliest age to believe that brutality is a natural force. That brutality exists in the world like gravity, or electricity, or magnetism, in the air, in the walls, flowing all around us, unseen, and that it's simply waiting to be given direction, to be applied to one person or another. And that those who do not learn to apply it to others are thereby condemned to be its recipients.

When they met, Unruh felt for the first time in his nearly seventy years of life the sense of encountering a kindred heart.

Sung was similarly perplexed and amused, Unruh would also learn, by the incapacity of most people to imagine the world's history in the awesome expanse of its entirety, rather than simply as an experience bracketed by the fleeting instant that you happen by random chance to be alive. And Sung's vocation as a killer seemed to him no more immoral than the kind of ritual exploitation that constituted so much of so-called normal life. In fact, a life dedicated to the perpetuation of other people's systematic misery—the life, say, of a politician who by corruption condemns whole towns to some toxic poisoning of their water supply, or of a business tycoon whose fortune is built on the labor of interred children in some far-away country—seemed to Sung far more immoral than a life spent enforcing the ultimate punishment of a widely understood code by which people had readily agreed to abide.

Which is to say: the life of a professional killer.

Which is to say: John Sung had never killed anyone who did not expect to be killed. This was the simple truth of his employment. Now, whether death was an appropriate punishment for betrayal, or overweening ambition, or chronic indebtedness, was a question that Sung, given his background, did not feel morally equipped to answer. But the fact remained that each person to whom this punishment was meted out was well aware of its eventuality as the ultimate consequence for their actions—and this seemed to Sung not immoral, or evil, but rather like one of the more rational and elegant manifestations of the free will that we collectively like to imagine we possess.

For this reason and others, Unruh developed a further fondness for Sung.

This fondness was not at all undermined—it was, in fact, amplified—by the realization that the reason their mutual employer had paired them was, in all likelihood, to instill in Sung a more valuable brand of ruthlessness. Esau Unruh was little understood by the men who employed him, but what the simplest minds among them could comprehend was Unruh's remorselessness. They imagined it must be some sort of inoculation from human empathy, which he might be able to share with others—Sung, for one. As Unruh aged and withdrew monastically from life, they hoped to build or engineer another Unruh. So, his employers, in their lack of understanding, conspired to try to instill his most appealing characteristics in another, younger murderer. To see, in effect, if what Unruh possessed would rub off on John Sung.

The entirely unexpected result of Unruh's pairing with, and tutelage of, John Sung was that he and Sung fell in love.

This, at least, is how Unruh's relationship with Sung would be characterized by third parties to him later, and he never took issue with it—though whether "love," that storied word, was the proper description for his feelings, he did not feel qualified to say. Given that the first and fundamental example for him of what he understood to be "love" consisted of a hateful man who ritually beat and broke a haunted woman, he'd long abandoned the idea that "love" between two people was something he might understand, let alone encounter, let alone aspire to experience. He had dispatched those two "loving" people, his parents, from this earth himself. And he had dispatched many others after them. And he expected one day himself to be similarly dispatched, by man or God or time. Where "love" fit into that, he couldn't say.

But what Unruh did understand was that, in the person of young John Sung, he had, bewilderingly, and for the first time ever, collided with another living soul whose continued existence on this earth he valued more than his own.

Was that love?

If so, then yes, they were in love.

Their physical relations also struck Unruh as materially different from those in his past, and not just because of the obvious fact that Sung was not a woman. Unruh didn't imagine that their few brief naked explorations constituted anything similar to the kind of rhapsodic encounters he saw elaborately celebrated in movies or songs on the radio, all of which had struck him as an amusing collective anesthetic delusion cooked up to keep people in line. Sung, for his part, seemed incapable of conceiving of intimate physical contact that was not intended primarily to bring him pain. So their initial encounters were awkward, to say the least. But heartfelt, too. And Unruh, during these clumsy fumblings, came to believe that perhaps these interactions offered Sung a different framework in which to consider himself in relation to the world. As not an object of disdain or abuse. But as something better. That perhaps they offered him a different way to see himself. The way that Unruh saw him.

As for Unruh, the essential lacking at his center was so familiar and profound that he not only never imagined it might be any different, but he accepted this lacking as intrinsic to his being. As, perhaps, the very essence of his being. The very thing that made him Esau Unruh.

But what he found he was learning at this late improbable moment in the company of Sung was that the lacking was temporarily . . . *forgettable.*

For a few moments.

Just a few.

And that, in this forgetting, he came to consider that maybe the lacking was not *everything.* Not all the time.

It was not the whole of who he was.

In any case, Unruh was always happy that their hapless physical encounters, bumbling and comical and fleetingly transcendent as they might be, happened in the sanctified privacy of their bedroom, outside the purview of anyone but themselves, and certainly of no concern to their mutual employers.

Or so he believed, perhaps foolishly.

After all, Unruh had for so long existed as someone the world saw as possessing a singular useful purpose—to negate—that the idea that any other aspect of his self would be of interest to anyone seemed ludicrous to him.

So when an outraged employer—a man of great vanity and

legendary stupidity, but also of high ranking within the criminal enterprise with which Unruh had long been embroiled—berated Unruh at length and with great righteousness over the telephone in sputtering, profane terms about this scandalous moral abomination to which he was privy, Unruh was simply surprised. There was nothing to take offense to, really, since the reaction seemed wholly irrational.

Unruh would admit, however, that he did take something like pleasure in dispatching the two incompetent lackeys that the employer subsequently unleashed in an effort to wipe the moral stain of Unruh and Sung from this earth. Those two unruly, workaday thugs, armed with pistols, who were no doubt tickled to get the assignment to go off and ice some faggots, but who instead met their own end in a motel parking lot in an almost comically brief exchange of gunfire.

Unruh further took some pleasure—a strange and prickly and alien sensation he might even recklessly classify as delight—at his subsequent visit, with John Sung in tow, to the obscenely decadent seaside home of that same profanity-prattling employer. A fortress where several overly muscled bodyguards wandered the grounds with facial expressions of great serious purpose. In all his years in this vocation, which now numbered over fifty, years that had seen his hair winter to silver white, Unruh had never understood the apparent instinctual connection drawn by criminals between beefiness and safety. Muscular men have evinced one skill in this world, Unruh thought: the ability to accumulate muscles. And muscles have never been bulletproof.

A frontal assault with firearms was the simple and effective prescription here. The bodyguards proved, as bodyguards often do, to be primarily ornamental.

After the bodyguards, once Esau and John were inside the house itself and had found the loudmouthed criminal and a few rash functionaries besides, the mansion became a notorious and fabled scene of dispassionate slaughter.

Later, back at Unruh's home, it was Sung who suggested the police.

Fear was not part of the discussion. But Unruh understood the likelihood that death awaited them and, furthermore, that between now and death, they faced a lot of running. The nature of criminal enterprises is such that insubordination can never go unpunished. Also, Unruh and Sung imagined that between them they held enough valuable knowledge about the workings of several national criminal enterprises that they might bargain for some sort of clemency.

Some new anonymous exile, together.

Hawaii, maybe.

That seemed like a noble goal.

So they went to the police.

Where, instead of clemency and exile, they were immediately separated, and Unruh never saw John Sung again, save once.

As it turned out, perhaps not entirely surprisingly—a fact that Unruh should have foreseen, and for which he's upbraided himself mercilessly in the long, muddied years since their separation that day—the federal agents they encountered, while flabbergasted to find two such infamous fugitives appearing unbidden at their doorstep, were not entirely sympathetic to the contingencies of their unlikely love story. These agents were, in their way, as aghast at this romance as were Unruh's former employers. And they were certainly not inclined to proffer mercy.

Unruh saw Sung one final time. Sung was hooded. Unruh glanced at him briefly, through bars. Sung was slumped, on a bench, his wrists in manacles, a white cloth hood over his head. Then Unruh was led away.

Their collective testimony, being quite valuable, did earn them a deal of sorts. The deal was this: Sung was relocated alone to Hawaii, his identity changed, his record expunged, to live out the rest of his natural days at an undisclosed location with an ankle bracelet under permanent house arrest. The two of them may yet have been allowed to live out their days together, in exile, but for the intercession of an ambitious scientist in the midst of a new experiment, seeking criminals of extraordinary circumstance.

Dr. Judy Holliday.

A specialist in memory.

Unruh was redirected to her care.

It was later explained to him that, given his sordid past and quite legendary exploits, he'd been chosen for a pilot program. The program involved amnesty, of a sort. His memories of criminality would be erased, with one exception. It had been determined that his crimes were of such singular remorselessness and brutality that the only effective deterrent, should he be allowed into this new program, would be the promise of safety and continued freedom, such as it was, for his friend John Sung. That was the deal. He would remember Sung, barely, but never see him again. He would be allowed to remember that there is a John Sung. And if Unruh misbehaved, even slightly, his friend Sung would be executed. That was how the agents insisted on referring to Sung: as Unruh's "friend." Unruh never protested this—he said very little during his interviews, beyond revealing the identities and histories and crimes of everyone he'd ever worked for—but he could sense the agents' barely modulated disgust, embedded in that euphemism "friend."

In order for this deterrent to be effective, the scientists assured Unruh that they would arrange for him to retain his memories of Sung. They'd erase his early life, his criminal exploits, all that would be gone, but he'd keep his memories of these last few years, the years blessed by something like happiness. The years with Sung.

This promise was all he had ever hoped for in his incarceration, and when they explained this to him, Unruh cried.

This decision—to indefinitely shelter two notorious killers in separate and relatively benign lodging, rather than lock them up forever in the isolation ward of a supermax facility or hang them both until dead—was not universally applauded among those few law enforcement officials who were privy to its arrangement. One such disgruntled official leaked news of it to the press. Unruh, who'd existed outside the public consciousness for the entire span of his career, suddenly became a kind of celebrity. His exploits were recounted in detail with outsized horror during nightly cable news debates. None of this he was aware of, locked up in solitary. Plus, he found the initial treatments at the hands of the memory specialists had left his mind a bit . . . muddied.

As it happened, despite their blithe assurances, these scientists weren't entirely confident they could erase *most* of his adult memories while leaving his attachment to Sung intact. So they mucked around in his mind for a while, engaged in some initial exploratory tinkering, tested a few pet theories, then closed it up and called it a day.

The effect of all this clumsy mucking is that Unruh, despite their assurances, only remembers bits and pieces of John Sung. For example, he remembers that such a man existed. He remembers that this man was dear to him. But what he looked like, his laugh, his touch—all of that is beyond Unruh's recollecting.

He cannot remember Sung's face.

His only memory is of the man in the hood, and of the fact that he cared about that man very much.

The looming murderous figure being evoked breathlessly on cable news and during hastily adjourned congressional hearings—the ravenous bogeyman conjured from the rantings of the hysterical press—that man would have been all but unrecognizable to Unruh himself, muddled and murmuring alone in his containment cell.

He never watched his own hearings.

He was simply loaded on a school bus. With seven other similarly befuddled folk.

There was a woman on the bus. To Unruh, she looked pregnant.

There was a man, dressed as a sheriff.

The eight of them were driven for hours over the Texan plains.

Then he was interviewed, briefly, by that weary-looking sheriff in his crumpled brown uniform, who welcomed him, along with all the others, in a garishly lit and chilly trailer, to a new town with a strange name, where the sheriff promised all of them they would not only live, but flourish.

He was given a new name.

William Wayne.

After a vice president and a movie star.

The sheriff stamped a paper, which he then signed and filed away.

"Welcome to Caesura," he said.

Wayne was assigned a modest cinder block bungalow in a very quiet part of town. There were so few of them living there back then.

On his very first night in his new home, he sat down at the kitchen table with a piece of white paper and a pencil.

He sat and stared at the paper for hours, pencil poised. Struggling to conjure, with great effort, the memory of a hooded figure in chains.

Then he started with the pencil. A few scratches, at first.

Hoping to draw a picture of the face of his friend John Sung.

"John Sung is dead," this woman says to him now.

John's daughter.

So he had a daughter.

Wayne shows her his drawing. Unfolds it on the coffee table. Smoothes it flat with a twisted hand.

He's worked on the drawing for eight years. It is remarkably detailed.

Lifelike, even.

"Tell me one thing," Wayne asks her. "Did he look like this?"

She studies the sketch. She strains to remember. Then she confesses, "I don't know. I don't remember him. That's why I brought you the photo. I hoped that you would."

Wayne sets the photo, the one she slipped under the door, the one Wayne hung in the window as a sign to her, as a beacon—the photo of young John Sung, smiling—next to his own drawing.

The likeness is remarkable.

"That's him," she says.

"Let me tell you what I do remember about him," says Wayne.

She starts to cry.

They both cry.

27.

FRAN LINGERS in the bedroom doorway, watching Isaac play, one last time. He's seated on the carpet of his bedroom with his race car, spinning it in noisy doughnuts, the car racing in circles to nowhere. Lost in his world. A child's world. That's all she ever wanted to build for him. Somewhere safe to get lost in.

"Isaac, honey," she says. "I need you to pack your things."

She says it as calmly as it is possible for her to say it in the context of this moment. She is mindful above all not to frighten him. "Just a few shirts and some pants. Quick, quick. Pick your favorites. I'll get a bag for us. Then we have to go."

"Go where?" he says, the car clutched in his hand.

"We're going to ask Sheriff Cooper to take us for a drive."

"In his truck?"

"Yes, that's right."

Walking briskly home from the library, a few torn-out articles stuffed in her pockets, she'd thought about going to find Cooper herself, but she wanted to be here, at home. So she flagged down

Walt Robinson on the main street as he wandered away from the intake trailer, looking somewhat dazed, even for him, and asked Walt to deliver her message. "Find Cooper and tell him we're ready," she said. "Tell him we'll be waiting at my house."

"Ready for what?" Robinson asked.

"He'll know," she said.

Now Isaac scrambles to his feet in his room. "What about my cards?" he says, hiking up the loose waist of his corduroy pants.

"Which cards?"

"From my treasure box."

She remembers his box, the one that was missing from under the dresser.

"Where did you put it? I checked its usual spot, but it wasn't there," she says.

"I took the box outside," Isaac says. "I buried it. I dug a hole in the yard."

"Why did you do that?" she says.

"I didn't want to lose the cards."

"But why would you lose them?"

"I didn't want the man to take them away."

Fran's stomach curdles.

"What man?" she asks, as gingerly as she can manage.

"The man who came to town. The man who gave the cards to me."

"Who did?"

"The man in the suit. At the movie theater."

She crouches on her haunches, grabs his shoulders, pulls him closer. Don't panic him, she thinks. Don't panic him, even as she herself is on the edge of losing it. He's already flinching, like he's worried he'll get in trouble, like she's about to lash out, and there must be a reason he hasn't told her any of this before.

"Tell me about that man."

"He gave me the cards. For free. As a present. After the movie."

"No, honey," she says. "You got those cards from the store. Remember? Spiro ordered them for you."

"Those were different ones. New ones," says Isaac. "The man gave me the first pack. I put it in my box."

"You didn't show me?"

"I put it in my box and put it under my dresser," says Isaac, his brown eyes brimming. He's in trouble, he knows it, he doesn't want to be in trouble.

Fran collects herself, or tries. "Where was Sheriff Cooper? When this man gave you the cards?"

"Someone was asking him something. A woman. He was distracted. The man gave me the cards and walked away."

"What did this man look like?"

"Like he was going to a funeral."

"Like he was sad?"

"No, like he was dressed up in a black suit. He didn't look sad."

"And he gave you those trading cards?"

"Yes. He cut my hair."

Fran squeezes his shoulders more tightly; she can't help it. "He did what?"

"He cut my hair. He said it was his job. Sheriff Cooper was distracted. It was crowded in the lobby."

"But, Isaac, your hair's not cut. Mommy would have noticed."

"He cut a little piece of my hair." Isaac grabs a clump of his brown curls in the back. "Right here."

Fran looks at it, fingering through the hair—there, she would barely have noticed, she *didn't* notice, his hair's so shaggy now, but there it is, a little chunk of his hair is gone, just a tiny snip.

"Did you tell Sheriff Cooper?"

"The man told me it was a secret."

"Did you tell anyone?"

"No. I put the cards in the box."

"Isaac, that didn't seem strange to you?"

"I don't know what goes on outside," he says. That's what he's always called the rest of the world: outside.

She considers her son. He's absolutely right. He doesn't know. How could he?

"Get your things," she says. "Let's go. We have to go right now."

"But my box—"

"We have to go. We have to leave it buried."

We'll get Cooper, she thinks, trying to calm herself. *We'll get to Cooper and we'll get in the truck and we'll just go. That's what he's always advocating.* She hasn't thought much further past that. But she knows if she asks him that he'll take them.

Isaac starts to cry now, fully. Softly at first, disbelieving, then he lapses into quiet hysterics. "I need those cards. I *need* them." Isaac's sputtering now, his face snot-streaked, his voice careening into the highest frequencies of childish urgency.

"We can't, Isaac—"

"But the *robots*. The robots will protect us. They have rocket-arms and lasers. They'll *protect* us and we can't leave them behind."

She looks at her son. She tries once again, for the one millionth time, to climb inside the workings of a child's mind. To know what's best to do right now. She has no idea. Finally, she grabs his arm.

A minute later, they're both outside, on their knees, together, Fran glancing every few moments up and down the empty street. The two of them, scrabbling with their fingers at the dry Texas dirt, digging up their modest yard, unburying a treasure.

Cooper stares at the door of the police trailer, crisscrossed with yellow SECURITY LINE DO NOT CROSS tape, and thinks, finally, *Fuck it.*

He pulls out a jackknife and slices through the tape, clears it away, then tries the knob.

At least they didn't padlock it.

The trailer's dark inside, but otherwise more or less how he last left it. The bloodstained chair, Gerald Dean's final resting place, still sits opposite his desk. He opens the desk drawer where he keeps the extra boxes of .38 rounds, but the boxes are gone, which he figured they would be, but he's no less disappointed.

He pulls his revolver out of his holster and flips the cylinder open.

He fired two bullets at the coydogs, missing both times, shoulder barking.

Dietrich fired two more bullets that hit.

Then there was the bullet for Gerald Dean.

Which leaves one bullet in his gun.

Just one.

Goddammit.

He rummages around in the drawer again, sifting the contents, searching, but finds nothing.

All right, then.

One bullet.

One bullet is worse than no bullets, he thinks, because at least with no bullets, you know you're beat.

One bullet can give you foolhardy ideas.

He flips the cylinder shut and holsters the pistol.

There's no reason to think your story isn't just as likely to hold up today as it was last night, he thinks. *As long as Robinson and Dawes stick to the facts, we should be done with these agents by nightfall, tomorrow at the latest. Maybe we can even get rid of Dietrich in the bargain. This could all work out okay.*

Then you take Fran, and the boy, and the money, and go.

Dawes appears in the doorway of the trailer behind him.

"They're ready for you," she says.

"Just give me a minute," he says, still hunting for anything else useful in his desk.

"Cal, they told me to send you right away."

Cooper looks up. "I believe that's the first time in recorded history you've ever called me Cal. Now you've got me good and nervous." She says nothing, so Cooper presses her. "Anything you'd like to share with me, Sid?"

Dawes looks him over. She feels, in this moment, very sad. And more than a little scared. She expected to find opportunity in that trailer. Maybe to find a way out. A path to something better, even. She found something else instead. Dawes thought about this on the walk over here—what she would say to him, and how much. She thought about what she knows about him. And as he stands waiting for her to answer him, she thinks—and is sure that she is right—*he doesn't know. He doesn't know what I know. He's like the rest of them. He doesn't know.*

"I think they're here to take the boy," she says.

"What?"

"They asked me about Fran. Not Colfax. Not Gable. Not Dean. Just Fran."

"What about her?"

"Where she is."

Cooper considers what Dawes is saying. He considers the truck. He considers the gun. He considers what it would take to find Fran and Isaac and go, now. He considers what he saw in the black cases in the intake trailer.

"So what did you tell them?" he says.

"I said I don't know. But I don't think that's going to slow them down. They know she's in the town. They just have to figure out which house."

There is no history between Dawes and Cooper now, no backstory, no hidden motives, no secrets, just the two of them, in the trailer, just this moment.

Cooper asks her, not sure what he'll do if she says no: "Are you with me? Or with them?"

She nods. "With you."

She'd thought about this on the walk over, too.

Cooper unholsters his pistol and holds it out to her grip-first.

"You ever fired a gun before, Deputy?"

"No, sir."

"Well, don't tell anyone that. Take this. Find her first. Start at her house. You know where it is. Go now and when you get there don't let anyone else in. Not until I get there. I'll come with my truck soon."

Dawes takes the gun. She's never even held a gun before. It's heavier than she expected.

"There's only one bullet in there," says Cooper. "Don't tell anyone that, either."

"And what about you?" she says.

Cooper takes off his heavy gun belt and lays it coiled on the desk. It's no use to him anymore. He thinks about taking his star off as well, but leaves it in place for now. "You said they want to see me, right? I guess I should go find out what they want."

28.

WAITING, WAITING, WAITING, he hates waiting, Dietrich thinks. Back in his bungalow, he stands in front of the full-length mirror on the wall. Head shaved, shirt off, at rest and calm and ready. Fingers tingling. He jangles his arms in front of the mirror like a boxer before a fight, watching himself. This is something they never let you have in solitary, he thinks—a full-length mirror. To see yourself. If there was a mirror in solitary, then there would be two of you. A companion. He looks over all his tattoos, the portraits etched on his skin, their eyes turned up to him admiringly. *At least I have all of you,* he thinks, and the portraits listen to him intently.

In solitary, all they give you is a concrete floor and concrete walls and a metal door and a hole to piss and shit in and two books to read and one hour a day to walk in circles in a cage outside. Otherwise, NO HUMAN CONTACT.

It said so right on the door to his cell.

He waited there, too. Waiting, waiting, waiting. Only his tattoos to keep him company.

Until these people sprung him.

Papers signed, deals made, favors swapped, money exchanged—whatever happened behind the scenes, he didn't care. All that mattered to him was that the door to his cell rolled back like a stone from a tomb.

Later, they explained to him everything that would be required of him, but he barely listened because if the choice was do this or go back into a tomb, then that wasn't really a choice at all. He remembers feeling . . . exhilarated, somehow, or heartened, maybe, sitting in the room in his jumpsuit, as they detailed their requirements, because finally someone had recognized a proper way to channel his, shall we say, enthusiasm. And all this after Dietrich had lasted less than a year in the military, even though the military had seemed like the perfect fit for him, everyone thought so. Lots of space and sand and emptiness and ammo and plenty of targets to choose from. They say they want you crazy, but they don't really want you crazy. Not Dietrich crazy. Sure, they'll overlook a certain amount of enthusiasm, but Dietrich doesn't have a certain amount of anything, and he certainly doesn't have a small amount of that.

An asshole lawyer—this was before the concrete closet and the piss hole and NO HUMAN CONTACT—once described him to a judge as *dead-eyed and remorseless,* and as he sat beside the lawyer in his borrowed suit, all his tattoos covered and muted, he thought, *Well that is the most inaccurate statement I have ever heard.* Remorseless, maybe, he'd grant the lawyer that, for how can a man truly know if he feels remorse? Having presumably never felt it?

So remorseless, maybe. But dead-eyed? *No, sir. That is demonstrably not accurate.*

Dietrich's seen many things. He's done many things. Through it all, his eyes have been very much alive.

He should have asked that lawyer before he killed him, *Tell me, do my eyes look dead to you?* As it was, it took two days for Dietrich to get the reek of that lawyer's cologne off his hands. It's hard to strangle someone when you're wearing handcuffs, but not impossible. If you're enthusiastic.

Kill your own lawyer and you'll wind up in prison. Kill a guard and you'll wind up in solitary.

Do the kinds of things that Dietrich's done and, apparently, you'll wind up here. In a town like this.

Waiting.

Luckily, in prison, he had his tattoos to keep him company. All these prior recipients of his attention. Twenty-three, at last count, or a torso and two arms' worth. The lawyer was number nineteen. The guard was number twenty. Each one of them, immortalized in ink and lovingly memorialized. Men, women, a few children, nearly two dozen faces, all smiling beatifically, their eyes turned up toward him, their likenesses etched over ribbons, flowers, dates. Some of them he knew for years, some he knew for a moment. But always the defining moment, he likes to think.

His dead. They travel with him everywhere.

He twists his torso before the mirror to inspect the latest additions, healing under the large white bandage on the small of his back. The flesh beneath still tender. He peels the bandage away. It was hard to find a virgin patch of skin to fit three new faces in.

Three faces: the sheriff and his two deputies.

Getting them done already, before he even arrived here, was premature, he acknowledges that, and cocky, too, but we all need to be a little bit cocky sometimes. And it's not like he expected there to be a tattoo parlor in this godforsaken outpost.

The others he'll just have to try to remember, once he's done.

When he's finished here, he won't have an inch of blank skin left to cover.

There's a knock at his door. Dietrich reattaches the bandage, pulls on his white linen shirt, then opens the door. It's one of the agents. The spiky-haired one. He's carrying a large black case. He's wearing sunglasses and has a toothpick jostling around in his mouth like a fool. Dietrich recalls a time in the prison yard before solitary when they still let him mix with people, when he plucked a toothpick from a man's mouth, then used it to put out both the man's eyes.

"About time," Dietrich says.

"Dick Dietrich? Is that what they're calling you now?"

"Let me ask you something, and be honest," says Dietrich. "Does that sound like a Negroid name to you?"

Rigo ignores the question and steps into the bungalow, toting his large black case, and Dietrich closes the door behind him. "I understand you've been causing some trouble, Dick, since you've arrived," says Rigo. "The sheriff asked me to check in on you personally. He seems very worried about you. Oh, and I brought you a present."

He sets the black case on the coffee table and steps away from it. Dietrich opens it. Pulls out the AR-15 he finds inside. Hefts it to his shoulder. Sights it.

"Is this it?" he asks.

"You need more?"

"God gave me two trigger fingers," Dietrich says. "I don't like to leave one idle."

Rigo hands him a 9 mm pistol from his waistband. "That's mine, so take good care of it." He looks around the modest bungalow. "You ever gone canned hunting, Dick? It's a very popular activity out here in Texas. You go to someone's ranch, some huge parcel of land somewhere that's all fenced off, and then they loose a bunch of livestock for you to hunt down. Deer, elk, bears, whatever you request."

"That doesn't sound very sportsmanlike," says Dietrich.

"No, but it has its appeal," says Rigo. "By the way, that thing with the dogs—that was excessive, even for you."

"They weren't dogs. They were coydogs."

Rigo sucks on his toothpick. "What's the difference?"

"You told me to sow chaos. I sowed chaos."

"I didn't tell you to set animals on fire."

"The opportunity presented itself."

"And while we're on the subject," says Rigo, "when eight-year-old boys vandalize a place, they don't typically write *Damnatio Memorae* on the wall. Were you just being cute, or were you trying to get caught?"

"I don't see how it matters either way," says Dietrich. He's focusing on that toothpick. He's starting to feel annoyed. One benefit of solitary is that you don't have to answer other people's idiotic questions. "So when do we get this party started?"

Rigo turns and looks this man over, with his shaved head and his cockeyed smile and his loony tattoos. He seems every bit as crazy as they had been promised. Or warned. Sometimes, it's so hard to tell the difference.

"The boy. And the sheriff. They're off-limits," Rigo says.

"Fuck me. The sheriff, too?" says Dietrich. "He and I have a real rapport."

"He's with us."

"Does he know that?"

"Not yet."

Dietrich nods. No need to openly question orders. Because accidents happen. Crossfire, and such. "Got it. The boy. And the sheriff."

Rigo walks back to the front door, then stops with his hand on the knob. He takes one more moment to indulge himself and contemplate how exactly he'll put Dietrich down when the moment comes. Quick headshot, like a beloved dog, or something in the body, something low and painful, that leaves you to bleed out like a bitch? *I'll just go with the flow,* he thinks. *Do what feels right in the moment.*

Rigo picks the toothpick from his mouth and tosses it casually on the plush carpet, then says, "Twenty minutes. Not before. I need time to thank the good sheriff for all he's done for us."

29.

IT'S A SUNNY DAY and the late afternoon's bright, but Fran's got the curtains drawn tight, as she waits on the sofa in her living room under the light of a single lamp. Isaac's curled up and reading his library novel beside her, his unearthed treasure box nestled on his lap. She's so lost in the wreckage of her recollected memories that she doesn't hear the knocking at first. Isaac prods her. "Mom, there's someone at the door. Mom—"

She listens. Sure enough. *Fucking finally,* she thinks, and jumps up from the sofa. Cooper's here. She knew he would come. Lord knows, they've had their history. But that's one thing she's learned about him. He knows when he's needed.

"All right, Isaac, grab your things and let's go," she says. He grabs his backpack, all packed up. As for her, she didn't pack anything. There's nothing here she cares to take with her, except the book from the library. She'll keep that.

Another knock. More insistent.

Okay, Cooper, we're coming, she thinks.

She motions Isaac over toward her, then gathers herself, and opens the door—ready to crack a joke to Cooper about how he certainly took his precious fucking time riding over on his big white horse.

But it's not Cooper. It's that woman. The one in the black pantsuit. The agent. She's got two other agents behind her, the red-headed one and the big one. Immediately Fran knows something terrible is about to happen.

"Fran Adams?" says Santayana.

"That's right," Fran says.

"I have someone who wants to speak with you." The agent holds out a flat electronic tablet. She swipes the screen, once, twice, before it pops brightly to life.

"We're good, sir," Santayana says to someone, not Fran.

Fran looks at the agent, then back at the screen. There's a man sitting at a desk. He's looking straight into the camera. Straight at her. Friendly face. He clears his throat. She knows this man. It's the man from the TV in the Laundromat. The man from the article.

Mark Vincent.

The American Miracle.

"Hi, Carla," he says. "Long time no see."

"Calvin Cooper."

Cooper sits in a plastic chair. Rigo sits opposite him. The rest of the intake trailer is empty. The other agents are elsewhere, so it's just the two of them, under the bright, buzzing fluorescents. Rigo's sunglasses have been removed, folded, pocketed, so Cooper is free now to contemplate the strange and icy blankness of Rigo's eyes. Rigo smiles, cordially, though his smile is lacking something, Cooper can't place it, but whatever it is that's missing is the very thing that usually animates a smile.

Cooper asks: "So what do you want with me, Rigo?"

"Nothing."

"Really? So why did you call me here?"

"For your own protection." Rigo crosses his legs, placing one ankle on the opposite knee. His limbs give him the angular aspect of a mantis. He checks his watch, then crosses his arms, as though to indicate that he's said all he has to say.

"That's it?" says Cooper.

"That's it."

Cooper stands. "I appreciate the sentiment, but if you'll excuse me, I have things to do."

"Be my guest. I just can't vouch for your safety if you leave."

Cooper pauses. "What does that mean?"

Rigo looks him over. "Tell me, Cooper, what are you planning to do with all that money?"

"What money?"

Rigo laughs. He wags a long finger at Cooper, like Rigo's a pit boss dealing with a card shark who's already been caught but is still trying to wriggle free. "Two hundred thousand dollars. That's a hell of a retirement package."

"I don't know what you're talking about," says Cooper.

"Don't worry, I don't care about the shootings," Rigo says. He checks his watch again. "I mean, I care about them a little bit. I paid for them, after all."

30.

FRAN WILL NEVER REMEMBER what he said after he said hello to her, and for the rest of her life, she'll always wonder. That face, those eyes, that smile, and then he spoke, for what seemed like forever, but she doesn't remember a word of it.

Because in that moment, when he called her Carla, it came back to her. All of it.

She was a student, a scholar. Imagine that. A poet. She loved books. Ideas. Criticism. Sontag, in particular. Young and mired for what seemed like an eternity in the weeds of a PhD. He had an air about him. There was the money, sure. But what the money also affords. A chance to look beyond the next moment. That was the luxury he represented.

Great things awaited him, too, everyone could feel it. She felt it, like an electric charge. He was a natural politician. He courted her, like an electorate. He won her, like an election.

They were inseparable at first. She was at his side, always. Her devotion to him became its own kind of endorsement as he sought to launch his political career. He had money, plenty of that, which, for many voters, was qualification enough. They were happy to lift him up onto their shoulders in hopes that a shimmer of his pixie dust might shower down on them.

They married. In the hour before the ceremony, doing her makeup, alone, she had her first tremor of doubt. There was a part of him that was not accessible to her, she knew that, she couldn't deny it. *Maybe that's what it is to be such a success,* she thought. *Everyone wants all of you, all the time, so you can never truly give everything to anyone.* But he definitely had his own sequestered life. His own sequestered self. Kept his own hours. A locked office at home. She didn't pry. She understood she wasn't privy to those activities, nor should she be. She wondered about affairs, of course, but that didn't seem at all like the man she knew. If anything, he seemed uninterested in those kinds of pursuits, in the bedroom, except when it came to talk of family.

They would definitely have a family.

They kept a gun in the house. For protection. You must. A public figure like that? She liked to practice with it at the firing range while he was away on business. *Bang, bang.* Blow off steam. When they fought, which became more and more frequent after the marriage but not so common as to become truly alarming, the firing range became her retreat. At the range, she discovered, you can imagine whomever you want to superimposed over that paper target. You wear earmuffs. No one bothers you. They just give you some bullets and leave you to your business.

Bang, bang.

A few years into the marriage, as he got serious about running for the Senate, she became more suspicious about affairs. How could she not? With him absent, so often? So many women around him with the exact same look in their eyes that she'd once had? How could she miss it? She *owned* that look. She *invented* it.

She quelled her suspicions with more long hours at the firing range. She became friendly with the owner. He flirted, and not subtly, either. Adjusting her stance from behind. Her husband was busy gearing up for his Senate run. They had the money, they had the organization, they had the endorsements. An entire apparatus was being built up around him. He was never home, ever, and she wasn't studying anymore or even pretending she'd go back and finish her degree, or doing much of anything, really, except shooting. The having-a-kid part was going nowhere, too, not that it would have helped. Her therapist called it depression, and gave her pills, then different pills. She checked his phone when he left it unsupervised, looking for texts, photos, anything. Finding nothing. Why was she so jealous? Maybe she was the one who wanted to stray.

The shooting instructor started giving her rounds of ammo on the house.

How did she find out in the end? It took some doing. The locked office. The passwords. He wasn't one to get tripped up by some stray sext. She knew she had to get clever. There were unsavory characters hanging around all the time now, like that one bodyguard who was super-creepy, Perry Garrett, and that weird little toad of a man, Lester Vogel. Her husband long ago sold the analytics firm that had made him unimaginably rich and was now spending most of his time focused on his Senate bid and, if not that, on different boards. Different committees. Donating to some institute he'd lately become obsessed with. The Fell Institute. He swore its techniques would change history. But he kept everything else in his life well hidden. A black box she became obsessed with opening. After all, how can you be married to a black box?

And no one else would have opened it, no one would have found out, not ever, no one could have, except for her. Except someone with that kind of time on their hands, and that kind of access, and that kind of motivation, and that kind of paranoia that keeps you obsessively prying. To everyone else, he seemed normal, admirable. Those who knew—they must have, that small circle—they were silenced by money, or the promise of power, or the shackles of similar sins.

Maybe he even wanted her to know, to find out, in his arrogance, in his sickness. Maybe he half-suspected she would find out, and assumed that, if she did, she'd say nothing, and maybe he would have been right.

Because if it had only been affairs, she probably would have stayed silent.

The locked office. The late nights.

She got access, finally. Cracked passwords. She found files. On his computer.

Those videos. The children.

She never knew he had those kinds of appetites.

To be honest, she'd never let herself believe that anyone did.

And she did say nothing, at first. It would ruin him, but it would ruin her, too, assuming anyone believed her. So she turned the interrogation on herself. How had this happened? How did she not know earlier? Maybe she saw something in him before and refused to acknowledge it. Or maybe she was rotten, too, somehow, to be attracted to him. To find herself in his orbit. After all, she fell in love with him. *You are damaged, too, you must be,* she thought.

She said nothing to anyone else. How could she? What would she say? Who would believe her?

And at the firing range, she began to imagine the paper target was herself.

Bang, bang.

And that started to feel like the only way out for her.

God may forgive, but He rarely exonerates.

And, who knows, maybe that's how it would have ended for her—with the tycoon's increasingly distant and press-averse and pill-dependent wife finally taking her own life, a quiet, shocking suicide, in some tragic, unforeseen swoon. Cut to the sorrowful interviews during which he'd pause, and choke up, and struggle to compose himself. Start writing the redemptive feature stories about his loss, and moving on, and his selfless and well-intentioned warnings about how best to study your own loved ones for the tragic signs. He'd have been fine, and she'd have been free, so maybe that's how it should have ended. Maybe that's what would have happened.

If the test hadn't read positive.

Because it was only when the blue indicator on the pregnancy test said positive that she dropped the stick in the toilet and flushed it and went to the bedroom and got the gun she'd practiced with for so many hours and walked up behind him as he sat in his office at his desk where she'd found all his secrets and shot him in the back of the head.

She remembers now.

The bang. The numb ache of the recoil. The smell of gunpowder.

She must have missed him.

A little bit.

Even with all those hours of practice.

She didn't know she missed at the time. She was going to shoot them both, she remembers. Him and her. Him first.

But the truth is, she hesitated, when it came to her. She had the time to do it. But she wavered.

Thinking of that baby that only she knew she had inside her.

And in that single moment of wavering, an aide had time to intervene; he heard the shot, ran in, grabbed her wrist, yanked the gun away from her chin, where she'd finally planted it, so by the time she pulled the trigger again, it was too late, she was just shooting at the ceiling.

Then the ambulance. Then the hospital. Then the prison.

Then the deal.

No memory of any of it. Until now.

It never went to trial. The apparatus intervened. His aides brokered something different. They must have known he might survive. They must have seen it coming.

Instead, she'd be warehoused away, her memory wiped clean, part of a new program, run by that institute her husband had donated so much money to, the one he'd been so obsessed with. Because the most important thing to them at that point was that she could never tell anyone. What she knew had to disappear. It didn't matter how many years they sent her body away for. It was her memories they cared about. They had so much invested in him, and nothing invested in her. So it couldn't go to court. What mattered was that she could never reveal, to lawyers or reporters or to anyone else, just *why* she did what she did. What she'd discovered about him. About his appetites.

So a deal was engineered in lieu of a trial. After all, he was still alive, barely, on life support. But there was hope. She didn't know that. Soon, she didn't know anything.

They arranged to have her mind erased, so she could never tell anyone what she knew.

Trouble is, none of them knew about the baby.

And the baby was born in the Blinds.

"Carla, you look well," he says to her now. That face. That smile. That voice. Bringing it all back.

Then he says a little louder, to the agent holding the tablet: "Yes, that's her. That's definitely her." Then he says: "And who's this little man?"

Santayana angles the tablet's camera down toward Isaac, who cowers, clinging to his mother's leg.

"Hey there, you must be Isaac, right?" says the man on the tablet screen, warmly smiling as Santayana centers the tablet's camera on the boy's face. "Isaac, I'm so pleased to see you. I'm your father and I can't wait to meet you in person. These people are here to bring you home."

31.

COOPER SITS in the trailer with Rigo.

Cooper says finally, "How did you know I'd say yes?"

"I didn't, until you did."

"And if I hadn't?"

"We'd have found some other reason to intervene. The shootings are a convenient excuse, of course, but we could have cooked up something else. Some reason for the Institute to shut it all down. You fucked us up pretty good with that faked suicide, though. It's hard to come charging in, guns blazing, just because some lonely old man offs himself."

"So someone hired you to kill Colfax and Gable and Dean."

"No, dummy, I hired *you* to do that."

"But why those three?"

"Colfax was a test," Rigo says. "Just to see if you'd actually do it. I figured if you weren't willing to kill a psychopath like Colfax with sixty bodies on him, then we'd need to go to plan B. But you were. And you did. So we moved on to Gable. Then Dean."

"For what? Bounties?"

"For closure." He motions to the walls. "Is this trailer bulletproof?"

"I doubt it," says Cooper. He doesn't doubt it; he knows it isn't. There's only one building in the whole encampment that's fortified in that way, and it's not the one they're sitting in right now.

"Then we might want to get to higher ground," says Rigo. "Don't worry about the money, by the way. It's still waiting for you. The full two hundred. It's still yours. A deal's a deal."

"So what are we waiting for now?" says Cooper.

"Are you familiar with the phrase 'active shooter'?" says Rigo. He switches to an official-sounding tone. "During our recent visit to investigate the troubling incidents in Caesura, including several deaths and some unexplained acts of vandalism and animal cruelty, one of my men was overwhelmed by a particularly dangerous resident, a recent arrival, who then went on a killing spree. Thankfully, we were able to intervene and subdue him with our superior training and firepower, but, given the heavy casualties to the town's populace, the decision was made by the Institute to shut down the program." Rigo pauses, then says, "At least, that's the story we're going to tell everyone, once we're back in the outside world. Don't worry, Sheriff. Not to spoil the ending, but we're going to make it out alive."

"Who's we?"

"You, me, my team, and the person we came for."

"Fran Adams," says Cooper.

"No, but you're getting warmer."

There's a long, suspended moment of silence before the next thing happens, while Cooper contemplates just how fucked he is, how fucked Fran is, how fucked they all are, how fucked the town is.

And then the next thing happens.

Far away, but audible, and unmistakable.

Pop pop pop.

Gunshots.

And again.

Pop pop.

Cooper looks at Rigo. Rigo shrugs. He pulls his sunglasses out of his pocket. "Don't worry, Sheriff. Dietrich knows who to avoid. The boy, for one."

And the realization of what exactly is about to unfold surges into Cooper's heart and overwhelms him, like water flooding the lungs of a drowning man.

"What about the boy's mother?" Cooper finally brings himself to ask. "What happens to her?"

Rigo winces. "Honestly, I don't think she's going to make it."

32.

ON THE FOURTH KNOCK, Ginger Van Buren answers. She finds Dick Dietrich standing in her doorway.

"Good afternoon, ma'am," he says politely.

"You killed my babies," she says. "Shot them dead in the street." She's dressed in a filmy caftan. Her face is deeply lined and pale and her eyes are red-rimmed from two days of crying.

"I'd argue that, by the time I found them, their fate was already determined. May I come in?" He stands in shadow, framed in the doorway, a silhouette against the sunlight. She squints at him. The sun today is so bright.

"Honestly, I'm not up to visitors."

"Just for a moment," he says. "There's something coming and I thought it only fair to warn you. When it gets here, it's best that you're inside."

Well, why not, Ginger thinks, and, to be honest, she's not even really thinking anymore. She looks him over, this strange man, his head shorn, with all his tattoos, and thinks back over her life, or what scant parts of it she can recollect, and all of it seems like a dream since the other night. This whole strange coda, this house, this town, these people, it all seems like an errant epilogue to a much longer, more elaborate story that she can't, for the life of her, recall. Even her pets are gone. All she can hear now is the absence of their howling. It's deafening.

Well, why not, she thinks, and invites him in without another word, and when she turns, he's already closed the door behind them both so the living room's plunged back into its former gloom. He's already pulling something from the back of his pants and wielding it and she sees now that it's a gun.

"I'm sorry, but the thing I warned you was coming?" he says. "It's already here."

Well, why not, she thinks.

Dietrich knows the three shots are loud enough that people will notice.

Three shots.

Two more.

Well, why not.

The gun stuck back in the waistband of his pants, Dietrich walks back out into the sunlight on the porch, where he left the assault rifle propped up against the wall beside the front door, so as not to startle her. He hoists the rifle up by its strap and slings it over his shoulder. Then he spots that other woman, what's her name, the new one, the pretty neighbor, the nervous one from the intake trailer with the nice expensive hair, the one they promised to move across town, coming out in her housecoat to her porch to see what the noise is all about.

Cooper's mind searches for a plan. Comes up empty.

But Cooper's fists have already formulated a plan.

The plan: Punch Rigo. Then punch Rigo again.

He knows he needs another, better plan.

If Cooper's learned anything in the course of his life, it's that the plans his fists come up with are never to be trusted. So he stalls. "What are you going to do about Dietrich?"

"Let him roam. For now," Rigo says.

"Do you really think you can control a man like that?"

"Control? No. Kill? Yes. That we can do. You have to understand, Dietrich's the man nobody wants—not the military, not the prison system—so it was easy to obtain his services for our special purposes."

"What's in it for him?" says Cooper. "Money?"

"There's money involved, but someone like that? Money is never his motivation." Rigo perches on the edge of a desk, leaning back on his arms, legs crossed at the ankles, like a man who's got nowhere to be and all day to get there. "As far as our friend Dietrich knows, we're all leaving together with what we came for, one big happy family. I've got two of my best men tailing him to make sure that doesn't happen. But for now, we'll let him, you know, work out his issues. All you and I need to do is sit tight and make sure we don't get caught in the crossfire."

Cooper's still searching for that plan. Still coming up empty.

While he searches, his fists get impatient.

Decide to act alone.

Fucking fists, Cooper thinks, as he hoists one. *Okay, here we go.*

Rigo's surprised at the swing, a clumsy, glancing one, given that he and Cooper were just moments ago discussing their newly revealed role as co-conspirators. Rigo dodges it easily and the blow doesn't really connect. When Cooper takes another shot with his left fist, because what the hell, this is apparently the plan now, Rigo fends that one off easily, too. Then Rigo reaches for his pistol, which isn't there. That's right, he gave it to Dietrich. So he holds up his hands instead.

"Cooper—Cooper!" Rigo says, wheeling back. "You and I are on the same side. We're about to walk out of here—"

Third swing. In Cooper's experience, if the first two don't land, you shouldn't expect better results with number three. Yet here it comes, nonetheless. "Fuck you, Rigo," he says, roundhousing like a drunk. "Get out of my town."

Rigo feints again, easily. He's all arms and angles. "Don't worry," he says, inching back to keep his distance. "Once Dietrich gets his jollies, we'll take care of him. We're not going to leave him alive."

But Cooper keeps coming, keeps swinging. "You never should have come here, Rigo. You never should have stepped out from behind that fax machine." His fists are angry, jumpy, anxious, and Cooper's not inclined to hold them back. "The smartest thing you ever did," he says, taking another hack at Rigo, "was make me look each of those three men in the eyes. Colfax, Gable, Dean. Because when they saw what was coming, they knew that they deserved it. Even if they didn't remember why, they *knew*. And that made it easy for me." Cooper lunges again, flailing. Rigo dances away. "And the dumbest thing you ever did, you fucking idiot, was come here and show your face to me. Because now I can look *you* in the eye, Rigo. And I see exactly what you deserve."

Rigo circles behind a desk. "In about an hour, we're leaving. You can either come with us or we can leave you here with Dietrich until he's done. Believe me, he won't stop until he runs out of bullets—he won't even stop then. He'll rip your fucking throats out with his teeth."

As if on cue, from the distance: *pop pop pop pop pop.*

Cooper knows what the sound means. It's the town being slaughtered, one by one.

"Leave now, for all I care," Cooper says. "But you're not taking that boy."

"Not to mention the two hundred thousand dollars," says Rigo. "You ready to forfeit that?"

Cooper stops. He's winded. His punching is getting him nowhere. He needs a new plan, pronto.

"I didn't think so," says Rigo. "So let's stop this—"

"I have a different idea."

"What's that?"

"I'm going to kick you in the balls," Cooper says.

Rigo squints. "You're what—?"

Then Cooper kicks him in the balls.

Cooper learned this in a lifetime full of barfights. If you try to kick someone in the balls, you almost never connect, because everyone instinctually protects their balls. But if you *tell* someone you're going to kick them in the balls, they get momentarily distracted, because they're busy thinking about how much it sucks to get kicked in the balls. Then whammo.

Rigo whimpers and drops.

Cooper kicks him in the balls again.

Well, that didn't solve much, not in the big picture, thinks Cooper, *and it definitely cost me $200,000.*

Rigo murmurs on the floor.

Cooper kicks him in the face, for good measure.

That one was free.

Then he runs out of the trailer, into the empty street, toward the gunfire, toward Fran, and toward the boy.

33.

AGENTS COREY AND BIGELOW WATCH DIETRICH from a distance as he ambles his way down the road, stopping occasionally to heft his rifle and fire staccato shots into bungalow windows, moving with the lazy languor of a boy skipping stones in a pond on his way home from school. If Dietrich spots someone in the distance skittering across the roadway toward shelter, he sights the rifle and cuts them down expertly. Corey and Bigelow lay back, a good fifty yards or so, weapons holstered, ostensibly as Dietrich's backup. Their real task, however, is to tail him and, once he's managed to cleanse a good portion of the residents, take him down. There's no way they're letting a psychopath like Dietrich come back to the civilized world. He'll be cut down in a valiant but belated effort by the agents to save the poor people of this town. This will be the official story, anyway.

So neither Corey nor Bigelow is what you'd call alarmed as they watch Dietrich at work. In fact, they both regard his display of cold skill with a kind of professional envy. Dietrich is alert yet relaxed, his movements efficient, his aim unerring, and his results inescapable. Both agents, at various times, have been involved in tasks that required certain proficient and lethal resolutions, so killing, per se, does not unsettle them. They are struck, however, by Dietrich's peculiar strain of passionate competence—how he moves with the air of a man who is expert at, and deeply loves, what he is doing. The agents comment on it to each other in low tones. Neither Corey nor Bigelow is concerned in the least that they'll be able to take down Dietrich when the time comes: there's two of them; they're well trained and well armed; and, as best they know, Dietrich has no idea what's coming. Which allows them to regard his movements through the town as a kind of performance. A seminar, of sorts. Professional development.

They aren't worried at all, even when they momentarily lose sight of him at fifty yards when he seems to circle behind a distant bungalow. They aren't concerned when they travel down the road a bit farther and he's not on the opposite side of the bungalow or, as expected, in the yard of the house adjacent. They're not frightened, not yet, as they realize that Dietrich seems to be actively trying to evade them, though, at this point, Bigelow has the presence of mind to unholster his gun. Corey, for his part, does start to wonder, with an almost clinical curiosity, if maybe they, too, should have come armed with assault rifles. They'd discussed it but decided against it. But they're not scared, not really, as they instinctually separate from each other and scan the yards of the clustered houses, looking for signs that he's ducked inside somewhere, both of their pistols now drawn—and by the time they're both beginning to feel the first invasive tendrils of cold fear, almost simultaneously, the crisp shots from Dietrich's rifle, one-two, have felled them. After that, whatever they might have been feeling is left to pool in the dirt.

Dietrich makes a show of stepping over their bodies as he walks back to the middle of the thoroughfare. The AR-15 is held lightly in his hands. He looks at the dying agents with contempt. He wonders just how stupid Rigo is.

Stupid enough to give him an assault rifle, apparently.

No one's coming out to their porches to investigate the noises anymore. Everyone's hiding behind closed doors and drawn curtains, or running in the shadows for shelter like frightened children.

So it's just Dietrich walking down the middle of the road like death come calling. Periodically raising his rifle and squeezing the trigger and *pop pop pop* into doors, into windows. He likes to watch the doors splinter, the windows buckle.

He walks up the steps of a porch to a house. Fires the rifle through the door four times.

Pop pop pop pop.

Watches the door blister. He reloads the rifle. Then kicks in the door.

Why this house? Why not this house? he thinks, as he steps inside.

He walks into the living room. Finds it empty.

So he walks into the kitchen. Finds a woman crouching in the corner, by the cabinets, crying. He recognizes her. It's that librarian.

"What horrible thing did you do in your past, I wonder," Dietrich says, "that you wound up living in this place?"

She looks up at him. Says nothing. Just cries.

He hefts the rifle.

Pop pop.

Canned hunting, just like Rigo said.

"You need to come with us," says Santayana. "Both of you."

"No," Fran says.

"Ma'am, I'm not asking."

"No," Fran says again.

Then they all hear the noise in the distance.

Pop pop.

Everyone knows what it is.

Santayana looks at the boy, then back at his mother. She opens her blazer, giving the mother a glimpse of her holstered pistol. She'd rather not pull it out in front of the boy, but she will, if need be. That's the message. She closes the blazer.

"We can protect you both. Think of the boy."

Pop pop pop, still in the distance.

Fran's voice catches so hard as she says what she says that she barely nudges out the words. "He's the only thing I ever think about."

"Ma'am, please," says Santayana. The two other agents form a solid wall behind her.

There's nowhere to run, and nothing to do, and Fran knows the world has come for her. No matter what, the world will find her. If not here, then at the next place, or the next place after that. Her eight years of hiding out are over and it's all coming for her now. She wonders what she should have done differently, until her wondering is interrupted.

Pop pop.

"Really, this is what's best for everyone—" says Santayana.

"No, I don't think so," comes a different voice. Santayana turns toward the street to look. They all do.

And there, in the street, is Dawes. Holding a revolver. Leveled at the agents on the porch. She's wearing a puffy brown winter coat, too, for some reason, even though it's got to be ninety degrees in this sun. She keeps the revolver steady. Dawes has never held a gun before, let alone held one on a person. Santayana can tell that. Even Fran can tell.

"Fran, bring Isaac and come down here with me," Dawes says.

"Where are you planning to go?" Santayana asks, with a contemptuous barb in her voice.

Pop pop pop in the distance again. Dawes does her best not to flinch at the sound. "Come on, Fran."

Fran grabs Isaac's arm and they start toward the steps, and Santayana grabs her by the elbow and Fran yanks her arm free and slaps Santayana, hard, with the back of her hand, as hard as she has ever hit anyone. Santayana falters, then straightens, and yanks her weapon free, and turns it on Fran, then sees the boy's eyes widen. In anger, she swings her gun toward Dawes in the street and fires. A loud shot in the quiet of the afternoon, much louder than those distant pops.

Dawes's brown puffy jacket coughs a small burst of white feathers, and then is stained suddenly red. Dawes yelps like a kicked dog, her cry chasing the loud bark of the shot.

Santayana turns back to Fran. "Now let's go—"

"No." Dawes is still standing. Her gun leveled again. She knows not to pull the trigger, not yet. She only has one bullet, after all.

The other two agents pull their guns now and draw them on Dawes.

Fran bolts, dragging Isaac. They scramble down the steps to stand with Dawes. The three of them, in the street. Other neighbors have come to their windows now, drawn to the source of the nearby shot. Dawes struggles to keep the three black-suited agents on the porch all clustered together in her gun sight. Her arm is shaking badly. She can't tell how bad the gunshot is, but she's still standing, so that's something. As an EMT, she learned about trauma, and how gunshots are the worst, because they have no regard for their surroundings. They're not polite. They tear everything up.

She keeps her eyes on the agents. Her arm shakes. The gun dances.

"Santayana, stand down." Another voice now. A new one, from behind them all, farther down the street. Dawes can't turn to look, she doesn't dare to, but she knows who that voice belongs to.

Cooper.

Fran turns to see him walking slowly toward them all. No gun. His hands held up, palms out, in surrender. Speaking calmly. "The four of us, we're going this way, to wait out what's coming," Cooper says, pointing a thumb back over his shoulder. "Back to the chapel. Me, Dawes, Fran, and the boy. It's not safe for any of us out here."

"I can't let you do that," Santayana says. "He's coming with us."

Pop pop pop, in the distance. The intermittent sound makes their tiny tableau seem comical, inconsequential.

"Where's Agent Rigo?" Santayana asks.

"He sent me," says Cooper. "To gather up everyone and get them inside. We've got bigger problems right now, you know that." Cooper takes a few steps closer to the porch, his hands still raised. Once his back is to Fran and the boy, he's says quietly, but tersely, in a clipped whisper, to Santayana: "We're in this together, remember? Just let me take the boy somewhere safe. There's a place we can hide while all this plays out. After that, we can take him out of here."

Santayana considers this. While she does, Cooper says: "But we have to get out of the streets. Now."

Pop pop pop pop pop. Getting closer.

Santayana holsters her gun.

Cooper turns back to his party and claps his hands once. "All right. Let's go. Come on." Then he shouts and motions to the people watching from their windows. "Everyone—follow Dawes." Some of them come outside, hustling, while others just stare dumbly, paralyzed, or close the curtains again. Cooper turns back to Santayana. "I'm going to gather everyone in the chapel. It's in the center of town at the end of the main street. I need to get everyone safe while we deal with Dietrich. After that, we'll sort this other business out. All right?"

"All right," says Santayana.

The group of them starts to walk away down the street, Dawes hobbling, leaning on Fran, the four of them trailing a caravan of frightened citizens. Cooper says to Dawes, "You okay?"

"I can walk. It hurts."

Cooper pulls out a ring of keys. "Take these. Take everyone to the chapel." She nods. "Grab anyone else that you see," he says. "As many as will fit inside. Once you get to the chapel, ring the bells." Then he lowers his voice, almost whispering. "Then you lock that fucking door behind you."

"What about you?"

"Just lock that door. I'll get there."

She nods.

"You did good," he says.

"I know," she says.

Cooper turns to Fran. Says in a hoarse whisper, "Keep him safe. That's all you need to worry about."

"Cooper—" It all comes now, undammed, in a sob. "I remember."

He tugs her close and kisses her hair. "Just keep him safe."

Pop pop pop.

He turns back to Dawes.

"Now give me the gun," he says.

Dawes hesitates. Then she understands. "Cooper, that's *suicide.*"

"Just give me the gun."

She hands it to him. He opens the cylinder, checks it again, snaps it shut.

"You saved me the bullet," he says.

"I'm sorry that's all I have for you."

"Well, if I'm lucky," he says, "I'll only need one."

34.

BUSTER FORD HEARS THE SHOOTING and he knows it's coming closer. He sits in his living room, cradling his Bible, thinking about the fences. How, after all these years here—and he's been here eight years, the full eight, it's hard to believe, but eight years already, how time flies—you stop noticing them. You stop noticing how the fences rise and cut into the endless horizon, claiming their portion of the sky. You stop mentally noting how their mottled shadows stretch across the dirt every day at dusk, like a net thrown over the town. He's always wondered about the utility of the fences, because you're ostensibly free to leave at any time.

Of course, the fences are supposedly there to keep people out, too. But apparently that hasn't worked out too well.

Pop pop pop.

He cradles the Bible. He's thought of leaving the town, many times. His memory is more intact than most. He remembers almost his entire childhood. He's in his early sixties now, so a natural erosion has kicked in, on top of what they took away. But he grew up in Pennsylvania, he knows that, just outside Lancaster. His father slowing to steer the car around an Amish carriage as it clip-clopped along at the side of the highway. He remembers the candies he used to get as a kid at the Amish market on weekends and how, later, as a teen, he'd watch the Amish girls in their bonnets, how pretty they looked. He remembers one girl, in particular, he'd see every weekend at her family's booth, who was the most beautiful girl he'd ever seen. He tried to talk to her once, but he wasn't sure what to say. His friends made crude jokes about those Amish women. He never made those jokes.

His memories get a bit blurry after that; that must have been when his life went astray. But he knows, if he ever does leave the Blinds, he'll head to Lancaster, and look for that woman.

Pop pop.

The bungalow has too few rooms for him to hide in, he knows that, too. He could run, but there's the problem of the fences. You can only run so far. Besides, he's old, and no longer much for running.

The silences after the shots are the worst part. Then more shots, sharp reports, getting closer. Like the knock of a census-taker, stopping at every door on the block, approaching yours.

He sits in the living room with his Bible and summons all his energy and tries to remember. *If only I could know what it is that I did. How I ended up here. Inside these fences.*

He hears more gunfire like insistent knocking, louder still, until he realizes that the knocker has found his door.

When Bette hears the rapid staccato of shots, far away at first but getting closer, she moves to rise from Wayne's couch. She thinks that she will run. Or find the sheriff. Or find the agents. The ones who are supposed to take her home.

Wayne reaches out and stills her with his hand. She sits again. He's holding his pencil in his other hand, over the half-completed sketch.

She looks at this bowed, gnarled man, with his wild silver hair, his burrowed eyes, and waits for him to do something more. He doesn't. He's still.

He's listening.

Pop pop pop.

Cooper watches them walk away down the road, the ragged caravan, toward the refuge of the chapel. Santayana and her agents trail behind, at a distance, almost like shepherds, keeping watch.

Then he walks quickly in the other direction.

He could try to get the drop on Dietrich. Hide somewhere, like a hunter, wait on Dietrich, try to surprise him, but Dietrich's armed to the teeth and an expert shot to boot—he proved that on the night of the coydogs. And Cooper's bum shoulder is barking and even on a good day he can't reliably knock a can off a fence at twenty yards. So taking on Dietrich, with one bullet?

Dawes was right. That's suicide. And as much as the notion has held a certain appeal to him in the past, he's not much interested in that particular ending today.

He walks briskly away from the distant sound of the echoing shots.

Never carried a loaded gun, not for eight years on the job. Never had use for one.

He turns onto the next block.

Pop pop pop pop pop, he hears it again, and tries not to think about what each resonant barrage means. How Dietrich is roaming freely, stalking the town, murderous, fatal, like a sickness. How the town is dying slowly around him, plague-struck, helpless. No apparent rescue on the horizon.

Cooper mounts a set of stairs.

Well, not entirely helpless.

If there is one thing the Blinds has going for it, Cooper thinks, it's that there's no shortage of people living here who know what to do with a gun. Or did once, and can possibly be prodded to remembrance.

Some of those people being worse than Dietrich. Or were, once.

He marches across the porch and knocks hard on the door.

35.

THE CHAPEL IS a low-slung cinder block building, not much more than a bunker, really, painted white then tinted brown by years of wind-borne dirt. The structure's facade makes no exterior concession to holiness. No stained glass or saints or hung crucifix. Just a dented red metal door, with a single small square window in the center of it, at eye level, like a peephole. Two long but narrow recessed windows flank the entrance, and there's a scrubby stretch of withered grass out front. The building's set about twenty yards off the main road at the west end of the town's central thoroughfare, a stone's throw from the busier commercial outposts. Dawes has been inside this chapel exactly once before, during her initial tour of the grounds, on her very first day of work. She never returned. She's not much for faith. Though as she unlocks the impressive deadbolt on the door, she suspects she could use some faith right now.

She swings the heavy door open with a grunt and hustles Fran and Isaac inside, along with about a half dozen or so stragglers they've picked up. Most everyone else in town is holed up in their houses, but there were a few people just wandering the streets in a daze. Panic will do that to people. Dawes tried as best she could to wave them down but many of them just scampered off, skittish, as though scared she was beckoning them to their doom. Who knows—maybe she was. If there's a plan to all this, she's not privy to it, beyond getting everyone inside this building and locking the door.

The small party she's collected spreads out inside the room, which, like the building's exterior, is spare and rather notably unchurchlike. Three rows of plastic folding chairs face a wooden lectern. Other than that, it's just a large bare room with musty gray carpeting and dingy white cinder block walls that, she suspects, hasn't had too many recent visitors.

Once everyone's inside, Dawes locks the door. It's a formidable lock that takes a little doing. Then she sits—slumps, really—into a plastic chair, and only then realizes how painfully her side throbs. The brown coat is stiff with blood over the bullet hole. She unzips it, gingerly. Fran pulls up a chair. "Let me have a look at that," she says.

"What, you're a doctor now?"

"No, I'm a poet, apparently."

Dawes shrugs the coat off.

"Why are you wearing a winter coat, anyway?" asks Fran, as she tugs the coat off Dawes's arms and tosses it aside to the floor.

"You ever read a biography of Andrew Jackson?" says Dawes weakly. It's all catching up to her now.

"No," says Fran.

"Jackson once challenged a man to a duel. He knew the man was a better shot than him. So he wore an oversized coat, and let the man take the first shot. Which hit the coat, but only winged Jackson. Then Jackson took his shot and shot the man dead. For some reason, I remembered that fact just as I was running out the door to come find you. So I grabbed this coat."

Fran pries the torn cloth of Dawes's uniform shirt away from the wound and sees it. It's ugly.

A grizzled, heavyset black man, maybe fifty, walks over and interrupts them both. He's unshaven. Clearly angry. Fran knows him. Chester Holden, Chet for short. He likes to garden out front of his house. She's seen him out there on his knees, in his dungarees. That's about as much as she knows about him. He's wearing a work shirt and jeans and, Fran only notices now, he's barefoot. He must have run out of his house to follow them without his shoes on. He must be petrified, she thinks.

He says to Dawes: "At some point, are you going to tell us just what the hell is going on?" Behind him, other residents stand, listening.

"I don't know," says Dawes. "But these agents aren't who they say they are. And someone's loose in the town right now. He's armed. Sheriff Cooper's dealing with it."

"Yeah? How?" says Holden. "And what are we supposed to do? Just sit here and wait?"

"You can go back out there if you like," says Fran sharply.

A younger man steps forward from the cluster that loiters behind Holden. A big guy with a goombah vibe. Dawes recognizes him from intake day, back on Monday, which seems like a lifetime ago. "Isn't whoever he is just going to come here and kill us all?" he says. "We're big, fat sitting ducks in here."

"No, we're not," says Dawes.

"He's right," says Holden, angry. "We're sitting ducks." A few voices from the group concur.

"Cooper told me to bring you here for a reason," says Dawes.

"To a fucking church?" says the goombah. "Why? For last rites?"

"Look, I know for some of you, memory isn't your strong suit, but think back to your orientation. This isn't just a church," Dawes says.

Dietrich walks out again into the middle of the street, his rifle hot, thinking, *There is no joy in shooting an old man in a chair holding a Bible.*

Not joy, exactly. There is some joy. But sport.

There is no sport in it.

And as much as he looked forward to stalking through the town, he's finding the residents old and weary and, in their way, far too welcoming. Those two agents were a challenging diversion, but they're dead and there's only four more like them. Plus, the sheriff and his two deputies. He had planned to hold off on those three till the end, since he already has their tattoos, and it would be kind of funny for them to watch the whole town die. But at this point he's getting impatient and starts thinking of the most efficient way to bring it all to an end. The only question is whether he should take the kid. He should probably take the kid. He definitely gets a sense that whoever is bankrolling all of this, the only survivor they really care about is the kid.

He spots a person running, way up the block, hunched over, like how they saw it once in some movie about survival. He hefts the rifle. Sights the person scampering.

Pop pop.

Finally, some sport.

Then he spots another figure. In the distance. Walking toward him. Hands up. Like he's begging for mercy.

Dietrich sights the rifle, then stops. Lowers it.

Squints.

Now, lookie here. It's the fucking sheriff.

Cooper ambles forward in the silence, his empty hands raised in surrender. It's so quiet you can hear his boots squeak in the road. The early-evening simmer rises off the road in throbbing waves. He spots the figure in the distance, Dietrich, waiting for him, patiently. At this distance, at rest, with his rifle hoisted up and pointed skyward, Dietrich looks like a creature with an extra appendage. His silhouette dances in the heat.

The town has the smell of blood now. Cooper catches the scent on the feeble breeze. He waves a hand meekly. Summons his voice.

"Dietrich!"

Dietrich faces him, square in the center of the street, with no pretense of caution or concern.

"Sheriff Cooper," he says. "You come to arrest me?"

Cooper inches closer, hands still high. "No. I've come to cut a deal."

"Too late. I already got the tattoos."

"Look, Dietrich. I just need time. To get out. Me, and the boy, and his mother. Just the three of us. I have a truck. Just let us go. Us three."

"No." Dietrich savors the finality of his reply.

"Come on. You don't care about that boy."

"I don't. But someone does."

"I've got information you can use, Dietrich. This town is full of bounties. I don't mean petty criminals, either. I mean targets whose lives are worth tens of thousands of dollars, even hundreds of thousands, if you take their scalps home to the right people."

"As you may have noticed, I haven't really concerned myself so far with collecting scalps."

"Have you ever heard of William Wayne?"

Dietrich shakes his head. But he's curious.

"How about Esau Unruh?" says Cooper. "Does that name mean anything to you?"

Dietrich listens. The money doesn't matter much to him. This job was sold to him as a flat-fee undertaking, and while the payment offered was impressive, even flattering, it was meaningless, just more numbers to pile up in a bank account. No, it was the anarchy of the endeavor that appealed to him. Not the planning beforehand, or the payment afterward, but this—these few roiling hours of absolute freedom. This new information intrigues him, however, a little bit. "Yes, I've heard that name," he says. "In prison once. He's supposed to be, like, some super killer. The person in question, who told me about him, spoke of him like a ghost."

"He's here. In this town. He's in hiding right now. I can tell you exactly where he lives. And there's, I don't know, there's got to be a dozen men in the outside world who would pay a million dollars each to see him dead. Hell, they'd pay you a bounty just to hear the story of how you did it. You'd be the man who killed Esau Unruh."

Dietrich listens to this, too. Unruh's got to be a hundred years old by now, from the way that guy spoke about him in prison, like he's been alive the whole century, haunting the countryside. Probably he's now just some old man sitting in his own shit in a bungalow, babbling about nothing to no one. Not much sport to that. But, yes, a good story. A good trophy. A *great* tattoo.

"And why are you telling me this, Sheriff?"

"Because I want to live, and I don't have anything else to bargain with."

"And what are you asking me for again?"

"Just time. Ten minutes. To get to my truck. Me, the woman, and the boy."

"You have to leave that boy. That's non-negotiable."

"The woman will never leave without her son."

"Then leave them both."

Dietrich shrugs. Final offer. Cooper, a man with no leverage, considers the options. His hands still held high. Then he acquiesces, visibly. Dietrich sees it happen. A slumping, an internal collapse, a moral crumbling.

For Cooper, it's a well-practiced look.

"All right. That's fair. Just me," says Cooper softly. "I'll go. Ten minutes. That's all I need." *It's so hot out right now,* he thinks. Their two shadows stretch in the street grotesquely. Cooper and Dietrich, out here chatting, like old buddies. Cooper's sweating. His hands tremble. Weary from being raised in surrender for so long.

"Which way? To Unruh?" says Dietrich.

Cooper nods toward a cul-de-sac. "Last house on the next street over. He's alone. No one ever bothers him. He's home right now."

"I just came from that block," says Dietrich.

"Trust me, he's there. Look, you can take care of him, then get back to your business. I just need ten minutes to get to my truck. You see me again, you kill me. Deal?"

Dietrich's not even sure where the sheriff intends to go. The fences are locked. The agents aren't letting anyone leave. If he does try to go, they'll shoot him down as quick as Dietrich would.

"Yes, all right, it's a deal," says Dietrich. "You go."

Cooper bows, like a supplicant being dismissed. "Ten minutes," he says, then turns to walk away, then breaks into a jog and runs. Dietrich watches him go. He fires a few shots from the rifle straight up in the air, as though celebrating, *pop pop pop,* just to remind whoever's out there that he's still here, he's still in their town, and he's still coming. In fact, he's on his way right now.

36.

FRAN HAS ALWAYS HAD an awareness of vague evil in the world, as well as the knowledge that her one job in life is to protect her son from it. There is a freedom to this clarity. Like joining a religious order—the freedom of complete and unquestioning discipline. Whether you previously had a purpose, or wanted a purpose, in life, like it or not, you now have a purpose.

Keep him safe.

Eight years can go by in an instant. She remembers Isaac when he seemed no heavier to hoist than a loaf of bread. She remembers his first words, his first steps, Isaac as a toddler playing in the yard that rings their bungalow. She remembers tugging on, then discarding, pair after pair of inadequate trousers, all of which seemingly just moments ago had fit him perfectly. These images are the pages on her internal calendar. Not days, not months, not years—these milestones mark her time here. Isaac breaking his arm, and Nurse Breckinridge setting it, and assuring her no X-rays were needed, and Fran's almost overwhelming relief at not having to leave the gated town with her son. Or Isaac, planted in the corner of his bedroom with his books, reading and re-reading the pages, making the most of everything because months would pass between the arrival of anything new. When some new toy did arrive, ordered on the sly by Spiro, they'd unbox it together and invent some new mythology around it. Neither of them had any idea who the Ultrabots were, or the Cosmos Squad, or the Jungletrex Ultimate Warriors, or whatever off-brand knockoff Spiro managed to purloin, so they just made up their own stories together. They sat and determined who the good guys were and who the bad guys were. You can always tell the bad guys, she told him, because they're the ones who look bad.

She knew then that this wasn't a good life lesson, but if they stayed here together in this gated town forever, maybe it wouldn't matter.

But now, in this chapel, she realizes there's nowhere left for them to go. No further hole to hide in, no further fallout shelter buried below this shelter, no hiding place left on this earth where the world won't arrive one day and find you. He never struck her as an evil person, all those years, even up to the moment when she shot him. He certainly never looked like the bad guy. But now she sees. She knows. She understands. About evil, or whatever you care to name it. It comes. It's relentless. It doesn't care if you forgot it. It searches, and it finds you, and it arrives on your doorstep one day, and it lights up a screen, it calls you by your real name, it smiles at you, it says hello, it eyes your son and promises to take him home.

Cooper arrives at the chapel at the same time as Robinson.

"You look like you just ran a marathon," says Robinson.

"Fuck you, too," Cooper says. "Where have you been?"

"Trying to find people. Figured we'd all rendezvous here." He nods to a small group of people, four or five, who are trailing him.

"That's all you found?" says Cooper.

"All that were alive."

"Where's Nurse Breckinridge? We're going to need her."

Robinson shakes his head.

"How about Ginger Van Buren? Vivien King?"

Robinson shakes his head again. Cooper decides to stop asking about specific people. "And what about Santayana and the other agents?" he says.

"I saw them headed that way, toward the intake trailer. I figured they went to find Rigo. Tell him we're massing here in the chapel."

"You think they know about the chapel?"

Robinson shrugs. "If they did, I imagine they'd be here, trying to stop us."

Cooper nods, then pounds on the red metal door.

"What happened to you?" says Santayana, in a pitying tone, in the intake trailer, as Rigo sits bloodied and doubled over in a plastic chair.

"He kicked me in the fucking nuts. Twice," Rigo says, trying to affect an uncompromised posture. "I've just been waiting for you."

Santayana suppresses a smile. You don't often get to see a man who's just been kicked in the nuts, but she always enjoys it. All that male weakness, so comically concentrated in one convenient anatomical target.

"I thought the sheriff was supposed to be with us," she says.

"It turns out he feels some attachment to that kid."

"And no one thought to tell us that?"

"No one knew. And it gets worse."

"What?"

"He's got a thing for the woman, too."

"Well, fuck him, then," she says. "He can die like the rest of them." She's annoyed now. Rigo assumed they could just ride in, make trouble, wreak havoc, unleash Dietrich, and slip out again. She understood, however, that in a community that's lived in isolation for eight years, there are bound to be some emotional entanglements. *Fucking shitty intel,* she thinks. *It will fuck you every time.* Two years spent to track this whore down, and then Vincent finds out she has a *kid.*

His kid.

Now, here we are in this clusterfuck, she thinks.

The other two agents, Burly and Gains, linger in the background, slightly abashed, like children in the presence of bickering parents.

"Where are Corey and Bigelow?" she asks.

"They're trailing Dietrich."

"Okay," she says, "at this point, I vote we just let Dietrich finish up, then we take care of him, then we take the kid, then we go. We torch this whole town on the way out. We'll say the residents lit it. We can say they went full Waco on us. Just burned their own compound to the ground."

"Sounds like a plan," says Rigo. He stands, gingerly, feeling emboldened. "I want that sheriff, though. I want to strangle that fucker myself. I want to personally drop his dead body in a ditch."

"Don't worry, you can have him. And he won't be hard to find," she says. "None of them are now."

Rigo turns to the other agents. "Everyone else in this town is to be considered target practice. Understood? Scorched earth. No witnesses. No regrets."

Santayana says to the agents: "You two go find Corey and Bigelow. Tell them to take care of Dietrich and wrap things up. Then meet us back at the chapel in the center of town."

Rigo turns. "Why the chapel?"

"Because everyone who's left in the town is holed up there," she says. "Convenient, right?"

"Oh, *fuck me.*" Rigo looks caught between distress and fury. He also looks like someone just kicked him in the balls again. "Santayana, did you not read the fucking briefing?"

"Of course I did," she says, trying to remember if she read the whole thing right to the end.

"Did you read the part about tornados? That this place is in Tornado Alley?"

"Yes." She definitely did not read the part about tornados. *What the fuck is Tornado Alley?* she thinks.

Rigo starts pacing. Fretting. Muttering. "Oh, fuck me."

"What?" she says. For once, she's earnestly confused. And genuinely annoyed. And ever-so-slightly concerned.

He turns to her sharply. "That's not just a fucking chapel. It's a fucking safe house."

37.

DIETRICH WANDERS SLOWLY BACK DOWN the middle of a street he just came from, his eyes on the last house on the left. He wonders how he should do it. Quick shots aren't much of a story. He should do it by hand, up close. How old is Unruh, anyway? Dietrich wishes he had a knife. Some hefty combat type of knife, with a serrated edge on it. He's used so many improvisatory things to cut so many people that it's funny for him to think about how long it's been since he held a proper knife.

What he could do with a proper knife.

There should be some sense of ceremony. He wishes he knew more about this man. He remembers the guy in the Colorado supermax who wouldn't shut up about Unruh. Said he'd run up against him once, or knew someone who had, or heard about it—his stories never added up too much, sense-wise. He said Unruh came from the North, stood seven feet tall, had a tattoo of a bloodstain on his face. Even to Dietrich, whose tattoos never failed to enthrall once their stories were revealed, the idea of a facial tattoo seemed impressive. Like war paint.

I was born at the wrong time, Dietrich thinks, as he mounts the stairs to the porch. There have been times in human history when it was simply understood that you moved from man to man and each man fought without rules or mercy or restraint. That was simply the way of the world. *Maybe we'll fight a little bit today,* he thinks. He'd like to find out how this old man smells. These will all be good details for the story. *And, if it gets out of hand for some reason, I'm the one with the guns.*

He walks up to the door. Knocking seems polite. He'd like this man to answer the door. Frankly, he'd like to be invited in.

So he knocks. And waits.

Notices light through the peephole.

Sees a shadow swallow the light.

He steps back slightly and squares himself to the door, and with his rifle held waist-high in two hands he fires twice.

Door blisters.

He hears a thud.

Light blooms again in the peephole.

Too easy.

He'll fudge the story later, he thinks.

He's about to kick in the door when he catches the sight of himself in the large picture window. His double, his companion, like in the full-length mirror, but even larger. It's nigh on dusk by now so the window catches the last light of the sun and reflects the street scene. Reflects Dietrich. He regards himself, his rifle held low in his hands, and he looks to himself like a war-stained soldier of old. Battle-tested. He straightens up, as though for a portrait. He notices dots of blood here and there all over him, his arms, his white linen shirt, now road-dusty and bloody. The tattoos of the faces crawl up from under the linen, up his neck, out his sleeves, like a little brood of children, looking up at him. His dead. His legacy.

He smoothes a hand over his shaved head. He steps closer to the mirror of the glass. Inspects his face. Not dead-eyed. Not at all. Turning the name of this vanquished old man over in his mind. A name like a primal grunt. Like a death rattle.

Unruh.

Dietrich looks closer still at his reflection in the window. He looks tired. There are bruised bags under his eyes. Well, no wonder, he thinks. He's been working so hard.

And as he leans in and studies his face more intently, a strange thing occurs. He sees his face, reflected back at him, suddenly buckle, then crumble, sagging as though in sudden despair, starting right from the very center, dead between his eyes, then spiderwebbing outward, his whole face falling, slowly, with great deliberation; he watches with focused curiosity and puzzlement as his face disassembles itself into a dozen jagged sections, like a jigsaw patiently unsolving itself, and then he realizes it's not his face that's falling apart, it's the mirror, it's the window, that's breaking and collapsing and now the whole window glistens and sparkles and shatters, then erupts in a million brilliant shards. And only now does he realize that this is all happening—has all happened, it's all over—in a moment, an instant, the very last instant of his life.

Dietrich's lean body goes limp, then buckles, as the bullet passes brightly through his brain, having traveled already through the glistening glass and then his forehead and then out of his head in a great red spray, then continuing onward in a hurry, as though Dietrich's thin skull was just a minor detour on a longer, more urgent journey. As he slumps, a bright red mist forms a speckled cloud over his falling body, like a final thought bubble left to linger in the air. His body clatters to the porch with a thump, but he's long past dead now, long dead, his last thoughts lost, his corpse already cooling on the porch. Only the empty tattooed eyes of his victims remain open, bearing witness.

Once the whole window has fallen in shards like a brittle curtain, Unruh steps out over the jagged sill and onto the porch, bending himself through the now-vacated windowpane, with Cooper's revolver, gifted to him, along with its single bullet, held limp and smoking and empty in his left hand.

Unruh's body is crooked and old and he strains in the sun to unfold himself to something like his former stature. Having dispatched Dietrich, he doesn't give the corpse another thought. He's more concerned with the warmth of the sun on his face, which is a feeling he hasn't felt in a great long while. The spreading warmth on his cheeks and forehead, and on the wine stain that's marked him since birth. He stretches in the sun—

—and to a distant observer, Unruh seems to dance now, his body spasming in a joyful jitterbug that belies his obvious age. As he dances, the two agents move closer, their drawn weapons firing rhythmically, each round catching Unruh as they carefully sight the old man and squeeze their triggers methodically and expertly put him down. He topples like an ancient oak, felled, his body folding over Dietrich's and lying still.

And as Burly and Gains inch closer, cautious to the end, they spot the blood-splashed photo clutched in Unruh's out-flung hand, the photo of a smiling man, and they both wonder if this was some last target, some last victim, for this cold killer, before they stand over the bodies and empty their weapons into the pile, just to be sure.

When Burly kicks the door of the bungalow open, they find Bette Burr standing in the gloom inside. She's unarmed, hands raised innocently. The body of Agent Bigelow, dragged in from the street, lies just inside the doorway, where Bette had hoisted him up and used him as a shield, propping his bulk up just long enough against the door to darken the peephole, so that his corpse absorbed Dietrich's shots through the door. Then she let the body drop with a hard and noticeable thud. It was Unruh's idea, the part with the body, but she enacted it; he was far too feeble. She went out into the empty street and dragged the body inside and hefted it up against the door, then let it drop with a heavy thump, while Unruh waited by the window with the gun, Unruh and Eleanor inside, the two of them accomplices at last.

With everyone else dead and her unarmed, the agents collect her and take her with them, not suspecting that this unassuming woman with an open face is anything more than a simple witness to this carnage. Not knowing that, today, pressing her full weight behind the hefted corpse against the peephole, she understood for the first time that some part of her father lives on in her, waiting to be acknowledged, and accessed.

Cooper does a head count.

Him, Dawes, and Robinson all made it here—that's three. Fran and Isaac, too. That's five. Beyond them, there's a half dozen or so other residents arranged in little anxious clusters. Cooper glances over them, counting: There's Greta Fillmore, Chet Holden, that goombah from intake day, Hannibal what's his name. There's Doris Agnew and Spiro Mitchum, who, God bless him, showed up in his apron with two armloads of groceries in large paper bags, in case they're hunkered down for a while. There may be others still alive and hiding in their homes out in the town, but they're on their own for now, Cooper thinks—he can't do anything about that, not now, he saved everyone he could before he came here. There's eleven of them in total in the chapel, versus six agents, so they have numbers, at least. But they don't have a firearm between them, or even a sharp stick, and they don't have a phone, or any way to contact the outside world, and Cooper has no idea who'd they contact if they could.

And of all the people who made it inside the chapel, he knows there are maybe two or three of them, tops, who will be of any use if the situation gets dicey. Dawes is done; with her wound, she's barely conscious, and he's not sure how bad it is or how long she can hold out. Robinson's useful, and maybe the goombah. Otherwise, he looks around at these confused and panicked people in their bathrobes and dungarees and the irony of it almost makes him chuckle. Here he is, stuck in a safe house with nearly a dozen crooks, cutthroats, and infamous killers, and not a single one remembers who they are, let alone what they used to be so good at.

Cooper walks over to check on Dawes. Fran's bandaged and swaddled Dawes's wound as best she can with the first-aid kit on hand. Fran looks up at Cooper.

"She needs a doctor," she says. Her face is grave.

"Well, we don't have a doctor and our nurse is dead," Cooper says.

"But someone's coming, right?" comes an anxious voice from the crowd behind them. Cooper turns. It's Doris Agnew. "Someone's coming to save us, right?" she says. "Like, the police? If we can just wait it out?"

"Let's hope so," Cooper says, but he knows there's no reason for hope. He's tempted to be more truthful with her, with them all, but he's already decided that if they're going to be stuck in here awhile, with little options and limited supplies, he can't let hope be the first thing that runs out.

Rigo hears it in the distance; it's unmistakable: the spatter of a firefight.

"What the fuck is going on?" he says. Santayana strides ahead of him, walking in the main street, unperturbed. The streets are quiet now, abandoned. Long shadows yawn across the road as the sun clocks out on its shift and retires for the day.

Santayana stops and regards the low-slung building from about thirty yards away. "Remind me—we've got flashbangs. Smoke. Some tear gas. Assault rifles. Plus, our own sidearms. Anything else? Can't we just smash those windows and smoke them out?"

"It's a safe house," says Rigo, behind her, exasperated. "Built for tornados. And other contingencies, apparently. Walls are bulletproof, windows shatterproof. And we'd need a tank to take out that door. You really should have read the briefing, Iris."

"I'm sorry, but tornados were not the first fucking logistical concern on my mind."

She turns to see Burly and Gains approaching at a slow jog, with a third person, a young woman. Burly's got Dietrich's semiautomatic rifle slung over his shoulder. Well, that's something, she thinks.

"Where's Dietrich?" asks Rigo.

"He's dead," Burly says.

"You took him out?" says Santayana. She's impressed.

"No, some old guy got his hands on a gun and shot Dietrich right on his front porch," Burly says. "He's dead, too. The old man."

"And who's this?" says Rigo, looking over at Bette Burr.

"She was in the house," says Burly.

"I have a voice," Bette says. Then, to Rigo, "I'm Bette Burr."

"Of course you are," he says. "You're staying out here with us." He turns to Santayana. "All right. This is not so bad. This is a workable situation. We've got firepower, we've got time, and with her"—he gestures to Burr—"we've got some leverage. Let's see how much the townsfolk truly care about each other."

Santayana ignores him and says to Burly: "Anyone else in this town with a secret hidden handgun we don't know about?"

"Shouldn't be," says Burly.

She signals for the semiautomatic rifle and Burly hands it over. She hefts it to her shoulder, sights it. A Bushmaster; she likes the feel of it. She targets the chapel and fires. Tight bursts. Loosing a loud rattling fusillade. The bullets clip and claw at the building, send concrete chips flying, thump dumbly at the windows but don't penetrate.

She stops. Acrid smoke and the ear-ringing echo of the shots persist. She hoists the rifle back over her shoulder by the strap.

"Just checking," she says.

She turns to Burly and Gains: "You two go get the rest of our weapons from the intake trailer and bring them back here." They jog off, obedient. She says to Burr: "You—sit down in the dirt and don't talk." Then Santayana turns to Rigo: "No more fuckups. No more negotiations. No more happy-grab-ass. From now on, it's just corpses and results."

"And what about us?" says Rigo. "We gonna use our powers of persuasion to coax that boy out of that building?"

"In a way," she says. "First, we need to find some lawn chairs."

"Great. Then what?"

"You brought those files, right?"

"Which files?"

"You know which files."

Rigo thinks a moment. Then it hits him. "Oh, *fuck.* You are so fucking devious." He wags a finger at her, smiling. "You are one devious bitch."

Then he scampers off without another word, and only a hint of a lingering limp.

Once he's gone, Santayana hooks a thumb in the rifle strap that's hung over her shoulder and turns back to further study the bullet-pocked chapel. In her gravel-dusted patent heels she walks slowly toward the dented red door. She steps to one side and puts two hands up, cupped, on the milky glass of the adjacent window. The glass is thick and cloudy. Inside the lights are out. But as she peers into the building she can make out a huddle of people, clustered together. They seem to see her, too, her small silhouette on the glass, backlit by the last of the setting sun.

She waves.

The sky darkens.

People sleep. They curl up on the carpeted floor, find corners, hunker down. Cooper sits in the gloom of the chapel, amazed at how people can get rest under such conditions. He's never been that way. Give him a minor worry and he's up for the rest of the week. So, naturally, he's given up on sleep in this situation. These are his people. He brought this on them. He brought this to the gates of their town. He sits in a chair in the dark and thinks about that and keeps watch.

Dawes is sleeping. Isaac, too. Fran's lying on the floor with her arms around Isaac, but she's awake. When she notices Cooper watching her, she rouses herself, untangles herself from her son, and walks over and sits next to him.

"So what's the plan?" she says, as quietly as she can.

"This is the plan. Getting us inside of here."

"So what's the plan to get us out of here?"

"See, now that requires another plan. No one told me I had to have two plans."

Fran smiles, a grave smile, defiant, given the circumstance. "I can't wait to get out of here so I can be done with you forever, Calvin Cooper."

"I can't wait to get out of here and be done with me, either," he says.

He raises his fingers and strokes her cheek softly. It's the kind of gesture they never would have allowed themselves before, not in full view of the other residents, but, fuck it, who cares now. If they get out of this alive, no one will care if he stroked her cheek. And if they don't get out alive, he'll be glad at least that he did it.

"Why did you leave me?" she asks him.

"I never left you. I stopped sleeping with you. There's a difference."

"So why did you stop sleeping with me?"

"Because I knew you had to leave eventually. And I didn't want there to be any part of me that didn't want that to happen."

"Did that work for you?"

"Not in the least," he says.

She waits a moment, watching people sleep, then asks: "Will they send help?"

"That depends. Who's 'they'?"

"Anyone."

Now he tells the truth. "I don't think so, no."

Her face, usually so stoic, falls. He can see it, even in the dark. She says simply, to no one, "But Isaac."

"I know."

"He doesn't deserve this. Maybe I do, maybe we do, but he doesn't."

"I know," says Cooper again. He has nothing else to say. He could try to reassure her—he can promise to keep them safe—but at this point, what's the worth of that promise?

All he can do is do it.

Fran does her best to smile again because she knows that's what she's expected to do in this moment but she fails, even at that, and she can feel herself bodily falling. She feels like the whole abyss of her life, all those empty, erased years, are opening now to swallow her whole. And there's a comfort in that welcoming darkness. She doesn't even mind it so much. If it was just her, she'd just let go, and fall.

Just don't take my son, she thinks.

So they sit side by side, and he takes her hand in his, and she finishes her crying in silence, and they watch the room together, as people sleep the final hours before the coming day.

FRIDAY

38.

COOPER WAKES WITH A START. He must have dozed off. The windows in the chapel are blindingly bright. He's still holding Fran's hand. She's still sleeping. Isaac is standing over them both, awake. Watching and saying nothing. Cooper drops Fran's hand, embarrassed. Then he stands, and is about to push past Isaac, but he stops. He stops and hugs the boy. Isaac stands stiff as Cooper pulls him in. Then Cooper lets him go, turns, and shakes Fran awake.

In the room, a few people are already up, milling around, looking out the murky windows. Spiro Mitchum's in the corner having a hushed but angry argument with Greta over a jar of instant coffee. He says to Greta: "Look, it's not my fault. I didn't know there wasn't a kettle."

Cooper walks over, and Greta turns to him, angrily, pointing a bejeweled, bent finger at Spiro: "This dipshit—" Cooper holds up a hand to calm her. "This is only day one, Greta. Let's not turn on each other yet."

The goombah, Hannibal Cagney, stands at the window, watching the street. He waves to get Cooper's attention, then motions him over. "Something's happening outside. Thought you'd want to know."

Cooper peers out the window. The bulletproof Plexiglas leaves the street cloudy and distorted, but he can see that someone in a black suit, must be Rigo, is standing in the middle of the street. Someone else, also in a suit—looks like Santayana—is sitting behind him, in the street, in a folding lawn chair. There's an empty chair next to her.

They must have slept out there all night, Cooper thinks.

Rigo's holding something in his hands, waving something. He yells out, "Rise and shine!"

Whatever's in his hand looks to Cooper like a tablet or a book. Cooper squints. Or a file folder. That's what it is, Cooper sees now. A manila folder, held open in Rigo's hand, like he's a street-corner preacher balancing a Bible. Rigo is shouting something else, too, but it's hard to understand inside the fortified chapel, behind the thick bulletproof window.

Cooper strains to make it out.

"Cooper! Cock-a-doodle-doo!" is what Rigo's shouting, over and over again.

Cooper turns back to Dawes and Fran, and to the room. "I'm going outside. To see what this is. Lock this door behind me."

"You can't—" says Fran.

"They don't care about me," says Cooper. "And they know that whatever they do to me, you're not going to open this door. Right?"

Fran doesn't speak, so Dawes, from her seat, still swaddled in that bloodstained puffy jacket, says, "Yes. That's right."

"Good." Then Cooper turns, unlocks the door, opens it, and steps out into the sunshine.

"Sheriff Cooper!" Rigo shouts, as Cooper slips out from behind the red door. "Good morning."

"Morning, Rigo. How are your balls feeling today?"

"Ask your mother," says Rigo. Then he points to the folder in his hand. "I've just been reading up on some of your citizens. Quite a motley crew of pervs and killers you've got living here. But you knew that already, didn't you?"

Cooper squints and sees that two more agents, Burly and Gains, are standing guard behind Santayana's lawn chair. Between them, as though the agents are her chaperones, stands Bette Burr. Beyond them, at the edges of the street, a few of the other surviving residents are gathering to watch. People who must have been holed up in their houses all night. They look shell-shocked and terrified. There's maybe twelve, maybe fifteen of them, by Cooper's quick count. With the eleven inside, that means it's likely that about half the town is dead.

Rigo motions toward the crowd. "I asked my agents to round up everyone this morning for a demonstration. I assured them that the danger had passed and they'll be fine and we'll be leaving soon, just as soon as we get what we came for."

"Rigo, go home." Cooper understands he's performing for the whole town now, those both inside and outside the chapel. "Tell your boss that you failed. Move on to whatever comes next. These people can't help you, and they don't want you here."

"To the contrary," Rigo says, hoisting the folder in his open hand. "I think they'll find this really enlightening." He glances down at the file. "Errol Colfax," he reads loudly. "Remember him? Who wants to know a little bit about his background? Born Kostya Slivko. Nickname: 'Costco.'" Rigo flashes a showman's look to the crowd, as if to say, *Curious!* then keeps reading: "Sixty-four murders and suspected murders." Rigo makes a face like he's impressed. He looks around, playing to the crowd, his face an exaggerated mask of mock surprise, shielded by his surfer's sunglasses and topped with those white-blond spikes. "I guess it's true that you never do know your neighbors, huh?" He looks back down at the folder. "So what happened to old Kostya, I wonder?"

The street is silent. Cooper wonders how much of this the people inside the chapel can hear.

"Colfax committed suicide," Cooper says flatly. He doesn't like this. He knows Rigo's playing him.

Rigo adopts a face of dramatic disappointment. "Here we are, in the sun, and it's a new day, and we're still going to tell the same old stories? How about a little truth-telling instead?" He looks back at his folder. Flips through some pages. "Here we go," he says. He looks up at the crowd. "Is there a Laurence Barkley here?" He looks around. "Laurence? Barkley?" No one stirs. No one answers. Rigo sighs to himself and returns to his list. "Hmmm. Must be dead. Okeydokey. How about a Lyndon Lancaster? Is there a Lyndon Lancaster living here?"

Cooper knows Lyndon Lancaster by sight, and knows he's standing a few yards away at the edge of the street, in a bathrobe. Cooper's eyes flick involuntarily in Lancaster's direction. *Don't move,* he thinks. *Don't answer. Don't do it.* Cooper sees now what Rigo intends. He'll call out and expose the whole town, what's left of it, every resident, every secret, one by one. Destroy all of them. *All of us,* Cooper thinks.

"I'd call you by your real name, but I know that you don't know it," Rigo says. "But if you'd like to know, show yourself."

There's a long, tremulous moment as Rigo waits, and then Lyndon Lancaster steps forward.

He's tall, thin, mid-fifties, unshaven, graying hair hanging loose over his eyes, with a terry-cloth robe wrapped around him, even in the heat. He looks like someone's once-dashing dad who's let himself go since the divorce.

"That's me. I'm Lyndon Lancaster," he says.

"Are you sure?" says Rigo. "Just kidding. Nice to meet you. Why don't you come on over here? There's a lot you can learn about yourself in this file." Rigo waves him over. Lancaster approaches, reluctantly. Soon he's standing in the middle of the street, next to Rigo, like an awkward volunteer at a magic show.

"Lyndon Lancaster," says Rigo. "Sounds like a soap star, to be honest." Then he reads from the file. "But your real name is Sam 'The Wolverine' Lemme. Am I pronouncing that right? *L-E-M-M-E*—rhymes with 'phlegmy'? Look at me—why am I asking you? Like you'd know."

Lancaster says nothing. He just stands nervously. Cooper watches Santayana, a few yards behind the two men, reclining in her lawn chair, regarding the proceedings calmly, an AR Bushmaster rifle held flat across her knees. At her feet, Cooper notices, is a large black rectangular legal-file box. Stuffed with files, from the looks of it. All their files, Cooper imagines. The blind files.

Rigo reads from the file: "Twelve confirmed murders. Most of it routine button-man stuff, for the most part. Rhode Island mafia, lower rung, actually. Some real boring penny ante midlevel shit, to be honest. Cool nickname, though. The Wolverine!" Rigo says this like a ringmaster hyping the big top's most remarkable freak. "I wonder how you got that name?" He continues to read the file. "You did kill this one woman, named Sandra Antonia Francesca, because she happened to be married to a guy who owed you money. That guy, they found later in twelve different garbage bags. Never linked that one to you, though. As for the woman, they had you dead to rights on her, due to the fact that you pissed on her dead body after you raped her." Rigo mock scrutinizes the page before his eyes, as though in disbelief. "See, now, that's just dumb, Sammy. Piss has

DNA in it, you know. Then again, it says here it was a pretty messy rape, so DNA was likely not an issue." Rigo closes the file, then looks up straight at Lancaster. "Apparently, that was your thing. The pissing part? That's why they called you the Wolverine. You used to piss on the people you killed. As a kind of—what would you call it? Sadistic flourish." Rigo wiggles his groin comically in a pantomime of pissing. "See, wolverines piss on their food so no one else will eat it. True story!" Rigo looks around at the crowd, then back at Lancaster. "One of your thug playmates must have been an amateur naturalist. Either way, that's how you got the nickname. Wear it proudly."

Cooper watches Lancaster, whose face is drained and pale now and who looks perilously close to vomiting. Lancaster tugs the robe around himself despite the relentless morning sun. Then Lancaster looks around at the assembled crowd, which has fallen deadly quiet, and his eyes search each person in the crowd as though one of them might break ranks and step out and save him. As if to say, *You know me. I'm Lyndon Lancaster*. But no one knows him, not really, he realizes, not even himself. Not until now. And as he scans the crowd, it seems to be recoiling, receding in disgust, or at least that's how it looks to him. He has no recollection of these crimes. Yet he doesn't blame these people. Because there's no part of him that doesn't believe what Rigo is saying is true.

He looks to Rigo, pleading. "I'm not that man," he says weakly. "I'm Lyndon Lancaster."

"Does that even sound like a real name to you?" says Rigo. Then he pulls out an automatic pistol from his waistband. He holds it, grip out, toward Lancaster. "I'm going to give you a choice, Sammy 'The Wolverine' Lemme. You can take this gun, and you can shoot me, certainly, that is an option—though my agents might take issue with that, and they'll not only kill you, but that lovely girl that they're currently standing with. But, if you like, you can shoot me, maybe piss on my body when you're done"—Rigo looks around clownishly at the crowd, as though goading them to cheer—"but what's that old expression? Don't shoot the messenger!" Rigo laughs. Then he turns back to Lancaster. "Or you can go another route"—Rigo thrusts the gun out toward Lancaster—"and take this pistol and do what the state should have done to you three fucking years ago when they first arrested you, rather than cutting you a deal and wiping your sins away and depositing you here to live in blissful anonymity among this motley crew of murderers and rapists. Your choice."

Cooper calls out urgently: "Lyndon, just walk away."

Only his friends call him Lyndon and Cooper hopes that might snap him awake.

Lancaster looks at Cooper blankly, looks back at Rigo, then looks at the gun.

Cooper shouts now: "Lyndon, they don't want you. This isn't about you. Just go home."

Instead, Lancaster reaches out and takes the gun. He examines it, in his hand, like it's a gift he wasn't expecting and isn't quite sure what to make of, but is increasingly delighted to have received.

Cooper: "Lyndon, don't!"

Lancaster holds the gun to his temple.

Rigo sticks his index finger up under his own chin. "It's much better right here," he whispers. "Much higher success—"

But Rigo's last words are swallowed by the sharp report, and the boom of the blast echoes idly over the main street, drifting like smoke over the watching crowd. Lyndon's brain matter scatters in an antic plume before spattering to the gravel like summer rain. His body falls.

Rigo stoops and picks up the gun, gingerly, pinched between

two fingers. He pulls a handkerchief from his inside breast pocket and wipes off the gun ceremonially. He toes Lancaster's body. A puddle of blood widens on the gravel. Rigo puts the gun back in his waistband. Then he looks up at Cooper.

"That's one," he says. "Any time, Sheriff, you can call this off."

Cooper says nothing.

"No?" Rigo turns and walks back to Santayana, who's still seated in the lawn chair. He hands her Lancaster's folder, which she sticks back into the legal file. Then she pulls out another one, a new one, and hands it to Rigo. He flips it open and reads, turning back to the assembled crowd.

He says loudly, "Is there a Doris Agnew here?"

They hear the shot, even inside the chapel, and everyone jolts, before the room abruptly stills. Hannibal, who's been watching at the window, recoils. "Holy shit," he says quietly, to no one.

Finally, Fran calls out: "What happened?"

"Some guy just shot himself in the fucking head," Hannibal says. The room murmurs. A soundtrack of confusion, the prelude to a panic.

"Why?" Fran says, though what answer she's expecting, she can't imagine.

"I don't know, from something that guy was reading maybe. It's hard to hear," says Hannibal.

"What could he be reading?" says Spiro, fearful, from the back of the room.

But Fran knows. And soon Spiro knows, too. The whole room knows. And no one says anything. The knowledge of it, dawning on all of them, spreads silently through the room like a dreaded contagion.

"He's calling another name now," says Hannibal.

"What name?" someone asks from the back.

"Don't—" says Fran, but it's too late.

"Doris Agnew," says Hannibal.

At the back of the chapel, at the sound of her name, Doris Agnew stands.

"Doris Agnew," Rigo repeats.

Nothing. No one answers.

"Last call for Doris Agnew," Rigo yells.

Behind Cooper, the chapel door groans open. He turns quickly to block her but the door locks behind her and she steps forward and past him, with the blank momentum of a sleepwalker. Cooper grabs her shoulders and yanks her and says, "Doris, no," but she shakes his hands loose and keeps walking toward Rigo, undeterred.

Toward the promise of knowledge.

Cooper watches her. He knows her well. She's a sweet woman. Mid-sixties by now. She's been in the Blinds maybe six, seven years. A bit of a notorious gossip. Her soft southern accent gives a hint as to her former life.

"Read it to me," she says to Rigo, facing him, in her musical lilt.

"Your name," Rigo says, "is Louise Evelyn Hucks. You were a nurse, apparently. Do you know what an 'angel of death' killer is?"

"No," she says.

"It's tough to know an exact number, but thirty-eight seems like a good guess," Rigo says. "Infants, all of them. Maternity ward. Poison, and whatnot, a few suffocations. They think maybe you couldn't have a baby of your own, is what drove you to do it, though that seems like some amateur armchair psychoanalysis to me." He shakes his head dramatically, as though in mock wonder at the scale of the crime. "How the hell you swung a deal to end up here, though, is beyond me." He scans through her folder, flipping pages. "Ah, here we go. The old insanity defense. I guess they bargained for a transfer here. Maybe they wanted to see how the memory-wiping process would affect such a damaged mind." He slams the folder shut. "How about you, Louise? You feeling crazy?"

"No," she whispers.

"You're pretty lucky, actually," Rigo says. "At least you didn't flip on anyone, so there's that. Of course, on the other hand, that means you offered them nothing in return for your life—"

"Just do it," she says softly. Even Rigo is surprised.

"I'm sorry—?"

"Just do it," she says. "I don't have the guts. Not like Lyndon. You do it for me."

Rigo glances over at Cooper, shrugs, then addresses the silent crowd. "What do you think, folks?"

Cooper starts to move toward Rigo, who draws the gun again and points it at Cooper, and Cooper halts.

"Don't torture me. Just do it," Doris whispers.

Rigo turns the gun crisply on her and shoots her dead in the street, the shot sounding like a whip crack as she falls.

Burly and Gains move swiftly to cart her body away, hoisting her and retreating to the doorway of a nearby building, where they've already deposited Lyndon's corpse.

"You all saw that," says Rigo to the crowd, shrugging, still holding the pistol. "She *asked* me. She *begged* me. And no court in the country would convict me. I mean, thirty-six infants? *That they know of.*" He turns to Cooper. "Come on, Sheriff. We're not here to execute the whole town. For one, it's going to start to get very messy. And, given how hot it is, pretty smelly, too."

"You're not getting that boy," Cooper says quietly. "Just go home."

"That's your counteroffer?" says Rigo. "You are a fucking terrible negotiator, you know that?"

"Give him the kid!" someone yells from the street's edge. Cooper flinches. This is exactly what he's most afraid of. That the crowd will turn.

In her lawn chair, Santayana smiles. And she moves her ankles closer to clutch the large black legal box at her feet. You can always threaten to kill people, she thinks, but that's an amateur's bluff. There are too many stupid people who are willing to die these days, and too many stupid things they're willing to die for. So the real trick is to figure what is worse for them than death.

Like what's in these files.

She clutches them closer.

This is working so much better than she let herself imagine.

Cooper can't place the source of the voice from the crowd and, for the moment, he's glad he can't, because he knows he would stride right into the mob and find that person and break him.

Rigo shrugs. "Listen to your constituency, Sheriff." Then he strolls back over to Santayana. "Let's read another one." He addresses the assemblage in a raised voice as he waits for her to dig a file out. "Do y'all know that 'file' is an anagram for 'life'? That just occurred to me." He gives a self-satisfied nod. Santayana keeps shuffling, her lacquered nails riffling performatively, like a lottery girl spinning the basket full of numbered balls. "I mean, you can't *all* be serial killers, right?" says Rigo, still waiting. "Just, like, statistically speaking? I assume some of you must be, like, penny-ante B&E guys, or Wall Street bullshit artists. But maybe not. I guess we'll find out."

Santayana finally finds the file she's looking for, slides it free of the case, and hands it to Rigo with a flourish. He flips it open.

"Oh, this should be good," Rigo murmurs.

Then he repeats it loudly, for the crowd, for effect, tapping the paper with his slender finger: "This should be good!"

Ever the showman, he rustles the folder and clears his throat.

"Calvin Cooper," he says, in his ringmaster's tone. As though he's introducing, to the waiting patrons, the next act for their astonishment and amazement.

39.

ORSON CALHOUN HEARD THE SHOTS, OF COURSE. That sporadic chatter of ordnance. Then silence. Sometimes long silences. Then another burst. All day yesterday. It went on for hours.

And he's not hiding, he just has work to do. He figured the shots would find him eventually. In the meantime, he wants to get his workshop back in order, as best he can.

Order. Without that, what do we have?

So this has been his dedicated task for the past several days, ever since someone broke in and ransacked his shop in the early hours of the morning, laying waste to his carefully organized tools, overturning his tables, trashing his repair projects, scribbling nonsense words about *Damnatio* and *Memorae* all over his walls. For a long while, after he first discovered the carnage, and after he reported it to Cooper, he just stood and stared at the wreckage despondently. Cried, even, sure—he cried. Jobs he'd long been toiling on were lost causes, in total disarray. Gears and nuts and finer pieces that he'd laid out patiently, over weeks, just so, carefully assembled and displayed on oilcloth on his worktable, had been scattered, haphazard, in the dust. All that work, all that order, undone. Like time itself was moving backward toward chaos. The universe undoing itself.

Besides which, his tools were everywhere—and what is a man without tools? Every hammer, every wrench, every screwdriver, every awl, all of which had their own prescribed slots on the pegboard, their own designated nails to be hung from carefully, their own individual outlines on the pegboard traced lovingly by Orson's own hand, so that when a tool went missing you could see exactly where it once belonged and where it would one day return. Well, that entire wall was bare. Nothing but ghostly outlines, left on the wall like the reminder of a crime. Like the chalk outlines of corpses after a massacre.

The emptiness of it all overwhelmed him.

So he had only one recourse. Get back to work.

Now, after a day or so, he is maybe halfway back to normal. Almost all the tools are replaced in their proper spots. There's a hammer missing here, pliers absent there, but, as a whole, there's something like order in evidence. Something like tranquillity restored to his troubled mind. The individual projects, too, have been reassembled as best he can manage, the apparent detritus grouped and bundled together by job. That took time. But at least it's a starting point, he thinks. He knows in some part of his heart that this workshop will never be fully restored, and he suspects he may not live long enough to restore it. But the work of attempting this restoration has given him solace and quelled his roiling soul.

For the past few days, that's been enough.

He stands now with a weighted hammer in his hand. It's a twenty-eight-ounce framing hammer, a good weight for most everyday jobs. He searches for its proper spot on the wall. Only a few spaces are left vacant now. He notes a ballpeen hammer hanging in the wrong spot on its nail. *Stupid, Orson,* he thinks, then pulls it off and hangs it in a loop on the waist of his overalls until it can find its proper place. The hammer, the right one, that belongs in that spot is still missing, apparently, and this realization sparks a surge in his skull of the same stabbing painful despondency that's been plaguing him for days. The sense that not only will this task never be finished but that all tasks, always, are fraudulent, a joke. But without *tasks*—well, he won't allow himself to entertain that notion.

Instead, he searches the board for this hammer's proper spot, its home, and in that quiet moment, he hears the name of the sheriff—*Calvin Cooper*—called out loudly from somewhere outside. It comes from the street in a voice that he doesn't recognize. It must be one of those visitors, he thinks. These men who arrived yesterday and brought the gunfire with them. He assumes eventually they'll come for him. If they want to find him, he's here, in his workshop, working. And, to be honest, that's exactly where he'd want to be if they should come.

But something about the name of the sheriff draws him away from his task and to his workshop door. The sheriff has also been good to him, kind to him, giving him tasks and projects, even with things that weren't desperate for fixing. The sheriff seemed to understand the turmoil in his mind, and how the work would calm it. So he was always good about finding broken things for Orson to fiddle with, bringing them to him like offerings. Just so Orson could puzzle over them for weeks and thus pass his hours away.

So Orson walks over to the doorway of his shop to see if he can spy the nature of the proceedings he's overheard. Who is calling the sheriff? There's some hubbub, he sees, over by the chapel. A small crowd of residents gathered there. A few of those visitors assembled there, too. A woman sitting in a lawn chair, for some reason.

He watches a minute longer, holding the hammer loosely in his hand, putting the work of the workshop aside for just a moment, and listens.

Fran watches at the window. They can't hear everything, but she heard Cooper's name, she's sure of that. She enlisted a few of the older residents in the chapel to watch over Isaac, and take him to the back; they even found a deck of playing cards stashed in a cabinet. Isaac had never seen a deck of cards before. He stared at it in wonder.

Now Fran's free to linger at the window and watch, which feels like a bad idea, yet she can't pull herself away. Whatever's happening out there is not good, that's obvious. Two people are dead already. And they just called out Cooper's name.

Robinson hears the name, too, and comes to the window and joins her.

"What's going on?" he says in a quiet voice.

"I don't know. They just called Cooper's name."

"Calvin Cooper," Rigo says again, loudly, like a judge about to pronounce sentence.

Cooper steps forward.

"Let me save you the trouble," says Cooper, in a steady voice, but loud enough that everyone can hear. Rigo's surprised at this, which is good, Cooper thinks. *Just give me this one moment of advantage.*

He strides toward Rigo, until they're standing just a few feet apart.

"What are you doing?" asks Rigo.

"Confessing," says Cooper. Then he addresses the crowd. "Calvin Cooper," he announces, parroting Rigo's tone. "Born John Lyon Barker in the great state of Vermont, forty-five years ago this week. Like everyone else here, I changed my name on the day I arrived, because just like all of you"—and here he gestures to the assemblage—"I needed a fresh start. A last stop and a fresh start—isn't that how the welcome speech goes?" The street is silent, save for Cooper's voice. Rigo closes the folder slowly. He seems unsure what to do next. Which is more or less the intended effect, Cooper thinks, as he watches Rigo waver. Santayana simply regards the proceedings from her lawn chair, silent, like a judge on the bench. She, too, is not sure where this is going, but it's hard not to be transfixed. It's like bearing witness to a self-immolation: a man in the street, doused with gasoline and now standing, trembling, the lit match pinched between his fingers.

"Let me tell you all what's in that file," Cooper continues. "Calvin Cooper, age forty-five, currently resides in Caesura, Texas, known locally as the Blinds. When I was sixteen, I fucked my best friend's girlfriend and lied about it to his face repeatedly, until one afternoon he shot me in the shoulder with a crossbow as revenge." Cooper taps his left shoulder. "I've still got the scar to prove it. My friend claimed it was an accident, but I know it was a warning, and, either way, it hurt like a motherfucker, and still does. Luckily, it wasn't my pitching shoulder—I say luckily, because later that year I fathered a son, by a different girl, a teenager, we were both seventeen, and I abandoned her and the child both. And the reason I gave her for why I couldn't stay was because I had to pursue my baseball career, which was bullshit. Even then I knew I wasn't good enough, not really. But she didn't know that, and she bought it, at least long enough for me to leave. She did a great job, though, without me. In fact, she did such a good job that she wrote a whole book about it. It's called *Raising Icarus.*

You should check it out. It became a big bestseller. It's all about overcoming adversity to raise a wonderful kid. She's become a kind of parenting guru. As for me, that's the only way I know my son. From reading about him in a book. And that's the only way I deserve to know him."

Cooper is crying now; he doesn't care, because his voice stays steady, and that's what matters. As long as his voice stays steady, he doesn't care about the rest.

"Where was I?" he says. "Oh yes, at age twenty-six, my baseball career long over, I started work as a prison guard, because why not? I figured maybe I would prosper surrounded by people worse than myself, and the only place I knew where such people were collected was in a prison. I was not well suited for the job, though, given I was weak and frightened and full of anger, and so, one year in, I got jumped and beaten badly by an inmate, who slammed my head in a door, repeatedly, which is how I got this scar right here." Cooper gestures to his forehead and the jagged souvenir. "The inmate jumped me because he took drugs to make him strong, which also made him angry, and I had called him an unconscionable name because I was stupid and scared as shit, every single day. He jumped me, and beat me senseless, and probably would have killed me if not for the intercession of the other guards. And a month after that, I turned a blind eye when, in retaliation, my coworkers pummeled the living shit out of that man and beat him half to death." He pauses here, remembering the broken face of the man. He remembers it so well. "Last I heard, that man can't walk or talk or even get out of bed or feed himself. The settlement from the state covers his medical bills, and I was allowed to take an early retirement, without benefits or honor. I headed south and wound up here, and that man wound up drooling all over himself, kept alive by a machine. If anything in that story sounds to you like justice, you just let me know which part."

The sun throbs, the heat comes in waves, like water lapping a shore, and Cooper sweats, and though his eyes stay locked on Rigo, he recounts all this in a voice loud enough for the entire street, even those in the chapel, to hear. He knows Fran can hear him. He wants her to hear. He wants everyone to hear. "Let's see, what else might it say in your file, Rigo?" he says.

"You didn't even get to the best part," Rigo says, watching him, fascinated.

"That's right," Cooper says. "The best part."

Inside the chapel, Dawes calls out weakly to Fran Adams, who's standing, transfixed, at the window.

Fran turns. She didn't catch what Dawes said. "What's that?"

"Stop him," says Dawes.

Fran steps in, closer, responding as much to the labored urgency in Dawes's voice as to what she's saying. "What?"

"He doesn't know," says Dawes.

"He doesn't know what? He doesn't know his own past?"

"No." Dawes thinks back to the library, the search engine, the crime blotter, the cold, bright screen. "Not all of it," she says.

Cooper continues, emboldened now. He has complete command of the street. "After all that, I moved to Austin, where I took a cushy job as a security coordinator for a software firm, a job that was gifted to me out of pity by an old baseball teammate from community college. I spent the better part of the next decade doing nothing but staring at monitors, drinking, and fucking people over, not least myself."

"Sheriff Cooper, we're not here to conduct a therapy session," says Rigo, trying to wrest away control of the performance. "We're here to discuss your crimes—"

"Of course. My crimes. Well, you know what's coming, Rigo. You, better than anyone." Cooper continues, to the crowd: "At age thirty-seven, I took this job because I knew in ten years I could retire. That was the deal. And I knew I could hide out here in the middle of nowhere with a bunch of people who are inarguably worse than me. And that worked out okay for eight years or so, except I met some decent people in the Blinds. Some good people. Despite their pasts." Cooper clears his throat, his voice catching. He starts up again: "Then, two months ago, I murdered Errol Colfax."

The crowd murmurs, shocked, it's unmistakable.

"I shot him in the head where he sat and then I lied about it and said it was a suicide," says Cooper. "I did it because someone paid me to do it. A lot of money—fifty thousand dollars." The crowd is chattering now, enlivened. "Until yesterday, I didn't even know who that person was, or why they wanted Errol dead. But I did it because that person had told me all about the real Errol Colfax. Who he really was, and what he'd done in his past life. I used that as motivation, or as an excuse. I honestly don't know which anymore." As Cooper speaks, his recitation seems to draw the crowd in closer. His confession becomes an incantation that threatens to conjure something fearsome from the air.

Orson, listening, exits his workshop's doorway. Unthinking, he starts walking slowly toward the gathered crowd, hammer hanging heavy in his hand.

The other residents inside the chapel cluster at the window around Fran and Robinson.

The entire town is listening now.

"Then, four days ago, I killed Hubert Gable," says Cooper. "I shot him in the back of the head, at the bar, for the same reason as Colfax. Someone paid me to do it. I don't regret killing him, not really, because I know what he'd done, too. And I shot Gerald Dean after that. It was not in self-defense. I was paid to do it, just like Colfax, just like Gable. Two hundred thousand dollars. Paid to me by this man, standing right here, right now—Paul Rigo."

A restless breeze stirs some refuse on the road but no one in the crowd moves or makes a noise or seems even to breathe. Cooper stares into Rigo's sunglasses, standing close enough now to see his own tiny self, reflected back at him in the dark convex lenses, standing alone in the middle of the street.

"Paul Rigo doesn't work for the Institute, by the way, not directly," says Cooper. "He works for a man named Mark Vincent. A very rich man who sent Rigo and his partners here to take a boy from our town. To take a boy who was born here, and has no prior life to speak of, and certainly no prior sins to hide. Paul Rigo and his accomplice, that woman, Santayana, and these other agents have come here to steal that boy away from his mother and from all of us. And to cover their tracks, they loosed that man, that killer, Dick Dietrich, among us. Like a virus, like fucking smallpox, to wipe us out, or at least keep us busy so they could take the boy and then have a reasonable excuse for having done it, should anyone back in the real world ever ask them what transpired here." Cooper turns now to address the crowd. "They mean to take that boy, and leave this town, and burn it to the ground if they're able. And maybe they'd be right to do so. Maybe that's what we all deserve. It's certainly what I deserve. But not the boy. Not the boy." Cooper turns to Rigo, pointing straight at him, but says for the whole town to hear: "And make no mistake, no one in the outside world is coming. No one even knows what's happening here. And those who do know don't care, and they never did. Not about us." He gestures to Rigo, Santayana, the agents. "And I helped these people, and I brought them here. Without knowing that I was doing it. They had me kill those men to bury their secrets, and the secrets of their boss.

But I'm not going to help them anymore. So you tell me," he says now to the crowd, "what do you think we should do?"

Behind him, Rigo laughs. A genuine laugh, but showy, outsized, meant to get Cooper's attention. Which it does.

Cooper turns. "What's so funny, Rigo?"

Rigo looks him over, fascinated. "You really don't know, do you?"

Fran watches from the window. The entire chapel is silent behind her, unmoving. As though their fates are being determined right now, as though they're awaiting a jury deliberating in another room, the verdict being decided just beyond this murky glass, beyond their ability to influence it or to further plead their case. So they just wait. All their diverse paths have led them here today. To this shared chapel. To some shared fate. The only thing between them and that fate now is a locked red door.

Fran puts her hand on the lock, then listens.

"Look around, Sheriff," Rigo says, gesturing to the main thoroughfare. "This is your town. You built it."

Cooper just stares at him. He's at a loss as to what is coming next. To what more is in that folder that Rigo brandishes like a holy book.

"The only reason there is a Caesura," Rigo continues, "is because Johann Fell was killed. This place"—he swivels now, theatrical, arms thrown wide to the crowd, to the town, to its empty streets, its forlorn buildings—"was the brain child of Dr. Judy Holliday, Fell's protégée. A place where criminals, the worst of the worst, could roam free, their sins wiped away, living here under her close supervision. Fell never wanted to see it realized. He thought it was a monstrous idea.

He had other, purer intentions for his method. Refugees. Torture victims. Children escaping war crimes. People who'd been senselessly damaged—he thought he could save those people. That was his dream. Not killers, not"—Rigo nods to where they've dumped the bodies of Lancaster and Agnew—"rapists and baby murderers. Johann Fell had a different vision. But he was struck down violently. A frail but brilliant man, killed in a brutal, random act. In the streets of Austin, Texas. A hit-and-run. Life is funny that way. They never did catch the driver."

Rigo watches Cooper as he speaks, fascinated by Cooper's face. The burgeoning realization. Rigo wishes Dr. Holliday could be here. He knows she wouldn't want to miss this.

Rigo continues: "The man who killed Dr. Fell was named John Barker. He was a drunk, a disgraced prison guard, basically a drifter at that point. He lived alone and worked as a security guard for a man who subcontracted some tiny, inconsequential part of the Institute's operation, and his off-hours were taken up by barfights and blackouts. I'm sure he barely remembers those years himself. He ran down Johann Fell. He did it for five hundred dollars. He was selected precisely because he was the kind of man who'd take that kind of job. After he'd killed Fell, he crashed his car into a tree. Probably in hopes he'd kill himself. But he didn't. He lived. The crash left a nasty scar across the back of his head. The local cops picked him up, he was well known to them, but then the Institute intervened. Dr. Holliday enlisted him in a brand-new program, which, thanks to Fell's untimely death, she now had the liberty to pursue. He had his memory of the crash and the deal erased. It was easy, since it had happened so recently. Just a day or two—gone. Then she moved him here. He became Caesura's very first resident. The difference with him was, they never told him how he'd ended up here. Instead, they gave him a tin star." Rigo shakes his head, then reveals it: the final, damning point in the closing argument to the jury of the crowd. "His job was to watch over you. He failed even at that." Rigo turns to Cooper. "Though you are different from everyone else here in one respect. They just live here. But without you, this place wouldn't even exist."

Cooper listens. This all seems to be happening very far away. Rigo's voice is clear and unrelenting and yet, somehow, the high sun seems to have flared again beyond its usual brilliance and illuminated the road between him and Rigo, opening it up like a chasm, and out of it pours bright light that disorients him. The whole scene now seems to be swallowed by this overwhelming light. He has no—this isn't him. This isn't him.

"I don't remember," he says quietly.

"Of course you don't," says Rigo. "All this time, you thought you were the sheriff. But you were just another resident. Another rat in the experiment. Frankly, you should thank me. Now you're finally free to leave."

Cooper, untethered, falls to his knees. He stares at the dirt. The sun is so bright. He remembers the tree now. The crash. The frail man in his headlights.

Behind him, the red chapel door swings open.

Every eye in the town turns now toward the chapel, save for Cooper's. Even Santayana, near giddy from this exhilarating turn of events, rises from her lawn chair to see who's exiting the chapel.

Fran closes the red door behind her.

"Stop," she says.

Cooper turns now, too, hearing her voice, knowing it's her, and when he sees her he knows she's heard everything, and he knows it doesn't matter anymore. He is reminded now that what matters, all that matters, is the life of the boy behind the door. Cooper understands this with a clarity so sharp and unfamiliar to him that it's startling. A clarity that brings him back to his feet. A clarity that spurs him now to say, "Fran—"

"Stop," she says again.

And Cooper's not sure if she means for him to stop this confession, or for the agents to stop these proceedings, or whether her aim is to barter the boy or perhaps herself or simply to appeal to some higher human reason. And he never learns which of these is true because at that moment Rigo raises his gun and points it at Fran.

Rigo says, "I think it's time to end this. I think it's best you bring that boy out to us right now."

And there's a moment when Cooper looks at Rigo and thinks to lunge, to fight, he's close enough, maybe, to reach Rigo and topple him, to go down fighting—he'll die, of course, Cooper knows that, he deserves it, he will die, Rigo has the gun and there's three more guns behind him, all ready to put Cooper down, but that doesn't matter at all, he knows, because all that matters is Fran and the boy. And the only thing that stays Cooper's hand in this moment is a lack of assurance that his actions would save them. He must know beyond a doubt that they'll be saved.

Rigo stays still, his arm steady, the gun pointed.

"Bring the boy. Now," he says.

And Fran says, "You don't raise your gun to me. You don't even raise your voice to me. I fucked your boss, and I shot your boss, and I left him for dead, and you're nothing but a functionary. You're a letter from a dead man in the past that I choose to ignore. There is nothing you can do to hurt me. So you can put your gun away right now because you will never get what you came for, not ever. Don't you see that? You either leave here without my son or you die here. Those are the only outcomes." She steps forward. "Do you understand that now? You can shoot the sheriff dead, and you can shoot me dead, but this town will prevail. This town will swallow you whole. You want to read us *files*? You want to reveal our histories to us? The only thing those files should be telling you is that you are a fool to stay even a moment longer. You're not shaming us, Rigo. You're reminding us of who we are. And that doesn't end well for you."

At her words, the crowd, previously cowed into retreat, seems in some barely perceptible way to stir.

Rigo, his pistol raised, seems in the grip of a genuine confusion. "You want every person here to know what *you* did?"

"I know what I did," she says. "I know who I am. Tell anyone you want."

In the long moment that follows, the silent air seems almost to beg for a gunshot. The crowd is tensed for it. Even Fran seems to know that it's coming. In a strange way, she doesn't care, because she knows the boy will live now. Without Cooper, without her, if that's what it takes, but she knows the town will triumph. She feels it, and understands it now, and for her, for the crowd, for Cooper, even for Rigo, for Santayana, the understanding is clear among all of them, like a newly signed treaty. A gunshot would be meaningless, extraneous. A gunshot would only signal the unloosing of the ferocity that now simmers potently among those gathered in the street.

So the silence persists.

And in the silence, absent the expected gunshot, the red door swings open again.

It's Robinson, in his rumpled brown uniform.

"Enough of this," he says, looking exhausted, as he closes the door behind him. He walks into the street, past Fran, toward Cooper and Rigo. "She's right. Put that gun down," he says to Rigo, calmly.

"You'll get your turn," says Rigo, not even looking at Robinson.

"My turn for what, exactly? My name is Walter Robinson, but

my real name is Raymond Roebling. I'm fifty-two years old, I never murdered anyone in my life as best I know. I've never even struck a man in anger, though I have a feeling that's about to change." He walks calmly toward Rigo. "You're not going to shoot this woman; you're not going to take that boy. This is crazy, and you need to give it up."

Rigo swings the gun impotently toward Cooper. "Make him stop."

"It's over," Cooper says.

Rigo swings his gun back toward Robinson. "Don't come any closer, I'm warning you—"

Behind Rigo, Santayana watches. The agents behind her, framing Bette Burr, reach to place their hands on their holstered weapons.

Robinson's close enough now to Rigo, a dozen yards or so, that they could play a game of catch. And Cooper feels a sudden spark of dread and says, "Walt, *don't,*" but Robinson waves him off and says to Rigo, "That's it. It's over. All of it."

Rigo swings the gun back toward Cooper, as though pleading with Cooper to intervene, as though they're allies now, but Cooper does nothing, so Rigo swings the gun back toward Robinson, who's now just a few feet away. Still calm. Still walking.

"Rigo, please—" says Robinson, and then the shot, long anticipated, finally arrives.

Rigo startles. The crowd recoils.

"Oh no," says Hannibal weakly, inside the chapel, at the window, watching.

"What?" says Dawes, from the chair in which she's resting.

Robinson's body has already fallen in the street, even as the sound of the killing shot dissipates over the crowd like a flock of birds dispersing.

Santayana lowers her discharged pistol.

Robinson having understood what Fran knew, what Cooper knew, what they all understood, that it would take a gunshot to end this.

Or to begin it.

"Fuck this," Santayana says. "It's too hot, and I'm too fucking tired, and while all of this is very entertaining, Cooper, you go get that boy right now or I will personally execute every last shit bag in this fucking town one by one until you—"

But her last words are lost in a war cry, the whole town hears it, like a mournful keening, and those who turn to seek its source see Orson Calhoun striding purposefully, now jogging, now breaking into a run, his hammer held high, catching the sun, and in the few fleet seconds it takes for him to close the ground between the edge of his workshop's yard and the woman with the gun, Orson enjoys a sudden surge of clarity. About all those hazy half-memories he holds, of all those days spent with his father, in the basement, learning about tools. Of what his father used them for. Of who he used them on. Of a thwack, a cry, a sobbing. Of the rusty smell of the rag he held for his father to wipe down the tools. The stiffness of the sodden rags. All the techniques of the trade, passed on in the flickering subterranean light from father to son. And it brings to Orson not understanding, exactly, but a sudden sort of dread and welcome peace, of who he is and why he's here and how he came to be this way, a feeling of release that in some more wicked and honest era might be termed a reckoning.

Santayana turns sharply, as per her training, toward the sound of the escalating scream, her pistol seeking a target, but it's too late for her now, too late, as Orson buries the claw end of the hammer in the front of her skull, and Orson notes how the hammer's teeth announce their arrival with a heavy wet *thunk,* and how the woman's eyes roll back peacefully, before the weight of her body tugs at the smooth wooden handle in his hand and he releases it and she slumps almost gracefully to the ground.

At a distance, Agent Burly sights Orson and puts three quick shots in Orson's back, solid center. And though Orson turns, and flails like a struck beast, it's over now, he's done for, two more quick shots arrive with more certainty, one in the neck and one in the head, and these put Orson down for good. But someone has a shovel now, scavenged from the commissary. Someone has a pickax, similarly obtained. And as the two agents, Burly and Gains, swing their weapons in search of new targets, the crowd seems to collapse upon them, folding inward like a closing fist, until the street becomes a scene of loosed anarchy. The sounds alone are primitive, the thuds and grunts and crackings. The wielder of the shovel wallops Gains from behind and the pale redhead goes down, his wispy hair splashed a deeper red, and as he lays unconscious in the gravel, the shovel's sharp blade finds him, again and again, as though someone's driving a spade stubbornly into frozen soil. Three other men from the crowd have swarmed on Burly. The men are unarmed but attack the agent with some long-suppressed and brutal expertise. He's no match for them and offers only a waning resistance before he crumples. Elsewhere, a posse has toppled the lawn chairs and descended on the file box. Hands tear at it, fingers riffle in a frenzy. The box is upended, files loosed into the air, pages fluttering over the road, before searching patiently for a place to land. Pages settle in widening pools of blood and absorb the blood and are thus obscured.

Rigo watches all this wild-eyed. The folder on Cooper he holds in his hand is dropped and its contents scatter. Rigo fires blindly into the collapsing crowd and Cooper takes this opportunity to tackle him, and Rigo topples easily, as though he's already conceded, and on the ground Cooper wrests his gun free with barely a struggle, then stands up over him and aims the gun at Rigo in the dirt. Rigo shrivels.

There's nothing to stop him, Cooper thinks. Certainly no sense that this is not who he is.

This is who he is.

He understands that now.

But he doesn't kill Rigo.

Instead, he says, "Enough."

And then, just like that, it's over.

The street stills.

The frenzy recedes.

Cooper stands at the center of the wreckage, the bloodied sheriff, standing astride Rigo, still clutching the gun.

In the quiet, he counts corpses.

Orson Calhoun. Lyndon Lancaster and Doris Agnew. The five agents: Santayana, Burly and Gains, Corey and Bigelow. Plus whatever carnage Dick Dietrich left in the streets to be discovered. Plus Dietrich himself. Plus William Wayne.

Plus Dean. Plus Gable. Plus Colfax.

Plus Robinson.

Poor Robinson.

He and Dawes are the only true innocents.

Save for the boy.

The boy, still safe in the chapel.

After a moment of accounting, Cooper reaches down and grabs Rigo and hoists him to his feet. Then Cooper turns to Fran and gives her a signal, and she turns and walks back to the red door. She knocks and it opens for her, and she enters the chapel, and moves past the rows of disarrayed chairs and the huddled crowd to find her son at the back of the room, and clutches him for a long moment.

Then she stands and sounds the chapel bells, to signal all clear to the town.

For a time, the only sound in the street is bells.

40.

THE SIX OF THEM take one truck together, so as not to arouse suspicion. They travel in one of the black SUVs left behind by the agents, a six-seater. Fran drives, with Cooper beside her, watching the plains pass. Spiro and Dawes sit behind in the middle seat, Dawes propped against Spiro's shoulder, her breathing shallow. Her bleeding's been stanched but none of them knows enough to know how bad her situation is. Behind them, in the last seat, sits Hannibal Cagney and Paul Rigo. Rigo is handcuffed, his head leaning on the window. The six of them drive together for two hours on an empty road without passing another car. Every so often, signs appear to promise them an eventual city.

No one speaks. The tires hum on the road.

Finally, Cooper says, "Here."

Fran pulls over to the shoulder, the truck rumbling to a halt. Cooper gets out and walks around to the side door where, aided by Hannibal's prodding, he wrests Rigo from the backseat.

Cooper stands Rigo up, straightens his suit, squares his shoulders, like he's readying him for a prom date. The sun is just starting to decline in the distance, exhausted.

"Not here," says Rigo. "This is nowhere."

"We could drive another hour, it wouldn't make a difference," Cooper says.

Rigo raises his manacled wrists. "You're going to leave me like this, too?"

Cooper turns his back and walks to the passenger side and gets back in the truck.

"You're stupid to do this," Rigo calls out. "You think I won't come after you?"

"I hope you do," says Cooper, through the open window, and then the truck pulls away.

Later, as Fran drives, she asks, "What do you think he'll tell Mark Vincent?"

"I don't think he'll have a chance to tell him anything," Cooper says.

"But if he does, do you think they'll come back again?"

"It's his son," Cooper says. "Wouldn't you come back?"

They arrive two hours later at the emergency ward entrance of the first hospital they encounter, at the farthest outward edge of Amarillo. Cooper helps Dawes inside to the admitting desk. He doesn't know Dawes's real name so he just writes down Sidney Dawes on the forms. When pressed for details by the attending nurse, Cooper tells her it was a hunting accident: that they work security for a private corporation which operates a remote facility, and some hunters strayed too close to the grounds, so he and his fellow officer went out to ward them off and she got clipped by an errant round.

Once she's admitted, he stands at her bedside.

"I'm sorry I let you down," she says.

"You saved Isaac," Cooper says. "Without you, he'd be gone right now, no doubt. And Fran would be dead. You saved them both."

"I've never even held a gun before."

"May you never need to hold one again."

"Everything you said out there was true? What you said in the street? And what he said?"

"Yes, it's true," Cooper says.

"Are you going to turn yourself in?" she asks.

"To who?"

She doesn't answer, then turns her head toward the painted wall. He waits.

"I wanted to be change," she says.

"You are," he says. "And you're not finished."

He promises, over her protestations, to return and visit her again tonight. He'll be back in a couple of hours, he says, once his one last errand is done. Then he leaves her to her bed and the ministrations of the staff.

Now it's just Cooper and Fran and Hannibal and Spiro in the truck, driving over empty road. Two gas cans splash and rattle in the back of the SUV. The empty cans, from Orson's yard, filled up at a filling station just beyond the hospital.

It's nearly dusk. The sun, so bright and buoyant in the daytime, slides like a spent coin behind the horizon. The day's last light blossoms pink and red and disperses in all directions, and it's hard to tell, from behind the windshield, if this last light is fending off the darkness, or simply surrendering to it.

They pull into Dr. Holliday's driveway. Only Cooper and Fran disembark.

Dr. Holliday greets them outside her front door with a smile.

"Calvin, I've been expecting you," she says. "And you brought a guest."

"I'm Fran Adams," she says.

"Ah, yes," says Holliday. "The source of all this trouble." She gestures to the patio. "Care to join me? The sunset is spectacular from this vantage point."

There's no offered drinks, no further niceties, just three people seated at the table. Flickering torches illuminate the patio.

"Will they come back?" asks Cooper.

"Not if I don't let them," says Holliday. "I'm the gatekeeper, Calvin. I always have been."

"So you let them come in the first place?" says Cooper.

"I didn't seek them out. They approached me. You have to understand, Mark Vincent has been a very generous benefactor to this program since its inception. He shared my vision, even when Johann did not." Holliday wears a long, flowing white linen top, with a heavy pendular necklace made of large turquoise stones of obvious value. The torches cast shadows that flicker across her face. "Mark was obsessed with the idea that your worst memories might eventually be erased. That they might no longer be part of who you are. Given his"—she searches here—"*proclivities,* and his eventual ambitions, I suspect he saw the possibility of erasure as a kind of get-out-of-jail-free card. Or a stay-out-of-jail card, as it were." She smiles at Fran. "He didn't anticipate his wife's more crude intervention."

"But who were the other ones?" says Cooper. "Who were Colfax, and Gable, and Dean?"

"Colfax was just a common killer, you know his history," Holliday says. "As for Gable and Dean—Vincent's representatives contacted us six months or so after his incident, when it started to look like maybe he would survive after all. They offered us some further individuals whose knowledge of Vincent's appetites might prove problematic. One of them was Lester Vogel, who was Vincent's regular pipeline for his materials. The other was a bodyguard, Perry Garrett. Apparently, he and Vincent shared certain enthusiasms and had hit it off, and Garrett had acted as a kind of go-between. Both Vogel and Garrett were arrested and quickly funneled into our program. When we were done with them, neither of them had any clue who they'd been before, let alone that they'd ever known the other. But then Mark Vincent woke up."

"That was years ago," says Cooper.

"There was some question as to the viability of resuscitating his political ambitions," says Holliday. "He had an extensive rehab, as you may know. Once a political comeback seemed possible, even inevitable, there was a new urgency to put the past to rest. Also, he became very interested in his former wife's whereabouts. As you might expect."

"I'm right here," says Fran. "You can talk to me directly."

"Yes, I guess you are—you finally are. In the sense of being the woman, Carla Milne, who came to us eight years ago. The bloodstained poet. You remember everything now, don't you? My triggers worked exceptionally well."

"What triggers?" Fran asks.

"The newscasts. The headlines in the papers. The book at the library. To be honest, I had no idea what it would take to reawaken your memory, or if it was even possible. We'll have to discuss this in detail some other time, Ms. Milne. I'm very curious about your experience. What happens when you get yourself back in full, in all your . . . complexity."

Holliday turns back to Cooper. "And then there's you, my dear Calvin. My first. You always remember the first."

"I was just another variable," says Cooper. "For the experiment."

"You were much more than that. First, you helped me solve my dilemma with Johann. He simply ran out of vision at a certain point, and I ran out of patience. Then, once you'd done that for me, you were a chance to find out whether, stripped of your identity, you'd relapse to the capabilities you'd previously exhibited. I was the one, of course, who pointed Rigo toward you. They'd clumsily approached Ellis Gonzalez, after they'd learned he was running illicit mail into the town, but he refused. So I told Rigo to try you instead. I was so curious to see how you'd respond to his proposal."

Cooper watches Holliday talk, her elegant face framed against a backdrop of verdant foliage, the torches dancing, the curling leaves and tender flowers of the patio enveloping the three of them on all sides. This expansive garden is such a contrast to the arid plains around it, he thinks, it almost feels like an entirely different planet. Like they're the only three people in some newborn world. Him, Fran, and Holliday, sitting here, in a virgin garden of Eden. Adam, Eve, and a third entity, regarding them. God, or the serpent, or both.

"So if those men were stashed safely in the Blinds—" says Cooper.

"Please don't call it that," says Holliday. "I've never liked that name, you know that."

"So if these men were stashed safely with us, without memories, why did Vincent's agents come now?"

"Because they found out about the boy," Holliday says. "The murders in the town created a convenient pretext for them to intervene. A backstory for Vincent, to explain why he'd taken the boy from his mother. They came in to take the boy home to his father. In a certain light, it's not an ignoble goal."

"And Dick Dietrich—"

Holliday frowns. "That was their innovation. They felt a certain amount of discord in the town, precipitating their extrication, would benefit their efforts. I thought it was foolish."

"Is that what you call it? Discord?" says Cooper. "Loosing a fucking killer in the town?"

"Loosing another killer. Let's not mince words," Holliday says. "The town had no shortage of killers."

"And you authorized all of this?"

"Yes, as the last phase of the experiment. Ten years, that was the deal, remember? We just moved up the timetable slightly. Vincent was eager to retrieve his boy, and then there was the business with William Wayne. The strangest mind we ever encountered and, in a sense, the most interesting. Our leverage over him was about to expire, and I knew he was not to be contained otherwise. So I arranged to send in Eleanor Sung to deliver her father's message to him. At that point, the whole experiment seemed to have run its course. What happened to Wayne, by the way?"

"He's dead," says Cooper.

"A shame. A mind like that. You see, that's what Johann, for all his brilliance, never understood. The minds of the innocent are simple and so easily explained. The minds of the guilty, however—they are endlessly fascinating, once you really roll up your sleeves."

"So that's what we are to you, Judy?" asks Cooper. "Guinea pigs? Lab rats?"

"Variables. As I've explained. Each of you, in the original cohort of eight, posed a different challenge. For Wayne, the goal was to leave him with one memory, just one—the memory of a memory, really, and by that, to secure his compliance. We were not entirely successful, in that case. For you, Calvin, the goal was to erase only one memory, just a few hours, really, and thereby convince you that you'd lost no memories at all. With you, we succeeded admirably."

"And what was I?" asks Fran. "You erased my memory completely. So what was my variable?"

"You were pregnant, of course."

Fran can't keep her tears from betraying her. "You knew," she says softly. "And you still sent me there."

"Of course we knew. You had a full physical before you entered the program. We just didn't tell you we knew. What options did you have, really? Prison? Abortion? In any other scenario, you'd lose the child. You should thank me. I saved your son. I was fascinated to see what choices you would make, given the care of a child in that place."

"These people were entrusted to you," says Cooper. "We all were."

"You were made available to us, there's a difference," Holliday says sharply. "The residents of Caesura are people the existing justice system did not ask for, did not want, and had no use for once they'd served their purpose. I wanted you, I asked for you, and so I got you. And I gave you all a great gift. I gave you almost ten years to pretend that you aren't who you know yourselves to be, and to live accordingly." She turns to Fran. "You say you remember everything now?"

"I do," says Fran.

"Yet the proteins in your brain where those memories were stored are literally gone. In a physical sense, they do not exist, as surely as if I cut off your arm right now. The memories are gone, and yet, they're not, like a phantom limb that won't stop itching. And there are certain stressors—like my triggers—that can bring everything back. Some of these stressors we knew about. Some of them we even planted. Some of them—well, some are just trial and error, I guess. That's what those agents were. Trial and error."

"So you would have let them take my son?" asks Fran quietly.

"The purpose of a laboratory is to observe," says Holliday. "Not intervene."

Cooper seethes. "If you wanted to shut the experiment down—"

"Not shut it down, Calvin. Conclude it. Take it to its natural end."

"—then why not just set us all free?"

Holliday looks to Fran, then back to Cooper. She smiles. "Calvin, you were always free."

Fran sits silent for the moment. When she finally speaks, she says: "How did they know about my son? Did you tell them?"

Holliday laughs, a laugh like chimes. "No, of course not. I would have preferred for the boy to stay, simply to observe him further. But once they learned you had a son—well, given the timing, Vincent's paternity seemed plausible. Still, they needed to be sure."

"The man. At the mall. Who cut my son's hair," Fran says.

"Just to test it. Just to be certain. Vincent was fully recovered at that point and very interested in the boy's provenance. To his credit, a long-lost child now only complicates his political fortunes. But he seems genuinely . . . attached." Holliday reaches across the table and lays a comforting hand on Fran's arm, like a counselor. "At some point, I would love to talk to you about that moment of realization. When it all came back to you. In a sense, that's what this"—she gestures here at the house, the labs elsewhere, the distant town, the Institute—"was always all about." Holliday turns to Cooper. "So what's next, Sheriff? I'm guessing my liaisons were not successful in their objective, or we wouldn't be talking right now."

"What's next is we go home," says Cooper. "To the town. And you stop. Like you said, the experiment's over."

"I do intend to shut down the facility, if that's what you mean. As for the residents—"

"There aren't many left alive. Maybe half," says Cooper.

"—the residents will be free to relocate wherever they like."

"They have nowhere to go."

"The world is a big place. They'll find somewhere."

"No," Cooper says. "That town is ours. We live there. And we're going to stay. And you're going to leave us alone."

Holliday recoils, bemused. "That's ludicrous, Calvin. You can't survive without outside assistance. The weekly shipment of supplies, for starters, all of which is funded by the Institute—"

"Oh, you're going to keep funding it," Cooper says, leaning forward, calmly, and placing his large hands flat on the stone slab. "The Institute will keep it open, and fund it, but it becomes a line item on your budget, nothing more. Otherwise, you bury it. And you install Eleanor Sung as the new liaison between the Institute and the town."

"Why her?" asks Holliday.

"Because I trust her," says Cooper. "And she feels a certain loyalty to the town now. She'll live out here in the world and work for you, but you don't interfere with her at all or even contact her unless absolutely necessary. And then you never give our town another thought."

"Calvin, there is no more Caesura, you need to accept that," Holliday says, impatient. "It's over." Her face clouds noticeably, like she's lost interest in his pointless meanderings.

"As far as you're concerned, that's true," Cooper says. "Also, I want the files. All of them. On everyone."

"I gave the files to those agents."

"You gave copies to those agents. So make more copies. I want them all."

"To do what with?" She seems genuinely curious.

"To keep them. And to show them to whoever wants to know. People have that right. To know. Or not. But it will be their choice."

Cooper stands.

"And one last thing," he says. "You tell Mark Vincent that we wish him the best of luck in his upcoming race. And you tell him that if he ever comes to our town again, or sends a proxy, or a proxy's proxy, we're going to kill those fuckers, too, and mail them back to him in pieces, and then Fran and I will get in a car and tell the world everything we know. About him, about you, all of it. So you tell him, we're very sorry, but he needs to forget about his son."

She laughs. "Forget a child? That's not an easy thing to do," says Holliday. "As you well know, John."

"Well, maybe you can help him with that," says Cooper. "That's your specialty, isn't it?"

Cooper turns to Fran, who's still seated. Once again, Cooper wishes for a hat. This would be the perfect moment to put on a hat. Instead, he says simply, "Come on, Fran. We're done here."

But Fran lingers a moment longer, regarding Holliday. As though assessing some new species of creature she never imagined existed. A creature whose capacity for cruelty is so vast that it alters Fran's conception of what's possible. Of what you might one day have to deal with. This revelation doesn't dishearten her, though, or paralyze her, or cripple her. Rather, like all revelations, it nourishes Fran, it strengthens her, because it further feeds her understanding of the world.

"Leave us alone," she says finally to Holliday. "That's all. But that's everything. Do you understand? Leave us alone."

She stands to join Cooper.

"And what about all this carnage you've caused?" says Holliday, from her seat, in her jewels, with her implacable smile.

Fran leans toward her.

"Just forget it," she says.

And only then, in the ensuing quiet, do the three of them hear the first crisp whispers of the fire.

They look up from the patio to see Spiro and Hannibal, each holding an empty gas can, their faces sweaty and their hands and clothes dirty and stinking of splashed petrol. The fire rages higher behind them, flames pawing and slurping at the house. While Cooper, Fran, and Holliday talked, whiling away the evening hour, Spiro and Hannibal circled the compound, dousing the garden, soaking the foliage. The fire's rising now. The vast garden cowers and withers under the heat. Fragile flowers bow humbly. Palm leaves clench like fists.

"You'll see Eleanor Sung in a few days," says Cooper to Holliday, over the sound of the fire's snapping. "Until then, we're headed back to see a friend in the hospital. So I can offer you a ride to Amarillo, if you like. Or you can stay here and watch this place burn to the ground."

Holliday seems amused at the extent of this vast tantrum. She gestures toward the compound. "You know this is nothing, right? This is not even a fraction of our research and everything is backed up in any case. This is merely one of my many homes. This isn't even where my work is stored. You can't touch my work. And it will continue, no matter what. So all this accomplishes nothing. Except warming your childish faces, here for a moment, like children at a bonfire, telling stories. Like spoiled children, acting out."

"That may be so, but either way, your ride's about to leave," Cooper says. "And I don't suspect you'll want to sleep out here tonight."

The five of them head back to civilization. Cooper and Fran in the front, and fuel-soaked Spiro and Hannibal sitting in back, stinking, with Holliday wedged in the middle, her white linen top stained with smoke. They drive with the windows cracked to disperse the fumes of the gas. The miles pass silently between them. Like they're a broken family fleeing a catastrophe.

It's not long before the raging fire is hardly a flicker in the rear-view, as they drive a hundred miles in the opposite direction, and leave the roaring plains to reclaim its ceded ground.

41.

IN THE MIDDLE OF TOWN, another fire is burning.

This is what greets the four of them when they return.

The blood-soaked files have been gathered up and swept into a pile and set aflame. The people have ransacked the intake trailer and collected all the agents' armaments, pistols and ammo and a few assault rifles. The town has the look of a war camp. A few townsfolk now stand with rifles over their shoulders, like sentries, watching the fire. Others wear guns stuck in their belts. They stand ready, for whatever new siege might be coming. All the while, the bonfire burns. It dispenses its secrets to heaven in the form of sparks, which flutter and mingle above with the innumerable stars.

Cooper watches. There are graves yet to be dug. They'll bury the bodies themselves. It's long past time that Caesura had a cemetery, he thinks. No headstones for anyone, though. No official markers. Let each of the dead decide in the next life what name they choose to go by.

As for the town, he imagines they'll survive. As a goal, survival seems like more than enough, at least for now, at least for tonight. Dawes will be the new sheriff, if she wants it, Cooper's already decided that. They checked in on her at the hospital after leaving Holliday, and the prognosis was better. Hopeful, even.

She'll come back, and she'll be sheriff, and they'll also open the gates. Maybe even take down the fences, and the residents will come and go as they please. If anyone cares to venture out beyond the town, to encounter whatever's waiting for them, whoever's looking for them, that will be their choice. They'll always be welcome back.

As for Cooper, he'll move in with Fran, if she'll have him. He hasn't proposed it yet. There's no need to decide it tonight, or to decide what happens after that. All he knows is that he'll go about it slowly, the whole project, not just with her, but with the whole town, and with himself, he understands this. With no forced urgency, but a humble process of determining who in the town can forgive him. Whether any trust yet remains. Perhaps there isn't any, and if not, he'll deal with that, too. But everyone here has their own pasts to grapple with. He won't rush them or force them to grapple too quickly with his. He has his own grappling to do.

The fax machine will be dispatched, of course, that is the next order of business. In fact, he has half a mind to lug it out from the police trailer right now and toss it onto the flames. He trusts Eleanor Sung to run things from afar, and if she needs to reach them, she can drive out and visit face-to-face. For his part, he doesn't intend to bother her. They'll need some emergency lifeline, he guesses, though he's increasingly inclined to believe that whatever the town needs, it will find within its borders or not at all. They should be able to puzzle out the problem of survival together. For starters, they've got $200,000. The money's still there, still accessible, he double-checked from a pay phone during the trip into town.

It could all disappear tomorrow, he knows that, too, but he suspects it won't. Call it a bribe, or hush money, for services rendered and secrets kept. Those funds should suffice for a while. After that, they only face the same challenges of every new hopeful settlement that's ever been established in human history. Which is a fact that Cooper finds heartening, perhaps foolishly so.

Frankly, he's less concerned with how they'll survive than with who will come next to challenge them. Not just Rigo, not just Vincent, but all the accumulated enemies of the town who still harbor festering vendettas. Given there's no one in the outside world to shield their secrets or their whereabouts.

Then again, he thinks, we're a town of notorious cutthroats and criminals and killers, who only now have an inkling of who we are and what we've done. And what we're capable of.

So let them come.

As for the files, all the files, they'll go in a box, he thinks, into his drawer, in his office, with a lock, and he'll hold the key. It will be his last and only responsibility to the town. Given the riot today, some people here already know all there is to know about themselves. Some know half. Some know nothing. But those who ask will always have access.

That will be his rule. The only rule of the Blinds.

Fran holds Isaac hefted in her arms like a much younger child and together they stand next to Cooper. He hasn't asked if she'll have him, or even if she plans to stay, and tonight's not the night to ask.

Instead, they watch the bonfire.

"It kind of feels like a holiday," she says.

"Bonfire Day," says Cooper. "We should mark it on the calendar."

"We could celebrate it every year."

"But what are we going to burn?" Cooper asks her.

"Whatever needs burning," she says.

Hours later, as the fire fades, there is no further revel to speak of, though a few townspeople linger as though at a festival. It's deep into the early morning before the last one heads to bed. And even though there's no one among them, not Cooper, not Fran, nor any of those who remain, who doesn't still fear some coming intrusion, some enemy galloping toward them from the past, for the first time in the town's history, they sleep with the gates wide open.

Cooper buries the padlock in the ground himself. At dawn, in the desert, just beyond the fence. He digs a shallow hole, and before he covers it over, he tosses in his sheriff's star besides.

Let Dawes earn her own star, he thinks, not this tarnished hand-me-down.

He pats the dirt with the toe of his boot. Then he plants a homemade sign above the hole. A sign he made an hour ago in Orson's workshop, with some old timber and black paint. He pounds the sign into the ground with Orson's dented hammer. Then he pockets the hammer, turns, and heads back toward the town.

He leaves the sign out front of the open gates to greet anyone who cares to call.

As a welcome, or a warning, or both.

The sign, hand-lettered, simply reads:

WELCOME TO THE BLINDS

ACKNOWLEDGMENTS

My sincere gratitude to the invaluable people who helped shepherd this book into the world: My agent, David McCormick. My editor, Zachary Wagman. Miriam Parker, Sonya Cheuse, Emma Janaskie, Meghan Deans, Martin Wilson, Sara Wood, Michelle Crowe, Suet Chong, and Daniel Halpern at Ecco. Howard Sanders and Katrina Escudero at UTA. Boris Kachka and Michael Idov, for the brief and necessary Russian lesson. The good folks at the Ditmas Workspace in Brooklyn, who provided constant encouragement and endured my invasions at irregular hours. My friend and reader Howard Akler. My RC. And, of course, as ever, my wife, Julia May Jonas, the notorious, indispensable, perpetually inspiring JMJ.